THE
TWO-KNOCK
GHOST

To Rosalie:

You are a real sweetheart. I still want to share my Yankee stuff with you. Your friendship means a great deal to me.

Jeff Lombardo

THE
TWO-KNOCK GHOST

JEFF LOMBARDO

Copyright © 2016 by Jeff Lombardo.

Library of Congress Control Number:		2016914622
ISBN:	Hardcover	978-1-5245-4052-4
	Softcover	978-1-5245-4051-7
	eBook	978-1-5245-4050-0

All rights reserved. No part of this book may be reproduced or transmitted in any form or by any means, electronic or mechanical, including photocopying, recording, or by any information storage and retrieval system, without permission in writing from the copyright owner.

This is a work of fiction. Names, characters, places and incidents either are the product of the author's imagination or are used fictitiously, and any resemblance to any actual persons, living or dead, events, or locales is entirely coincidental.

Any people depicted in stock imagery provided by Thinkstock are models, and such images are being used for illustrative purposes only.
Certain stock imagery © Thinkstock.

Print information available on the last page.

Rev. date: 09/09/2016

To order additional copies of this book, contact:
Xlibris
1-888-795-4274
www.Xlibris.com
Orders@Xlibris.com
746655

CHAPTER 1

THE KNOCKS ON the front door were so loud that they woke me violently from my sleep. With squinting eyes, I saw that the clock atop the TV said 3:36 a.m. "Who's there?" I angrily yelled. No answer. I jumped out of bed shouting, "Hold on, I'll be right there." I quickly walked the twenty steps to the door. I peered through the peephole to be safe. I saw nothing but my long empty balcony stretching before me. I opened the door and stepped outside, looking down the stairs and up and down the walkways between the three buildings nearest to mine, hoping I might catch a glimpse of a prankster running away. There was no one. In fact, the night was still. Not a leaf was moving on any tree, not a blade of grass shimmering.

My mind, already racing and upset, tried to calm itself by analyzing the situation. The conclusion it came to was that it had gotten itself all worked up over nothing. It was probably just a dream, but it had frightened me. Two mere inappropriately timed, rather loud clanks on the front door had awakened me, but rankled me as well.

Sleep was important to me. So was quiet. Absolute quiet was the best. I had to get up in three hours. It had always been difficult for me to fall back asleep after I had awakened during the night, but tonight would be even more difficult because the knocks had sounded intrusive and unfriendly, and I had been awakened frightfully. Pondering for some moments when the last time was that a couple of nighttime sounds like that had scared me awake, I concluded I couldn't remember a last time. It had never happened.

* * * * *

When the alarm clock blared on to sports radio 620 WDAE at 6:30 a.m., I didn't wake with my usual ear tuned to the latest sports news. I was still feeling agitated about the thudding knocks on my front door a few hours earlier. Had there really been someone there? Was it friend or foe? If it was friend, had they been in trouble? But if they had been, why hadn't they stayed? If it was foe, who was it that I had annoyed so much that they would have wanted to puncture my sleep time with such nasty behavior?

I proceeded with my shaving and showering with my ears beginning to hear the baseball scores from the night before and, more importantly to me, how the Rays had played. Gradually, thoughts of my upcoming workday began to mingle with the scores and my conjectures of the night before.

I had a busy day coming, six patients in my clinical psychology practice in downtown St. Pete. I had checked my calendar yesterday to see who was on the schedule for today. This is what I always did before leaving the office because I like to think about what I was going to say to people the next day during sessions.

I've never been one to let things go easily, especially something wonderful or unique or unsettling. The dual knocks from the night before kept tumbling through my mind throughout the day. By the time I had seen my six patients, written some notes, and left the office, I was still pondering the origin of those knocks. I wondered if it was a prank or a friend in crisis or a loud random dream. Would any one of those be a one-time event? I wondered how long it would be before thoughts of the happening would drift from my mind and leave me alone.

* * * * *

I have a problem with alcohol. It started innocently enough in 1967 when I was a freshman at Kendall College in Evanston, Illinois. It was Christmas break and every boy except two of us had already gone home. I don't remember why I was there, but I was. The night I had my first drink ever, I had a friendship only date with a young woman I had known in high school in Northbrook. Her name was Kathy Blazer. My dad, a pretty good musician, taught Kathy's sister, Theresa, the clarinet. Dad, who had played in several bands and was still doing so, had met Mr. and Mrs. Blazer at one of his square dancing gigs and had befriended them. Not only did my dad teach Theresa but his friendship with Mrs. Blazer had helped me land a job in 1965 as an orderly at Eden View Convalesant and Geriatric Center in Glenview. Mrs. Blazer was the administrator of the place and I remember promising her to do the best job I possibly could to take care of her people, and I did.

Kathy was not a pretty young woman. She was tall and gangly, prompting a great number of kids to derisively call her "the bird."

But I liked her. She was smart and funny and infinitely likeable once you got past her physical oddities.

Kathy was attending Northwestern and living in a dorm a few blocks from Kendall. Our plan was to go out for pizza and fun.

On my way down the hall near the exit sign, Robert Workman stuck his head out of his room.

"Hi, Turf," he said, calling me by my baseball nickname.

"Hi, Robert."

"Where are you off to?"

"I'm going out for pizza with one of my friends from Northwestern."

"Would you like a drink before you go?"

"No thanks," I said.

"Come on, Turf, just one."

He was pleading, and I felt sorry for him. Earlier in the school year Robert had gotten into an argument with Kelly Stevenson, an extremely popular student and Kendall's starting second baseman, over a pretty coed they both fancied. They were arguing in the parking lot near the dorm, things got heated and Robert, in his exasperation, threw a punch at Kelly. It wasn't much of a punch, barely a glancing tap. But Kelly ducked and backstepped at the same instant and tripped over a yellow concrete parking bumper he had no idea was there. He fractured his left leg. About fifteen students, both boys and girls, had followed the argument as it spilled from the dorm to the parking lot where every one of the observers thought there might be a fight.

Now the flimsy fight was over, but a great deal of damage had been done. Kelly, a gregarious, popular athlete was in jeopardy of losing his ability to play baseball for the upcoming season. Even before his fall, he had the favoritism of the onlookers. Kelly was easier to like. He was outgoing, smiley, happy-go-lucky. Robert Workman was quiet, studious, a nonathlete, slow to smile, shy. He wasn't a bad guy at all, just more difficult to get to know and like.

The broken leg broke Robert's spirit, as word of what happened spread quickly around the campus. The far greater majority of kids not only sympathized with Kelly but they ostracized Robert Workman somewhat unfairly. What made things worse was that Kelly got the girl and Robert got a blanket of depression for the rest of the semester.

Now it was only the two of us left on campus, and he was pleading for companionship. What could spending a few minutes with him cost me? I'd been a disciplined athlete all my life. The controls I had on myself were huge. I had never drank before in a social setting or even at home. I had never so much as opened a bottle of my father's alcohol and tried it.

"Do you like rum and Coke?" Robert asked as I seated myself on a chair at his desk by the window.

"I never tasted rum," I answered.

"In that case, I suggest you try it first mixed with the Coke, otherwise it might be too strong for you."

So without ever having tasted plain rum, I had my first three ounces of it mixed with five ounces of Coke in an eight-ounce glass.

I liked it. In fact, it was love at first taste. I was actually thirsty in that moment. The cafeteria was closed for Christmas break and I hadn't had anything to drink or eat all day and it was nearly 5:00 p.m.

I drank the eight ounces quickly, as if it were simply a glass of Coke. We talked about the fight and how sorry Robert was that he ever raised his hand to Kelly. When my glass was empty, Robert filled it again—same proportions.

All of five minutes had passed since I had finished the first full glass. The second glass took about seven minutes to finish. The conversation continued to revolve around Kelly and Robert's fight and the loneliness Robert felt when he was not only shunned by the entire student body, but dumped by the girl who had chosen Kelly.

After twelve minutes, I had consumed six ounces of rum and ten ounces of Coca-Cola. I excused myself to pee, and when I came back three minutes later, my glass was filled again with what I'm certain were the same proportions because the third drink tasted identical to the first two. I was still enjoying the hell out of my new tasty drink, but during this glass, our conversation was broken repeatedly by some of the greatest belches I can remember making in my life. The conversation was still deep, almost soul searing, but it began to be punctuated by burps and giggles.

Nineteen minutes in, I had consumed nine ounces of rum and fifteen of Coke.

"Time for me to go, Robert."

"Oh please, Turf, one more."

"I'll be late to pick up Kathy."

"Come on, it'll take five minutes."

That made sense to me. As soon as he said five minutes, I looked at my watch and made up my mind to finish that upcoming drink and our conversation and be as close to on time for Kathy as I possibly could be.

Belches and laughter were now the main activities of our final minutes together. I held true to my promise to myself, and five minutes to the second later, I had completed my consumption of twelve ounces of rum and twenty ounces of Coke and walked out of Robert Wickman's room and the dorm, and I was on my way to see Kathy Blazer.

The cold air slapped my face hard when I stepped outside.

I began my six block walk to Kathy's dormitory on tightly packed icy snow. I hated that kind of snow because I had to shorten my normal long stride and take much shorter steps, which always seemed to tighten my groin. Slipping and sliding from time to time also did nothing to help me feel like the athlete I wanted to be. But this walk to Kathy's was beginning to be different from my other treks there. Within a block from my dorm, I began talking out loud to myself, "I'm on my way to see Kathy Blazer. Isn't that going to be fun? We're going to have pizza. I can't wait because I love pizza."

I'm telling you, I was animated too, demonstrative and loud. The closer I got to Kathy's dorm, the louder I became. The liquor was kicking in.

When I got to the girl at the front desk of Kathy's dorm, I told her in a flirtatious way who I was there to see. I remember that she chuckled—probably thinking something like "Kathy's in for one heck of a wild night with this guy."

Kathy was down to the lobby a couple of minutes later, a little surprised to see me chatting it up with a group of three coeds.

"Hey, Robert."

"Kathy, Kathy, Kathy, how the heck are you?" I asked.

"I'm fine, thank you, but it looks like you're doing a whole lot differently than you usually do."

"Thank you, ma'am. I'll take that as a compliment."

I began to stand, feeling the world spinning wildly. I turned to the three coeds I had been flirting with and said, "Excuse me, ladies, but my date has arrived and I must take my leave."

Immediately, I told Kathy, "Before we go anywhere, can you show me where the bathroom is please?"

She started to give me directions, but I stopped her immediately.

"I mean, can you hold my hand and take me to the bathroom?"

Though surprised, she took my hand and led me to the nearest bathroom. For me, the hand holding was of necessity. I had no way of knowing that it was the first time Kathy had ever held a boy's hand. Each of us was feeling quite different things in that moment leading to the bathroom. I had a bursting bladder a couple of feet beneath a head that felt like it had just stepped off the teacup ride at Disneyland. Although I wasn't aware of it at the time, Kathy "the bird" was walking across the busy lobby of the girl's dorm, hand in hand with the handsome pitcher for whom she had always had a secret crush.

When we got to the bathroom, I went in by myself, but I was so drunk and woozy I didn't trust myself to stand without falling while urinating the usual way into the toilet. Instead, I did my business into the sink, holding on for dear life during my emptying cycle.

I remember feeling guilty for having done things this way, so I tried to make things right by running the hot water for about a minute while scrubbing the sink with toilet paper and soap. When my guilt was assuaged, I put my head near the sink and soaked my face in cold water hoping that would help me cope better with whatever these new sensations I was feeling were. It didn't, although the cold water felt refreshing in the moment I was splashing it on my face. A moment later I opened the door and stumbled into the exceptionally receptive arms of Kathy Blazer.

I don't remember much more about that night. What I do recall is that we went to a restaurant, had a wonderful deep dish pizza, were joined by friends at times, and that I was a ridiculous idiot throughout the night. I remember what seemed like dozens of times that I slid from an upright seated position to lying on my left or right side on the booth bench with my feet planted firmly on the floor. Repeatedly, Kathy would reach over the table and pull me back to an upright position. As I look back through the haze of time, I recall that I was giggling hysterically each time Kathy pulled me back upright. She finally left her side of the table opposite me and came on my side to sit on my right.

Most of the time I slid to my left, but several times I fell to my right, where her lap was invitingly awaiting me. It felt comfortable down there.

Most of the times I slumped down there, Kathy was in no rush to raise me. In fact, she must have been wearing perfume down there because she smelled oddly sweet. Come to think of it, it might have been Jungle Gardenia—a popular fragrance of the times.

I can remember her massaging my curly hair, tugging at it gently and affectionately. She'd scratch my scalp with the long fingernails that tipped her lengthy fingers. Her tenderness actually reminded me of my maternal grandmother and her loving nature. Only God and Kathy knew how many times I fell asleep in Kathy's lap that night. I was not thinking negatively that Kathy wasn't a babe and I was not having fun being with her. I was having a blast, albeit a rum-enhanced blast. It was a blast nonetheless, and it seemed to go on that way for hours.

The last part of the evening was a relative blur, except that I remember that I walked Kathy back to the dorm long after our dinner was over. It had been six hours since I had begun the night by drinking twelve ounces of rum with Robert Workman. Even the frigid Evanston winter night's air didn't thrust me back to normalcy. In fact, I was more dependent on Kathy than ever for support. The temperature had dropped at least fifteen degrees since we had entered the restaurant, so not only was I holding on to Kathy for support, but we were snuggling for warmth.

To any passersby observing us as we hiked the six icy blocks back to her dorm, Kathy and I would have appeared to be another of thousands of Northwestern and Kendall couples. The fact that we weren't didn't matter or bother me at all.

I insisted on walking her back to the dorm. I have no recollection of how long I might have stayed in the lobby with Kathy getting warm, talking, flirting with other coeds or whatever else I might have done. I do recall Kathy asking me about 1:30 a.m.—a half hour before her weekend curfew—if I thought I could make it home okay. I self-assuredly said yes and left a few minutes later. I do not remember kissing her good night.

It was cold outside again, like a hard slap in the face. Instead of helping to sober me, to wake me, it exacerbated my drunkenness. I was seven and a half hours out from my drinking with Bob, and I was still shit-faced. I wobbled and weaved along the sidewalk laughing at my own lack of equilibrium. I longed to get back to my cozy dorm room and fall into the sack.

Instead, I slipped on some ice and fell into the snow. It was ice, but I had a huge coat on, so that part of my body didn't feel too badly. I wanted to get up immediately, especially when my hands slumped onto the snow. I looked into the skies to the spinning stars and a blurred moon and all my incentive to navigate away from my predicament dissipated. I was more dizzy and tired than cold. I fell asleep almost immediately.

Through my sleeping stupor, I heard her gentle voice and felt her poking my shoulder.

"Are you all right?"

I roused enough to see an angelic young woman's face, which was illuminated by the not-as-blurry moon behind her left ear.

"Can you stand up?"

"I think I can."

And as I tried, I could feel the cold worse than I ever had in my life.

I couldn't do it. I was still woozy, unable to stand, weak, and nearly frozen.

"I think I might need some help," I said through chattering lips.

Two tiny hands reached out to mine. The angel planted her feet as best she could and tugged with all her might. I rose slowly and completely. At fully standing, I was looking down at the tiniest of angels. She was five feet two inches tall with long, straight blond hair and the kindest and prettiest eyes a human being could possess.

I liked her immediately.

"Where are you going?"

"Back to the dorm."

"I'll drive you there," she said. "You're in no shape to walk."

I told her thank you as I held her right hand with my right hand and held my left arm across her back, with my left hand squeezing her left shoulder tightly. For some reason, maybe because my body was sore from its earlier fall to the snow, I was afraid of falling. I also didn't want to embarrass myself in front of this beautiful young woman more than I had already.

My unknown benefactor led me to the passenger side of a yellow Volkswagen. I plopped my butt onto the seat with my feet still in the snow outside. The lovely woman pushed my feet into the car, closed the door, and headed for Northwestern.

"What dorm are you going to?"

I said, "Kendall College men's dorm."

"Kendall? So you're not Northwestern?"

"No," I said then corrected myself and said, "Yes, I'm not a Northwestern guy."

She chuckled and turned the bug around on the silent street.

I don't remember what we talked about those fleeting three blocks to the dorm. I mainly remember that looking at how cute she was was the one thing that was keeping me awake. But that part of my brain won out over the other part of my brain that yearned for sleep. She was adorable and now that I was awake, I felt a powerful attraction to her. Her features singed their way into my mind. No amount of alcohol could stop that. I also realized that she was not an angel, but a genuinely strong, caring young woman, who was in the process of doing me the biggest favor anyone had done for me in my lifetime.

Altogether too quickly we arrived at Kendall. Again she was at my door in a flash to help me out of the bug. I held her hand and shoulder the exact way I had a few minutes earlier, and we walked to the front door of the dorm.

"What's your name?" she asked.

"They call me Turf," I said.

We knocked on the front door and the nighttime security guard went back behind the front desk while keeping a watchful eye that little coed didn't go upstairs with me.

I said, "Thank you, ma'am, for helping me."

She said, "You're welcome, Turf."

I bent down and hugged her gently, still having enough sense not to kiss her.

Then she turned and walked out the door.

Little could I have known in that instant that on the night of my first drunk, I had met the love of my life—Christine.

CHAPTER 2

THE NEXT DAY I woke at noon with a banging hangover. It was my first and I didn't like it. I shaved and showered and headed downstairs, hoping to avoid Robert Workman and both having to explain to him what happened last night and try to say no if he offered me another drink of rum and Coke. After all, I had, in fact, enjoyed the taste of the blend of liquor and soda. Thankfully, he wasn't there, so I headed out of the dorm once again into the frigid Evanston air on my way to see Kathy Blazer. We had made another friendship date a week ago for 1:00 p.m.

When Kathy came downstairs she had on a red-and-white short summer skirt. It was totally inappropriate for this time of year. On a pretty girl with a good figure, seeing that outfit would have turned me on. But on Kathy, it looked rather odd. But no matter how the dress looked being worn by her it was still a thing of absolute beauty. Kathy strode proudly through the door from the stairway to the lobby doing the best she could to wear that dress well. I had never seen her like this before. She had a smile on her face the size of Texas and her eyes were literally sparkling. Something wonderful that she was feeling on the inside was manifesting itself significantly on the outside. As she approached me, I saw that she was wearing the reddest shade of lipstick I had ever seen. And she wasn't walking toward me, she was bounding. She was obviously ecstatic about something. Kathy Blazer almost looked pretty. "Hi, Turf," she said as she continued making a beeline straight into my personal space. She grabbed me confidently about the shoulders and kissed me with an odd blend of passion and affection right smack on the lips. I couldn't believe it. I was shocked. And it had tasted good.

"Why are you so happy today, Kathy?"

Immediately the look of happiness and joy on Kathy's face evaporated.

"You don't remember?" she said.

Suddenly I felt a pit in my stomach.

"Remember what, Kathy?" Looking back, I might have seemed insensitive to her feelings in that instant, but I honestly had no idea what she was talking about.

"You asked me to marry you last night and I said yes."

Instantly, I was both saddened and terrified. I was saddened because I had hurt her feelings and terrified that maybe she would figure out some way of forcing me to go through with a marriage.

"Oh my god!" I said. "I sincerely have no recollection of having asked you that."

"We were in the restaurant. It was about eleven o'clock."

What had I done? All I could remember about last night was acting goofy, being loud, eating an occasional bite of pizza, and falling over repeatedly into Kathy's sweet-smelling lap. I also remember her fingers tugging at and playing with my hair and gently massaging my scalp. Had the memory numbing effects of the alcohol been so strong that it had blotted out events that apparently had ranked among the most important of a young woman's life?

"Turf, don't you remember that we kissed over a hundred times and you were rubbing my calves and thighs when you were lying in my lap?"

I could have been cruel and said, "But, Kathy, surely you realized I was blitzed out of my mind." But I didn't. I only apologized repeatedly and profusely. I didn't want to hurt her any further.

Not only had damage been done to her, but it seemed to be increasing as she lobbied for validity to whatever happened last night with snippets of heart-wrenching explanations.

"Do you remember you said you loved my lips?"

"I'm sorry, but I don't, Kathy."

"Do you remember saying you loved the feel of my legs?"

This she asked a little too loudly, and before I knew what I had done, I looked away from her to see if anyone was in earshot. Kathy's eyes became sad before I could answer yet again, "No, Kathy, I'm sorry but I can't."

She looked at me deeply in that intense instant; I peered into her not pretty eyes and saw how I had caused harm to a good human being.

I honestly had no recollection of anything I had said or done that evening except what I have already acknowledged. Still, that did not assuage the guilt I felt at having hurt her. She was my friend and a friend of my family. I hadn't planned to hurt her.

Damned alcohol.

A few more snippets emerged from her lips as well as more apologies from mine. Suddenly, she got up slowly from the couch. Her cheeks were now a two-lane highway of tears. She was sobbing.

"I'm sorry, Turf. I've got to go back upstairs. I don't think we should see each other again."

What had I done to have possibly hurt Kathy this much? I analyzed the questions as quickly as possible. What I concluded was that she had been a damaged human being before last night. Somehow, I had lifted her up and, within fourteen hours, dashed her further down than she had ever been before.

Again I told her that I was sorry—meaning it with every fiber of my being, hoping she would forgive me, shrug it off, and smile again.

But she didn't. There was no reasoning with her.

Kathy Blazer turned away from me and headed to the door at the end of the dorm's lobby, wearing the saddest face that I had ever caused to that point in my life.

I sat there stunned, speechless, embarrassed, lonely. Somehow, I had hurt a friend. And I felt like crap.

Then she opened the door and disappeared behind it.

I never saw Kathy Blazer again.

At that moment, I didn't know what to do with myself. For several minutes I sat there almost crying, desperately trying to visualize any of the actions Kathy told me that I had done. I couldn't remember a single kiss or rubbing her legs and thighs. I could imagine it. And I could imagine how that pronounced attention could have affected her. But I simply couldn't visualize any of it, except falling repeatedly into her lap.

Was that what a blackout was? It certainly seemed like one. I had never had anything like that happen to me before. I was going on logic. In fact, I concluded that that is exactly what had happened. In the middle of my first drunk, I had blacked out for hours and had wound up hurting a friend of mine terribly. And she had not forgiven me when I asked for her forgiveness. That was another of life's lessons I learned that day—that people don't always forgive you, even when you ask for it sincerely from the deepest part of your heart.

* * * * *

CHAPTER 3

AFTER SITTING IN the lobby near the old Steinway Grand Piano for several minutes and pondering what had just happened, I decided to pour my heart out by playing a few songs. I had never had a lesson on the piano, but beginning at the age of sixteen, I began fiddling around with a piano in a small dark piano practice room at Glenbrook North High School that was barely large enough for the piano and the bench. I had been upset about a beautiful tiny girl named Jane Rosene and initially wanted to find a quiet dark place to cry my sorrows away. But while I was asleep with my head in my arms on the piano, I had a dream. It was simple—that I could write a song that would express my feelings for Jane. When I awoke, I started tapping keys, listening to whether when I tapped them they made me feel happy or sad. That part of it was easy, and I realized early on that those notes that I played would always be happy or sad notes.

The hard part was creating a melody or, as I was thinking at the time, a musical story of how I was feeling. I knew what a melody was. I liked music. Instinctively, I knew how a song was structured and balanced. I believed I could write music by osmosis. Even without formal training, I believed I could create a tone poem of what was occurring deep in my soul.

The next hard part was putting chords to the little sequences of melodies I was writing. It was terribly difficult at first. But it came. I forced it to come. There was a logic to it. If I wrote something that didn't sound right, I eradicated it. But if I put something together that I liked, it sounded as if those notes had existed there for all time just to be put into the exact sequence that I had placed them.

It took me four months to write my first song. When I finished it, it was lovely, powerful, frisky, classical sounding. I named it "For Jane." I couldn't wait to play it for her. I was pretty sure the song wouldn't make her love me; she was already enamored with a handsome young stud who was a national skateboard champion. But I wanted to impress her. I wanted to give her something she had never had. A song of her own, written for her from deep within the heart of somebody who loved her.

We were friends already and I told her one lovely May day that I had written a song for her and I wanted to play it for her. I asked her if I could play it for her in that same piano practice room in which I had written the whole thing in almost absolute darkness. Don't ask me why I did that. It is probably just something that started that first day and I merely kept it going from a wintry January day to a near end of the school year day in May.

But Jane said no to the dark, tight practice room. "I have a grand piano in my living room at home. Why don't you come and play it for me there?"

Now, the pressure was really on. Here I was still a pimply faced, relatively awkward kid and Jane Rosene wanted me to come to her home and play for her on a grand piano. I had never played a grand piano. The mere thought of it intimidated me. And what if her mom was around and wanted to hear the song too? And what if her dad was there? Or she had brothers or sisters? Or what if she had friends over and they wanted to listen to the song. And God forbid she asked her boyfriend to come over and listen too. Suddenly, an intimate moment I had wanted to share with Jane in a darkened room had turned into a concert with a possible audience of several people. My God, this was the first song I had ever written. I had wanted it to be for her, not for her whole family and their friends.

For once in my life, fate smiled upon me.

"We could do it tomorrow after school about four o'clock. My mom and dad will still be at work. They don't get home until 5:30. That will give us plenty of time."

I was still nervous about brothers and sisters. I asked, "Will anyone else be there? A brother or sister maybe?"

"No, Turf. I'm an only child and we don't even have a maid so it will just be you and me."

My confidence came surging back. It was a beautiful song. I wanted to play it only for her. It was a sacred event. My wish, with some key variations, was coming true.

Tomorrow came altogether too quickly. The school day dragged while the nervous pit in my stomach grew. At 3:15, the school bell rang and I was out of the building in a flash. I had to catch a different school bus that day, Jane Rosene's bus. She lived five miles away from me in a different direction. I hadn't even anticipated how I would get home from Jane's. I simply wanted to play my song for her. I would gladly walk the five miles home, practically fly it home if she liked it.

When we got onto the bus, Jane said, "You sit with me today."

Oh my god, was this really happening? Of course there were numerous curious onlookers wondering first of all what I was doing on that bus, and secondly what I was doing sitting next to the most stunning girl at Glenbrook North, all of Northbrook for that matter. (Although, my mother and my sister ran a close second and third to Jane.)

So Jane decides to stop them all in their tracks with a single sentence said loudly enough that everyone could hear. "We're going over to my house where Turf's going to play a song he wrote for me on the piano."

Here we went again. All anonymity was now gone. The pit in my stomach grew into a canyon of nerves. Now everyone on the bus knew what was going on. In minutes, when kids started arriving home, phone calls would be made and within hours all the cool kids including Dick Whatever-the-heck his name was would know my once hoped for very personal business with Jane.

The Rosene residence was the sixth stop of the route. We got off the bus to a few lighthearted giggles and even a touch of applause. It actually made Jane and me laugh.

In a moment we were inside her enormous home after she first pulled out a large stack of letters from the mailbox. We headed straight for the living room past numerous pieces of lovely art, statues, and a blend of antique and modern furniture, all remarkably compatible.

And there it was—the Steinway Ebony Grand Piano. The centerpiece of the room. The only item on it was a Liberace style sterling silver candelabra adorned with eight unlit pure white candles. This was to be my instrument in a matter of moments.

"Who in your family plays?" I asked her.

"All of us," she answered. "My mom's the best. My dad's real good, too. I'm the least accomplished. I've really slacked off the last couple of years because of school and cheerleading. Would you like something to drink?"

"Do you have cream soda?"

"I do," she said, and she headed for the kitchen. While she was gone, I went to the piano bench and sat. The piano was huge—twice as big as the console upon which I had written her song. I played a few simple chords and played parts of a couple of scales with my right hand. My left hand was dead to scales, just there to provide simple chording. The keys were firm and springy, nothing like the old slow keys of my dark room piano.

Jane returned with my cream soda and a coaster. I took a much needed sip then placed the coaster and the drink on the piano.

As she moved to sit on the couch she asked me, "Are you ready?" The house was quiet. The living room was almost like a sanctuary with the piano being the altar. I said, "Yes I am," and then I said, "Here I am, Lord," and immediately offered a quick prayer to God to help me make it through this.

I began . . . the first notes. No mistakes. The passion was immediately there as was the beauty and the depth of boyhood love that I had for this young girl.

From the corner of my sight line I saw her lean forward and rest her head in her hands that were supported by her elbows on her knees. A smile came to her face as the notes became playful and suddenly it almost seemed as though she might cry when the notes became pensive and evocative. She was with me and the song, every inch of the way, feeling what it was saying to her with each of its phrases. I had purposely put a multitude of segments into it to illustrate all the elements of love that I felt for her as well as characteristics that she had.

The song began to end, phrases of powerful notes that could be likened to the end of a love story film of great magnitude in which the lovers had conquered a multitude of challenges. It was a progression of dynamic musical elements. I'll never know how I wrote it except that wild wonderful things were flowing inside me for this girl and somehow they made their way through my system out the tips of my fingers then almost magically into the logic of the song. And then, it was over.

I looked at Jane. She was stunned. And I was 100 percent certain in that moment, no matter what else was going on in the rest of her life, she loved me. And it felt good for both of us.

"Again please, Turf" was all she said. I happily obliged. This time playing the frisky notes a little friskier, the sad parts with more pathos, and the powerful parts with greater emphasis. This time, when I was finished, she rose from her seated position, walked to where I was seated on the piano bench, put her arms around my neck, and kissed me hard . . . on the cheek. I took it, gladly, but all fantasies of true love ever existing between us dissipated in that instant. I knew what I was to her. I was someone very special, but I was not Dick the Skateboard Champion.

She returned to her seat on the couch and said, "Could you play it for me one more time, Turf; this time with a little feeling?" I laughed. I thought I had put about everything I had into my first two renditions. In fact, I felt like Van Clybourn playing a concert for his special lady. Somehow, there was more translated from my being through my fingertips to those keys the third time I played that song. When I was finished, I was exhausted. I think Jane was, too. She had been completely imbued not merely with the story the notes of the song conveyed to her, but the depth of feelings I had for her.

In a moment, her mother was home.

"You've got to hear this, Mom. Turf wrote it for me." Jane's mother sat her purse down on a chair and sat on the couch next to Jane. Together they looked like older and younger sisters, two gorgeous women, the same size, the same hauntingly blue eyes. I played the song one final time that day. When it was finished, Jane's mother sat there shaking her head with her mouth open slightly. She appeared to be stunned that a boy of seventeen had such deep feelings for her daughter that he could write into a song like that for her.

Over the past two years I had written about ten songs. None of them as complicated or multimooded as for Jane, but each of them depicting some feeling I'd had about a thing, person, or event.

Now I was playing through the songs one by one, pouring out my feelings over having hurt Kathy. I was hoping that by playing, my own sorrows would leave my body through my fingertips.

When I finished the ten songs, I was nearly exhausted. I had played them with all the passion I could muster. I finally paused for more than merely a moment as I had when I was between playing the songs. I stretched my arms over my head, twisted my back to the left and the right to relieve the tension that had built up there since Kathy's announcements. When I stretched to the right, I realized that there were seven people in the piano room—five women and two men, all college students. There were two couples and three girls sitting in three separate flowery print chairs. Christine, the girl who had driven me back to the dorm the night before, was in their midst.

When I finished with stretching and as it looked as if I might have completed my playing, the seven listeners clapped for me. It was the largest group I had ever played for. For a moment I lost my breath. I had never been applauded by that many people and I was a little embarrassed, but I caught my breath almost immediately and was filled with a very different kind of pride, knowing that my music had positively impacted seven total strangers.

Slowly, the group began to break up, all the individuals heading to wherever they had been going before the music had distracted them. Christine stayed, waiting for everyone else to leave before she spoke to me.

"How are you feeling today, Turf?"

"Believe it or not, I had an odd hangover for about an hour when I first got up, but it's gone now."

"Do you do that kind of thing often?" she asked (with extreme curiosity).

"Christine, last night was the first time in my life that I had ever drank. I stopped at a lonely friend of mine's room and had a few drinks of rum and Coke, but I must have overdone it because I really did myself in."

"When I saw you in the snow I was really worried about you, Turf."

I could see genuine concern in her eyes.

"I'm okay today, thanks to you, Christine. God knows what might have happened to me had I slept the night out there. I could have had frost bite."

"You could have died, just another drunk Evanston student dying in the snow."

"Thank you, again."

"I think you sort of repaid me with that beautiful music. I could never have imagined when I helped you to my car that you could create something that lovely."

"How did you know that those songs were mine?"

"They were like nothing I have ever heard before. In fact, they were like tone poems, little stories, each one."

I was stunned and flattered. She had nailed it. Each time I sat down to write a song, that was exactly my goal . . . to be able to tell a musical tale. I wanted to create the imagery of whatever I was thinking and feeling at the time. I simply wanted to create a story with a beginning, a middle, and an end. There needn't be any words. I never knew how a song would start or where it would go. I would begin searching. When I found something that sounded like what I was feeling, I put it into the song. Each song took weeks to create. There were thousands of wrong notes, renegade notes that had no business trying to force their way into my very specific story. And yet, after many weeks of struggle and alien notes and many spiteful moments between me and the piano, each song would come to an end. And when that happened, it seemed as if every solitary note in its final sequential position had been destined to be in exactly that place for all eternity. I told you that once before. But I've thought about that fact hundreds of times.

"You missed the first four or five songs, Christine. Would you like me to play them?"

"I would."

I turned back around and started playing the songs, beginning with "For Jane" and in the sequence that I always played them. I never turned around the whole time I played. There was no clapping, no commenting at the complexities of any song. When I finished with the five songs I thought that she had missed, I turned around to see Christine crying.

"What's the matter?" I asked, getting up from the piano bench and sitting in the flowery print chair next to hers.

"When I heard some of your music, it made me feel things from my past that I haven't felt as deeply about in a long time . . . things that have happened to me when I was a little girl, a childhood friend of mine drowning when I was nine, my grandmother dying last year. Then one of your songs almost made me laugh. It wasn't that it was funny, it was fun. And that song made me feel a whole lot of other different kinds of feelings. That song brought me back all over the place—to tea parties I had with my mom for years as a girl, summer vacations, riding on my first Ferris wheel when I was ten, sock hops, fun stuff. But it was that all the songs cumulatively were so evocative of my emotions. I never have been to a concert before today. But now I honestly feel that I have been to one."

She glanced at her watch.

"Do you have to be somewhere?" I asked.

"I need to study in the library for about three or four hours."

I wanted to be near her so badly. "Do you mind if I join you?"

"Where're your books?"

"Back at Kendal. I can go get them."

"I have an idea," she said. "Why don't I give you a ride to get your books and we can study in Kendal's library?"

"One-half of that idea would be wonderful, telling me to get my books. But the library is locked up tight as a drum. There is only a skeleton staff of security guards working on the premises. I'd have to go to your library."

"That'll work."

"I have one more idea and a couple of quick questions. Do you have Sunday night dinner on your meal plan?"

"No I don't."

"May I take you for pizza when you are finished studying?"

"That'll work too, Turf," she said with a girlish smile inhabiting her face.

So that's what we did. We studied for four hours then drove through a dark frosty Evanston to the restaurant then shared a Chicago-style deep dish pizza. By the end of our first study date and meal together, we had developed a genuine fondness and respect for one another.

CHAPTER 4

I WAS HAVING another recurring dream. In it, the devil was lifting me off the bed, tormenting me with a powerful magnetic force over which I had no power. Then merely by willing it, he threw me against the ceiling then slammed me into all four walls—all the while tormenting me with insidious laughter emanating from his hideous face.

What had I done in my life that I had been so bad that I deserved this brutal punishment while I was still alive? If I was going to hell when I died, couldn't he at least wait until I got there and then torment me for all eternity? Why now and why so often?

I've always enjoyed probing into my deepest self and into the deepest selves of others. After all, I did become a psychologist because I cared about people and wanted to help ease their deepest pains. But as I probed my own self now, even during my nightmare, I couldn't figure out why the devil was torturing me and why he had so often, especially recently in this relatively similar recurring sleep horror. Could it have been something as simple as that I had been raised Catholic by strict parents, priests, and nuns whose stories about the devil had always scared the crap out of me? And the names they used for the devil—Lucifer, Beelzebub, the Prince of Darkness. Could there be other words or phrases that could terrify a six-, seven-, or eight-year-old boy than these? And then there was the concept of eternal hell—that the devil could torture you forever and ever and ever ad infinitum—with relentless blazing fire. You didn't even have to do too much to get there. You could make it for disobeying your parents, which my friends and I did all the time when we were little. Then some zealous nun, "hooded warriors" my buddies and I would call them, would tell you that if you had disobeyed your parents and you hadn't confessed that sin (those sins in my case), to a priest and you got killed in a car crash, you were going straight to Lucifer's inferno. Looking back, we kids played so many games in the street where we were darting constantly around moving cars. I can quickly remember how the "hooded warriors" threats even affected my fun games when I was a little tyke. In the middle of Union

Avenue, darting to grab an errant baseball toss, I would wonder whether the future split second would be the one when I was going to hell.

The devil had been firmly implanted in my psyche. But I thought I was past all that. I should be past all that. I had worked hard in my conscious life to eradicate all belief that the devil could ever hurt me, that there even was such a salacious being.

Yet here I was, a grown man, well adjusted, I thought, and I was dreaming about the devil throwing me around the room, tormenting me, torturing me. The dream was so real and I was hysterically frightened. When I'd awake from these recurring nightmares, the pain and fear would linger for hours. Even days after they happened, I'd be pondering exactly what it was that had happened and why it had occurred at all. During this point of my life, it was happening every few weeks so that I was never so far away from it that I couldn't always be pondering it like I did the myriad other complex things that were occurring in the life of a simple psychologist.

Here I was right in this instant, in the middle of this horrific dream. I was in hell, and it was my bedroom and the devil and I were fist fighting. I'd get one punch in that barely grazed him and he'd get five punches into my face and body that felt as if each blow was a jackhammer causing excruciating pain.

I would not give up. Somehow I would right myself and punch him hard in his red evil face. Then he'd get this glorified sadistic look on his face and unleash another devastating flurry of blows upon my head, torso, kidneys, and groin. He knew how to punch and cause pain. Even the devil needed to catch his breath, and when he paused for an instant in his brutality, I'd gather the wherewithal to slug the bastard a time or two only to be pummeled again by his next onslaught.

Over and over this happened. A series of similarities that seemed unending and hopeless against him, I had no chance to defeat him.

Then suddenly, in the midst of my assault from the Prince of Evil, I heard it again. Knock, knock. It terrified me beyond the misery I was already enduring. All I could think of was that it was some of Lucifer's legends trying to get into the bedroom to help him hurt me. But no one came into the bedroom. I thought that if it were part of his minions they would have no problem breaking my bedroom door down or seeping in through the walls like spirits do.

On top of my continuing beating and my conjecturing about the spirits that might be joining Satan at any moment, I also thought that someone might be in trouble at my front door. It was that thought that must have trumped everything else that was happening because it was enough to wake me. I yelled, "Hold on a minute, I'll be right there," as I awakened, frightened from my dream. I hustled to the front door, this time not peering through the peephole figuring I had just been battling with Satan. I wasn't afraid of any human being at this moment.

I threw open the door and, for the second time in two weeks, both times after two loud knocks. There was no one at the front door. Suddenly, I was more frightened than I had been moments before. Were the knocks from allies of the devil trying to get into my dream bedroom trying to help him? Or was it a totally different demon from a different dimension entirely wanting to get into my house to torment me? But with the courtesy of knocking? Or lastly was it a person who hated me for some reason and who wanted to annoy me by knocking on the door only twice then racing away before I could rouse myself and get to the front door? I didn't know and that bothered me.

Here I was, a man who'd spent much of his life trying to figure out what made other people tick inadequately, and I couldn't even figure myself out with the devil dreams and the Two-Knock Ghost. I went to the fridge and mixed myself a glass of Publix soy vanilla and soy chocolate milk and watched about twenty minutes of news and weather on Bay News 9 before I felt calm enough to turn out the light and try to fall back asleep.

CHAPTER 5

ALCOHOLISM HAD SNUCK up on me. Before I was twenty-four, I had drunk only once—that night I had the rum and Coke with Robert Workman. I didn't have a single drink after that. I had no need for alcohol, not even to think about it. I had a great life. I married Christine three months after I got my BA. She was working as a nurse at St. Joseph's on Lakeshore Drive. I had a fantastic relationship with my mom and dad and all four of my grandparents. Christine and I were planning a family whenever nature ordained it. We didn't want to try to manipulate anything. We wanted to meet life as it arrived, no fears. We both loved Chicago and the lake front, the wonderful hotels, the Shedd Aquarium, the Adler Planitarium, the Museum of Science and Industry, the Buckingham Fountain, the shopping. We loved the Wild Cats and the Bulls and the Black Hawks, the Bears, Maxwell Street, Pizzeria Uno and Duo, and believe it or not, both the Cubs and the White Sox. We'd pull for each team in their respective league, except in later years when interleague began and when they played each other. It may became the best team win on any given day and because we loved both teams we couldn't lose.

On my twenty-fourth birthday, Christine arranged a party for me—nothing fancy, just a get-together of my parents, her parents, both sets of my grandparents and about six of our mutual friends. Our modest three-story house in Bridgeport easily accommodated the total sixteen people that hung out in the house that night. We had my favorite then, black forest cake and chocolate milk. Of course, Christine knew what everyone she had invited liked to drink so there was every kind of beverage on the table from beer to wine, coffee to tea, lemonade to ice water, chocolate milk and apple juice, which was my second favorite drink at the time. It was the late sixties and my party was a lovefest of sorts with people who all got along well.

There were no political debates or silly arguments about meaningless things. There was just a bunch of giggles and talk about everybody's favorite novel—*To Kill a Mockingbird, Dr. Zhivago, Catch Twenty-two, of Mice and Men*. Everybody was intelligent, kind, respectful of each other's feelings. It was one of my best birthdays ever.

It was a Friday night. No one had to go to work the next day. No one had to rush out of there to get home to catch a good night of rest. The party was mellow and lingered till a bit past midnight when the first yawns occurred, and shortly thereafter the conversation shifted to dialogue as to whether it might be time for people to start leaving. It took about forty-five minutes till about 1:00 a.m. for everyone to say their good-byes and share hugs and kisses. My mom, dad, and grandparents were the last to leave, each of them lending a hand to help Christine and me clean the party mess.

I couldn't help but reflect on what wonderful people they each were—my mom and dad, Kathy and Bob, and my maternal grandparents Phil and Lena, my paternal grandparents Sid and Dorothy. Several years before my twenty-fourth birthday party, my mom and dad decided to downsize now that their kids were grown and move out of the house from Wheeling to Glenview. They wanted to be closer to Lena and Phil, who had a slew of medical issues in their early seventies. They found a house one block from my parents' house. Kathy could walk there, which she and Bob had done hundreds of times in the past four years. Bob and Kathy's plan was to help out Lena and Phil as much as they could in order to keep Lena and Phil in their home as long as possible. My grandparents knew they weren't healthy, and they knew the sands of time were slipping through their hourglass. They had sincerely expressed their disdain for ever living in a nursing home and my mom had figured that being close by to be able to help them if she or Bob were needed was a perfect solution.

My dad didn't have any problem with Mom's plan. After twenty-six years of being married to her, he was still deeply in love with her, more so now than ever before. They were utterly happy with their relationship and my dad went right along with the plan, not because he let my mom dictate the terms of big decisions, but he knew it was the right and really good thing to do. Besides, Bob's mom and dad lived on Glencoe Beach, thirteen minutes away from their new little house in Glenview.

When they left my party that night, they stepped outside into a glorious winter scene. The sky was clear with a bright three-quarter moon shining. Though the temperature was only 28 degrees, there was no wind and a crispness was in the air that seemed to elevate all of our spirits more than the chill made my family feel they had to rush to the car.

Even though we had shared hugs and kisses inside, we shared more of them outside in the beauty of the night. I remember kissing my grandfather and my dad on the neck then blowing fart sounds with my lips on the same necks that I had just kissed. It tickled each man literally, made them giggle, and reminded them how they both used to do that to me when I was a little boy. I was sure that my grandfather had taught that playful gesture to my dad. What I wasn't sure about was how many generations back that goofiness went.

I was so happy that night when they drove away. There was so much love for me packed inside that Lincoln Continental. I took Christine's hand, pulled her close to me, and kissed her romantically before we walked back into the house, arm in arm to go to bed.

I was deep into a contented sleep when the phone rang about 4:45 a.m. It was pitch-black outside, clouds having come up and hidden the earlier bright moon. It was totally dark inside the bedroom. I hoped it was a rare wrong number because I wanted to return to my sleep as quickly as possible.

"Hello?" I said.

The series of statements I heard next were a blur of information then and are still a blur of information now. I was reduced to nearly childlike responses as the slew of the most horrific of phrases were revealed to me.

"Car crash on the outer drive. Caused by a drunk driver. Hit your parents' car front left quarter panel causing it to flip at least four times."

"What?"

"Your grandparents weren't wearing seat belts in the backseat. Grandpa broke his neck."

"Huh?"

"Grandma broke her back and spine."

"Huh?"

"Flew around the inside of the car like rag dolls causing broken bones and head injuries to both of your parents."

"What?"

"All killed."

"What? No, no, no, no, no. There's got to be a mistake."

It was not a mistake. Through a fog of emotions, I had heard enough to know the facts as they truly were. Four of the people I loved most in the world had been senselessly snatched from me. I could see how it had unfolded. The four parents had decided to cap off the night with the scenic drive home along Lakeshore Drive, hoping to see the moon illuminate the frozen snow-covered lake. Although it was a much longer ride home, I could feel each of their longings for twenty minutes more of the beauty of nature as well as the splendid architecture of the buildings along the outer drive of Chicago's Gold Coast.

I listened carefully as the voice on the other end of the line told me where my parents' and grandparents' bodies were, and before I felt anywhere near prepared for it, there was a click and the worst phone call of my life had terminated.

I sat there for a moment with the receiver in my right hand, wondering if I even had strength enough to put it back into its cradle. I contemplated waking Christine but when I looked to my left, I saw that she was already awake, sitting up against the headboard.

"What happened, honey?" she asked with eyes looking more concerned than I had ever seen them.

I can't even write after, all these years, exactly how I explained it to her. The pain of repeating it in any form has never abated. I can tell you that when I was finished, tears were streaming down her pretty young face. No doubt she too had been hit with a cacophony of overwhelming feelings. They included complete compassion for each of my family members and how they had died. There was empathy for me and the fact that my monumental grief moment would change me and that I would have to live with it forever. And though she never told me this, there had to be her unbridled joy that it wasn't her parents and grandparents who had also been at my party and who had also come in one car. She might have even been thinking, *Thank God, there had been no drunk drivers out that night between Bridgeport and Oak Lawn.*

That was the beginning of it—the unfathomable, unfillable, unrelenting, unending emotional and physical hole in my stomach. It's been said before, by millions of people, I imagine, and scores of my own patients, I am certain, but when this kind of emotional pain strikes you, it is as if someone has aimed a shotgun at your stomach, point-blank, and pulled the trigger. You are blasted by numerous pellets, ripping a virtual hole in your stomach and all the other vital organs that surround the area. Time ceases to move. Then almost instantly, you contemplate what you have lost, how infinitely much you have lost. Then you are struck by an inability to breathe that is so all encompassing that you wonder if you will ever be able to take your next breath, then all the breaths you had previously been looking forward to breathe in joyfully before this moment. You go into near physical shock. You want someone you love to put you into a bed where you can lie in a fetal position so the stomach pain doesn't hurt as much, cover you with a huge blanket, then wrap their arms around you tightly while saying in an ultra-soothing voice for weeks on end, "It will be okay, Turf, you'll make it through this. I'm still here. I haven't gone anywhere. I'm not going anywhere. I'll be there with you through this whole thing." I wanted Christine to do all those things for me. But all she initially did was hug me tightly as I fell to my back in our bed, my tears flowing profusely, before she pulled my head to her breasts and held me there for nearly a quarter of an hour while rubbing my head and remaining silent. I realized even then that she was giving me the best she had in that moment—tenderness that I longed for and didn't think I could breathe without.

Slowly, I curled into a fetal position beside her, feeling less in control of myself than I ever had. And gradually, over the next several hours, days, months, and years, all the reassurances that I could ever yearn for from Christine that I would make it through this and be okay, that she was still there and wasn't going anywhere, came as often and with as much fervor as a human being could deliver them.

The problem was that I didn't believe any of it. I didn't trust anything anymore. I didn't trust Christine. I didn't trust myself. How could I? I didn't think I would ever leave my bedroom again, much less be able to leave my bed to go to the bathroom. I didn't trust my priest to be able to tell me anything that would assuage my grief. I didn't trust the morticians to restore the beauty to my parents' and grandparents' bodies and faces. Nothing. I trusted in and believed in nothing, including God—least of all God. I had always considered him a friend. But I thought now, *How could he do this to me?* I was contemplating from a place of raw emotion. There was no logic to any of my thoughts. I had been figuratively shot in my emotional stomach but felt unfathomable pain in my real stomach now. Where was God when I needed him? Where was he when my family with the sacred heart scapular hanging from the rearview mirror needed him a couple of hours ago? God was the one I trusted the least right now.

Not only had four intrinsic elements of my life been untimely and unfairly ripped from me, but there was no God comfort anywhere to be found or felt within me. He too had been ripped from me, ruthlessly.

As I have said and may repeat, there was no logic to my thinking, just pain. Some of the shotgun blasts had also hit my brain, releasing horrible chemicals I had studied for years in school. These chemicals, plus the pain I was feeling, had made me mentally ill. No matter what kind of young man I had been before, no matter who I was married to, no matter what funeral arrangements I would have to make or patients I would have to see, I was damaged goods.

For the next several months, I lived in a no-man's-land, barely functional. I continued with my graduate studies in psychology while working part-time in the Chicago Public School System. Christine worked at St. Joe's tirelessly and selflessly as she always did. But when the clock started ticking again it was in slow motion—click, click, click—one agonizing second at a time. You could almost hear the sound of some mystical time beating drum. Boom, boom, boom, one boom per second. The agonizingly slow annoying pace was palpable. Thud, thud, thud. Each thud a pang of pain. Pain, pain, pain. It was nearly all I could think of. Here I was, one of the luckiest men in the world because I was married to one of the kindest, most caring woman imaginable and I couldn't even transfer my pain into loving her more deeply. Instead, those early months following the accident were the origins of my slowly developing neglect of her. We were newlyweds and it shouldn't have been that way. Don't get me wrong. I was crazy about my wife—I still am—we had good times, scores of them and thousands of laughs. so many raucous and hysterical laughs. But I should have been much more attentive to her needs, taken more time to explore her heart, mind, and soul. And it was only after many years of the raucous laughter that I began to question its origin.

I almost feel guilty now that this is my story and not Christine's She deserves her own memoir. She is a great lady and a better person than I will ever be.

About six months after the accident, I didn't think I could go on. The hole was still there and time was still thudding its sluggish refrain. I tried to think of everything I loved, the Cubs and the White Sox for example. I went to games. It didn't help. I ate out a lot. I took Christine countless times to Pizzeria Unos and Duos. It didn't help. I tried to pray. It didn't help. I went to see outdoor concerts at Grant Park and Ravinia. It didn't help. I still loved baseball and deep dish pizza and writing music of many kinds, but the hole was still there. And though I felt so utterly empty, there seemed to be something inside the hole—pain. It was a duality of pain, one which sliced through the core of my emotional being to my depths and one which kept my physical stomach churning in endless ulceric gravitas.

As I searched relentlessly for pain-reducing remedies both with and without Christine, one night my mind flashed on something new to me then but with roots in my personal past. I remembered my night with Kathy Blazer, how goofy I must have acted, how I couldn't remember so much of what I must have done, at least according to Kathy. I even recalled how good the rum and Coke had tasted that night in poor Robert Workman's dorm room. I theorized that maybe one night Christine and I could go out to a little restaurant, order some rum and Coke with our pizza, have a bunch of giggles and laughs, and in the process I could find some relief from the pain of thinking of the deaths of my family with all the residual physical pain.

That afternoon I called Christine from work only moments after first conceiving my idea. She was at work but on break, so I didn't have my usual difficult time reaching her. I asked her if she'd like to come to dinner with me that night.

She said yes immediately then continued, "What's the occasion?"

I answered, "Absolutely nothing, except that I love you and feel like going out and having some fun." There was nothing untrue about my statement.

"Where to?" she asked.

"PU," I said, our fun initials to signify Pizzeria Uno.

And she said, "Okay, Turf, I'll see you when I get home."

I felt better already. I always did when I knew I was going out with Christine. Although she was not capable of filling the hole in my heart, nor should she ever have been expected to do so, she always was a wonderful companion and I loved her dearly.

That was my first experiment with rum and Coke. It was my second time drinking it. My initial use of them as a drink a few years earlier with Robert Workman had been an accident, but tonight I wanted to see if rum and Coke could help with emotional pain. By the time I ordered my drink, Christine had already ordered her customary water with lemon, which I usually drank, too. The difference between us was that she drank hers straight. She didn't even squeeze her lemons into the water. She just plopped the lemons into the water and that's the way she liked it. I would squeeze my lemons into the water, squeezing every drop I could out of the one or two wedges a server would usually bring to me. Then I'd add some substitute sugar to it, and bam, I'd have a glass of easily made lemonade.

"You're having a rum and Coke, tonight? That's different. I think that's the first time you've ever ordered a drink at dinner since we've been together."

"It is. I have a taste for it."

"You do? I didn't even know you drank."

"I don't."

"How'd you know you had a taste for it?"

"Do you remember the night we met? You picked me up out of the snow. Earlier in the evening I stopped in the room of one of my lonely acquaintances and he gave me rum and Coke. I obviously drank way too much, but I remember having a fun night overall. I know I've been moody for a long time now, and I figured if I had one or two drinks that I might be more fun for you tonight and feel less tension inside."

Christine went right along with me.

"If you're going to have a rum and Coke, I'm going to have one too."

She was already smiling like a child.

"It's pretty powerful stuff," I told her. "You'd better limit yourself to one, so you can drive. I'll limit myself to two. After all, I'm almost a foot taller than you, and I won't even think about driving. Is that all right with you?"

"Of course it is," she said, her blue eyes glistening in the dimly lit pizzeria.

We laughed through dinner. We mocked the Cubs who were having another mediocre season. We laughed about co-workers and their oddities. We giggled about whether Miss Kitty and Matt Dillon were having sex on Gunsmoke. We debated which was scarier, Outer Limits or Twilight Zone. And I actually felt better emotionally. I was high enough to be happy, to have fun with the young woman I loved more than any other person in the world. And Christine had fun, too. And from what I can now remember, it was the most I had seen Christine smile since before the crash.

By the end of the meal, Christine's share of our large deep dish pizza had absorbed her singular rum and Coke, so I felt good about her driving us home. After a drunk driver killed my family, I was never going to drive drunk, or allow anyone, who I considered even remotely tipsy, to drive me anywhere. This I swore to the core of my twenty-four-year-old being. I would never drive drunk.

We went home that night and made love. We were still giggly from the various conversations we had had at the restaurant and on the way home. And Christine was more frisky because I was behaving more jovially than in the last six months.

That's how my alcoholism started. Innocently enough. And with some marvelous side benefits. I always had my two rum and Cokes and she'd sometimes have one then drive us back to Bridgeport. There were restaurants in Bridgeport that we liked—an Italian joint, two Lithuanian spots, The Governor's Table, and David's—but whenever we went to a Bridgeport restaurant, we'd always walk. We'd hold hands, talk, and laugh, and I remember feeling excited even before getting to a restaurant because I knew that in a few minutes my rum and Coke would help anesthetize my still decimated emotions.

Five years into the restaurant drinking, I didn't have a single negative thought about what I was doing. I had worked hard and earned my PhD, writing my dissertation on drunk drivers and the effects they had on their victims, their victim's families, and their own families. Christine had helped me tremendously with my college tuition, and I was finally able to begin paying her back while saving some cash for our future family and our retirement, which seemed so eternally far away.

When I drank, always rum and Coke, I felt better emotionally. For the first couple of years, Christine accompanied me. I'd have two drinks, she'd have one, and then drive us home. That was our system. For some strange reason, I had a loyalty to rum and Coke. It was almost as if the drink was a friend to me. I had no desire to drink anything else or even try something different. But after two years into our restaurant drinking, Christine decided one night that rum and Coke, alcohol, was not her thing, and she stopped it, snap, just like that. With no problem. She had no dependency on liquor. She switched unceremoniously to lemonade and that became her drink for the next decade. There was also no judgmental negativity from her toward my drinking. After all, it was something I did only when we went out to dinner, which was on average, maybe seven or eight times a month. I didn't look or act like an alcoholic in any fashion. We didn't keep alcohol in the house. Through my twenty-ninth year of life, I had never purchased a bottle of rum. I acted like a perfectly well-adjusted man in every way. The fact that I had a couple of drinks a few times a month when we went out was never perceived by Christine or myself as a danger sign as to what alcohol might do to me in the future.

In what I perceived as fact at the time, alcohol seemed to be working for me. When I drank, I laughed and giggled in whatever restaurant we were dining. And Christine seemed to be enjoying me more when I was my extroverted self than the more introverted sober and somber self I had become since the accident. Our restaurant nights almost always culminated with us making love and falling asleep in a tender embrace. Those were some of my favorite nights with her. And they were some of my favorite times with myself. I hardly noticed the pain pit in my stomach on those wonderful rum and Coke nights.

The problem was that I was growing increasingly more dependent on alcohol to loosen me up, to relax me. I was consciously aware of this. But my body and subconscious were in those secret places within which truths are stored.

CHAPTER 6

SLIGHTLY AFTER MY thirtieth birthday, Christine and I had our first son. We named him Robert Phillip after my father and grandfather. Initially, I felt that his presence on this planet helped fill the void that was still in my heart.

He was adorable. He was almost born a gentleman. He rarely cried and when he wanted or needed something he sort of cooed for it, making discernable faces as to what it was that he needed. A scrunched face meant that he needed a diaper change. An open mouth, glistening eyes meant he needed a bottle, and before he was old enough for a bottle, it meant that he needed a breast. He had manners before he knew what manners were, and it seemed as if we were always teaching him something. He was consistently teaching us something as well. He was the greatest joy that we had felt in six years beside our love for each other. We agreed because Robert Phillip was undoubtedly intelligent, that we would not speak baby talk around him. Instead, we used complete sentences and even large words, as if we were speaking to a little man. There were plenty of toys and baby playing, but from the beginning of his life he was dictating to us the rules for how we should play with him.

Like me, he liked to throw baseballs and was good at it. I hadn't played much baseball since I finished college, but playing catch with him, even when he was two made me miss not only playing baseball, but watching the Cubs and White Sox like I used to. It also made me miss collecting baseball cards when they were the greatest thing in the world that a little boy could buy for a nickel.

Robert Phillip filled my heart and soul so much that I stopped drinking rum and Coke at restaurants. I was feeling more fulfilled, more purposeful in my life. I had a son to raise and a wife to love. I had a multitude of clients that constantly needed my encouragement. At times I thought I was the luckiest man in the world.

Things got better still. Slightly after my thirty-second birthday and four days after the date my son was born, Christine had another baby. This time it was a girl.

She was gorgeous and even quieter than Robert Phillip, the little gentleman. We named her Lena Kathleen in honor of my grandmother and mother.

But two nights after the overwhelming joy Christine and I had felt over the birth of our daughter, her breathing became shallow. Christine was sound asleep in her hospital room at St. Joe's and I was asleep in my bed in Bridgeport. The doctors' initially agreed that it was not prudent to wake Christine while they were working on Lena. What could she do to help? Nothing. The doctors decided my wife would be better served sleeping through the night, unless things grew more serious. Why wake her at 2:30 in the morning and cause her undue worry? They didn't call me either, same logic. After three and a half hours of hypothesizing, testing and x-raying, seven doctors—five men and two women—concluded that my daughter had a hole in her heart. Imagine that. I'd had a medi-physical hole in my own heart that I finally thought was healing because of my rediscovered joy, due to the births of my children.

When the call came to my office the next morning, it was as if an unknown medi-physical phantom shot me in my very real physical stomach once again. The emotional pain which had been abating for two years as I was beginning to build my family, exploded back with horrendous ferocity.

"How did you figure out it's a hole?" I asked the doctor who was also going to be her surgeon. He explained that he figured it out pretty traditionally. They found a murmur when they listened to her heart. When they took the x-ray, they found that it was located in the atria. The condition is called an atrial septal defect. He continued to explain that the left and right blood filling chambers of the heart are separated by a thin shared wall, called the arterial system. Lena had a hole there in the wall between the atria—those are the upper two filling chambers of the heart. Because of the hole, some oxygenated blood from the left atrium was flowing through the hole in the septum into the right atrium where it was mixing with oxygen poor blood and multiplying the total amount of blood that was flowing into the lungs. This more powerful blood flow was creating a swishing sound. That's what a heart murmur is. And that's what they heard in Lena.

"In cases where there is a small hole, the problem usually resolves itself as the child grows. But in Lena's case, there was concern because we rated the hole as large. We're going to have to be vigilant because Lena's heart is having to work harder because of the hole and the contributing factor that Lena has a tiny heart to go along with her tiny body," the doctor explained.

Lena hadn't been premature, but her birth weight had only been six pounds two ounces. We hadn't worried about the weight because in every other way she appeared to be healthy as well as beautiful.

"What will you do now, Doctor?" I asked, my own heart fluttering.

"We monitor closely in intensive care, get some more weight on her and repair the hole as soon as we feel she's strong enough to undergo the surgery."

"Mr. McKenzie, I can almost 100 percent assure you that Lena will be fine and that not only will there be no complications, but she will grow up to be a healthy normal child. I've performed similar procedures scores of times."

That is exactly what he said. They were the kind professional words of a brilliant competent doctor. But did I hear that? No. I heard the word "almost" before "100 percent assure you." I heard "multiplies the total amount of blood that flows to the lungs." I heard "heart murmur and Lena's heart is having to work harder and Lena has a tiny heart to go along with her tiny body." That is what I heard and that is what my weakened emotional being clung to.

"Thank you, Doctor. I'll be there as soon as I finish work."

Thud, thud, thud—the second hand banged to a sole penetrating crawl. Worry, the depth of which I had never experienced, assaulted me like a blitz to a quarterback. Instantly, a god-awful loneliness permeated my being. I had to talk to Christine right away. I buzzed my secretary and told her to tell my next client I might be a few minutes late. Christine and I talked for forty-three minutes. We both cried; she first, then I. Then the ebb of pain hit her again then me again. And this happened again many times. We were on a teeter-totter of pain. First one of us hit the ground with a bang then the other one.

My poor wife, I thought, *she could have never imagined that by becoming a part of my life, she would experience so much pain*. The word pain, the feeling of pain, were becoming sad refrains in our lives.

I had not had a drink in over a year. But now I wanted one terribly. I felt like a coward, dependent on the emotional relief a few chemicals from a bottle of alcohol could give me. I felt myself becoming afraid,

afraid for my daughter and any physical pain she might endure, afraid for Christine and the emotional and resulting physical pain she would undoubtedly feel—and I was afraid for myself. I was this big six foot two, 190-pound man, thirty-two years old, in great shape, and I suddenly felt afraid to be alone at the end of the night.

When I finished with my last client about 5:30, on my way to the hospital to see Christine and Lena, I did something I had never done before. I stopped at a liquor store and bought a bottle of rum and a six pack of Coke. I threw them onto the backseat when I returned to the car, thankful they were there, almost like friends who would later provide me with comfort and assistance with sleep.

At the hospital, I went to see Christine first. Her eyes were bloodshot from crying. I went immediately to her bed, bent over, and hugged her tightly for nearly a minute. I felt a single one of her teardrops hit my neck while we hugged. Even though a large, wise part of me knew that I shouldn't, I somehow began to feel responsible for what was happening with Lena. After a few moments of talking with each other, Christine and I went to see Lena. She was already in intensive care. She appeared tinier than the other times I had seen her. Perhaps it was because I knew she was markedly more vulnerable now than when I had, only forty-eight hours earlier, felt unbridled joy when I welcomed her to the outside world.

Christine and I stood there holding hands and not speaking a word. We simply looked at Lena, wondering what, if anything, there was to say. Somehow our locked fingers expressed a pact of solidarity that together we would do whatever it took to see our infant daughter through this first crisis of her life. I can only speak for myself, but I was also thinking selfishly about what I would feel if Lena didn't survive her operation. I can surmise that Christine might have been thinking similar thoughts, but she had drifted into a profound silence. Though our hands were clasped and we were standing side by side, it was as if she were absent from the scene in the way that really mattered—her mind. She was inhabiting another dimension, probably similar to the one I had lived in for most of the last eight years. It's a dimension where the chaos of loss and pain battle with your ability to focus on present moment happiness. It's a dimension where worry is a cruel king and all of your other thoughts are lowly subjects he is abusing.

* * * * *

Later that night I went home and carried my bottle of rum and my six pack of Coke into the house for the first time. Many hundreds of times would follow. I did not turn the TV on, I did not eat. I walked to my bedroom and closed the door after fixing my drink on the counter near the fridge. I was not thinking that I was a moral coward or that maybe I had been for the last several years. I was thinking that I was sad, that I was just doing what I had to do, that I had every right to do this. I was a grown man. I had a busy day tomorrow, and I needed to sleep without worry, if that was possible. What happened was that the pain of the loss of my parents and my dad's parents slammed into my mind like an emotional tsunami. The impact of the wave washed away every good thought that might have been in my mind a moment before the impact. I could not think of Christine, or my beloved Cubs, the White Sox, or Pizzeria Uno, or how much I loved my career. I could only think of the actual loss of my family and the possible loss of Lena. I drank while under the covers, leaning against two propped up pillows. The sheets and blankets were pulled to my chin. I was suddenly desperate for some feeling of security. How foolish I was to think rum and Coke and sheets and a blanket could provide me with any degree of what I was desperately seeking.

When I fell asleep that night, I dreamed of the devil for the first time. I was in the hospital, and Christine and I were looking at Lena, who was in a glass isolation room. There was a doctor bending over her, listening to her heart with a stethoscope. When he finished listening, he stood and turned around. It was the devil—no horns, but the unmistakable sneering red face looking at the two of us and wordlessly saying, "I've got the situation in my hands now and there is nothing either of you can do about it."

I woke up wildly frightened and angry. I was angry because I had stopped going to mass and confession years ago. I didn't even believe in the devil, thinking deeply on a conscious level that he was a ridiculous concept created to control people's behavior through scare tactics. But my dream of him had scared the crap out of me. I was angry because I didn't know why something I didn't even believe in would have the power to frighten me. I woke thinking, "What if there really was a devil and he had control over Lena's fate?" I also didn't believe in Jesus, but in a good, compulsively creative God who could hear me if I prayed and might conceivably intercede on my behalf with this devil SOB if I asked him.

So that night I prayed in my bed, as I once again pulled the covers to my chin. I said, "Dear God, please don't let that demon hurt my baby. She is so innocent. Why would he want her, anyway? There're so many other people out there who are better candidates for his tormenting. Christine and I don't deserve this. We're good people. Please help us."

I was still quivering with fear. I thought I was a stronger man than this. But being an incessant ponderer, I fell asleep again that night knowing that part of my problem was that I didn't know for sure what the truth about God or the devil was. Every thought I ever had as a grown man about God and the devil and even life and all of its shoulds and shouldn'ts was conjecture. I didn't believe in anything specific. Everything I concluded about the great spiritual unknown was theory. Nothing was a true conclusion. I really couldn't ever tell any of my clients that what I was telling them about life was absolute truth because I was not at all certain what absolute truth was. I believed in it because I was certain it was out there somewhere, but what I truly believed was that the absolute truths of the great unknowns were something that man's small brains would never be privy to. When I gave my clients advice, I felt that primarily I would be giving them suggestions about how they could function better as citizens of their own communities, their states, the culture of the United States. Did I know who God truly was? Most certainly, I did not. But I theorized that I was part of nature, something so profound that I did not create. And if God had created this, He would definitely allow me access to him and on this night of my first devil terror, I hoped like an innocent child that God would hear my prayer and spare Lena from significant pain or death.

I fell back asleep and sometime during that fitful night, I heard two innocuous knocks at what sounded like my front door, but I was too exhausted to wake up and answer them.

CHAPTER 7

CHRISTINE GRADUATED SEVENTEENTH in her class at Northwestern. She was smart—big ten cum laude smart. She graduated seventeenth in her class out of hundreds. She loved to study all kinds of things. When she put her mind to it, she could achieve anything.

She had gained a reputation for being the go-to gal at work. if someone was sick in hers or almost any other hospital specialty. She was a fast learner and had more on-the-job training for different specialties than I could begin to express. She was beyond dependable. I will never understand how she pulled off doing all the things she did on the job and with our family. We did have a tremendous amount of help with Robert Phillip during his early life. Christine's parents, Dan and Judy O'Reilly, lived in Hyde Park. Getting from there to Bridgeport only took a few minutes. They were almost always available for babysitting not because we asked them for their help but mainly because they asked us for the joy of spending as much time as possible with their grandson. They were keeping Robert Phillip for a few days while Christine delivered Lena.

Christine's father was an accountant. That's where Christine received her acuity with numbers. Dan O'Reilly was smart, made a good living, and was incredible at investing and making money from those investments. He and Christine were very close. He spent hours with her from the time she was nine years old teaching her about the stock market and the value of saving money. On numerous occasions he would tell her, "'Teenie,' saved money never sleeps. It works for you around the clock." He was still telling her that when she was in her early thirties and she was listening.

Because of her love of and near wizardry with money, I gladly let Christine handle all of our financial affairs. She would talk to me about everything and I would listen, but handling the money was her thing. Because we lived modestly and had successful careers, our holdings grew rapidly. Most importantly, Dan O'Reilly was always there to answer questions that Christine might have. They were a playful tag team when it came to sharing options and ideas and solving financial equations. Christine's father was always a good friend to us on monetary and many other levels.

Christine's mother was also a nurse. There was no doubt that Judy had taught her daughter how to take care of people tenderly. Judy was pretty like Christine. In her forties when I met her, she was in excellent physical condition, a byproduct of her enjoying running for exercise at every opportunity. She also liked to lift weights. So besides being an excellent example to Christine how to care for people tenderly, she was also an example for Christine how to eat healthy and stay strong. Judy was five feet two inches tall, the same height as Christine. And she was a little dynamo. In her fifties when our children were just born, Judy was in a position to work when she wanted—thanks in part to her husband, Dan, and his skills at making money. Their family was the opposite of Christine and me. Dan was the financial guru, planner, and manager. Whereas in our family, Christine was the financial expert.

I wondered how Judy did all the things she did. She was like three women in one. She especially starred at Thanksgiving and Christmas where year after year she was the gracious hostess for wonderful parties at her home in Hyde Park. Judy was a beautiful woman inside and out, and I often thought how lucky Dan was to have her love, as I was to have Christine's. Put Judy and Christine side by side and they looked much more like sisters than mother and daughter. Though both women were independent thinkers and late twentieth century contemporary progressives, their religious beliefs were fairly simple and almost identical. Both women had been born Catholics and believed deeply in Jesus Christ as their Lord and Savior and the pope as the leader of the spiritual world and all of the basic tenants their church espoused. Neither of them attended mass every Sunday but the reason for that for each woman was that their work schedules had often prevented them from doing so. But each woman was sure to fulfill the obligations required to be official practicing Catholics. They were two extremely benevolent women who were near real life saints. They gave constantly and profoundly of themselves to countless souls. The only difference between them and canonized saints was that they weren't performing miracles, and they weren't dead. What they were performing were endless acts of transformative love for their patients, friends, and families. Neither of them believed in ghosts, except the Holy Ghost.

My wife came from good stock. She was a giving person. Her goodness most times seemed effortless. But right now, when Lena's future was in question, I observed how difficult it was for her to hold it together. This generally playful woman was having a hard time controlling her weeping. Usually bubbly and effervescent, Christine had become remarkably quiet and instead of being a rock that I could lean on, I found myself often standing silently next to her, holding her hand and weeping along with her. I was still so damaged from the loss of my parents and grandparents that it seemed as though there was nothing of substance within myself to tap into for moral support or encouragement. Of course Judy and Dan O'Reilly were always nearby to help, but I was frustrated with myself for not having a spiritual fountain in reserve that I could drink from to fortify myself so I could be stronger for my wife at this time.

Still, Christine was my greatest role model. Even during this difficult time that knocked me awkwardly from any sense of healing that I had experienced with the passing of the years, I could still feel strength emanating from Christine. And I wondered, shamefully, whether she thought less of me because she could sense my weakness within my silence.

* * * * *

Three times in the next week before Christine came home from the hospital, I brought home a bottle of rum with me. I'd go to work, go to the hospital, see the girls, then stop at a liquor store and buy some rum and Coke. I almost thanked God for the companionship of those bottles because with them, I didn't feel so alone. I wasn't thinking about any impending alcoholism. I was wondering how to get through the next hour without fracturing within myself from fear of the unknown.

Had I been a stronger man, not such a moral coward, I would not have needed the rum. I could have turned to prayer, worked out more, read a self-help book, gone to church, confessed my sins, received Communion. But I didn't believe in the religious stuff anymore. And there wasn't much time to work out because I was spending nearly sixteen hours a day between the office and the hospital.

It was Christine who was the strong one—always. I don't want to give the impression that I am not a good person. I am. I always was and

I always will be, but it's the truth. I love my wife, my kids, my family, people in crisis, people in general. I am not a racist. I hate war of any kind, and I'd do anything I could for my family not only when they were in trouble, but I like to create fun things to do with them too. But Christine was the stronger one. And Christine was more creative too. She planned our dinners when our schedules permitted. They were always tastier and more balanced than what I threw together when I was in charge. She would conceive of our vacations, plan routes if we drove, take care of flight schedules, and picked hotels when we flew. She did all of the shopping for the kids' clothes the first few years of their lives. As I've said before, and I will probably say it again, she was a human dynamo. Finally at the end of the day one might think she would drop in bed like a brick. But she rarely did. Her dynamism didn't end at the bed. She came into it wearing something adorable and began doing everything she could to please me prompting me to do everything I could to please her. And when the sharing of love ended, only then did my wonderful wife collapse into sleep. When she slept, it was deep, so deep that she only needed five hours or so of it. Then she'd pop up refreshed, shower, make us coffee and toast or eggs or bacon or all of the above, then proceed again with one of her usual days of unceasing goodness. No person I knew in my life deserved more love than Christine O'Reilly McKenzie.

To the utter and complete joy of each of us, Lena's surgery on her tiny heart went perfectly well. She was okay, and she would be okay forever. There was nothing to worry about, but I didn't stop worrying. I especially worried about her size. She was so small. And during the nine weeks between when I found out about the hole in Lena's heart and the surgery to repair it, I became used to having a bottle of rum in the house. Before Christine returned from the hospital, I kept the bottle on the night stand or the right side of the bed near where I slept. A few hours before Christine came home I moved the bottle to a food cabinet in the kitchen. Christine asked me about it one day very matter-of-factly "no big deal." I told her I was back to enjoying a drink now and then and she accepted it rather easily, no further questions. I purposely refrained from telling her that the bottle of rum in the cabinet was the fifth bottle I had bought since the morning the doctor had called me the first time about Lena.

* * * * *

Life settled back to our normal routines after Lena came home. Christine continued on her trek of being a human dynamo, and I continued as a productive worrier. Judy and Dan continued to love their grandchildren, babysit for them as much as possible and always without complaint. Even Lena had a bit of a growth spurt between nine months and a year old. But the biggest surprise came in August of 1977. Christine told me one night while the kids were staying with Grandma and Grandpa that she was pregnant again. It was bedtime and she had come into bed wearing an adorable blue teddy. She had spent our entire evening together acting as a happy little butterfly flitting around the house looking as if she was planning to tell me something interesting. In this situation I had no way of knowing what she was going to share with me. After all, she was so successful at work and seemed to be always getting raises and promotions or switching departments or going back to school to learn a new skill that it could have easily been one of those types of things. Besides promotions and raises, she loved to share things with her parents. I especially liked the tales she would recount when she worked in the emergency room. They were of limb or life-saving details, that if I were a writer, I could have written marvelous short stories about.

Tonight though, there was something different about her. The butterfly was glowing. She made me my favorite dinner of stripped steak and green bean casserole and added our favorite touch by lighting the candles on the dining room table. I didn't rush her by asking her what it was that she had to tell me. I never did. I just let her plan unfold at her pace, which I had become used to, after over a decade of marriage. She loved to share her stories. And I loved to listen to them. They came all the time. I've read many novels in my lifetime, but none of them delighted me, or held my interest, the way listening to Christine's stories did.

At the table our conversation was extremely casual. We talked about the Cubs, the White Sox, national politics, Chicago news, world news, etc. I had a glass of rum and Coke with my dinner to take the nagging edge off worry.

After dinner, I helped her clear the dishes. Then I washed them and the broiler pan and the casserole dish. She dried them and put them away. Then we retired to our bedroom. I brushed my teeth and gargled some mouthwash, then jumped into bed to work on some notes from work. Thirteen minutes later, Christine emerged from the bathroom wearing her blue teddy, hair down and brushed out to incredible luxuriousness. I only had one lamp turned on, located on the nightstand to the right of our bed. It didn't give off much light, just enough to work by. But when Christine emerged from the bathroom with that remarkable glow about her, the room became unmistakably brighter as did I, as I had on so many other nights, as she approached our sacred coziness. She pulled down her side of the covers, slid underneath them, pulled them up over her body and slithered right over to me. She hugged me before I could finish writing my last sentence of notes and put my clipboard on the nightstand. But I stopped immediately, got rid of the clipboard, and turned to snuggle with Christine. She sure knew how to celebrate making an announcement.

"I have an interesting story to tell you," she said.

"You do?" I answered. I couldn't have possibly guessed.

"You silly." She giggled, knowing full well I knew something was coming.

"An amazing thing happened at work today."

"It did?" And I readied myself for another of her real life hospital thrillers.

"I found out something fascinating about one of the patients there."

"You did? What is it?"

"She's going to have a baby."

"Who is it?" I asked, thinking it might be a local TV anchor, a famous lawyer, or some city councilwoman.

"Well," she said coyly, "the real irony of this story is that she lives in Bridgeport."

Now, my curiosity soared. In a split second, I recalled all the even remotely famous women who lived in Bridgeport that I had seen while shopping at Dominick's or eating at the Governor's Table or David's. There were quite a few actually.

"Can I give you a clue or two?" Then she kissed me playfully on my right cheek.

"Sure," I said. "Shoot."

She had my undivided attention. She was lying on her left side, her right leg draped over my thighs and the fingers of her right hand were tugging on my twelve or so chest hairs.

"She goes to church at Saint Anthony's." That was the Catholic church located on Twenty-Seventh and Wallace. Ironically, Christine preferred attending Saint Anthony's because she liked the sermons there better than those at Saint David's on Thirty-Second and Emerald.

"Can I ask a question?" I asked, so happy to be participating in her little game.

"Go ahead." She giggled.

"Do you ever see her there or talk to her there?"

"Not really, no."

That answer threw me. "Now you've gotten me completely off track."

"Want another clue?"

"Please."

"She likes the same clothes as me."

I was thinking, what? But I didn't say anything because I wanted to run the clues back in my mind. Here's what I had so far. An amazing thing happened at work, something fascinating with one of the patients there, going to have a baby, lives in Bridgeport, attends Saint Anthony's, but doesn't ever really see her there or talk with her.

Now Christine wasn't shy. After all, you do remember she picked me up, literally, in the snow in Evanston one morning at 1:00 a.m. And she had enough self-confidence that she could speak openly and at ease with anyone. But why hadn't she ever spoken with this woman at church which could so often be a relaxed environment? And what was really baffling me was that if this mystery woman was a patient at Saint Joe's, why didn't Christine know her? I dispelled that thought quickly when I reasoned that Saint Joe's was a big place. Certainly a nurse—even one that moved from department to department as much as Christine did—could not know every woman who found out there that she was pregnant. My mind was ping-ponging associations seeing if I could trigger any better guesses as to who it might be or at least better questions to ask Christine.

I continued to ponder while Christine tugged at my chest hairs. I was sure I had one or two less by now. Christine was patiently quiet. Slowly, a connection was forged. It started with my remembering something I had briefly forgotten. Christine had stated that the woman liked the same clothes as she. But if she never really spoke to the woman or even saw her in church, how could Christine possibly know that they both wore the same kind of clothes?

Before that instant, it was as if Christine's clues were being transported on the cars of a long freight train through a pitch black tunnel. Click, click, click, click. It wasn't the sounds of the train wheels going over the railroad ties. It was my metamorphical mind sounds, moving in rapid-fire succession attempting to glean truth from darkness.

Suddenly my heart almost leapt out of my chest.

"Christine, you're pregnant!"

"I am!" she said, as if I'd just given the winning answer on a TV game show.

I reached my arms around her and pulled my glowing bride on top of me, squeezed her somewhat tightly and kissed her with the perfect blend of passion and tenderness. When our lips parted, she combed the fingers of her right hand through my hair.

"How far along are you?" I asked.

"Seven weeks."

She continued, combing my hair while I kissed her again—this time with more congratulatory passion, if there is such a thing. I could feel her happiness transferring itself from her body simultaneously into my flesh and my soul. We were both so happy that we became one within minutes. Afterward, Christine fell asleep before I did, still lying on top of my body.

Although I was exhausted, I forced myself to remain awake for a few precious minutes. Having always been a worrier, I wanted to blot out all negative thoughts and live utterly thrilled in the instant that was upon me. I didn't have to do any work at all to achieve it. There was simply an energy of true blissful joy passing between Christine and me. Even though she was soundly asleep, I could feel her love of me and her happiness for carrying a new life inside her. As sleep approached, I clung to my ebbing wakefulness, knowing beyond a doubt that I was experiencing the greatest moment of my life.

CHAPTER 8

THE TWO-KNOCK GHOST would not cease tormenting me. It was making its annoying presence known at least three or four times a week—far more often than I was having the devil dreams. Over thirty years had passed since the greatest moment of my life. Now I was stuck in this new reality without Christine but replaced with the devil dreams and the Two-Knock Ghost.

I was now in my fifties, living in a modest two-bedroom, two-bath, 1,200 square foot condo in a retirement community called the Beaches of Paradise in Saint Petersburg, Florida. Christine was living a few miles away in a 3,600 square foot, $400,000 home on Snell Island. The kids were grown, all graduated from college, married, and living in various parts of the world. They were all as happy as Christine and I were, in the first couple of years of our marriage, prior to my family's accident.

Now Christine and I were living alone, sort of. At least she was alone. A large portion of my current life, I was living with the devil and a pesky ghost. Christine had asked me to leave about a year before the spirits intruded on my living space. She told me that my drinking had become too much for her to live with any longer, that I needed to get my act together, conquer the drinking, and alter the behaviors that had driven a wedge between us. She was gentle with me saying that if it took me a few months to find my own place, she wouldn't have a problem with that.

She didn't have to ask me twice. I could see the anguish in her eyes when she asked me to leave. And I didn't want to hurt her any more than I knew I already had by denying her the request that was killing her to ask of me. We had talked with each other about my drinking a few times in the past. But each of the handful of times was several months apart, covering two, maybe three years. Obviously, I hadn't placed enough credence in her words. For a long time I had thought that I was faultless. I never raised my voice to Christine. I never cheated on her. In fact, we slept in the same bed together every night, and as far as I could figure, I was always, at the very least, affectionate with her.

She told me that after I got back to my old self and completely conquered the drinking, we could resume the living together part of our marriage.

"I'm still in love with you, Turf," she had told me. "And I know you're still in love with me, but I've hit my nadir with you, and by sending you away, I'm hoping that will help you hit rock bottom soon, forcing you to change and come back to me fully, 100 percent."

I was beyond hurt. I was devastated. Part of that devastation came from the fact that in the first place, I didn't think I was an alcoholic, and in the second place, I couldn't figure out what I had done to Christine that hurt her so much that she would ask me to leave, what I thought was, our happy home.

I had a tremendous amount of work to do. According to Christine, I had to probe my alcoholism and I had to figure out why a guy who didn't even believe in the devil or ghosts was being besieged by them.

My usual confidence in myself had been shaken to the core. I was a psychologist for God's sake; I was the one who had been helping people for decades, and I didn't even begin to know where to start to transform myself into a better man without the baggage of alcohol and the spirit world.

I decided, after Christine asked me to leave, to stay focused on pragmatic things initially. I needed to find a place to live, and I needed to continue my practice. I was planning to work another ten years or so then spend the rest of my life traveling the world with my wife. The traveling and wife part of that equation was now in jeopardy. But I had to work because I loved it. And I didn't want to shortchange my patients.

I found the condo at the Beaches of Paradise, and I put as much of my restless heart as I could into my practice. Three months after I moved away from Christine, I was living in limbo in most areas of my life. But my psychology practice was thriving. The nights were the worst. I had begun to fear their approach. I never knew when the devil would attack me in my most vulnerable state—sleep. And I never knew when the Two-Knock Ghost would strike. It was always the same, *knock, knock* and nobody comes in. *Knock, knock* and no face or form was revealed. The Two-Knock Ghost wasn't merely pesky, it was annoying, frightening. I was in the midst of a devil dream, brutalized by the unmistakable form of the red devil with his ivory horns and his tail snapping side to side like a cracking whip. Then there it was—*knock, knock*—upstaging the devil's sadism. Sometimes I was having a good dream. It might have been one of many of Christine and me sharing a tender moment. Then *knock, knock,* usually at my front door but occasionally at my bedroom door. The beauty of my moment with Christine had been destroyed. And never once did the ghost have the decency to show itself. Why? I tried figuring out a reason. I could not.

As the days passed the ghost became more intrusive. Five months into my life at the Beaches of Paradise, the ghost knocked on my closed office door in downtown Saint Pete. I had fallen asleep while writing notes on one of my clients who was suffering PTSD after being robbed at gunpoint as a customer in a convenience store holdup. I was actually dreaming of my client, of ways I might be able to help her. *Knock, knock* so loudly, so close, and in my workplace. Before those mind blowing thuds on my door, my office had seemed like a sacred place. It was where I did most of my best thinking. The knocks scared me immediately to consciousness. I leaped from my desk and bolted for the door. Of course, and for the umpteenth time there was no one there. Why again? These knocks really scared me as for the first time, I equated myself with the kids in the Freddie Kreuger movies. Had I turned the corner where every time I fell asleep I would be harassed by the Two-Knock Ghost?

I began to wonder if there could be anyplace where I could sleep or even nap when I would be exempt from the obnoxious ghost. I first thought I might find a Catholic church and take a nap there. Even though I no longer believed in Catholicism, I surmised that maybe the Two-Knock Ghost would be frightened of bothering me when I was on sacred ground. Then I came up with what I initially thought was a great idea. The beach. Plain and simple, there were no doors on the beach . . . no place to knock. I was sure that I had figured out two places that I could go to escape my pesky nemesis.

I still wanted to contemplate my PTSD patient more. I decided on the spur of the moment to drive to the beach, bring my notes and a pen, pull out a beach chair, and continue my thinking.

I left my office and drove straight down Central Avenue all the way to Treasure Island. The beach was serene, the temperature about 70 degrees and the beach was nearly deserted. It was 7:15 and almost sunset by the time I got there. A gentle breeze lifted the waves just enough so that they made a soothing splash when they broke upon the shoreline. I was extremely concerned about my robbery victim, Mary Bauer. She was a pretty woman, five feet two inches tall, maybe 105 pounds, thirty-three years old with blond hair and gorgeous blue eyes, nearly comparable to Christine's. She taught third grade at Melrose Elementary on Saint Pete's south side. She was the perfect prototype for a third grade teacher. She was witty, creative, and engaging with her students. She did everything she could not only to teach her students the required curriculum but to help teach values that would fortify them throughout life. Most of them came from the immediate area surrounding Melrose. It was a rough area. Poverty and drugs abounded. She found that her students were nearly desperate for the love and attention she willingly gave of herself.

One day after work she noticed that her gas gauge was on empty. She decided to take Sixteenth Street and head for a little gas station/convenience store on Ninth Avenue and Fifteenth Street South. She had never stopped there before, primarily because it wasn't her turf, and that fact was obvious. There were often four or five thugs hanging around there or directly across the street. They were often very animated, usually unkempt and scary looking. But this particular day nobody was hanging around the store or across the street. There wasn't even anybody pumping gas. She decided to stop for gas and a Dr. Pepper. It would be five minutes in and out.

Pumping the gas was easy. She could have paid at the pump, but it had been a challenging school day and she wanted to indulge in the Dr. Pepper treat. She walked into the store, smiled at the Indian storekeeper, located the cooler, and made a beeline for it. She was about to pick up the can of her favorite soda when she heard a commotion a few feet from her. She turned to see three masked men racing into the store, each carrying a handgun and heading straight for the cash register.

"Give me the money!" one of the men shouted at the terrified man who stood in front of countless cartons and packs of cigarettes.

"Hurry up!" another man shouted.

Mary could only stare at the action, frozen in fear, wondering what might happen to her as well as the petrified store owner. She could not see any of the three robbers' faces but she could tell they were black; their hands fully exposed as they wielded their weapons.

The attendant quickly opened the register and began pulling the bills from their individual slots within the drawer, implicitly complying with the gunmen's demands. Unfortunately, he was too slow for the robber who stood directly in front of him. Without warning, the masked man raised his gun and in a single, swift unbroken movement reached over the counter and smashed his gun into the left side of the attendant's skull. The impact was of such force that the recipient crumpled into an unconscious heap on the floor. Then the gunman leaped over the counter, grabbed the bills from the attendant's clenched fingers, and returned to the cash register, pulling out every remaining piece of currency and coin from both the drawer and underneath it.

It was while this was happening that the third thug noticed where Mary was in the tiny store and hustled toward her. He placed his gun against her temple and yelled at the top of his lungs: "Give me that purse, bitch." As Mary obliged, he screamed at her, "I bet you've never had a real man before, have you?" As if he actually expected her to answer. His left hand immediately went for her breasts while his right hand held his gun against her brain. When the other two robbers finished cleaning out the register while making certain the storeowner was still passed out on the floor, they immediately moved to their buddy and Mary. They expanded on the rudeness of their partner, raising Mary's skirt and putting hands and fingers onto and into places on her quivering body they had no right being.

The first man to reach her snatched her purse from her left hand and shoulder while the other two men continued their groping. Even though Mary wasn't sure she would have life beyond the next few seconds, she tried frantically to observe any facets she could distinguish about the three men. It was difficult. The only visible characteristics she could see were the similarities in the men's heights and weights. Each was about six feet one and weighed a solid two hundred pounds. Beyond that there were no discernable differences. As much as she wanted to focus on the idiosyncrasies of each man, she felt herself closing her eyes through much of her ordeal. Though the abuse seemed to be flowing relentlessly, she was able to find a miniscule of comfort in the moments in the dark room behind her shut eyes.

What, in reality was taking only two minutes, felt like an eternity to Mary Bauer. The sum total of the negativity that had befallen the loveable teacher her entire lifetime did not equal what was happening to her these one hundred twenty seconds.

A car pulling up to get gas spooked the three robbers and as the last man to reach Mary bolted for the door, the first man pulled his gun away from Mary's temple, brought it back toward himself then swung it with full force into the same temple he had moments before threatened shooting. Perhaps it was a good thing that Mary's eyes were closed at the moment of impact. The thin flap of eyelid had protected her eyeball from being scratched as the gun slammed into the side of it. Mary dropped to the floor, hitting her knees first and then her chin and nose. Her neck snapped ruthlessly, tearing muscles all the way to both shoulders. Three thin streams of blood began to emanate from her head wounds as she lay on the floor oblivious to the robbers making their escape in a 1996 dark blue Saturn. She also had no clue as to the emotional pain that would assault her a few minutes later when she awakened in an ambulance on her way to Bay Front Hospital. Contemplating what to say that could help her was the primary reason I had driven to the beach. To avoid the Two-Knock Ghost, if I fell asleep, was my secondary reason. I knew myself pretty well in most areas of my life—so I thought. About one thing I was absolutely positive: that I could fall asleep anywhere and quickly. Since I had passed into my fifties, that fact had become even more real. And tonight was no different. As I thought about Mary, I watched a series of clouds pass silently in front of the three quarter moon. It was almost like watching a choreographed sky dance, except there was no music. It was, nonetheless, hypnotic and within the half hour, I had slipped from the conscious world into a wonderful dream in which Mary Bauer and Christine were best friends. They were driving through a desert in a 1967 Mustang convertible. Christine, who I was certain had never fired a gun in her life, was loading a .357 Magnum while telling Mary uncharacteristically: "We'll find the sons of bitches, I promise. And when we do, I'll make sure they suffer for what they did to you." They looked like Thelma and Louise, except shorter and Christine was talking in a voice that sounded eerily like Clint Eastwood's character, Dirty Harry.

As I was dreaming the dream, I was excited that I might get to see my tiny wife extract some vengeance upon the robbers who had hurt Mary. Instead, the two women pulled into a small gas station in the middle of nowhere. Christine had to use the bathroom, so while Mary pumped gas, Christine began walking to the women's bathroom on the side of the building.

"Don't go inside the store until I finish my business and go with you, okay?" It was a gentle command.

"I won't, Christine."

But as my wife sat on the toilet, she became me and in an instant I fell asleep on the pot and began dreaming. I dreamed of an army of angels, all wearing uniforms and swords in the style of the Roman soldiers in the time of Christ. Their leader spoke to me, "We'll help you find the robbers, Turf. And when we do, we'll make them answer to a higher authority." As quickly as the angels had materialized, they vaporized.

Suddenly and inexplicably, I was dreaming about how vulnerable I felt when my daughter, Lena, was a baby and I was worried incessantly whether she would survive and how I could ever survive if she did not.

It was then that I heard it. *Knock, knock.* It shocked me. My dreaming dream self jumped up from the toilet and bolted for the bathroom door. I opened it, but once again, no one was there. My dream self shouted "shit" loudly and frustratedly and my real self woke so abruptly that I almost fell out of my beach chair onto the sand. I was so angry for many different reasons. My first thought was that I had been wrong about the beach being a safe place to dream. I had not thought prior to this moment that dreams have buildings and those buildings have doors that a ghost can knock on. It didn't matter that the beach was doorless. I was angry, as well, because I wanted to see Christine and Mary wreak some havoc on the three bad guys. I was angry because of the way this initially exciting dream had gone awry. Christine had morphed into me while sitting on the toilet. What was up with that? It was as if I stole a beautiful dream from the two women and made it about me. And then the Two-Knock Ghost stole the dream and put its frightening imprint upon it.

Lastly, I was angry that I didn't come up with any ideas of how to help Mary. During the Thelma and Louise part of the dream, I thought something interesting might be revealed, but moments later, when the action of the plot was upstaged by Christine's transformation and the Two-Knock Ghost, the only possible idea I came away with that could even remotely help Mary, was to suggest that she hang out with strong women in the future. I certainly was not going to recommend to Mary that she start packing a .357 Magnum.

The Two-Knock Ghost had ruined my dream. And I couldn't help but wonder why Christine had changed into me. Was there something inside my psyche that made me change the dream, setting up the appearance by the Two-Knock Ghost? For the first time, after thinking that thought, I wondered if I could have any responsibility for creating the Two-Knock Ghost. Could the ghost be some manifestation of something from within me, some weakness or need?

Not only had the ghost ruined my dream, it destroyed any tranquility that being at the beach had provided. I actually wanted a drink right then. I wanted to leave the beach and stop at any one of a number of bars that dotted Gulf Boulevard. I wanted that drink badly. I grabbed my beach chair and headed for my car. I'd be having that drink in a few minutes. It was only about a six mile ride back to the Beaches of Paradise from Treasure Island, and I'd be picking a bar on the first half of the ride home as opposed to the second half. I didn't have to go to a bar. I had plenty of rum and Coke at the condo. But I wanted to sit at the bar, think some more about Mary and some of my other clients, take my notebook with me and write down ideas while I sipped my drink. I knew if I did that at home, I'd be asleep by 10:00 p.m. I'd never fallen asleep in a bar before, and I had no reason to think that tonight would be different. I decided to go to the "R Bar," a local favorite only two minutes from the beach. I ordered a rum and Coke from a tall, friendly, young bartender whose name tag said "Dan." There were three other people at the bar other than me. Two were a distinguished-looking couple in their late fifties and the third was probably a local who looked like a beach bum, or maybe a fisherman, with rough hands, in his forties, sitting on the last stool at the far end of the bar at the opposite end from me. I made brief eye contact with the couple and we all smiled, gave a head nod and went on with our business.

My drink came and I began sipping and jotting ideas. I missed Christine. Though I was here to think primarily about Mary, my mind wandered continually to Christine. I was four months out of the house from her, and I still had no clue what I had done to hurt her so much that she would ask me to leave our home.

Every other night until tonight, alcohol had given me comfort. But tonight, after several sips, each time I thought about Christine I almost cried. A couple of times, I looked up to see whether the handsome couple or Dan was watching my eyes well up with tears. But nobody was looking. They were all very busy within their own little realms. I noticed that the couple was being very affectionate with one another. They were about the same age as Christine and I. And when I saw them exchanging tenderness, I thought of Christine again; then ordered more rum to try to achieve that point of a high where sadness transforms into tranquility or at least numbness.

I could not achieve that point on this night. Finally, nearing 11:30 p.m., I decided to pack it in and head home. I paid and tipped Dan, gathered my notes, and headed out the door for my car. It was only eleven or twelve minutes from the bar to "The Beaches" and I couldn't wait to get home because I was growing tired. Slightly less than a mile away, a couple of hundred feet before the light at 140th Avenue, right in front of the Candy Kitchen (a wonderful retro candy store and ice cream shop), a bike darted in front of my path. I slammed on my brakes, while at the same time the bike rider panicked and squeezed both her brakes. I smelled burnt rubber emanating from my tires as I focused on the petrified face of the young woman on the bike. She was probably in her midtwenties and was wearing a terror-stricken face the depth of which she had probably never worn before. My car was stopped in the right lane in which I had been driving. I opened my door, quickly stepped out of the car, and mostly as a courtesy asked how she was.

"I'm okay, sir. I'm very sorry. I should have never cut in front of you like that, especially since there's no traffic. I'm just tired and I wanted to get home."

"It's okay, ma'am. I'm just glad that I didn't hit you."

"Thank you, sir. I'm sorry I scared you," she said politely. Then she was off. She might have been shaken a little but the incident was probably over for her, except for an occasional reflection in her mind in the next couple of days.

For me, however, it was a different story. I had been lucky. But for a couple of feet and a second or two, I could have killed the girl. Between the moment I slammed on the brakes and my driving away from the near tragic scene, only two minutes had elapsed and only two cars passed us, both coming south on the opposite side of the street. Neither of them had been a Madeira Beach police car. That municipality was known for patrolling their streets strictly and giving out late night tickets. I reflected, as I made the right turn at 150th Avenue and headed toward Bay Pines, about what might have happened had a Madeira Beach police officer gotten out of his car at the near accident scene and inquired what the problem was. He would have seen a young woman shaken up and breathing heavily, and he would have observed a middle-aged man with a worried look on his face. He probably would have questioned the woman first and unless she had told him the truth—that she had darted in front of me from an unseeable angle and relative darkness—he might have approached me totally differently. Under any circumstances, he would have eventually come close to my person. I asked myself, "What would he have seen?" He would have seen my eyes. They would have been glassy, with some redness from being tired. Having been trained in such matters, he would have detected a slight slur in my speech. He would have quickly seen that I was nonthreatening and professionally dressed, so he would have allowed himself to come close enough to me that he could easily smell the liquor that was on my breath. He would have asked me: "Sir, have you been drinking?" And I would have honestly answered, "Yes I have."

At that point, it would no longer have mattered that I was innocent of causing a near accident on the street. I would have been just another drunk that he would have to put through the paces of sobriety testing before hauling his ass off to jail.

By the time I reached Bay Pines Hospital, one hundred seconds later, I realized I had just done something I swore I would never do. I had driven drunk. And it wasn't the first time either. I had become the person who had killed my family so many years before. I was a lucky monster. I could have killed an innocent woman whose only sin was that she had made a careless decision to dart in front of me to save a few seconds because she wanted to get home. I could have been arrested, gone to jail, been fined, gone to trial, been found guilty and gone to prison for several years of my life. Why? Because I couldn't handle life without the crutch of alcohol.

By the time I reached the left turn lane at Bay Pines Boulevard and Park Street, I had begun to realize why Christine might have grown tired of me. I was not the same alcohol-free man I was when we had met. The decision to drive home high that night had been a bad one. I was already pondering what other bad decisions I had made around my wife that had made her less tolerant of me. Suddenly, I felt an emotional pit in my stomach, missing Christine immeasurably and feeling utter shame at the man I had become. These feelings, added to the fear of being pulled over by a cop for some driving infraction the last eight minutes of my ride home, ripped open that hole in my heart that had haunted and plagued me for years. I hadn't lost Christine, but we weren't together intimately, as we had been for decades. Suddenly, and for the first time, I felt our separation as nearly a death and my body quivered with a race of physical torment through my veins.

By the time I made the right turn onto Fifty-fourth Avenue, I realized that I was powerless over alcohol and that I'd better get my ass to AA quickly. In a moment I arrived at the Beaches of Paradise, as a wave of relief passed over me. I may not really have been in paradise, but at least I was in a safe haven away from law enforcement and potential vehicular disaster. The traffic incident, plus the ensuing reflections and emotions, had rendered me exhausted. Tomorrow would be a busy day with six clients scheduled, all with varying problems. I needed to be rested and alert to be able to give them my best.

I wanted to go right to bed, but I was jittery and more lonely and nervous about what had happened on the way home than I was tired. I went to the kitchen, opened a cabinet door, and took out my bottle of rum. Then I went to the fridge and pulled out the half-empty bottle of Coke. I selected an eight ounce glass, poured about three ounces of rum into it then poured Coke into the rest of the glass.

That oughta do it, I thought. I turned off the lights, made sure the front door was locked, and walked into my bedroom. I felt so lonely I would have taken a teddy bear with me to bed, had I owned one, and held it all night. But I didn't own one and pulling the covers up to my chin would have to suffice. I sipped on my drink and thought of Christine and Mary Bauer. I had so much to do to contribute to the betterment of both of those women's lives. Christine's, I had unwittingly ripped apart. Mary's, I wanted to help put back together. Christine's rebuilding might take longer, but I was determined to do it. It would require insights into myself that I either didn't know or hadn't admitted to myself. I swore that my journey of self-exploration and evaluation would begin tomorrow, but right now I wanted to knock myself out. I was tired of thinking and I wanted to escape consciousness and hide out in sleep.

That night the devil invaded my peace once again. This time there was no pummeling. There was no throwing me around the room. He merely appeared in the dream bending over my sleeping body. He was straddling me with one leg on either side of my stomach.

"Wake up, Turf. Wake up, sleepyhead. I have something I want to tell and show you." Slowly, I awoke from my dream sleep and immediately looked into his red, evil face that was only inches from mine. Each hand was forcefully pinning down one of my shoulders.

"I've got you now, Turf. I've got you now." He said nothing more. The sneer on his face slowly morphing into a show of his huge frightening teeth.

Then he snapped his head and upper body down and began eating my face. I couldn't move as I screamed beneath him in excruciating pain. Bite after bite he de-chunked my face. Finally he arched back upward, my blood and body parts falling from his mouth. He thrust his tongue out and licked his chops, all the while sneering victoriously. A moment later he bent down again with the intention of going for my eyes. It was at the very instant he was about to eat out my left eye that I heard it. *Knock, knock* on my front door, and Satan heard it too. Instead of continuing with his cannibalistic meal, his body snapped upright and he turned quickly to look from where the sounds had emanated. He appeared surprised, not as if he expected more of his minions to join him in devouring me from face to toe.

Thank God he had been distracted. He ceased his attack but bent over me a final time, pinning my shoulders once more to the bed.

"I've got you now, Turf. I've got you now."

Then he flew off me backward right through the ceiling without chipping a piece of plaster.

For an instant I felt relief that Lucifer had exited my bedroom. Though what was left of my face was in horrific pain, his assault ended. For one split second, I experienced a break. Then I heard it again, *knock, knock*. Utter terror grasped me again as I anticipated some monstrous demon blasting through the front door, sprinting through my living room, ripping off my bedroom door, and continuing the onslaught. The Two-Knock Ghost had never knocked two times twice before but again it didn't reveal itself. I, for some reason not understood by myself, was now more frightened by the Two-Knock Ghost than of the devil. I lay in my dream bed, on blood-soaked sheets, in unrelenting agony, trying to figure out why the occasional two knocks from the Two-Knock Ghost was more frightening than the devil and his myriad prior assaults upon me. I concluded that I was more afraid of the unknown than of the known. I actually feared that there could be something more devastating than Beelzebub. Maybe behind those knocks were dozens of demons, hundreds, endless thousands, waiting to ravage. My final dream horror that fateful night was the realization that each night I could dream many dreams; that each different night could be a new set of dreams. How many times could Satan and the Two-Knock Ghost—whatever it turned out to be—intrude upon my sacred sleep time?

At the moment, I conceived that halacious question, I woke with a start. I was lying on sweat-soaked sheets, and I popped up with such force that I almost passed out. I turned the light on and sat upright in my bed shivering with fear and worry. None of this was right—not waking in terror at 2:42 a.m., not waking without Christine beside me, not waking with an empty 8 ounce glass that only two and one half hours earlier had held what I thought was my greatest ally, but what could have been my worst enemy. It wasn't right. It wasn't merely the external things around me that were wrong, it was the flaws within myself that had caused the things around me to be far off kilter and ugly.

I had never felt worse in my life, not when my family was killed, not when I carried my suitcase out of the home that Christine and I shared, not when I worried that Lena might die. Never. I was sitting in my bed alone at the absolute direness of my life, when merely a few hours earlier I thought I had so much good stuff going on. Maybe I still did have so much going on inside of myself and around me to live for. But I didn't feel it at this moment. I had lost myself. It had been replaced by shame. My god, I had almost killed someone earlier that night—a young woman. I had almost taken her life. And for what? So my senses of emotional pain and worry could be dulled by the magic elixir of rum and Coke?

I was out of control. Maybe that's what the devil stood for. Alcohol. Maybe that was what's eating me alive piece by piece. Maybe the devil was me. I had already become the one thing I swore when I was younger that I would never become—a drunk driver. A surge of desperation sprung within me, beginning at the base of my stomach and erupting like a volcano. I gasped twice for air as the surge passed my throat then gigantic hot tears began cascading down my cheeks. I was no longer a man. I was a polluted shell. I needed physical and emotional detox, and I needed to refill myself with character, strength, and absolute honesty.

Don't get me wrong. I didn't think I was a bad guy. I knew I wasn't, although I had almost become a killer of a human being a few hours earlier. What I did know was that I was a weaker man than I had ever been before. I knew that I had hurt people that I had loved especially my wife in ways that only she was aware of. And what about my kids? I had three beautiful children and I never until this night thought that I had been anything other than a good dad. Had I hurt them too and not had a clue about it? Had I hurt them and they never told me, then drifted away from home one by one, clutching their secrets close to their fragile psyches?

Until this moment I thought I knew so much about psychology. I had been a product of a good home. I was well educated from books and learned scholars. I had helped thousands of struggling souls over a thirty-year career when they were passing through trials and tribulations. But suddenly I understood that I had only scratched the surface of what psychology was. I needed to go on an expedition to the center of my being. And I needed to begin immediately before I lost everything that was near and dear to me, including myself, forever.

CHAPTER 9

THE NEXT MORNING I woke feeling I had a horse collar draped around my neck. I had a busy day scheduled, but I knew that today would be busier than a normal day because today was the beginning of my delving into my plan of self-correction. The foremost question in my mind was, where do I start? For the first thirty minutes of my waking day while I shaved, showered, and combed and brushed my red and gray hair, I couldn't come up with an answer. It wasn't until I reached into the refrigerator that my starting point became clear. I had a taste for a glass of strawberry milk for breakfast. As I reached for the quart of one of my other favorite drinks, I noticed three cans of Coke on the same shelf. It immediately made me think of my rum, not to have a drink—I never drank in the morning—but because I thought that the first thing that I should probably do was to pour the liquid out of the cans then pour out the remaining ounces in the bottle of rum. I did those things. It was easy. I felt good about it. I felt better about myself. I was on the right path already.

But the next question popped into my head almost as quickly as the first one had been answered. What next? No answer appeared as I popped two pieces of wheat bread into the toaster, waited for them to pop up, buttered them, added some strawberry jam, and then slapped on two pieces of American cheese. That was one of my favorite quick breakfasts.

No answer arrived while I washed my dish, knife, and glass then brushed my teeth. In fact, I felt my mind wander off myself and onto my clients for the day and their myriad challenges. I concluded quickly that the rest of my journey of self-exploration might not be as simple as pouring three ounces of rum and three cans of Coke down the drain.

It was when I grabbed my briefcase before walking out the door that the answer to my next question arrived. I thought of my clients and what I was going to say to each of them. For years, almost since the beginning of my career as a psychologist, I'd kept a notebook about each person I'd counseled. When I thought about the notebooks, the second answer came almost simultaneously. I should begin a notebook for myself. I should first make a list of things I needed to do, things like pouring out those three ounces of liquor.

I thought for a moment how associative the brain was. Twice in the last half hour, I had seen one thing and it had made me think of something else that was related to it, such a wonderful aspect of the human mind, its associative nature. It was a gift of nature that kept getting better over time. How deeply it helped with investigations of everything from science to criminology, to human understanding of others and oneself. I would need this aspect of my brain during the exploration of my own being. I would write something down and that thing would make me think of another task that needed to be done. One thing would lead to another and that process would replicate itself innumerable times. Then I would sort the tasks ahead in order of importance. It would not be unlike organizing the plan of attack for a short story or novel. This would be how I would proceed with the outline of my journey of self-repair. I would work on this every day. Part of me wanted to call Christine and tell her my thoughts and new insights. But the bigger part of me concluded it was too soon to tell her anything. After all, what had I accomplished—not much of anything. As I drove down Tyrone Boulevard toward Fifth Avenue, I likened what I had accomplished thus far to a young kid who had just played his first game of baseball in the lowest league possible and had gone one for four, a single. One hit was all I had. I was merely starting out. I had a long way to go to reach the major leagues of personal growth. If I called Christine now, as I so desperately wanted, I would tell her what had occurred and she would gently praise me for what I had discovered about myself, but that would be all that there was; a tiny sliver of a positive single baby step in a trek of a thousand miles. If I told her anything, I would feel more shame than satisfaction.

I would wait to talk with the love of my life because I had not discovered anything about myself other than my own vulnerability. I did not know why I felt such vulnerability, why I walked around with an enigmatic hole in my heart, why I worried so much about losing my loved ones. I hadn't yet figured out a single way that I had hurt Christine and the kids. Worst of all, I was baffled by my devil dreams and a pesky ghost who always knocked but would never come in or reveal itself.

My day at the office was busy. I saw six clients, each with emotional pains and sorrows that needed addressing. There were differences about this day, however. First, every chance I had I wrote notes to myself in my own personal notebook as to what I needed to do to repair myself. Secondly, prior to today I had always considered that there was more than just a professional wall between me and my clients. I had always thought that I was healthy and my clients were messed up. Even when I was grieving the most about the deaths of my family, I felt that the grief, although overwhelming, was a natural consequence of the crash. I had long ago concluded that I would go through the grieving on my own. After all, I had a tremendous wife, another set of loving grandparents, good friends. I didn't need to see a psychologist. In fact I never once even thought about it. But today was different. Not only did I need to pick a place to attend AA meetings, I needed to see a psychologist to help me deal with the devil dreams and the Two-Knock Ghost.

After beginning to jot down ideas for my personal plan of attack, I rearranged them before I left the office. At the top of the list I put, "find a place to attend AA meetings." Number two was, "find a good psychologist." Number one would be easy. I had quickly learned where many of the AA meetings were held when I first started my practice in St. Petersburg. As you can imagine, many of my clients were dealing with alcohol issues, and if they weren't already attending AA meetings, I would not only recommend that they would attend AA, but I told them of a place that was conveniently located near their home or place of employment. I wanted to make it easier for them in case they threw out the objection, "I don't know where to go for AA meetings." I knew where I would go for my AA meetings immediately. There was a building off Ft. Harrison in Clearwater near the Scientology headquarters. It was on Turner Street, a few feet from the railroad tracks. Not only did I have the place listed on my sheet of AA meeting places, but I had been there several times in the last couple of months. I had referred one of my clients there. His name was Toby Magnessun. He was a handsome man, barrel-chested, six feet tall with playful, beautiful, youthful blue eyes and soft blond hair that was beginning to show signs of white creeping in. Toby was a St. Petersburg police officer—a good one. Only forty-nine, he had been on the job for twenty-three years. His jacket was filled with awards and commendations, excellent performance evaluations, and a history of promotions and salary increases. He was a good-hearted soul with a wife and three children, two older boys and their little sister. The boys' ages were eleven and nine. His daughter was six. For the first thirteen years, Toby and his wife, Alicea, had a wonderful marriage. Alicea was a critical care nurse at Morton Plant Hospital. She was a hardworking and kind woman and a great mother. Of course, in my mind I thought she was a Christine type—a rare, marvelous soul who brightened a man's day by merely being in his presence.

Unfortunately, two and one half years ago Alicea was diagnosed with breast cancer. That news hit Toby hard. All the scrapes he had been in as a cop had cumulatively not impacted him the way the news of his wife's breast cancer had. His pain did not come from the shallow belief that his wife might lose one or both of her breasts, but from the moment to moment nagging thoughts that he might lose her. Toby had never been a big drinker; but he'd had his share of outrageous college drinking nights, wedding binges, celebratory sports nights with buddies, and wild cookouts where he was the host. But after Alicea was diagnosed, he began drinking little by little the first few months then more and more beyond that. The amount of alcohol he was drinking began impacting his job performance. First the changes were almost imperceptible—a few minutes late here and there, a single step slower in chases. Nobody could tell initially, that he was drinking every day. A few months into Alicea's illness, Toby started chugging it down. He would drink about anything, a complete opposite from me. His favorite was beer. He liked Heineken the best. He also favored sangria. Often he would have a Heineken and chase it with a fruit filled glass of sangria. He loved fruity drinks—strawberry margaritas, banana daiquiris, Red's Apple ale and tequila sunrises. His way of drinking was to go to any one of a number of his favorite bars, hang out for an hour or two, buy drinks for his friends, even strangers, talk up a storm, drive home tipsy or loaded, send the babysitter back to her house then tuck the kids into bed, often telling them a story either about his day or a fairytale.

Many nights Alicea would already be in their bed either resting or asleep. At that point her cancer-fighting efforts were drastically draining her normal energy. Toby would brush his teeth, gargle extensively with mouthwash, and crawl into bed with his wife. Most of the time she was too weak to notice he was high. He was skillful at turning off his bar room braggadocio and turning on his charm and tenderness for his favorite human being. Toby's problems with alcohol were not yet impacting his family. They were affecting his work. His partner, Patrick Kelly, a hard-nosed, straightlaced officer of thirty-five was acutely aware of Toby's continual physical decline. Initially, a few months before he was convinced alcohol was the culprit, he had asked Toby if he had a pulled muscle after noticing during a two cop chase that Toby was more than a couple of steps slower. Even though Toby was fourteen years older than Patrick, Toby had always maintained a high standard of physical excellence. He had not always been able to keep up with Patrick on chases but sometimes he had been able to pass him even when he started a few feet behind Patrick. The reason he sometimes started behind Patrick was because Toby drove the squad car the far greater majority of the time. It often took him two or three seconds longer to get out of the car for foot pursuits.

The slightly slower foot speed of Toby was not what pushed Patrick over the edge of his concern into action. It was Toby's increasingly slurred speech, his worsening tardiness, and the troublesome look of increased fatigue and worry on Toby's face that motivated Patrick to ask Toby more pointed questions. They started out sort of like this: "Toby, I know I've talked with you a little about this before, but I'm concerned about your running lately. Are you sure you don't have some nagging injury you want to talk about?" Toby would always answer something like: "No, it's okay, Patrick. I've been eating too much pasta lately. It's just a phase I'm going through. I'll cut it out soon. I'll be fine." He was never curt, always smooth, slickly covering up the real truth.

But Patrick became relentless in pursuing, not only because he cared about Toby, but because he needed the highly functioning partner that Toby had always been. He had developed a genuine concern for his own safety while working with Toby, who had compromised his personal skills due to his drinking.

Finally, after countless attempts at getting the truth from Toby's lips, Patrick decided it was necessary to take a different approach. They were driving down Eighteenth Avenue South in St. Petersburg one day toward Ninth Street, an extremely rough part of the city to be sure.

"Toby, we've been partners for a long time. You're probably my best friend. You're like a big brother to me. I know you're hurting about Alicea. But lately, I've smelled alcohol on your breath, your speech is often slurred, you've been late for work, your running has really slowed down, and I don't like covering for you. I think it's time for you to get some help."

Toby stared out the window at the busy gas station on the northwest corner of Ninth Street and Eighteenth Avenue South for a moment, thinking about the scores of times he and Patrick had responded to calls at this location. He flipped his blinker on and a moment later made the right turn south onto Ninth Street, heading for Lake Maggorie. Toby and Patrick never argued. They were two straight up men who always talked things out logically and civilly. The fact that Toby didn't respond right away didn't bother Patrick. He knew Toby's ways and his silence only meant that he was analyzing the depth of Patrick's words.

Nearly a mile had passed before Toby broke the quiet that lingered in the squad car. In a voice that was sincere and almost imperceivable, Toby spoke.

"I've heard everything you've said, Patrick, and it's all true. I've felt myself slipping for months. I am drinking—a lot. At first it was because alcohol dogged the pain of worrying about Alicea. But recently the drinking seems to have taken on a life of its own. I'm not functioning right and I know it. I'm embarrassed that you've had to witness my decline. I appreciate that you've cared about me enough in the past several months that you kept trying to find out what was going on with me. But I couldn't bring myself to tell you. Now you've pretty much figured out the whole deal. My problem is that I don't know where to begin to go for help."

"I have a cousin who's bipolar, Toby. She's been seeing a psychologist in downtown St. Pete. She swears by him. That might be a place to start."

"It might be," Toby said. "You see, Patrick, I'm not only dealing with the drinking, I'm worried sick about Alicea. My god, I wouldn't know what to do if I lost her. I'm actually desperate to talk to somebody who might have some answers for me. I know I need AA too."

They slowed the car as they passed the park at Lake Maggorie. About twenty cars were parked there with about thirty-five black guys hanging out talking and gesturing graphically about God knows what. There wasn't a white guy among them. At 3:18 in the afternoon, nobody was causing any trouble, but about fifteen of the cars were later models and the officers wondered about what they might be planning, how many of them might have criminal records, who they might recognize from previous incidents, and how they could afford those beautiful cars.

"Always something going on at Lake Maggorie Park," Patrick said.

"You got that right," Toby concurred.

That's how Toby was referred to me, that same day, by the time they reached Pinnelas Point about five minutes away.

"I want to do this on my own," Toby said. "No department involvement. Will you stand by me with that Patrick?"

"You got it, my friend."

* * * * *

It was only a couple of weeks later that I referred Toby to the AA meeting place on Turner Street. That wasn't the first place that I was going to refer him. Toby lived in a two-story house on Snell Island, ironically, just a few blocks from the house that Christine and I bought when we moved to St. Pete. Toby's home was expensive. To buy it, he needed his wife to have a successful nursing career, himself to be a highly decorated and oft promoted police officer, and for Alicea's father to have been a highly successful surgeon at Ed White Hospital, who loved them both and loaned them $150,000 cash at zero percent interest to make the purchase.

Initially, I asked Toby if he wanted to attend an AA meeting close to his home on Snell Island or close to the St. Pete Police Headquarters, which was located between First Avenue and Central at Thirteenth Street across from Ferg's Bar. His reply was, "Neither, Dr. McKenzie. I'd like to go somewhere up north a bit, where there is less chance of running into people I know. I'd prefer more anonymity being a cop and all." I told him, "Sure. Let me look through my list and see what there is." When I found the place off Fort Harrison, I asked him, "Do you mind driving thirty-five or forty minutes?" He said, "No. In fact, I might enjoy it. Even though time is precious, getting clean is the most important thing that I can possibly do so that I can be stronger again for Alicea and the kids."

He had told me this nearly three months ago before I'd had my drunk driving experience. Now, when I reflected on his words about being stronger again for his wife and kids, I concluded that his words had been strangely prophetic for me. That was exactly what I needed to do for myself and my kids, even though my kids were young adults and away from home.

After I told him where the place was, he said something I could have never imagined he would say to me. He said, "Dr. McKenzie, I'm afraid to go by myself. Will you come with me the first time?" After I was momentarily surprised by what this big, strong St. Pete policeman had said to me, I quickly thought it through for a few seconds and said, "Yes I will, Toby."

I had liked Toby as a person from the first time I met him in my office. If we had met in one of countless other social situations, we probably would have become fast friends. In fact, the more I got to know him, the more I wanted to be his friend. He and his wife were only a few years younger than Christine and I, and they only lived a couple thousand feet from us. How convenient it would be to be friends with him and his family. And as friends we could contribute so much to each other's lives. But I resisted the urge to be friends outside the workplace and keep our friendship as professional as possible. But since I was highly prejudiced in favor of this guy and his success over alcohol, I jumped at the chance to hang out with him a little extra time away from the office. I also concluded that just maybe a thing or two might come up during our time together on the road and at the AA meeting that I might be able to convert into better serving him as a therapist.

The first time I went with Toby was for a 7:30 meeting. The room was a large several hundred square foot auditorium, with the stage on the south end. There must have been 150 people there the night we drove there together from St. Pete and acclimated ourselves to the building, the people, and their systems for letting the alcoholics tell their stories. And stories there were. One after another the pain and angst of each alcoholic poured forth. Toby watched intently as I wondered when he would jump in and take his turn. He was nervous throughout the meeting, leaning forward in his chair most of the time and wringing his hands repeatedly. He did not jump in. He did not speak. In fact, after we left the meeting and got into my car before heading home, he said the first words he had spoken in over an hour and a half.

"I'm sorry, Dr. McKenzie, that I didn't break the ice and tell my story tonight. I guess I was feeling embarrassed about opening up. I know I can do it next time. Will you come with me one more time for moral support?"

I didn't hesitate for a moment. I said, "I'll go with you one more time, Toby, but after that you're on your own. Deal?"

"Deal," he said. We drove home talking about the Bucks and the Devil Rays.

Oddly at the time, I was thinking mostly of Toby and his upcoming battle to get sober. Though I had heard the words that Christine had told me, though I had moved out of our marital home and bought a condo at the Beaches of Paradise, I still didn't believe that I was an alcoholic, nor did I have a single clue as to what it took to initially admit that to myself.

The second time I accompanied my cop client/almost friend, to his AA meeting was my last visit there for several weeks. Toby spoke. He spilled his guts about Alicea, his children, and his absolute powerlessness over alcohol.

"I began drinking more when I found out Alicea was sick because I knew how good alcohol made me feel. It helped me to overcome my shyness and become the life of the party. Even though I probably had nothing cogent to say all those times I was getting drunk on my ass, I believed I was being entertaining, that everyone liked me. And if in reality, I was being a big oaf, I didn't worry about it the next day or the day after that because all I could think of was how much fun I'd had. I wanted to continue to have fun even though my wife was sick because if I wasn't drinking I was sick to my stomach with almost constant anxiety over her. I could barely function as a husband, a father, or at my job, without being fortified with at least some alcohol to get me through."

He was a natural born storyteller. Okay, maybe not naturally born, maybe he learned how to tell a good story by making up or embellishing real life stories for his children. However he got to this point, I was proud of him on so many levels. He had laid himself bare in a huge assembly room of strangers. It had taken a great deal of courage for a shy man. He had been protective of his privacy, not once revealing himself to be a policeman. Luckily, on this particular night, there had been no one there who had recognized him nor had he recognized anyone. He had moved people with his words. He had told his story genuinely and without enhancements. As I watched him speak I could feel the pain he felt at the potential loss of someone dear to him. His furrowed brow, slivered eyes, and relentless frowns were the outward indicators of his unrelenting inner angst. And beside myself, there was no other listener who could not immediately identify with his woes.

By the time Toby Magnessun had finished his introductory story to this new and accepting audience, tears had begun rolling down his rugged cheeks. He could barely look up and outward into anyone's face, as some of those tears began hitting his shoes and the floor. I watched them fall as if in slow motion, not hearing his last several sentences, but being mesmerized by the cascading liquid emotion that was departing his eyes.

When he finished, his heartache drained for now, his head bowed with embarrassment and humility, the crowd erupted with applause. I joined. Slowly, the quiet speaker raised his head and peered through watery eyes to the applauding throng. He knew they cared and that he belonged. I was honored to be present at the beginning of a profound life changing event for this strong but gentle man.

On the ride home there weren't a hundred words spoken between us. In fact, Toby asked me as we began the forty minute ride to Snell Island if I minded that we didn't talk much for a while. I said, "Of course not. What you did in there was pretty impressive. I know it took a lot out of you."

"It did," he said, and we drove in complete silence until we said good night in front of his house.

Those first two meetings with Toby is how I found my AA meeting place. At the times of those first two meetings, I still didn't think of myself as an alcoholic. I was reflecting on why Christine had asked me to leave, but I had begun only to think that I could fix myself all by myself. I wasn't like Toby. My drinking wasn't affecting my performance at work. I was never late. I didn't have to chase anybody on foot. My speech was never slurred. I wasn't an alcoholic like all the people in that room on Turner Street.

Christine was, in all likelihood, perceiving me to be an alcoholic. But I wasn't like all those people. That's what I thought then and for the next several weeks until I almost killed the female bicyclist in front of the Candy Kitchen. Only then did I begin to be honest with myself and start the long road to better and complete my utterly unfinished self.

After I dropped Toby off, my entire being yearned to stop at my beautiful old house and see Christine. It was nearly 11:00 p.m. Christine was probably home, maybe in bed or even asleep already. Those possible facts were not nearly enough to dissuade my spirit from longing to see my darling wife. But the wise side of me won out once again, reasoning that an unannounced visit would only hurt each of us. At that time I had only been gone from the house a few weeks. I had accomplished nothing in the way of changing myself for the better. I had not even started the process. I did not even know where to begin and at the top of my negatives list was the reality that I was in near complete denial that there was anything wrong with me, much less that I was an alcoholic like those people I had just left. I was the same exact man that Christine had asked to leave. What would be the point of seeing her and hurting her as well as myself?

I traversed nearly the entire width of St. Petersburg on my way back to the Beaches of Paradise. I thought mostly about Toby and the stunningly beautiful story he had told about his life, his wife, and his dependence on alcohol. And I thought, secondarily, about how much I missed Christine, attempting at every reflection of her to distract myself away from the thought by thinking of Toby, and occasionally, what I was going to use tomorrow as strategy for a couple of my scheduled clients.

By the time I got home it was nearly midnight. I fixed myself a tall glass of rum and Coke and went straight to the bathroom to brush my teeth and then straight to the bedroom after that. I opened my briefcase, grabbed my notebooks for tomorrow's clients, and placed them on the bed. For the next forty-five minutes I would sip my drink and review the notes on the six people I would begin seeing in a few hours. By one o'clock, my drink was finished and so was I. I turned the light out and fell deeply asleep.

Sometime during the early morning hours, I dreamed I was sleeping peacefully and dreaming a pleasant dream of Christine. It was a simple dream. Christine and I were reconciled and on a cruise, outside our cabin on a balcony, watching a luxurious sunset while holding hands. It was an idyllic dream, quite possibly reflecting a scene I hoped to duplicate someday in my waking life.

Knock, knock. It sounded like thunder out of the clear blue sky of our cruise ship scene. The moment between Christine and I did not immediately dissipate. I squeezed her hand a little more tightly as if not only to reassure her that I was there if a storm should arise, but that by doing so I could cling to this scene a little longer. It did not last. A fear in my psyche had been triggered and my tranquil image of Christine and I was snatched away in a cruel heartbeat. Replacing it was the vision of my sleeping self waking up with a start at having heard the two malicious thuds that stole my Christine from me. My rudely awakened dream self opened his eyes and looked upward. Pinned to the ceiling spread eagle and ready to strike was Satan. He was his horrifying usual crimson self, except this night he held a long black pitchfork with blades like razors in his right hand. My dream self screamed in terror at the thought of another impending assault. I tried to roll over and scramble from the bed and the room but I couldn't move. I was limited to my stare of the devil hovering above me. Lucifer stared back at me with glistening evil eyes but did not move. He did not move and I wondered why. We were locked in a horrifying glare. It was one of the worst dream moments of my life. Fear gripped every crevice of my being as I waited for whatever physical tortures he was going to inflict upon me. My fear of what might happen was far greater than the reality of what was actually happening. I wondered why he continued to remain motionless.

And then I realized what he was doing. He was playing a mind game with me. He was psyching out the psychologist. He was attempting to hurt me more by not attacking me than actually attacking me. As the dream moments passed, I began to believe he would never move toward me. As I continued staring, he and his pitchfork began to appear to be a horrible sculpture that some demented sculptor had suspended from the ceiling to be viewed by me every time I looked upward from my bed to the ceiling.

Then *knock, knock* again like explosive devices and a different terror besieged me. The devil moved only his savage face toward the door. He seemed to be listening for more knocks. I thought if he heard them he would open the bedroom door. He neither heard another knock nor opened the bedroom door. Instead he looked back at me with his menacing glare and floated backward through the ceiling and out of my domicile. I was still paralyzed, waiting as usual for the Two-Knock Ghost, or whatever it was, to begin the process of assaulting me. But the ghost never showed and the dream bedroom faded slowly to black.

* * * * *

CHAPTER 10

AFTER FEELING THAT I had achieved a great deal during my first twenty hours of sobriety, I faced the night. Earlier in the day I had not only begun the list of things I needed to do to discover my real current self and who I needed to become, but I had also chosen a place to attend AA meetings. In itself I felt that was a huge decision. But when I got home that night, it began to feel like I was running an obstacle course of temptation for an alcoholic. All I wanted to do was make myself my favorite simple toast and cheese sandwich, maybe two. But when I opened the refrigerator door, I saw three cold cans of Coke staring back at me from behind the cheese. Immediately, I was reminded of the three ounces of rum that I had tossed down the drain the night before. I licked my suddenly dry lips as I grabbed the cheese and reached for the loaf of Publix Wheat Bread that I always kept in the fridge to make it last longer. I knew that I would have to get rid of those Cokes right away, because of the associative discomfort I was feeling right now, but after I ate.

I began to wish I was at that AA meeting right now getting support for what I was realizing was going to be a bitter fight. When I grabbed for something to drink, I took out a half gallon of orange juice, drinking it right from the carton—something I never did when I lived with Christine and the kids. I finished two sandwiches, having felt hungrier, after the Cokes made me think of my rum. I washed my plate, put the orange juice back in the fridge, and then threw the Cokes away. During the moments that dark carbonated liquid was pouring down the drain, I wondered if I even liked plain Coke anymore. It had been decades since I had drunk a Coke without rum. I truly had no idea whether I would like it now by itself. The issue now was that seeing it not only made me think of rum and yearn for some, it had made me want to leave the house immediately and buy a bottle. I didn't, but that tiny episode of seeing the cans of Coke in the fridge made me feel as though they were playing a mind game with me. The truth is they made me crazy. Crazy! I felt uncomfortable shudders course through my body. My stomach hurt and I already felt like I was in a losing battle, wondering if I could make it to sleep time without darting to my favorite liquor store like a mad man.

That was only the initial obstacle. In a night of usually normal transitions, I was about to find out that there would be many obstacles and they would be lurking everywhere. I was smart enough to know that by changing my normal patterns I might concentrate on drinking less, so instead of going to my bedroom after dinner and working on my client notes, as I had for years, I thought I'd go into the living room and turn on my seldom used TV. I didn't even know the programs anymore. I could tell you all of the shows I watched as a kid. But now I only knew of the comedies that Christine loved watching; *Seinfield, Cheers, Frazier*. I had no idea what days or times those shows were on or whether they were current or reruns on cable. It was just my luck to turn on the TV and there it was, the *Seinfield* ensemble, Christine's absolute favorite performers before my very expectant eyes. Seven minutes later I couldn't stand it anymore. The actors seemed to be running around their sets getting all worked up about nothing. I turned the TV off without trying another channel, and within the first moment after, I felt a singular pang of missing Christine. Another obstacle. I immediately wanted a drink, again, to make the pain ease off. My body felt nervous as I denied it what it wanted. Then I felt my usual pull to go into my bedroom and work alone. As I did so, I wondered why I lived my life the way I did. Why did I always go to my bedroom, feeling sad most of the time? I had three great kids that lived with me for twenty-five years or so, but after dinner, I would always go to my bedroom and work. It was often the same thing on the weekends, except when we went on vacations as a family. If there was going to be sharing with my kids and Christine, it was going to have to be in the kitchen or the living room before or during dinner. After that was my special time to be alone with my thoughts. Even Christine hardly ever bothered me the first hour or so that I'd be in that bedroom. Why I was contemplating that now I didn't understand. But I wondered why the pull to go to my bedroom each night was so strong. Unfortunately, my next reflection was whether that near addiction of going to the bedroom each night had somehow hurt Christine and the kids. How many thousands of times had I neglected to be with the kids when they were watching TV in the living room? How many times had I neglected to be with Christine when her schedule permitted her to share those TV programs with the kids? I remember hearing them laugh and thinking so often how lucky I was to have them. I now wished the four of them were here right now, laughing and watching TV. I would forego the bedroom and join them. And why did I feel sadness for the first few minutes every time I went into the bedroom alone? It wore off as I delved into my nightly work. What was wrong with me?

As I passed the threshold into my bedroom, I felt the familiar sadness but tonight I missed my drink. I might have missed it more in that moment than I missed Christine. How horrible was that? What kind of a man had I become? Being in my bedroom was suddenly an enormous obstacle for me. I missed my bottle and my drink and every time I thought about and missed Christine, I yearned for a drink even more. My body literally shook as I worked on my client files from today and my strategies for tomorrow. Fortunately, Mary Bauer was scheduled in the morning. She had made some progress decreasing her anxiety but her fears were still acute, especially since the St. Pete police had not caught the robbers who had assaulted her. Thinking of how I could better support her helped turn my mind away from rum and Coke and into work. I noticed that when I wrote that night, my hand was shaking. My writing looked like that of a schizophrenic and that made me want a drink. Another obstacle. They were everywhere. In fact, I was the greatest obstacle that I needed to overcome. I reflected that I'd taken my bottle of rum and my favorite eight ounce glass with six ounces of Coke in it nearly every night to my bedroom for the last twenty years or so. I never ever thought that I might be hurting anyone. I was working in my bedroom to help support my family financially and my clients emotionally. For all those years of living my life that way, I felt justified—until now.

It was difficult concentrating on my work notes. Moment after moment I would think of my rum and want to drink some, but I continued to work. Finally, about an hour into my bedroom time, I got up to pee. I went into the bathroom, did my business, and then went to the sink to wash my hands. As I did so, I looked into the mirror. There I was before myself, the real and true me, the man I had become was staring back at me. I looked myself over from head to toe. First I noticed that the effervescence of my youth was absent from my face. My skin was pale and sallow. There was no sparkle in my eyes and to my dismay, my nose had grown. I didn't have wrinkles or a jowl yet, but

I wasn't as handsome as I once was. My eyes continued trailing down my body. I had a little belly. It wasn't huge, but larger than it had ever been. I realized suddenly, that I had not run in more than two years. For almost all of my adult life, running had been a near ritual for me. Four or five times a week I would suit up in shorts and a tee shirt, if the weather was nice, or a sweatshirt and sweat pants, if the weather was chilly. I remembered the hundreds of times I'd wear multiple layers of clothing during my winter runs in Chicago. Then I reflected on the myriad runs I went on with Christine. What an odd pairing we must have looked like to the casual observer. Me at six feet two and Christine at five feet two. But we were together. That was the important thing. And we were having fun. It didn't matter if it was freezing outside. We had learned early on that no matter how cold it was, we could work up a healthy sweat beneath our layers of clothing. I thought of Christine. I missed Christine. I wanted a drink.

I then began to see my thoughts as obstacles. I kept realizing things as suddenly thoughts and realizations began cascading from within like a waterfall. I realized that it had been over three years since I had asked Christine to run with me. Three years was a long time. Then I remembered that I had said "no thank you" to her the last six or seven times she had invited me to run with her. I seemed to remember that it was always the same scenario. She would ask and I would say, "I'm sorry, honey, but I've got work to do." And I'd go into that goddamned bedroom and close myself off from sharing myself with her and the kids. Of course I'd have my glass of ice filled with rum and Coke beside me to help me through my oh so important work, but tonight I realized for the first time how many times I denied Christine the sharing of one of our most enjoyable activities together. Eventually, she stopped asking me to run with her. She continued running into her midfifties, but I gradually dropped off. That's probably why she had a perfectly flat midsection and why I was developing a belly and a paunch. I thought about all the times I had denied her my company on her runs, and I felt like a heel. I wanted a drink at that moment for those reasons also.

I couldn't stand my reflection anymore because looking at it made my new emanation of realizations more painful. Perhaps, if I crawled into bed I could shut out this world of new pain. I was wrong. I brushed my still strong healthy teeth and headed for the bed and sleep. I got under the sheet, clapped the light off, and tried to fall asleep. Something was missing. Could it have been the sedating effects of alcohol? It most certainly was. This was the second night in a row that I had not had a drop of rum. My body, mind, heart and taste buds were craving the liquid like a starving man who had not eaten in weeks. I felt as though one of my best friends had died. I was struggling. I was in crisis. In a silent condo in a too quiet retirement complex, I could hear the beating of my aching heart and the nagging of the words inside my head.

"You are like those people at Toby Magnessun's meeting house, Turf. You're exactly like them. You're an alcoholic, Turf. That's what each and every one of them is. That's what you are. Nobody drinks exactly like the next guy. Anybody can be one—priests, nuns, firemen, policemen, accountants, teachers, presidents. There's no 'those people over there' and you in some safe place of personal exemption. You are all together in the same boat, fighting the same sea of sorrows. 'Those people' are not your enemies, they are not estranged from you. They are you." I was scaring myself, as unfamiliar voices in my head were tormenting me more than a devil dream. I was fifty-five years old and like a small child trying to hide from thunder, I rolled over onto my stomach, grabbed the pillow to my right, and placed it over my head and ears.

For a single moment I felt more secure. But the tumbling waterfall of shameful thoughts would not diminish. For the first time ever, I thought that whatever the devil could throw at me tonight it could not hurt me more than the thoughts of the past thirty minutes.

I fell asleep in that position with my face buried into one pillow with my hands and arms squeezing the other pillow tightly to the back of my head. That night there were no devil dreams. Instead, two knocks occurred at 1:00 a.m., sounding like Howitzers and waking me from my sleep. They had come from the front door. I didn't turn around from my facedown position to acknowledge them. I knew what they were. I knew at least part of what they were. They were coming from some asshole ghost who kept knocking but never came in. Punk! I lay there for a moment before I fell back asleep, contemplating what it was in my psyche that might be causing this two-knock phenomenon. Was some kind of chemical defect in my brain causing something that merely sounded like two knocks? And why always two knocks? Why not three or four or even more? I didn't even believe in ghosts, so how could it be something I didn't believe in that was annoying me this much? But then, I was dreaming terrifying dreams about the devil and in my conscious life I didn't believe in him. I must have fallen deeply asleep because I was dreaming about Mary Bauer. I was an enormous angel, and she was her tiny self, looking much more like a child than she did in real life. She was shivering with fear, eyes filled with terror. As the angel I whispered, "Come here, my child." She slowly came. I gently closed my left wing to protect her, as I stood a full eight feet tall, my eagle-like eyes scanning the countryside for danger, my face transitioning from a comforting smile to an ominous scowl. My right wing looked like a huge feathered weapon, waiting to swat her attackers into eternal hell if they dared show their faces.

But the beauty didn't last. It happened again. *Knock, knock*—two more knocks, this time at my bedroom door. I awoke once more, wondering what it was and why. This time, I rolled over, put the second pillow over my face, and jonsed for a drink of rum and Coke. I needed it to help me sleep. I needed it to ease the pain of my fear and worry. I needed it to help erase the pain that my realizations of hours earlier had caused. I needed it more than comforting words or a tender hug. I needed it.

A third time I fell asleep. A third time I heard the knocks. This time they sounded like they were inside my bedroom. I pulled the pillow from my face and looked immediately to the door, wondering if this was the moment the Two-Knock Ghost would reveal itself. But there was nothing to be seen. *Coward*, I thought. But what would any ghost have to fear from me?

Over and over it happened the rest of the night. The two knocks were more frenzied. Though there were always only two, there was now a sense of urgency about them that had never existed before. It was as if the knocks were saying, "Let me in now, or else." Then I would think, *Or else what?* Everything I thought about the Two-Knock Ghost was conjecture.

The ninth time I was awakened that night, the knocks on my door were barely audible. Why? Had the ghost exhausted itself with its sixteen previous knocks? Do ghosts get tired? I certainly was. There had been no continuity of sleep that night and why had the ghost's frenzied knocks coincided with my second night of sobriety? Worn out beyond measure, I longed for one final segment of sleep before my alarm clock went off. This whole ghost business had convinced me that something was transpiring in my brain and psyche that was far beyond my alcoholism. In my quiet bedroom during the final hour before sunrise, I realized I needed to find a psychologist to help me deal with the Two-Knock Ghost. I closed my eyes and exhaled an exasperated whisper, "Come in, you son of a bitch and show me what you are."

CHAPTER 11

THE NEXT MORNING I awoke, nearly completely exhausted, but more determined than ever to begin to change my life. The night before I had been filled with growth for me because I had begun to realize behaviors that had undoubtedly affected Christine and our very sacred union. I awoke again with shame in my heart for all the things I had done to hurt a totally undeserving woman. Next to the shame was fear—a lot of fear. I dreaded what other awareness of poor behavior on my part that impacted Christine and our marriage would come to me. My heart was already breaking this morning. I wondered how many more realizations I could withstand as I began looking inward and becoming honest with myself.

No matter how I felt, I had to go to work. Work was my saving grace. Even when I was burdened with my own negative emotions, helping others through their difficult times always pulled me upward to a better state of feeling. Today would be no different.

Mary Bauer was scheduled for eleven o'clock and amidst all my personal problems I had an idea I couldn't wait to share with her. Today I would do two things I knew would set me on the path I needed to travel. I would attend my first AA meeting as an admitted alcoholic, and I would find a psychologist to help me with the Two-Knock Ghost and who knew what else.

For the first time in years, I felt like I was on the precipice of achieving something for my deepest self. For years I had been contributing to the betterment of everyone else, so I thought. And as soon as I thought that thought, I realized that if that were true, Christine would not have asked me to leave our home and maybe our kids would call me more.

Another realization. I determined that I would call each of my kids beginning today. With Robert Phillip, then Lena, and Shawn Daniel, I would take the high road with each of them. I would ask them not only how they were doing in their lives right now, but if they felt that I had hurt them in any way while they were growing up. However they would answer me, I would acknowledge it, own up to it, apologize for it, if required, and deal with it as well as I could.

It would be a busy day. As I entered into it, my exhaustion abated replaced by curiosity and hope. I felt a loneliness that morning too. It was the hole in my heart that I always felt even when I was the happiest with Christine and the kids. I often thought it got there after the crash that killed my family, but in these hours of prolific revelations, I realized that I'd always had that hole in my heart. I was always lonely for some reason. I couldn't figure it out. I had great parents, I had great grandparents. I had a great upbringing in Chicago. Why should I have gone through life with a hole in my heart that couldn't be filled?

As I drove toward my office in downtown St. Pete, I realized nothing ever seemed to fill that emotional emptiness. Not Christine, not the birth of my kids, not my educational or professional accomplishments, not even rum and Coke.

Was that hole my yearning for God? Had I made the wrong decision to leave the Catholic Church over thirty years ago? Was there something wrong with my brain? I began to think that there was because the underlying feeling of emptiness that was plaguing me for years just didn't add up. Did I need medicine? Did I need to see a psychiatrist, not a psychologist?

In the middle of myriad hypotheticals, I reached my office at First Avenue North in the Bank of America Building. I walked into my office reception area and greeted Amanda, my twenty-eight-year-old Italian office manager. She was a marvelous human being, already busy when I walked through the door at 8:15.

"Good morning, Dr. McKenzie," she said with a smile on her face. I could not help but think her voice sounded like a mellifluous exotic bird singing an early morning greeting to the sun. It was impossible to look at her and be depressed.

"Good morning, Miss Amanda," I said playfully.

She was a tall Italian woman about five feet seven and a half inches, very thin, but handsomely shapely. Her greenish brown eyes were beautiful and piercing. To merely look into their genuine captivating charm was enough to elevate one's spirit. She was the perfect woman for her job. She was kind and sensitive to each one of my patients, somehow knowing what everyone needed from her during their interactions even though they came to my practice with utterly varied complexities. Amanda had just finished her bachelor's degree in business from the University of South Florida. Three years prior to this point in her life she had fallen in love with a banker from Tampa named John Schiefele. John had three children ages six, eight, and ten when they met. His wife, Anntoinette, left him for a handsome stud nine years her junior to frolic in Europe. When Amanda first met John, John and Anntoinette were involved in a severe custody battle for their children. Anntoinette did everything she could to paint a horrid picture of John's character. But after months of interacting with John and interviewing the children extensively, the judge did not buy into Anntoinette's fiction.

As time passed, the runaway mother communicated less and less with John, their children, or the judge. Nearly three years into their relationship, John, Amanda, and the children were living as a very happy family. Amanda was an even happier woman these days because John had proposed to her the week before, for the sixth time, and she had finally said, "Yes, John, I'm ready now."

I couldn't have the success I have had in my relatively new St. Pete practice without her. She has been a tireless and selfless worker on behalf of me and my clients. I noticed that her hair color was a reddish brown today and cut short, whereas the day before it had been blond and beyond her shoulders. She looked like a completely different woman, except for those glorious eyes and that inviting smile.

"Your hair looks stunning," I said, forgetting all my problems in the moment.

"My sister, Melissa, did it last night. John told me it's like being with a different woman. I told him that it's more fun that way, no?"

"I almost thought you were a temp. Even though I know it's you, I almost feel like I should give you another job interview."

She giggled for an instant then turned totally professional.

"Here's your schedule for the day, Doctor. And here's your phone messages in the order of importance. I'll bring you your hot chocolate in a few minutes." We were back to our basic routine. I said, "Thank you, ma'am," and headed for my office.

My schedule had changed. One of my patients had cancelled because of the flu. That was perfect because it would free up some time for me in the early afternoon to look through the phone book for a psychologist.

The first part of the morning flew past. I saw two clients before Mary Bauer arrived at 11:00.

"Mary's here, Doctor," Amanda said after she buzzed me.

Mary Bauer came into my office looking tired and withdrawn.

"Good morning, Dr. McKenzie," she said softly.

"Good morning, Mary. How are you feeling?"

There was a long pause before she spoke again. Her eyes scanned the items in my office until they raised themselves to look out my window longingly toward Tampa Bay.

"I wish I felt better, Dr. McKenzie, but I don't. I worry every day whether those three guys who assaulted me will find me again and do worse things to me. I feel violated 24-7. I don't feel strong. I don't feel safe. I don't feel like I'm being a good wife to my husband. I still have nightmares of the event as it happened and morbid variations of it, and there is no doubt that I am not as good of a teacher as I was before all this happened."

It was my turn to take a long pause. What could I say to her now that I'd not said to her before? I had taken so many different tacks with her so far. But once again I would try something new that I hoped might help her.

"Mary, so far in our journey, we've approached this as you in the role of the victim, that something priceless and irretrievable has been taken away from you. What if we turned this whole thing around and look at the event as you've been given a great gift." She looked at me as though I might be crazy, but her eyes were curious and hopeful.

"Go on," she said.

I spoke tenderly as a father to a daughter. "The event you endured changed you forever. Of that there is no doubt. But there is no doubt, as well, that you have gained so much experientially. No one wants to be a victim of a brutal crime. But if you survive it, you have gained a keen sense of what it is. It becomes part of the very bag of your life experiences. When you teach in the future, think of the wise attention you can give your little third grade boys that may be the attention that helps to dissuade them from growing up to be bullies or pursuing a life of crime. People often say that sometimes the love of one adult in a child's life can save them from souring as an adult. Because of your experiences, your heart is more intuitive about the true power of teaching, with genuine love behind it. With your husband, think of all the kindnesses that he shows you. His touch is soft and affectionate. You've told me he is patient. These qualities are the antithesis of what you experienced in the store that day. Now, you have even more need and reason to seek out his physical love. The tenderness and passions that flow between a loving couple have intrinsic healing properties that are greater than almost anything else that life has to offer."

She sat silently. I wondered if I should continue sermonizing or whether I should draw her in with a question. Before I made a decision, I thought about how everything I ever said to a client was conjecture, my opinion. I wasn't God. What I was saying wasn't absolute truth. It was more like a stream of consciousness. Most of all, I didn't want to hurt or confuse this sweetheart of a human soul. She was staring at me silently with eyes that yearned for something to believe in, verbal medicine that she desperately wanted to help heal her. I decided to continue.

"You have become a specialist of sorts because you have had a rare firsthand training that has impacted you profoundly. If you look at it as something you have gained, it can immediately be labeled a strength."

"How so, Doctor?"

"Mary, my mother always used to tell me that everyone is your teacher. When she first told me that when I was a teenager, I thought of it as just more 'Mom speak,' but I kept thinking about it for days, weeks, months, years even to this day. Long ago, I concluded she was right. Then when I was in college, I had a wonderful teacher who taught me that if I ever really wanted to understand an event in its entirety, that I should keep looking at it from as many angles as I possibly could. Like this cup on my desk here." I lifted the cup and held it in the space between us. "It's the entire cup that is the cup's reality. Both of us see different aspects of its reality as we peer at it from our individual perspectives. Neither of us can see the whole cup. The way I am holding it now, we can't see if it's empty or full or partly full or what's in it. From my perspective, I can't even see if there's a chip on the opposite lip of the cup from me, and from your point of view, you can't tell if there is a crack in the handle that I am holding. So we keep turning it and raising and lowering it until we see the cup from every angle. Only then will we see the true reality of what the cup is."

I paused again, this time shorter than a moment before.

"Could you elaborate a little more please, Doctor?"

I was on an extemporaneous roll. I liked it. It was fun. These were some of the best moments of my life, but even after all the years of being in practice, I hoped I wouldn't lose my train of thought, get tongue-tied, screw up. All of those negative things had happened to me before, and it was always an unpleasant moment each time it happened. But I really didn't want anything illogical or downright stupid to come out of my mouth right now because Mary was counting on me. I wanted to be at my best, so I dug more deeply from within myself than I usually did.

"Do you remember when John Walsh's son, Adam, was kidnapped?"

"No, I don't."

"John was your basic average loving dad and husband a couple of decades back when his little boy, Adam, disappeared. An extensive search lasted quite some time until they finally found a singular part of his son's body—his head."

Mary gasped. I continued.

"You can imagine the heartbreak John felt and the anger as he experienced a father's worst nightmare. John Walsh was a victim. Every negative emotion imaginable must have been coursing through his veins. He could have retreated into a shell and suffered deeply for the rest of his life but he didn't. He turned that anger and rage and sadness into something absolutely positive and tremendous." I paused only long enough to take a breath, but before I could begin speaking again, Mary asked a question.

"What did he do?"

"Have you ever heard of the TV show, *America's Most Wanted*?"

"Sure I have. In fact I've watched it several times."

"The John Walsh I'm talking about is the host of that show."

"That's the same John Walsh?" Mary asked incredulously.

I nodded a couple of times.

"I had no idea."

"That's because when it happened you might have been just a little girl or not even born yet. I'm not exactly sure what year it happened. But the point is that John Walsh took something that could have been eternally devastating and turned it into a nightmare for a multitude of really rotten men. And when you keep looking at the cup that is that story, you can see the countless fathers, mothers, brothers, sisters, aunts, uncles, cousins, and friends that were spared similar heartaches because John Walsh had figured out a way to get these thugs off the streets."

"But, Doctor, a few minutes ago you told me that your mother always used to tell you that everyone is your teacher, then you told me the analogy of the cup and its reality and I get that, but what do you think that the man that killed John Walsh's son taught him, especially since they probably never met."

"First, Mary, you know already that you don't have to meet someone to learn from them. Think of all the literature that you've read and poetry. You never met Jack London or William Faulkner or Shakespeare or Jules Verne or Ernest Hemmingway or Emily Dickinson, but think of what they have taught you as well as the joy they have given you. Think about all of the textbooks you have read over your years in school. You probably never met a single one of those authors.

"Second and most importantly, I'd like not to answer your question about what Adam Walsh's killer might have taught John Walsh but instead, I'd like to ask you to tell me what you think that murderer might have taught Mr. Walsh because I think that the answer might be much more beneficial to you if it came from you rather than me."

Mary swallowed hard and assumed an expression not unlike she might have had when posed with a difficult question by her teacher as a school girl.

"Doctor, you've just asked me a type of question I've never been asked before. It's a kind of question that I've never even pondered before."

"Can you give it a shot?" I said lightly and encouragingly.

"I'll try," Mary said then raised her eyes again toward Tampa Bay as if the answers would come from the serenity she was seeking by looking at the water.

"I think Adam Walsh's murderer taught John Walsh never to quit on life, no matter how deep the pain is that you feel."

I sat silently, hoping for more.

"He taught John that evil can inspire good." She paused and thought as I remained silent.

"That murderer eventually taught John that the world can be beautiful despite great tragedy. He taught John that his crime didn't have to limit John's potential in life, but could increase it a hundredfold or more."

She was rolling now.

"He taught John how to change his rage into a form of creative revenge. He taught John that love of family and humanity doesn't have to stop because of personal heartache. In fact, love can and must increase after these kinds of events or the parents who are suffering from it will fall apart, as will the marriage and the other children involved, if there are any."

She sighed deeply, not as if she had completed answering my question, but as though she was beginning to apply those lessons to herself and it was an enlightening moment. She lifted her eyes again to the water. Our silences filled the room. We were both deep in thought. I couldn't have anticipated what she said next.

"I'm still afraid, Doctor."

It was then that I decided to take a leap of faith. I asked her, "Mary, do you believe in angels?" I asked not because I believed in angels, but because if she believed in them, what I was planning to say next might give her comfort.

"I do," she said softly, speaking in almost dulcet tones as she had the entire session.

I leaped.

"Mary, I want you to close your eyes and imagine that you have an enormous guardian angel standing directly in front of you. You have looked into his eyes before and you have not only seen the protective love he has for you, but the sadness he feels that you were hurt under his guardianship. You have prayed for him to come to you and show you himself and he has obliged. You have seen his face, again, a countenance of complete kindness. He spreads his wings, an invitation to come next to him. Once more you look into his beautiful caring eyes, but though you see the care, you also see a fierce determination to protect you from further harm. Slowly he closes his left wing around you, while his huge right wing remains open like a giant sword waiting to strike down any entity that would attempt to harm you. You feel safe beneath that wing in the presence of that magnificent enlightened being. When you leave here today, you can take those images with you and think of them. Maybe they will help you." I chose again to be silent as I watched Mary pondering against her closed eyelids. A few seconds later, she reopened her eyes and spoke gently as always.

"Thank you for that, Dr. McKenzie. I actually feel better, and I know better what I need to do to get my life back on track."

Our session was drawing to a close.

"Mary, do you remember that at the beginning of our session today I shared with you that my mother always told me that everyone was our teacher?"

"Yes."

"Even though I was just a teenager when she told me that, I thought it was interesting. I took that concept and kept turning it over and over in my mind the same way we both turned that cup many times over. It took me years to see that we learn so much from one another. But as I continued to ponder it, I one day realized that each of us too is a teacher as well. I am a teacher, you are a teacher—I don't mean our professions, I mean in everything we do, everything. Our behavior truly and absolutely affects everyone with whom we come in contact. I know you've been hurting for many weeks now, Mary, but you know what I'd like for you soon?"

She shook her head no.

"I'd like for you to shed your cloak of pain and fear and become the happy productive woman that you have always been. Then, at some point after that, without even trying, I'd like you to teach people how resilient you are. I'd like you to teach your students the powerful effects that having love behind whatever you are instructing can have. Beyond that, I hope for you to be the wonderful happy person that you are at your core because everyone who sees you will benefit from that. And lastly, and I'll shoot for the moon on this one, I want you to change the world by being happy. If you can reclaim that intrinsic joy that you have for life, you will change the world merely by existing."

I don't know if I had said the right things to her, but my advice had come from deep within my heart and Mary had sat there patiently intently taking everything in and analyzing it.

"That's a tall order, Doctor, but I understand what you're saying and it makes sense. Now all of it has to forge its way into the parts of my heart and soul where the worries and fears and hurts still live. What you've said today makes sense to me. But it will take some time for all of this to percolate inside me. I admit I feel better and I can't get that image of the angel, with his wing around me, out of my mind. Thank you for that and for everything else we talked about today."

"You're welcome."

She stood and extended her hand to me with her usual elegance and grace. "Thank you for your kind and thought provoking words, Doctor."

We shook hands, each smiling genuinely and warmly at one another, then broke our grasp and walked together to the door. Then as I reached to open it for her, I thought about the Two-Knock Ghost. Never before in my life had doors been a problem for me, but now and for the past few weeks I had often become apprehensive when approaching a door. Since I didn't know what the Two-Knock Ghost was, it could be anything or anybody. I told myself not to worry. The Two-Knock Ghost had previously only invaded my dreams. I needn't worry about waking doors.

I opened my office door and Mary passed through.

"I'll see you again next week, Doctor."

"Till then, Mary."

"Good-bye, Amanda," she said as she passed through the reception area.

"See you next week, Mary."

And she was gone. I hoped at least she was a little bit fortified by some of the things I had said to her. It wasn't the first time I had used a dream I'd had to comfort a patient. I believed in the power of dreams and how they could impact a person's life. I believed how perfectly, timely and appropriate they could be or how badly timed and horribly terrifying. I seriously hoped that sharing the dream had given something for Mary to take with her to refer to if she needed it on occasion.

It was lunchtime. Amanda had already pulled her brown paper bag from one of her desk drawers as soon as the door closed behind Mary. Most days Amanda "brown bagged" it and often continued to work although we had a service to take phone messages for us between noon and 1:00 p.m. Sometimes Amanda would opt to take a quick walk to one of the little cafés that dotted Central Avenue. Once in a while she would walk to one of the many downtown hot dog vendors for a hot dog or a Polish sausage and a soda.

"She's really sweet, Dr. McKenzie, isn't she?" Amanda said.

"She sure is, Amanda. Enjoy your lunch."

Once inside my office, I decided to do two things in the next hour. First, I would call my oldest son. Secondly, I would find a psychologist. If my alcoholism was the cause of my devil dreams then I was going to start attacking it immediately, first by making amends with my children, if I needed to. I wasn't at all sure but I knew full well about making amends and if I started doing that right away, I might put myself further onto the right path of beating my drinking and diminishing the devil dreams. What to do about the Two-Knock Ghost was a different story entirely. I knew what the devil was. But a Two-Knock Ghost? What in the hell was that? Where did that come from? And how absurd was even the thought of it? I forced all thoughts of ghosts and demons out of my mind and reached for my Rolodex and my son's phone number. Next to the silver Rolodex was a picture of Christine, me, and the three kids when they were all under the age of ten. We were on one of our summer vacations. In the picture, we were at Disney World. How ironic. Disney World was only ninety miles away now and Florida was my home. How beautiful we all were then. How young. All together. I wiped the nostalgia from my mind and called Robert Phillip. He was working in San Francisco as a dentist in the Medical Arts Building on Van Ness. He loved that city. It was 10:00 a.m. in San Francisco, and I realized that he might be in the middle of a procedure, but I called anyway. I was determined to knock down all of my problems related to alcoholism and the Two-Knock Ghost, as if they were a series of lined up Dominoes. Robert Phillip was one of the first Dominoes and my heart yearned for it to fall right now.

"Hello, Robert."

"Dad!"

"How are you firstborn?"

"I'm great, Dad, but you caught me on my cell phone while I'm drilling into a nasty molar."

"I'm sorry, Robert. I'll call you back tonight."

"Dad, don't hang up," he said quickly. "I'm yanking your chain, but I will have to drill that molar in about eight minutes. What's up? I heard from Lena that you and Mom separated a few months ago. Are you back together?"

"No, son, we're not yet, but I'm working on it. I called for a couple of reasons. First, how are Emily and the kids?"

"Emily's fine, Dad. Perfect, in fact, if that's humanly possible. Josie's as cute as a spring daisy and proud to be a kindergartener and I just put braces on Zack's teeth. He's a handsome boy, but he looks kind of funny when he flashes that silver smile. He looks like you, Dad. Like a Norman Rockwell kid, freckled and towheaded. What else is going on with you?"

My throat was tight, and I was nearly perspiring when I formed the first words of my next sentence. I knew that Robert was at work and that time was limited for him right now. I didn't want to put pressure on him, but I desperately wanted an answer to my most important question.

"Robert, do you feel that there was any way that I might have hurt you as a child or a young man?"

"Holy shit, Dad! Where did that come from?"

"I'm working on personal issues, Robert. There are things I have to figure out and correct before I go home with your mom. I miss her tremendously, and I want to speed up the process of getting back to her."

"Dad, you were a great dad. I remember you teaching me how to play baseball, coming to my Little League games, helping me with my multiplication tables, making us all kinds of wonderful breakfasts, taking us on vacations and little road trips to Starved Rock and Springfield, helping me pay for college. You were and still are a great dad. I have no complaints."

"Son, could you do me a favor for just a moment and dig deep and tell me if there was anything I ever did that bothered you, maybe threw you off-kilter a little bit."

There was what seemed to me like an eternal delay on the other end before Robert spoke again.

"There was one thing, Dad, a little thing really, when I compare it to the scope of all the good things you did for me."

I was so nervous, I wanted to jump in and ask him right away what it was, but I held back and waited for him to formulate his description. Again time, though it was only seconds, passed slowly.

"I always wondered why you spent so much time in your bedroom in the evenings. Sometimes, when I was a little boy and I'd have done something naughty and you'd scold me, when you'd go into your bedroom I thought you were mad at me. I thought you were avoiding me. But as I got older, nine or ten, I realized that you were merely just taking a ton of work in there and preparing for the next day. You were real good at coming to planned events that I had in the evenings, but it seemed like every night that we were home with no outside activity planned that you would go into your room and stay there until Mom came and got you to come to tuck us in. That's all there ever was, Dad. You did it my whole life so I got used to it. I wondered about it from time to time and sometimes I wished you would watch TV with us, but you never did, except for *Frazier Thomas* and *Family Classics* on Sunday nights. You seemed to like that. But that's it Dad, really."

"I haven't thought about *Family Classics* in years," I said.

"Hey, Dad, you remember what I said about that molar? It's ready for me now."

"You go work your magic, Robert. I'll talk to you soon."

"Dad, if I wasn't so darn busy with work and Emily and the kids, I'd call you more often, but I love you, Dad. I hope you know how much I do. Now are you sure you're all right?"

He asked me with kindness and sincerity in his voice.

"I'm working on it, Robert. I'm thinking that maybe after I get back with your mother, we can have a big family reunion."

"Wow! That would be super, Dad. I gotta run. I love you, Dad."

"Me to you, Robert."

I didn't want to hear his end click off, so I pushed my phone quickly away from my ear and placed it back in the cradle. It was a bit of a quirky move on my part I thought, but I figured I'd hurt less at our good-bye if I was in control of hanging up.

I still missed him more after the call than before it, but now at least I knew that I hadn't hurt him too much. He had a lot of great shared memories and he loved me. I thought it acutely interesting, however, that he brought up my nightlife in my bedroom, something that I had been wondering about lately myself.

I looked at my watch, figured I had about twenty-five minutes before my next patient. I heard my stomach grumble and suddenly felt hungry. I decided to forego my plan to find a psychologist and cater instead to my hunger. I would look for the psychologist later in the day. I decided to go downstairs and out the front door, turn left, walk a couple of hundred feet and grab a hotdog or a Polish sausage at a nearby hotdog cart. I nearly hated to turn right when I walked out of the building because then I would be heading in the direction of All Children's Hospital, where Christine worked. She might be there now. I had communicated with her so little lately, that I didn't even know what her current work schedule was. It seemed odd to me that if I was walking along Central Avenue, as I often did at lunchtime, I felt much closer to All Children's and Christine than I did when I was driving in my car. Walking only a mile or so from All Children's hurt more. I missed Christine more when I was on foot. I felt the pain of our separation more. I felt the futility of my life without her, more. I liked to stretch my legs at lunch, to look at the cute little shop windows, sometimes go in and browse or buy, have a quick lunch at a trendy restaurant. But I didn't like the emotions that walking West out of the Bank of America Building did to me.

    I decided to get two hotdogs with ketchup and spicy mustard and an Orange Crush. I got the simple meal, everything in a small brown bag, and turned to walk North up Beach Drive to find a bench, eat and relax while gazing at the water. I was feeling pretty good emotionally. I believed I had given Mary Bauer some comfort in our session. I had talked pleasantly with my son. Later today I would find a psychologist I hoped would provide some comfort for me, and tonight I would attend my first AA meeting as an admitted alcoholic. I would pour my heart out with the truth, the way I was finally beginning to see it. I would spill my guts in public for the first time no matter how challenging that may be. I would begin turning the corner and heading back to my darling Christine instead of allowing my denials to take me further from her. No wonder I felt kind of good. I had a right to feel kind of good.

CHAPTER 12

THE AFTERNOON SPED by. I dealt with my patients with the deep attention that they deserved, but I was continually distracted by the two other activities I promised myself I would do today—find a psychologist and attend my first AA meeting.

As soon as my last patient left my office, I got up from behind my desk and went into the waiting room to say good night to Amanda.

"How does my day look tomorrow?" I began.

"Light," she answered.

"Only three clients."

"What time is the first one?"

"Eleven o'clock," she said.

"What does tonight look like for you and John?" I asked.

"Just a quiet night at home with the kids. Dinner, homework, watch some TV, relax—nothing special."

"Why don't you take an extra hour and a half for yourself and come in at 9:30 or so. The answering service can handle our calls for ninety extra minutes one day."

"Thank you, Doctor. I've been wanting to do some business inside the Banking Center for a few days. That extra time will be perfect for me."

"Have a good night, Amanda. I'll see you when I get in."

"You too, Dr. McKenzie."

I was already thinking about sleeping in a bit tomorrow morning, anticipating an emotional night, hanging out after the AA meeting, making some new friends and getting to bed much later than I normally did. I figured there would be nothing wrong with showing up here at 10:00 or 10:30.

As soon as I said good night to Amanda, I returned to my office, closed the door, sat back down at my desk, and pulled a local phone book from a drawer. In the next few minutes I would choose a psychologist. Even though I was thinking that this decision would be a pretty big one, I didn't have any problem at all using the phone book. Throughout the years I had used the phone book to call all kinds of businesses—doctors, restaurants, car repair places, seamstresses, florists. If I didn't get along with my psychologist, I could just switch to another one. I'd switched doctors, never gone back to bad restaurants or overcharging car repair shops. After all, I just wanted to bounce some ideas off whomever I chose about my devil dreams and the Two-Knock Ghost. I wasn't going there to expect the guy to save my immortal soul, I, more than anything, wanted a sounding board. Lastly, I concluded that the AA meetings would help me deal with that. I wasn't thinking at all about asking the psychologist to help me in that area.

I started at the beginning—Angelo Alvarez, Anthony Artez, Michael Ather, Connie Augmon, Daniel Awtry, Robert Ayers. Then there it was, Antonio Banderas, the name of the movie star. I chuckled rather hard and immediately wondered what it would be like to be "psyched" by the action star. Secondly, and almost immediately, I wondered what this guy looked like. My eye kept scanning down the list, now not paying as much attention as I had on the first seven names, and for the next two minutes, as my eyes scanned the list of psychologists, my mind kept wondering what Antonio Banderas looked like and whether he was a good psychologist. I chuckled again and thought, why not? This might be interesting and maybe even a little fun. At least when I told the guy why I chose him. Then I chuckled again when I wondered how many women had picked him because of his name, and whether they had been pleased or disappointed with his looks when they met him.

Serious business or not, this was the guy I was going with. I would throw my emotional sticks out of the can into his office and pick them up one by one, with his help. I made a plan to call him tomorrow morning from my condo before I went into work. I felt better still. I was getting things accomplished.

I wrote Antonio's name, address and phone number on a piece of notebook paper and placed it in my briefcase where I could find it easily. I looked at my watch, not quite 5:30. Plenty of time to drive the eighteen or so miles to the AA meeting, get a bite to eat, and still make it to the beginning of the meeting by 7:30.

I laughed at myself repeatedly as I drove north toward a restaurant and my new AA site, wondering about Antonio Banderas, what he looked like, and what kind of person he was.

I decided to keep it simple and make a pit stop at McDonald's on Missouri. I ordered a filet of fish, a strawberry shake, a cup of water, and a large order of fries. As I sat in the restaurant, dipping my first fries into ketchup, I felt my first twinge of nervousness at what I was about to do in an hour or so. I had never bared my soul before to anyone, not even Christine. Tonight I would lay myself bare to a room full of people, mostly strangers. I might have one ally there if Toby showed up tonight. But then I thought that I might be more embarrassed to reveal my inner most feelings before him than a hundred or more strangers.

My next decision was to make sure I got to the meeting by 7:10, 7:15 at the latest. I would find a good seat, put my head down, not look at who was coming in, and contemplate how I would tell my story. The twinges of nervousness transformed into a family of butterflies fluttering haphazardly in my stomach. My meal tasted wonderful in my mouth, but that was not enough to offset the distress I was experiencing in my belly.

I arrived at the Serenity Club at 7:07. There were at least a dozen cars ahead of mine, but the lot east of the building was more than half empty so I parked there and walked into the building at exactly 7:10. I said hello to a few people who were sitting on the steps outside and a couple more who were milling about in the lobby. I smiled at them perfunctorily and headed for a comfortable seat. My head was up for the initial hellos, the smiles and the chair finding, but as soon as I was situated, I put my head down and started thinking. I found myself within moments trying to calm my suddenly restive soul. But I kept my head down even through the filling of the auditorium. I kept my head down and listened. Every footstep, each movement of chair over floor, multiple conversations with myriad words flying about the room was intensified. The magnified sounds were distracting me as were the people who were seating themselves all around me. I remained with my head down. Someone who didn't know me might see my position and think that I was depressed. I wasn't depressed in this moment. I was scared like a little kid scared. I felt like a third grader in a new school and in a moment I would have to introduce myself and tell some of my story to the class.

The moderator quieted the din in the room as he welcomed the people who were attending. He especially welcomed the newcomers and anyone who was feeling in crisis stating unequivocally that they had come to the right place.

Within two minutes after the moderator had begun with, "Hello, everyone. I'm Sam and I'm an alcoholic and your moderator for the evening," the first alcoholic began sharing his story. My head remained down as I listened, paying careful attention to how he did it. I remember thinking that the way he shared his story was nothing grand. It was merely a simple telling of his personal current woes and his struggles with staying sober. Whatever he said, it seemed genuine and from the heart.

By the time the first alcoholic was finished, I was not even remotely ready to speak. It took over an hour and four more alcoholics to speak before I had the courage to share my rather tame story in comparison to the first five people I had listened to tonight. My head had been down the entire time the previous speakers had shared their tales. Now, I was ready and felt comfortably prepared. This time, when the moderator asked if there was anyone else who wanted to speak, I raised my head and said, "I do."

I looked at no other face in the room but the moderator. "My name is Turf and I'm an alcoholic." The words came hard and I shocked myself by the last split-second decision to use the name Turf. Even Christine had not called me Turf for the last few years. It was as if Turf had died those years ago without fanfare, without a mention. But here I was, a paunchy middle-aged psychologist and I had just unexpectedly resurrected my long lost, beloved alter ego before the most important speech of my life.

In the few seconds which seemed like hours, before I spoke again, I felt all of my preparations fly to an unknown and inaccessible realm. Fear gripped me during the two or three deep breaths I took before my next words. I could not help but contemplate in that brief moment why I would do such a thing when I didn't even feel like Turf anymore. But even as I was pondering what I would say next, I was surprised when over a hundred people said, "Hi, Turf," almost in unison. I had just enough time in the next breath or two to plan my next strategy as I nodded my head once to acknowledge the gregarious welcome. I would tell my story starting with the present and going back to the beginning. It wouldn't be difficult. I wasn't delivering the Gettysburg Address. It was simply my story, I knew it well, just tell it.

"I haven't had a drink in two days and I want one badly now. This is the first time in over twenty years that I have gone two days without a drink. I'm living on my own right now because my wonderful wife of over thirty years asked me to leave our home and our marriage until I got my act together. I left out of respect for her, not because I believed I was an alcoholic. I actually thought I was a great husband and father. Then, a couple of nights ago, I took some work from my office into the R Bar in Treasure Island and in the next couple of hours had three or four rum and Cokes. On my way home I almost hit a female bicyclist in Madeira Beach. It wasn't my fault. She darted from a real dark spot on the opposite side of the street to get in the North bound lane so she could turn right at 140th. Why she chose that instant to make that move I'll never know, but she did. When my car almost hit her, she panicked and jumped off the bike. I sprang out of the car and ran over to see if she was okay. She said she was and even apologized that she almost caused an accident. As soon as she rode off, I felt real fear when I asked myself the question: What would have happened if I had hit her and a policeman had been called to the scene? Or what if a policeman had just happened to be cruising Gulf Boulevard and saw that I narrowly missed her? He would have stopped for sure to see if the girl was okay, primarily, and to check on me secondarily. The cop would have come close to me and smelled alcohol on my breath. He would have given me a sobriety test, maybe a breathalyzer. I don't know if I would have passed those tests, but if I hadn't, my whole life could have changed that night for the worse. I could have been arrested, taken to jail, been forced to go to PCAS for alcohol evaluation, lost my driver's license, got a DUI, my professional life would have been placed in jeopardy, my wallet would be severely pinched, and on and on. I realized that night how lucky I was that none of those things had actually happened to me. But sadly, I realized I was an alcoholic. I had become the kind of person I despised the most. I'll tell you why.

"This started the day after my twenty-fourth birthday. My parents and both sets of my grandparents and my wife's parents had come to my wife's and my apartment in Chicago to celebrate my birthday. We all had so much fun. Early the next morning a call from the hospital informed me that my parents and my dad's parents had been killed by a drunk driver on the Outer Drive. They had taken a longer route home because they wanted to see the snow on frozen Lake Michigan under a beautiful gigantic full moon. I cannot tell you how much I hated the jerk that killed my family. I was sick with anguish, feeling a type of pain I thought was impossible to endure."

"I had only drank one time before that. I was in college and it was Christmas break. I had a friendship date that night with a girl from Northwestern. On my way out of the dorm, a lonely acquaintance of mine invited me to have a drink with him. I'd never drank before. I was an athlete. I had a code I prided myself on. No alcohol or drugs. Period. Ever! But I felt sorry for this guy and broke my code.

"In the next twenty minutes, I drank eighteen ounces of Coke and twelve ounces of rum. I was drunk by the time I was a block from the school. I acted like a complete fool during my date and even asked the girl to marry me. Apparently she said yes. But that's another story.

"The point is that night I was feeling no pain and years later when my parents died, the emotional pain I was feeling because of it, felt like it was killing me. That's when I started to drink rum and Coke as a comfort drink—not every day or even every few days, but every time I drank it I felt my sorrows dissipate. Rum and Coke became my ally, my friend. Gradually when my friend wasn't around, I missed him. Eventually I made sure he was always with me. As the years passed, I'm guessing that I drank more and more. And if that's true, I didn't even realize it because the increased drinking happened so gradually. But my wife noticed it. She talked with me about it a few times, but as much as I loved her, I blew it off. The rum and Coke wasn't going anywhere.

"Then finally one day she asked me to leave. I looked into her kind but determined Irish eyes and knew she meant business. Even though I complied with her wishes within a few weeks, I couldn't understand why she asked me to leave. I thought I was being wonderful to her. I thought I'd been a good dad. I thought she admired me. She told me I could come back home once I conquered the alcohol and got my act together, but when I first left—because I didn't think I was remotely an alcoholic—I wondered if I'd ever get back home."

For a brief moment I paused. I pondered something, thinking that I had just relayed to a room full of strangers that I was an alcoholic. But for some reason I will never know, I could not tell them yet that I was having dreams of the devil and I was too embarrassed to share anything about the Two-Knock Ghost. I continued.

"When I got home the night of the girl on the bike incident, I was literally shaking. I had gone from complete denial to full admission that I was an alcoholic with the slamming of my brakes. That night I threw my bottle of rum down the drain of the kitchen sink. I haven't had a drink in two days, but I'm going crazy for one now. I don't know if I'll be able to make it through to the other side because I feel as if I've banished my closest friend to the other side of the universe and I miss him terribly. That's the story to this point. Thank you all for listening."

There was no applause like there had been a few weeks earlier for Toby. Only the moderator said, "Thank you for sharing, Turf." Hearing someone who barely knew me call me Turf was very strange indeed. In the first place, no one I knew had called me Turf in years and a relative stranger had never called me Turf. Turf had been dead for a long time. Tonight he had been suddenly reborn. I wasn't sure why I'd introduced myself that way but thought that maybe Turf represented a more innocent, youthful, healthier me. Perhaps I wanted to recapture those aspects of myself that were me when I was Turf. I thought that Turf could help me battle this disease, that I'd moments ago admitted to the public I had. It would be the youthful heroic Turf against the sallow skinned paunchy Dr. McKenzie in a battle for both of their lives.

A couple of minutes into my sharing with my fellow alcoholics, my nervousness had evaporated and I began looking into the faces of the people in attendance. The relatively equal spattering of men and women of all ages from teenage to eighties seemed genuinely interested in what I was saying. Because of that, most of my story was delivered without fear. But when I was finished, the tiredness of the day merged with the exhaustion of battling the urge to drink for the last couple of days. Those collided with the tiredness of having to move away from Christine and live on my lonely own the last few months. I felt like I could put my head down again, close my eyes and fall asleep right there. But I did not. I wanted to go right home and get in bed. I didn't want to seem rude or selfish, so I listened to the next speaker in her entirety then lifted myself to leave. I had chosen a back row of chairs, so my departure was innocuous.

I thought I was home free. But in the lobby, Toby Magnessun bounded up to me seemingly out of nowhere. He had the energy of a little nine-year-old boy happy to see his favorite uncle. Still, he restrained himself to almost a whisper obviously to protect my anonymity when he addressed me. "Dr. McKenzie, it is so wonderful to see you here."

"I don't know how wonderful it is, but it's better than being where I was a few nights ago."

"I was touched by your story."

"Thank you," I said humbly.

"I know you're probably tired after a long day, but I would really like to show you something. It's only a couple of minutes away, and I guarantee that at first look you will be absolutely fascinated."

"What is it?" I asked curiously.

"Can it be a surprise?" the exuberant nine-year-old kid asked.

"Sure," I said, my curiosity growing.

We walked outside.

"Where are you parked?" Toby asked me, sounding more like the adult he really was.

"I'm in the main lot. I got here pretty early," I said as we walked down the stairs.

"Me too, on both counts."

He maintained his high energy.

"Why don't you follow me?"

"Okay."

"It's only a moment up the road."

"Okay," I said, my anticipation suddenly sprouting.

He got into his 2001 black Lexus and I followed him in my far less luxurious 1998 red Buick Electra. He turned left from the parking lot and headed toward the beach up Turner. We both stopped at the light at Fort Harrison, though he could have made it if he had sped up just a tad when the light was yellow. He had not. My anticipation grew as we passed through the light. My wondering grew quickly as we entered a residential neighborhood. What was it he could possibly want to show me? He hadn't said he was taking me to a friend's house. And it was really too late to be stopping somewhere unannounced.

We turned left onto a tiny street off Turner, but before we turned, I noticed that the ocean was visible a couple of blocks away. We drove behind an old church and made a right on the first street past the church. There were "No Parking" signs on the right side of the street and I was right behind Toby when he parked on the left side of the street facing the wrong way. I didn't think we'd have any problems. It was an absolutely quiet neighborhood and there wasn't a car in sight. My eyes were trained on Toby as he got out of his Lexus. He pointed behind him slightly to his left with his left hand.

"There it is," he said. I raised my eyes from my fix on him and looked slightly to my right to where Toby was pointing. Across the street was the most amazing tree I had ever seen. At first perception it was stunning, an old live oak with a trunk that had to be sixteen feet around with dozens of muscled branches that looked as if they wanted to take over the world. The enormous limbs had grown to the south completely over the street, sidewalk and both between and above the electric wires that hung a couple of feet south of the sidewalk across the street. The branches didn't stop there. They continued growing another fifteen feet until they hung over the red brick house fifty feet past the wires to the west, there were at least five enormous branches that soared half the way over the roof of the house next door. Several branches jutted from the back of the oak, comprising a canopy over the high roof of the house where the tree lived, but it wasn't yet finished manifesting itself. It had also grown to the east. Its gigantic branches traversing the street and beyond. In front of the tree was a limb that for some unexplainable reason had bent down toward the earth from a height of twenty feet, reached the grass, then bent itself again and continued on the ground for another thirty feet. Then for some reason beyond my grasp, curled itself upward once again, as if reaching for the sky and grew into a leafy green height of eleven feet. Everywhere I looked my head was eventually raised to the heavens as I marveled at the growth of the spectacular entity before me.

Slowly and with awe Toby and I had approached the behemoth oak. Toby chose to be silent out of respect for the reverence of my first impressions. Over and over I looked at the remarkable aspects of the tree until, finally, I broke the silence.

"It's fantastic," I said. "How did you ever find this?"

"My sponsor took me here one day in the middle of the afternoon. I had the day off, and I was attending a twelve o'clock meeting. He told me that his sponsor had shown him the tree many years before and told me that it was inspiring. My sponsor told me that anytime I was depressed, I should come to this tree and view its strength and majesty, its will, not only to live, but to thrive, then ponder the infinite creativity of God and I would always feel better. In the last few weeks I've come here five or six times and I always feel better as soon as I see the tree."

"I feel better too," I said.

"It's being in the presence of God's handiwork, Dr. McKenzie."

"I couldn't agree more," I responded.

I could hardly break my scanning of the wondrous life force before me, but it was late and I was tired. I could have looked at the tree longer, but I knew where it was now. I would definitely come back and peer at it and ponder God's creativity again. I would show the tree to Christine, but only after I put the rum and Coke behind me. I would show it to each of my kids too, when they came to visit. It was that special.

"Pretty cool huh, Doc!"

"Pretty cool. Thank you."

"Doc," he had only this moment started calling me that as if his gift of showing me the tree allowed him the increased familiarity. I not only didn't mind it, I liked it. He continued.

"I know it's late but I want to tell you that they have beginner's meetings there that you may want to attend. They will really help you get started, and they'll introduce you to the Big Book and help you get into your first steps."

He was so excited to be able to contribute more to me. At that moment, I considered him a friend, but I didn't tell him.

"I can call your office and leave some info with Amanda if that's okay with you."

"That would be great, Toby."

I reached out my hand to shake his. He reached out his. And our handshake was that of two friends—unspoken, but understood.

I turned and started walking toward the car. Toby was walking beside me. Suddenly, a thought came into my mind and I blurted it out instantly.

"Toby, do you remember hearing about Mary Bauer?"

"Refresh me."

"She was the woman who was assaulted in that gas station robbery on Ninth Avenue and Sixteenth Street South a few months back."

"I do remember now that you mention it."

"Do you know what the state of the investigation is?"

"I've only heard that investigators are working on the case, but they're not making much headway."

"Could you do me a personal favor and look into it for me?"

"Sure, Doctor. Can you tell me why?"

"I can't, Toby, but it would mean a great deal to me."

"I have a couple of snitches on the south side that I can query. And one day, Patrick and I could drive to Lake Maggore and shake things up a bit."

"Thanks, Officer," I said, showing him the respect he deserved in advance of his helping me. "Maybe you could tell me if you have any news about it at our next session."

"I'll try my best, Dr. McKenzie."

I felt that another handshake was in order, especially since I instinctively knew that Toby would not only go out of his way for me, but put himself in danger, especially amidst the throng at Lake Maggore.

"Thank you, Toby."

The second handshake felt the same as the first, like true friendship was developing. I hoped it would someday. It was beginning to feel like we were two guys who had some key things in common.

I got in my Electra, drove back to Turner, then headed south on Fort Harrison. Toby was right ahead of me, until he turned left on East Bay on his way home to Alicia and his kids. I was tired, but happy because I felt like I had completed a day of personal accomplishments. My stomach was upset and I was looking forward to getting home and having a rum and Coke before bed. As soon as I formed that thought my entire body began quivering. Whereas moments before I had felt gain in my relationship with Toby, I now felt unbearable loss from my alcohol friend of decades. I forced myself to eradicate that thought and replaced it with the hopeful thoughts of a desperately needed good night's sleep and calling Antonio Banderas before work tomorrow morning.

That night I dreamed I was living in an enormous house, a billionaire's house. Each room was larger than Christine's and my entire house on Snell Island. The ceiling was a good thirty feet higher than our family abode, which was two stories. In the dream it was time for bed. I walked into my bedroom, a symphony of cream-colored bed, sheets, carpet, dressers, TV, clock, and walls. It was beautiful. I felt comfortable and safe. There was no notebook with papers from work, no pencils, nothing extraneous in the room. I was dressed in cream colored silk pajamas with matching cream slippers and I was feeling no fear as I crawled between the top and the bottom sheets. I watched myself fall asleep. The dream me was finally at peace. There was no motion in the room, only a sleeping man amidst a sea of cream. Suddenly, the devil appeared forty-five feet above the sleeping Dr. McKenzie. He was pinned against the ceiling spread eagle ready to pounce at any moment. He looked almost exactly like the horrible sculpture creature from past dreams that merely hovered tauntingly, but not attacking.

But tonight he added a different dimension to his game. He started hissing like the snake he was and that sound awakened my sleeping self. As soon as I opened my dream eyes, I saw him.

He had his preattack face on, and I was terrified. He was so remarkably out of place, his red body and evil contrast to the heavenly cream of the rest of the room. He increased his hissing until it became so loud that I covered my ears with my hands. I knew he would pounce in a moment and tonight I wanted to fight him. I'd had a good day. I felt better about myself. I knew I would at least get a couple of good licks in.

Suddenly the hissing ceased and the devil hurdled himself down toward the bed. As he boldly descended, the live oak I'd seen only hours before appeared and filled the room. As the devil approached me, the oak's pliant branches moved to block his approach. He changed his direction, trying to get to me from another angle. But he could not. Because the enormous flexible oak bent quickly to stop his assault. Numerous times the evil being tried to find an opening in the branches, but he could not. The limber tree, with a seeming will to protect me, was too swift for him. When it looked like he was becoming tired and frustrated, he paused as if to regroup and restrategize. It was then I heard the sounds. *Knock, knock.* For the first time since the Two-Knock Ghost had begun its poelike tapping at my front door, I did not feel frightened by its sounds. I had expected it. Feeling extremely protected by the tree, the dream Dr. McKenzie thought, maybe I should invite the ghost in. This would be the perfect time for it to show itself, whether it was one malevolent spirit or many. I thought however many entities you might be, you could take your chances with the tree. Good luck.

But nothing emerged. The Two-Knock Ghost had merely made its presence known. Again, it revealed nothing but the annoying reminder that it still existed.

The devil tried to come at me a few more times, but every time the live oak's branches dissuaded his attacks.

Finally the devil announced the end of his attempts to assault me with a bloodcurdling scream that almost jolted the sleeping me to consciousness. Then he passed backward through the ceiling as he had in previous dreams and the tree stood watchfully in the room after the devil retreated. Dream Dr. McKenzie thanked God and the tree for the protection of this night. Then he pulled the covers to his chin, relished the beauty of the cream room a final time, and then stared at the guardian tree until he fell peacefully and safely asleep for the rest of the night.

CHAPTER 13

THE NEXT MORNING I woke refreshed after a seven-hour sleep. It was a little past eight and I hustled through my normal grooming routine so I could be dressed and ready to go to work when I called Antonio Banderas's office. It was 8:37 when I pulled his number from my briefcase.

"Dr. Banderas's office. Dianne speaking," a pleasant voice answered.

"Hello, Dianne," I said, also in my most pleasant voice. "My name is Robert McKenzie. I'm wondering if the doctor is taking new patients?"

"He is," the polite voice replied. "I can help you in that regard."

"Thank you, Dianne."

"The best way to begin the process is to come in one day at your convenience and fill out some basic paperwork, and then we'll make an appointment with Dr. Banderas. We are here Monday through Friday from 8:00 to 5:00, but we usually close the office from noon to 1:00."

She was saying almost the same thing Amanda said to my new clients.

"Thank you again, Dianne. That sounds simple enough. I'll stop in sometime in the next few days."

"Thank you, Mr. McKenzie. I look forward to meeting you."

I had accomplished another baby step on the road to my recovery. Take that, Lucifer. And you, taunting Two-Knock Ghost. I looked at my watch. It was only 8:45. Oddly, for the first time in two years I felt the desire to go for a run. I didn't have to be at work till about 10:30. I could pull it off, even if I only did fifteen minutes. I quickly shed my work clothes and changed into a pair of shorts, a T-shirt, my tennis shoes, and a pair of ankle socks. It had taken me four minutes to change. I grabbed my keys and was out the door. I stretched my calves while leaning against the window sill outside my condo, then I pulled back my thighs lightly, walked down the stairs and began a very slow out of shape jog in the direction of Five Towns, a huge retirement community that dwarfed the Beaches of Paradise, directly across Fifty-fourth Avenue.

Breathing was difficult though it was not yet 9:00 a.m. The temperature was 83 degrees and the humidity was high. The hot sun shone through a myriad of cumulus clouds. I wasn't sure if it was going to downpour because I rarely turned on the TV or the radio, preferring silence. Breathing challenges or not, the run was fun. I was stiff, like a rusted tin man, but I reminded myself how much I missed this activity and suddenly yearned for my wife to be at my side. How could I have ever gotten to this point, where I let myself get paunchy and subtracted the joy of running together from Christine?

I had crossed Fifty-fourth Avenue, glanced at my conveniently located Bank of America to my left and began to make my first search of the Five Towns property. Initially, I noticed how many of the buildings looked remarkably similar. But as I jogged down the main street of the property, I observed that there were several sizes of the buildings. Some of the residences were over 10 floors high. About the middle of the well-kept property was a large circular lake with a sidewalk all around it. On the near side of the lake, an alligator relaxed on the grass, enjoying the intermittent sunshine. The back of the property featured buildings that were only two floors in height (There was no devil here. No Two-Knock Ghost. There was just luxurious nature and I was happy to be in it.) They faced the lake. For some reason, I liked those buildings best. Back at the Beaches of Paradise, none of the residences were over two stories high, and I reflected how lucky I was to be on the second floor in an end unit near what I call the promenade—the main, well groomed entrance to the complex had beautiful bushes, plants, and flowers.

In another minute and a half I reached the back gate and jogged for home. By the time I stretched my calves at the bottom of the stairs I had been jogging for twenty-seven minutes. I'd better hustle if I wanted to make it to the office by 10:30. I thought what my primary goals were for the day while I showered. I would call my daughter, Lena, and I would ask Amanda what my schedule looked like for the next few days. The first time I had a break of an hour and a half or more, I would drive to Dr. Banderas's office and fill out that paperwork.

My day flew past. I had no breaks scheduled until Friday afternoon, two days away. It would be from 1:00 to 3:00 p.m. With my regular lunch break factored in, that would give me time to eat, drive to the psychologist's office, arrive there at about one o'clock, fill out the paperwork, and get back to my office in plenty of time for my three o'clock appointment.

But the most important thing I did this day was to call Lena, my darling little girl who was now a successful high school biology teacher. She had turned out to be a healthy human being, although she grew to only 5 feet 2 inches tall, the exact height of her mother. She had always been a delight to me while she was growing up. There were countless wonderful things we had shared while she was a child, but I think my favorite was when she was nine years old and she asked Christine and me if she could accompany us on our run that day. We were shocked and thrilled that she had asked us. Over the next decade, Lena must have run with us a thousand times.

Still, I felt guilty at the possibility that I had let her down somehow. And long before I learned the intricacies of the concept of making amends at AA, I was going to do so with Lena today, if it was required. The moment my patient left at almost Noon, I got on the phone to my daughter.

"Hi, Lena, it's me," I said in my happiest voice.

"Daddy! It's wonderful to hear your voice." She sounded extremely happy, just like she sounded when she was a little girl and we told her we were taking her to Disney World.

"You sound great, precious," I said, excited that she sounded genuinely happy to hear my voice.

"How are you, Daddy?" She had been calling me Daddy since she was a little girl and never grew out of it.

"I'm fine, honey, how are you?" I didn't tell her about my not drinking. After all, I was only three days in. It wasn't a big achievement yet.

"I'm doing great, Daddy. It's the end of the school year, and I'm looking forward to vacation. I won't be teaching this summer."

"Any chance you'll be coming to see us?" I asked, referring to her mom and me.

"I'm not sure, Daddy, but maybe. I've been planning to drive out west and explore places like New Mexico, Nevada, Arizona, and Utah."

"Be safe, honey, that's all I ask."

"I will, Daddy. How come I'm so lucky to get a call from you today?"

"The most important reason is that I miss you. The second reason is a little more complex."

"What's that, Daddy?" she jumped in. She used the endearing term "Daddy" often and always with a sensitivity of tone that melted my heart. I thought for a moment how lucky I was to have this marvelous spirit in my life, and I felt some shame at having not reached out to her more; especially when I knew she loved me so much and would have been happier if her daddy took a more active role in her life.

"Honey," I said much more tentatively than anything I'd said thus far, "I'm making some changes in my life, for the better I might add, and I have a question that is kind of difficult to ask."

Why was I feeling such trepidation? Here I was, the same guy who just a few days ago had thought he'd been a great dad.

"Did I do anything to hurt you or disappoint you or bewilder you while you were growing up?"

"Where'd that question come from, Daddy?" She paused, waiting for an answer that was not immediately forthcoming. It was my turn to pause and there suddenly was a moment of awkward silence on the line.

"As I'm going through these changes, I have some personal issues I want to address and this is a big one for me."

"Daddy, I hope you're not hurting about this, because you were a great father to me and the boys. I remember so many wonderful times we shared, places we went . . . Brookfield Zoo Wrigley Field, Old Comiskey Park, Saugatulk, Mount Baldy. I remember the bedtime stories you used to make up for me and the ones you read to me from Golden Books. There were too many wonderful things to list right now because you caught me at school and I have a lot of planning to do before my next class." I knew well about planning.

"Honey, there's one question I'd like to come back to really quickly. I promise I'll only take one minute of your time. Was there anything I did that hurt you when you were growing up at home?"

"Daddy, there was never anything you did directly to me that hurt me while I was growing up at home." Her voice was soothing, almost as if she were comforting a small child. "But there was always one thing I wished we could have shared a little bit more."

"What was that honey?"

"Time watching TV together." Her comment almost made me chuckle. What a strange thing to say to me all these years later. But then I asked her to clarify as the minute was already almost gone.

"It was almost always Mom who watched TV with us kids in the evenings. Or if Mom was working, it was just us three kids sitting on the couch watching *Outer Limits*, *Bewitched*, or *Mr. Ed*. You seemed to be always working in your bedroom, night after night, year after year. No radio or TV in your room. It was always so quiet in that room. I always wondered what you were thinking in there all those hours. I almost became a psychologist just to try to understand you better."

"But did that hurt you, Lena?"

"It didn't hurt me, Daddy. I merely found it curious, that's all. But if we had something planned for the evening or if we went away on vacation, things were different. Most of the time you and Mom would hang out and do all kinds of stuff with us kids in the evenings, but every once in a while even on vacations, you would go into whatever bedroom was yours and spend a couple of hours in there. I always thought it was curious, that's all."

She had been answering to this point in slow measured sentences. Abruptly, it changed.

"But, Daddy, I've got to get ready for my next class. Can we talk more soon?"

"Absolutely, Lena. Thanks for sharing and good luck with school."

"Good luck to you too, Daddy. I love you."

"I love you too, baby."

And she was gone.

Though I felt generally good about what my beloved daughter had shared with me, my conversation was my second in a row with a child who called into question how much time I spent in my bedroom. I had been thinking about that recently, but after talking with Lena, it jumped to the forefront of my mind. What was it that drew me to that bedroom? Was my work of such vital import that I ignored my kids so much that two out of the three of them had divulged their curiosity about it in the past few days?

Now I started thinking that I have five things that might be buried in my subconscious:

1. My sliding down the precarious precipice of alcoholism.
2. Spending so much time in my bedroom.
3. Always feeling like I carried an unfathomable emotional hole in my heart, even though on the surface it appeared that I had everything to live for.
4. The devil plaguing my dreams.

5. And what was up with a ghost who knocked twice but didn't have the courage to come into my bedroom and identify itself?

I concluded that these were all questions I would present to Psychologist Banderas hoping he wouldn't think I was crazy after I explained to him the reason I thought the Two-Knock Ghost was frightening me so much.

My afternoon flew by and as the evening approached, I thirsted for a rum and Coke. I concluded that the only way for me to deal with those cravings was to drive to Clearwater to the Serenity Club. It was a long drive, almost an hour, but I knew it was worth it. Besides, it would keep me out of my bedroom where I not only had my worst cravings but felt the emptiness of the persistent hole in my heart. As I drove, it seemed like why's were dropping into my brain from everywhere. Why the devil dreams and why such fear of the Two-Knock Ghost when I'd never even seen it. Why did I feel such loneliness? Why had alcohol become a more constant companion than my wife? Why had two of my children told me they felt neglected because I spent so much time in the bedroom? My body not only craved alcohol, I literally shook with the desire to turn the car around and get into my bedroom with my work for tomorrow. I fought a difficult battle with those desires thinking that I was one sorry multi-addicted SOB. I thought, how do I replace my bedroom work times? No matter how sad I felt when I first went into the bedroom, I got a lot of work accomplished there. That work benefited hundreds of my clients over the years. Then *bam*! The guilt over neglecting my wife and children blasted into my lower stomach like pellets from a shotgun. I wanted a rum and Coke badly, just one. I could control myself. More fighting, all within my jumbled thoughts. I told myself to focus on one thing. How can I replace my bedroom working time? For a moment my mind was nearly silent. It was busy, however, sifting through myriad possibilities, making connections. And up through my thought shoots it came. Work in the car on the way to the meeting each night. I'd have about an hour. Sure I couldn't use a pen and paper, but I could plan for the day and what to say to my clients, in my head. I had never taken that approach before, preferring ideas through pen to paper, but I had often thought about my clients at random times throughout the day. But now I could simply jump in the car after work, feel no initial sadness upon entering the vehicle like

I did when going into my bedroom and immediately begin plotting my strategies for the next day. I would memorize things. Then somehow along whatever route I took to the Serenity Club, I could pull over and have a nice little dinner at some little restaurant or fast food place, take my precious little pen and paper into the restaurant with me and write down the thoughts I had just memorized during the first few minutes of my trip. When I'd finished eating and jotting down some notes, I could memorize more ideas the last lap of my ride to the AA meeting. It would be easy. Simply think, eat and write down some ideas, then think some more in the car the final minutes to the club. That shouldn't be too hard. Then suddenly the absolutely brilliant revelation came to my brain that I'd have another forty-five minutes to think on the way back to the Beaches of Paradise. What a great plan I'd developed in merely a few minutes. I felt proud of myself for coming up with the process that would help me get work done and keep me out of the bedroom. I still wanted a drink.

At the meeting, I did not speak. I listened. Story after story unfolded of people, like me, who were struggling with not drinking or not drinking and doing drugs, or not drinking and doing drugs and being codependent. The stories fortified me. It was exactly what I needed.

I scanned the throng for Toby, but he was not in attendance this night. I wondered for a moment where he was. Did his wife have a setback? Did his schedule change? Was he safe? I realized in that moment of reflection that the lines between client and friend had become extremely blurred between us.

By the end of the meeting, though I didn't want a drink, I was feeling a bit lonely. Thus far at the meetings I had attended, I purposely avoided introducing myself to anyone. I wasn't there to make friends. Besides, my personal shame and shyness had dominated, and outside of a couple of acknowledging nods to friendly smiles, I got in and out of the Serenity Club as fast as I could. When I got into my car and headed west on Turner so I could drive south on Fort Harrison, I realized that there was something I could do that night to assuage my loneliness. I crossed over Fort Harrison, getting a green light this time, drove a few blocks closer to the end of the road and turned left toward the Episcopal Church of the Ascension. As I approached the front of the church I began to see the tree. I turned left on the first street past the church. I parked the car, got out and started walking toward the tree. There it was in all its mighty splendor. It spread out with its multitude of branches as if they were enormous comforting angel wings waiting to surround and protect me. A few hours ago the reflection or spirit of this tree had made its way into my dreams and saved me from a whipping by the devil. I wanted to thank it. How do you talk to a tree? I guessed that's what you did because that is what I did in that moment.

"Thank you," I said. "Whatever you are or whatever is in you that made you care enough about me to come into my dreams and fight for me, I appreciate it."

Did I feel a little foolish? You bet I did. But I continued speaking to the live oak anyway, silently.

"I can see why you inspire people, why you make them happy. You are an icon among trees. If man didn't prune you, you would attempt to grow everywhere, take over Clearwater. Your roots would eventually tumble the houses around you and your powerful branches would forge across the road through the steeple of the church and upward to the heavens and God."

I was having fun fantasizing and making friends with the live oak that had already proved its friendship to me by swatting my nemesis like a gnat.

I only stayed there a few moments. It was a residential neighborhood and I didn't want to make the news as the perverted peeping tom psychologist from the Beaches of Paradise.

That night, I dreamed of the devil again. This time he was sitting on a high backed golden throne in an enormous red room with flames shooting straight upward from 105 foot black circles on the floor. His throne was raised six feet from the floor. His arms were resting, comfortably folded in his lap. My dream self was sleeping in another cream-colored bed with cream-colored sheets, and again I was wearing pajamas. Suddenly my dream self was startled to wakefulness. I looked forward and upward and there he was, sitting on his throne laughing at me hysterically. He did so for twenty seconds, paused, peered directly at me, then laughed again insanely, manically for twenty seconds. Repeatedly he did this, an unlikely but unaltered pattern. After twenty or so repetitions, I felt secure enough that the dream me could fall back asleep.

Bang bang! They sounded like gunshots. This time Robert McKenzie didn't wake up in fear, but the man in the cream-colored pajamas did.

And what was there to meet him but Lucifer on his throne hysterically laughing, same routine. The cowardly Two-Knock Ghost had once again announced its presence but had not revealed itself. And for this? To be laughingly mocked by the Prince of Darkness? Three more times during this not so funny sleep cycle, the Two-Knock Ghost clanked his wake-up calls for the man in the cream pajamas. Each time the result was the same. You know the drill. By the end of the night I was certain that the Two-Knock Ghost and the devil were working in tandem. Why else would the vengeful ghost wake me? Why not let the devil do it himself?

Though my real self had not been awakened the night of the devil's laughter, the effects on my real self were still quite painful. I woke emotionally drained and almost unsure of every aspect of my being. For the first time in my life, I craved a rum and Coke immediately upon waking. I felt weak and pitiful. I needed to see that psychologist soon, whatever his name was. I was a mess. And for the first time in my life, I didn't want to see anyone laugh all day. I was sick of it.

CHAPTER 14

FRIDAY DIDN'T COME soon enough. I had been to two more AA meetings and was getting a good handle on working in the car, organizing my ideas on paper at dinner, then thinking more good thoughts about my clients during my last lap to the Serenity Club. I had been to the live oak one more time, but I had not Thursday night because I had talked with Toby, and after twenty minutes of good conversation with him, I wanted to get home to sleep. Besides that fact, I had also become quite fond of working in my brain the forty-five minutes it took me to drive home.

But my big personal news was that Friday afternoon I was going to fill out my paperwork for Dr. Banderas. That day at noon, I stopped at Amanda's desk and picked up my client schedule for the next two weeks. I had requested that she perform that task Tuesday in order to give her plenty of time to complete it before Friday. As usual, she was prepared with my client schedule, printed out neatly and logically for the next ten business days. I marveled at how efficient she was. She was a secretary that I had employed for several months and I could not recall a single mistake that she had made. I said, "Thank you, ma'am," as I took the paperwork from her hand and headed out the door. I headed for my car, salivating for a Polish sausage and an Orange Crush. Today I would go to Joy, my favorite hot dog vendor in the city of St. Pete. Joy set up her hot dog cart each morning on the northwest corner of Sixth and Central. She was a well-muscled woman, toned in several visible places including arms, legs, chest and back. She wore thick glasses and sunglasses, almost always, covering what most people never noticed was a very pretty and kind set of eyes. Fact was, she was truly a kind person, always helping to raise money for some charitable organization she supported. She had a rough side too. Even though she had a reputation of always giving a hot dog and a soda to someone who was genuinely hungry, she also had to deal with quite a few thugs and druggies who wandered around downtown St. Pete along with the far greater majority of honest hard laboring people who worked downtown. Occasionally, some creep would ride by and snatch a handful of coins and paper money from her tip pail. When they tried to grab the whole silver-colored pail, they were nearly jolted from their bikes because that pail was bolted to the hot dog cart with a long thick chain and six strong bolts near the end of the chain. Joy's husband, Roger Michael, was her partner not only in life, but in the hot dog business. He set up his own hot dog cart on the southeast corner of Central and Eighth Streets. A big burly guy with long graying hair in a ponytail and a lengthy beard. He had muscles upon muscles. He and his wife were members of the Black Knights Motorcycle Club and they worked out and lifted weights four nights a week without fail unless they went on vacation on their motorcycles. No one had yet to try to snag Roger Michael's tip pail.

Joy was her typical ebullient self that glorious late May day. I had found a parking spot about seventy-five feet from her stand and had walked up to her feeling a bit happier than I usually did.

"What's up, Dr. McKenzie?" she said, her pretty smile trekking broadly across her suntanned face.

"I'm trying to give up drinking," I said.

"I didn't know you had a problem with it," she said, more seriously than her hello.

"I didn't either, until a few days ago."

"I don't drink that much," she said matter-of-factly, "but I can't imagine giving it up completely."

"Honestly, neither can I."

In the first place, I couldn't believe I had blurted out that I wanted to give up drinking. In the second place, I couldn't believe that I was having a casual conversation on Sixth and Central at a quarter past noon with Joy, the hot dog lady.

"I wish you the best of luck, Doctor," she said sincerely. "Now what can I get you before I get slammed?"

"I'll take a Polish sausage with either kind of mustard, some ketchup, and an Orange Crush."

"Coming right up, Doc."

Her use of the word *Doc* made me think of Toby. He hadn't mentioned anything about Mary Bauer in our last conversation and I had not brought it up. I knew full well that it was too soon after I asked him to look into it for me for him to have any information. It would come at his own pace.

By the time Joy handed me my wonderful Polish sausage and Orange Crush, there were six people in line behind me. As I paid her $3 with a $1 tip, she said sincerely, "You always bring a crowd with you whenever you stop by."

"I'm glad," I said as I began to depart, smiling.

"Stop by more often," she said.

I raised my hand with the Crush in it as if it were body language that said, "I will."

Then I was in my car on my way to my new psychologist's office. His office wasn't far up the road, located at 8601 Fourth Street North in the same building where a dialysis center was located. I was there by 12:50. The office door was locked, so I simply sat in a nearby chair in the outer lobby and waited.

At precisely 1:00 p.m., I heard the click of the door lock and the office was open. I walked from my chair feeling confident, happy. I knew that doing this was the right thing. Behind the desk in the waiting room was Dianne. I quickly noticed on her name plate on the desk that she spelled Dianne with two *N*s.

I thought I'd be a little playful. I said, "Hello, Dianne with two *N*s. I'm Robert McKenzie with a capital *M* and a capital *K*." She let out a good laugh and presented a pretty smile. We were instant friends.

"I'll bet you're here to fill out some paperwork, Mr. McKenzie."

"I am," I said, like a kid getting to buy a box of Good N Plenty in a candy store.

"You may not feel quite as frisky when you see how many pages there are."

"I won't mind," I said, feeling that answer because I really didn't want to sit there for an hour filling out forms like a young man enlisting in the service. But I knew the drill. As I thanked her for the forms, she asked me if I had a pen and I told her I had a couple of my trusted black Pilot pens. She said, "I like those too." And then we were really good friends. Bonded in two minutes.

I took a closer look at Dianne. She was a strong woman with a well-set jaw. She looked like she might generally be a serious person, but her response to my opening introduction revealed she had a low giggle point. I guessed her to be about forty-nine; twenty years older than Amanda. She was probably about ten pounds heavier than her ideal weight. She was put together well and was still quite attractive. In that moment I was looking at her more closely, I concluded that her quickness to fun during life's ongoing improvs is what made her substantially appealing. I took the small packet of paperwork with me to a leather couch across the room, sank comfortably into it, and began filling out the forms. They were not unlike the paperwork I utilized at my office. I did not have a single problem filling out the forms until I got to a singular question. Occupation? I agonized over it. I was feeling embarrassment, shame, and stupidity at being a tormented psychologist and not being able to analyze and conquer my nightmares. And the shame almost made me tremble long before I got to the question that asked me to describe in detail what was bothering me. I almost lied, making up a job that would fit a middle-aged professional-looking man like me, something I could easily bluff my way through if Banderas asked me about it. But even though I hadn't seen the Big Book yet, I knew that honesty was a large factor in sobriety so I told the truth, reluctantly. As I expected, it took about forty-five minutes to fill out the paperwork. This was something I had decided to pay for myself. Before I left the office, I had hoped that I would get a peek at Dr. Banderas, but I was not that lucky. I would have to wait until my first appointment.

"Do you have any questions before you leave, Mr. McKenzie?" Dianne asked me as I handed her my completed paperwork, upon which many of my life's secrets rested.

"I do, Dianne. Most importantly, does Dr. Banderas see patients in the evening?"

"He does on occasion, yes. He often makes himself flexible for his clients' needs." I liked the way Dianne had phrased that sentence.

"I, like Dr. Banderas, am a full-time professional person. I usually work Monday through Friday from 8:00 a.m. until about 5:00 p.m., sometimes later."

"Would you like your first appointment to be in the evening Mr. McKenzie?"

She hadn't yet seen in my paperwork that I was a doctor.

"That would be greatly appreciated, if possible," I said, thankfully.

"That way I'll be able to get you a much quicker appointment," she said as though she just moved Christmas to November.

She was scanning her schedule book with quick, skillful glances and within twenty seconds, responded: "How about next Wednesday at 7:00 p.m.?"

"Oh boy," I answered, pretty much like a little kid who was excited at the prospect of Christmas coming early.

"Good," she said, pleased that she was able to work out my first appointment to my satisfaction. "I'll look forward to seeing you then. She was a consummate professional secretary with a nearly regal bearing, finesse, and a youthful flair about her. Dr. Antonio Banderas was fortunate to have her working for him, as I was fortunate to have Amanda working for me.

My behaviors were beginning to change. I hadn't been to a liquor store in almost a week, hadn't had a drink in four days, hadn't hung out in my bedroom much, created a whole new approach to my evening work. I had begun to attend AA meetings and had made an actual appointment to see a psychologist who I could begin talking to about the devil and the Two-Knock Ghost because I wasn't getting anywhere with either of them. As I reflected on the changes that were beginning in my life, I wanted to see Christine. I yearned to see her, thinking that finally I had something to tell her that was significant. I was beginning to change my life. I was proud of myself. But I wasn't ready yet and I knew it. I had not conquered anything yet. I would have to achieve a great deal more than my first baby steps toward self-fulfillment in order to impress my tiny little dynamo of a wife.

I was on the right track. I may not have been in the right place to see her yet, but I would at least be in the right place to call her soon. I yearned to do that too. When it came to Christine, there was yearning everywhere . . . to call her, to listen to her voice, to be with her, to go out with her to an Italian restaurant, to hold her in my arms through endless nights, to recapture the glory of love that symbolized the wonder we had shared for over thirty years before she asked me to leave. I wasn't sure yet what all the reasons were, why she had done that. How could I be with her without having the complete understanding of an answer for that question if she were to ask it of me? I had so much work to do. I wanted to do it and change myself for the better as much for Christine as for myself. That's just the way it was. For each day of those thirty years, I had thought that everything I was doing in life was as much for Christine's happiness as for my own. Somewhere along that long road of years, I had slipped up to the point of having hurt my darling wife immensely. I was only beginning to understand the nature of those slip ups and the depth of the pain that I had caused her. But knowing that I was only at the beginning of the path of my personal awareness of how I had injured Christine did not reduce my yearnings for her. In fact, everything I was discovering about myself made my yearnings to be happy again with Christine greater.

As I drove back to my office in the middle of the afternoon to see my last two clients, I felt the emotional pain of my separation from my wife. Suddenly I felt physical pain . . . and I wanted it to go away. I had work to do and two human beings who needed help in life were coming into my office within minutes. I wanted a drink. I didn't want or need much, a half of a glass of rum and Coke would make me feel better. But I knew that I was crazy for thinking those thoughts. One moment I was feeling proud of myself for thinking I was beginning to accomplish something. The next moment I was falling apart.

* * * * *

The next five days were a blur. I kept myself busy with work and AA meetings, a couple of brief, no information about Mary chats with Toby, a singular stop to ponder God's craftsmanship at the live oak and an interesting phone call to my youngest son, which I'll tell you about in a moment. But all weekend long until I actually shook his hand, I looked forward to meeting Dr. Banderas almost as much as a college boy looks forward to going on a date with a pretty girl who he liked a great deal, which in my case had always been Christine.

It was lunch time Monday when I was finally free to talk with my son, Shawn David. For yet another reason I have never been able to figure out, he and I were able to talk with each other easier than I could talk with my two older kids. Don't misunderstand me. Talking with each of my children had almost always gone smoothly for me. They were all great kids, now pleasant and prospering young adults. But with Shawn I had always seemed more relaxed talking with him. As he grew into adolescence and adulthood I revealed more of myself to him than I did with his siblings. Perhaps it was because he was the easiest going of our three kids. He put the least pressure on himself. Oddly, and it was possibly because of that quality, that all kinds of things came easier to him, including more honest expressions from myself. There were few people who didn't like him immensely, except maybe bullies who were jealous of his casual style and the fact that younger and older women alike flocked around him. Oh, how could I have almost forgotten to tell you this, he was a race car driver.

I had no idea where my lunchtime call would find him.

"Hello, Shawn."

"Hello, Dad!" he answered with happy surprise.

"Where are you right now?" I asked, genuinely curious.

"I'm in the shop having lunch with the guys. We've been working on the car all morning."

"Is this a bad time for you, Shawn? Do you want me to call you back?"

"This is a great time, Dad. Let me grab my sandwich and soda and head into my office."

He kept talking as he walked toward his personal quiet spot.

"Where have you been keeping yourself lately? It's like you've fallen off the grid."

"You know your mom and I have been separated a few months now," I said, not hiding the shame in my voice very well.

"Right."

"When I first left, I honestly didn't know where your mom was coming from. That went on for some weeks, but now I'm getting a handle on things and I'm beginning to take responsibility for some of my actions, which I'm now certain hurt your mom."

"That's great, Dad!" he said, always the eternal optimist. "Do you want to share anymore specifics, or do you just want me to be satisfied with the fact that you're getting a handle on things?"

There was not a hint of sarcasm in his voice. He was being sincere, respectful in his way.

Here I went again, about to reveal my deepest intimacies with my youngest son.

"For me, Shawn, the biggest news is that I've admitted that I'm an alcoholic, and I've started going to AA. I've also taken steps to work on two other problems that have been plaguing me in my dreams—the devil and a Two-Knock Ghost."

"A what?"

"A ghost who always knocks twice but never comes in."

"And you're afraid of it?"

"Son, if you knew the various contexts in which the ghost knocks, it might scare you too."

"I understand, Dad. I've had some pretty horrible dreams in my life too—crashing dreams, ya know."

"I do."

"But I didn't think you even believe in the devil or ghosts."

"I don't."

There was a moment of silence between us. I was hoping he would never crash, and I thought that he might be thinking that you don't have to believe in something in order to dream about it and have it frighten the wits out of you.

It was I who broke the dead air.

"Shawn, there was a deep reason I called you today. I'll tell you honestly, I haven't even seen the Big Book yet, but I know about making amends. Something's really been bothering me lately. I am beginning to understand the various ways that I have hurt your mom and I'll begin making up with her for those things soon enough, but I've worried about you kids lately and whether there were things I did that hurt you as a child."

"Oh my gosh, no, Dad. I can't even remember a single spanking."

Hearing that made me feel good. It reminded me that I never spanked my kids. What I would do was sit them down and go through every step of a problem they were having, point by minute point, until they got what I thought was the full and proper perspective of a situation. I called it "logicalizing." Sometimes, it was worse than a spanking.

"Dad, I can't remember a single thing you did that hurt me emotionally. I do remember a myriad of things that you did that produced the opposite effects of negative emotions."

"Like what?" I liked when Shawn would get on one of his complimentary rolls and right now, though I wanted the truth of how I might have hurt him, I also was at an intersection of my life where a little positive stroking couldn't hurt.

"I remember great vacations and the board games we used to play when the days seemed to stretch out forever. We played Scrabble and Battleship and Score Four for hours on end. I still have a journal from when I was about fifteen where I kept a running record of who won and lost our contests. I remember all kinds of card games we used to play, that you and Mom taught us. We played a million games of 500 Rummy, Gin Rummy, Black Jack. But my favorite card games we played were Canasta with two decks and Samba with three decks. Do you remember those games, Dad?"

"I remember them, but I don't know that I would remember how to play them."

"I don't think I would remember how to play them now either. That had to be fifteen to twenty years since we played those games. I'll bet Mom would still know how to play Samba and Canasta."

"I'll bet she would," I said, missing Christine again and feeling nostalgia about the multitude of vacation days we played those games as a family.

"But here's what I like best of all, Dad. From the time I first told you that I liked auto racing, you started buying me little toy cars—Matchbox cars at first, lots of them, remember?"

"I do."

"Then you started me on my favorite collection of all, my Tootsie Toy Cars that were made in Chicago. I remember that when I left home I had sixteen of them. They're difficult to find. But after over ten years of being away from home, I've increased that collection to twenty-seven cars, trucks, tractors, and trailers. I love that collection. And when I look at it, I think of how you started it for me and how we would go to auctions, antique stores, second hand stores, and flea markets looking for all kinds of collectible cars and those gosh darn hard to find Tootsie Toy cars from Chicago and how we laughed and hooplaahed whenever we found one."

"I'm almost laughing now when you remind me of those times. They were a lot of fun, weren't they?"

"They sure were, Dad."

There was a two-second pause in our conversation before Shawn said, "Hey, Dad, guess where I've got my Tootsie Toy collection featured?"

"In your living room up above the fireplace?" I guessed.

"In my office at the shop. I have nine each on three different staggered shelves. I'm looking at them right now. They fit in really well here. They're happy to live here. I spend much more time in this office than in my living room."

"Thanks for sharing that story with me, Shawn. It actually gives me more strength to face some of my future challenges. But I want to ask you one last time. Was there anything I did when you were growing up that hurt you significantly in any way? I really need to know." I became silent and the air between us was dead for several seconds. I could almost feel Shawn thinking, reflecting on the long body of years which comprise a childhood. I remained silent, respecting his contemplative space, wondering what he would finally share when he breached the dead air.

"Dad, there was only one thing that you ever did that I thought was a little strange. It was how consistent you were about going into your bedroom to work on your client notes. You could be in there for hours. After 7:00 p.m., we hardly ever saw you. We'd all be watching TV or doing our homework in the kitchen or living room and you would be in your bedroom working, never a TV or a radio on. I do remember that after I was about eight years old, you would pour yourself a tall glass of rum and Coke with lots of ice and carry it into the bedroom with you. Is that the real reason you went into the bedroom, Dad, to drink?"

"I'd like to think it wasn't," I said a bit shamefully, "but I'm not totally sure anymore. I always thought I was going to work on my client notes for my next day of work."

"But you know, Dad, there were lots of Friday and Saturday nights when you went in there too."

"I hadn't realized that," immediately acknowledging in the moment he said that, that here was a definite way I had hurt my kids and maybe Christine. Right away I wished I could go back to those hundreds of nights and refrain from going into my bedroom and sit instead in the living room and watch TV or play with the kids. How many times I had smelled popcorn cooking in the kitchen and not left my bedroom to share it with my family. I was just beginning to feel sorry for myself when my son spoke.

"But you know, Dad, if there was something special going on for us kids at night or on a Saturday or Sunday—a sporting event, a recital, a play, a debate—you would always be there. I remember that sometimes Mom would have to work but your schedule was more regular and I can't ever remember a single important event of mine that you ever missed. I'm too young to remember all of Lena's and Robert's events, but I'll bet if I ask them, that they'd say you were always there for them too."

I felt a little better, but not much, because my children were now three for three in telling me they thought it was odd that I spent so much time in my bedroom at night. I asked Shawn if he could think of anything else that might have hurt him and he said, "Definitely not,

Dad." We chatted for a few more minutes. He told me about his current race car and all the problems it had on a daily basis. His tone of voice was subdued and perturbed about that. Then he told me how many hot chicks followed him around the circuit and his voice was upbeat and joyful about that.

"Dad, I'd better get back out there into the shop and get back to working on that Chevy before some of the guys cop an NA toward me."

"What's an NA?" I asked curiously.

"Negative attitude, the opposite of what it sounds like that you've got going on these days."

"Thanks for the compliment, Shawn. Go ahead, get back to work. I promise that I'll call you more quickly than I ever have before. I'm making that commitment right now."

"I love you, Dad."

"I love you too."

After we completed our call, I made a commitment within myself. I would keep the same promise about calling more quickly than I ever had before, for all of my children. They deserved it. And they deserved my more consistent best from now on.

Three calls. The same three answers. I was forced by the responses to go deep within myself to figure out what it was that pulled me into that bedroom night after night, year after year. No matter how deeply I searched my mind, the only conclusions I could come to was that I went in there to work, to better the relationships I had with my clients, to help to better their lives, to help their oft tumultuous lives to become more manageable. I was certain that carrying my drink into the bedroom was not my primary reason for going in there, but merely a byproduct of my always feeling that I had to go in there to work.

I switched my focus to the creation of my new routine. I would run every morning—I mean jog, because at this point that was all of which I was capable. I would try to walk about twenty minutes during lunchtime. I would go to AA meetings almost every night and I would do my thinking for my clients in the car on my way to the Serenity Club, transpose those notes at dinner and try to avoid my bedroom as much as possible as I tried to figure out what had been luring me in there all these years at the expense of my family. I also decided that I'd begin watching TV so that when I talked to Christine I could carry on a coherent conversation with her about what she liked and didn't like and why.

I was slowly trying to create a new life. That's what new routine was. That's what I had told clients hundreds of times. It's what I truly believed. It was time for me to put my beliefs into practice.

The few days between Monday when I called my son and Wednesday when I drove to my new psychologist's office passed by fairly uneventfully, except on Tuesday, I drove my paunchy self the three or so miles to Lake Seminole Park to jog on their paved trail. It was beautiful there, trees, a wonderful view of Lake Seminole from much of the park, a lagoon which featured an occasional alligator sunning on its banks. The trail was clearly marked; walkers and runners to the right; cyclists and roller skaters to the left. I had already been running for a few days and I'll bet I had already lost a pound. Besides, I had decided to cut back on the carbs, especially spaghetti and go for high protein. That ought to knock off a few pounds, if I kept jogging. That Saturday I decided to jog the two-mile trail. It took me thirty-three minutes to complete it. I was considerably worn out from the heat and my effort, but I decided to walk the two miles after I jogged it. That took forty-five more minutes. I was happily beat after those two joyful ordeals and glad that I had made the decision to walk over to the drinking fountain in front of the men's bathroom and drink as much of the lukewarm water as I could stand.

Sunday I jogged on Madeira Beach. I parked in the public parking lot at 146th and Gulf Boulevard and jogged all the way to the bridge at John's Pass. It was my first jog on the beach since I had been in Florida—maybe eight months. When I reached the rocks at the sand's end, I did a U turn and headed back to where I had started. When I arrived there, I took off my tennis shoes, walked into the warm late May water and took my first Florida swim as a resident. It was a weekend of firsts. I realized while I was swimming in the calm morning salt water, that I had not swam in the community pool at the Beaches of Paradise either. As I wondered why not, I realized that I had become a little introverted and reclusive since I had moved away from Christine. That fact was in evidence nowhere more than where I lived. The Beaches of Paradise had everything there—dances, dinners, pancake and sausage breakfasts, Bingo, bowling, golf, shuffleboard, a library, outdoor barbeques, a large club house, pool tables, everything designed to bring people happily together. But not me. I wanted no part of it. I merely wanted to live there so I could move out of there and move back where I belonged, with Christine. I wondered if several residents there might have thought that I was stuck-up or at the very least somewhat aloof or shy. But I couldn't begin to know the answer to that question because in the more than four months I had lived there, I didn't know anyone well enough to have the first clue as to how they thought about anything.

CHAPTER 15

WEDNESDAY CAME QUICKLY, but not easily. By the time I finished work and took myself out to dinner before driving to see the psychologist, I hadn't had a drink in over a week. I also had not hung out in my bedroom to do client work in almost the same amount of time. I had gone to six consecutive days of AA meetings, had spoken again about my problems with alcohol, had seen and talked with Toby three more times, and had visited my favorite tree once and prayed there for the health and happiness of my kids, Christine, and my becoming a better man. I had dreamed about the devil twice since I had made the appointment with my new psychologist and the Two-Knock Ghost had knocked intrusively within three of my dreams—the two of the devil and one where I was in my office with my new psychologist who looked to be exactly like the actor of the same name. Those knocks had especially knocked me off-kilter because I had just met my new psychologist—the famous actor—had found him exceedingly gracious. In my dream I was about to ask him for his autograph when the ghost knocked twice. How rude, I thought. What a punk. Between the devil and the Two-Knock Ghost, I could hardly have a pleasant dream anymore. One or the other would infiltrate my wonderful moments with their unique brands of terror. But tonight I would begin to address those issues as I drove the last mile to the psychologist's office. I looked forward to the day when those nightmares would no longer invade my sleep. Within the last three blocks before the office, I thought that it would be super if I could go back home to Christine without the baggage of the dreams of the devil and the Two-Knock Ghost. After having them, I would always wake up feeling an emotional drain that was equivalent to a hangover. I would be able to let the effects of the dream dissipate quickly. Although I'd never had a dream about the Two-Knock Ghost while I was at home with Christine, I'd had several about the devil. Each time I had them I felt those lingering effects of the dream detract from my ability to be happy in the present moment. And so many of those present moments were ones that I shared with

Christine, who deserved nothing less than my best from moment to moment.

In three more minutes the car was parked on the north side of the building at 8601 Fourth Street North. That building was one of a handful of sights in St. Petersburg where patients could go for kidney dialysis. But in the multi-floored building there were a variety of other office configurations, which included lawyers, new growing firms and several other small to medium sized businesses.

I took the elevator to the third floor, noticing that the hallways were painted a drab gray over an equally drab gray rug. It was a no frills utilitarian hallway. I opened the door to the office and entered. There she was again, the pleasant Dianne with the invitingly smooth southern drawl.

"Good evening, Dr. McKenzie," she said, flashing a thirty-two-teeth smile.

"Welcome to your first visit with Dr. Banderas."

"Thank you," I said, appreciative of her kindness.

"You're welcome," she said. I immediately wanted to sit on the front porch of an old southern plantation, share a glass of iced tea with her, and talk about anything she wanted.

"The doctor is reviewing your introductory notes right now. I'll let him know that you're here and he'll buzz me in a couple of minutes, as soon as he's ready to see you."

She smiled again and I took that as my cue to have a seat in the waiting room a few feet from her desk. Since I didn't have a clipboard with all kinds of paperwork attached to it, I took more time than I had the first time I was there to look around the office. It was at first glance a tremendous upgrade from the hallway. There were three large potted plants that rose from the floor to a height of about five feet. One, I was certain was a rubber tree because my mother had one for years that was almost identical. Another was a lush green ficus, rich with leaves. A third was a small elephant ears plant, the kind that I had often seen outdoors in Florida, but was seeing now for the first time as office decor. On the table was a bouquet of pretty mixed flowers, the kind you could buy for about $3.50 at Publix. Neatly staggered on the table around the red vase with the flowers were a variety of about thirty magazines, including seven or eight *Psychology Today*. Dianne also had a red vase with a bouquet of different flowers on the far right hand outer corner of her desk next to several pictures of her family. It was an uncluttered office with just the right amount of plant life to make a client feel as if they were in a relaxed, comfortable environment. About the time I was thinking my last thought about the office environment, I heard Dianne's buzzer go off.

"Dianne, I'm ready now. Could you send Dr. McKenzie in please."

"I will, sir," she said with utmost professionalism.

I was already standing and moving toward his door by the time Dianne said: "Dr. Banderas is ready to see you now, Dr. McKenzie."

"You remembered." I chuckled.

"That's what I get paid to do here," she joked back. She sprang from her chair and opened the door to her boss's office.

As soon as she did that, I noticed the person behind the desk rise out of his chair and step toward the door to greet me. It was Dianne who spoke again.

"Dr. McKenzie, meet Dr. Banderas."

When Dr. Banderas walked his last two steps to shake my hand, Dianne left the room and closed the door behind her. I almost giggled uncontrollably again, but stifled it, thankfully.

Dr. Banderas was the polar opposite of the famous actor. He was five feet two, stocky, with a full gray and black beard that was extremely well groomed. His eyes were the darkest of browns and large. They were friendly eyes, kind and wise eyes. I could tell these things immediately without reservation.

His head had lots of curly black hair, but only on the sides and in the back. He was missing a large oval-shaped portion of hair that extended from his forehead five inches to the back of his head where the hair started growing again. From the middle of his forehead to the sides where the hair grew there was a two inch gap of hair. He looked a bit like a monk in an expensive suit. As far as actors, he looked more like Danny DeVitto than Antonio Banderas.

As he extended his hand to shake mine, he said with a twinkle in his eyes, "Not quite what you had in mind, Dr. McKenzie. Am I right?" He shook my hand as I answered, "You nailed it, sir." A smile illuminated my face as I spoke.

He was extremely easygoing as he finished the handshake and walked back around the desk to his chair.

"I get that all the time when I first meet people. However, most people get used to me rather quickly."

I was still standing as he seated himself in his plush leather chair.

"Have a seat, Dr. McKenzie, either on the couch or in the chair, wherever you feel more comfortable."

I chose to sit in the chair. I was fascinated by the looks of the man before me and I wanted to look at him squarely in his gentle eyes, but the plants and flowers in the room were distracting me. They were everywhere. It was as if I'd just landed in the middle of a tiny, well-manicured jungle island.

"Kind of hard to ignore the surroundings isn't it, Dr. McKenzie?"

"It is," I said, feeling more comfortable in the moment to look away from Dr. Banderas and scan the room. Every color of the rainbow was represented multiple times within the bouquets that adorned the office and in the variety of growing plants that he had.

"I hope you like it, Doctor."

"You may call me Robert, if you like."

I had never seen a room like this that was packed with plant life. It was beautiful and serenely comforting.

"I feel relaxed here, almost like I'm on vacation," I said, still gazing at the multitude of plants.

"I wish I was more knowledgeable about the names of plants and flowers," I said.

"I'll make you a deal," the little man said in an inviting voice that was nearly devoid of an accent, except for a slight lilt that was reflective of a Spanish speaking past.

"Over time, I will share the names of my plants and flowers with you."

"That's a deal," I said, as I began to feel as if I was in a safe environment.

"Your paperwork states that you are a psychologist."

"I am," I responded matter-of-factly.

"It also said that you only recently acknowledged that you are an alcoholic, and you have come here primarily because you are being troubled by dreams of the devil and a ghost that knocks twice but never comes in."

"That's right, Doctor."

"That's quite a heavy burden for you to be carrying around these days, isn't it?"

"It has been lately. But I think I'm doing the right thing now by attacking the problem head on."

"I think you are too, Robert. But I must tell you that it is not often that I have a person who comes to me with their main complaint being dream terrors. And I have never heard of such a unique ghost as your two knock entity."

I didn't respond because he didn't seem to be finished, and when he continued, he unknowingly proved me right.

"I read your paperwork the evening you completed it and subsequently, because of the unique nature of the Two-Knock Ghost, I've pondered your case at some length in the days between when you expressed your thoughts and this meeting. I don't usually do this with clients, but I have come to a bit of a conclusion about your Two-Knock Ghost."

"What is it, Doctor?" I asked while thinking that what Dr. Banderas had said about the Two-Knock Ghost was highly unusual, especially for a psychologist who had only spoken with me for a couple of minutes.

"I was fascinated by the concept of the entity you described. I had never heard of the Two-Knock Ghost. I tried, probably like you, to figure out what this entity was. I used every bit of logic I could apply to the situation and because I had never heard of anything like your ghost, I concluded that the Two-Knock Ghost belongs to you alone. It is your ghost, and it has probably not revealed itself either because you are not ready to know what it is, or you have been using the wrong approach in your attempt to communicate with it."

I didn't know I had an approach to communicate with the Two-Knock Ghost. Wow! He had dove right into my stuff and he was wasting no time letting me know what he thought. I remained silent. He did not.

"We'll talk a great deal about the devil dreams, I'm sure. But I'm positive that the key to the Two-Knock Ghost is getting it to reveal itself. Of the strategy to accomplish that, I am not certain, but we'll work on that together. Okay, Robert?"

His voice was soothing. And the way that he spoke was both intuitive and well thought out. I could not help but contemplate what he had said. The Two-Knock Ghost was my personal dream. And I sat there considering how the human psyche feared deeply that which we knew existed but remained secretive about its true nature.

We continued talking. Dr. Banderas completely backed off from talk of the devil or the Two-Knock Ghost and spent most of the remaining hour getting to know me. I shared my childhood in Chicago with him and he showed genuine interest in every detail that I expressed. I told him of my profound love for Christine and my children. Eventually, I told him about the crash that killed my parents and my grandparents. He was more compassionate than anyone but Christine had ever been with me. At one point, after I had expressed what I felt when I found out that four of my most deeply loved family members had been killed in one horrendous crash, he responded with the following statement.

"Robert, the depth of loss after an event like what happened to your family, is unfathomable. The impact on a person's soul and psyche is immeasurable and the rippling effects of pain and feelings of devastation continue to haunt you throughout your entire lifetime. Because of the severity of the loss, a hole has been created in your heart that may never be filled."

Again, he had hit on something that had been bothering me my entire life—that unfillable hole in my heart. As soon as he said that, I spoke up because I wanted to clarify something.

"Dr. Banderas, you are absolutely correct about that unfillable hole in my heart. But I feel like I've had that my whole life. Even as a small boy, I would go to my bedroom and play with my Legos, my baseball cards, erector set, Fort Apache. But I'd always feel lonely when I'd first go into my room. I'd feel emptiness, longing. It would wear off after a few minutes, after I'd get into whatever it was that I was playing with, but that feeling of yearning for something and not knowing what it was, plagued me my whole life, long before my family was decimated."

"We have a great deal of searching of self to do, Dr. McKenzie. There are many closed doors inside you. But behind them are the answers you are seeking. Together, we will find the keys which will unlock those doors."

I enjoyed talking with him. I loved listening to his nearly mellifluous voice, and our first session proved that not only would we share camaraderie but he would look at my realities from completely different angles than I would. He would go into my history with intensity and sophistication. I was looking forward to our next session before this first one ended. I also thought how really odd it was that a person would lay themselves bare before a veritable stranger, telling that person countless deep problems and expect that person to help them overcome those problems. Going to a psychologist was a daunting task for both the patient and the psychologist. Yet it's done thousands of times throughout the world every day. The results of these mixings of usually random pairs are truly unknown at each beginning. I wondered what the results would be between me and this short, unhandsome, but caring gentleman.

When I left our introductory meeting, I felt good, buoyed by the fact that a man I had only met an hour before, had acknowledged that he had already thought deeply about me and my most profound terrors. It was only 8:42 p.m. If I cut across town, I could probably make most of the meeting at the Serenity Club.

As I drove across St. Pete toward Clearwater, I did not think about my Thursday clients. I thought about Dr. Antonio Banderas, the physically diminutive man who had become my new ally in combating the ugliest and most threatening of my enemies.

I did not speak at the meeting, but I enjoyed listening to the alcoholics who did speak, revealing their struggles with alcohol. I thought at that meeting that it was true we were alcoholics. But there was something inherently different about us. My decline into alcoholism, though similarly long and insidious, never saw me raise my voice to or hit my wife or kids. It did not keep me away from home in bars. It did not make me have a sense of bravado and pursue other women to conquer. Although I always felt available to and easily approachable for my wife and children, I might not have been, in their eyes. Though I was only a few feet away from my family when I was in my bedroom drinking, it might as well have been a million miles. My closed bedroom door meant to my family "do not knock, do not come in, do not even think of disturbing the man behind the closed door." I was like untouchable gold behind the impenetrable vault door at Fort Knox. Tonight, during that meeting at the Serenity Club when I did not speak, I realized that my great sin was that I'd neglected my family due to my duel compulsions of going into my bedroom to drink my precious rum and Coke, and for the betterment of my clients. It also became clear to me that instead of calling my children and asking them if there was anything I had done to hurt them while they were growing up, I needed to call each one of them in the next week and admit to and apologize for the sin of neglecting them the way I had all those countless hours when drink and God knows what else, lured me to that bedroom.

About 10:30 p.m., near the end of the meeting, at a moment when I got out of my head enough to look around the room to see the faces of who was there, I noticed Toby's face. He was looking right at me as if he had been looking at me for a long time and was glad he caught my attention. When he was certain our eyes interlocked, he made a small but significant gesture with his right hand for me to come over to where he was.

I first nodded my head to let him know I got his message and then rotated my head in a way I hoped he would understand that I would join him at meeting's end. When he nodded after my gestures, I figured he understood what I was trying to suggest.

There would be only one more speaker, a slew of announcements and the finale of the entire group's recitation of the Serenity Prayer and the Our Father.

One minute later I met Toby in the lobby. He looked tired and intense.

"Can we go to the tree and talk for a few minutes? I have some news for you."

"Absolutely," I said excitedly, believing the news he wanted to share had to be about Mary Bauer.

We went to our cars and drove the three minutes to our majestic live oak. We parked, with him in front of me. When he was finished parking, he did not waste a second before his hand was opening his door and his body was heading for me. He crossed in front of my car casting a small, sly, smile on his drawn face. He entered my Electra and sat in the passenger's seat, groaning ever so slightly as he did.

"Good news," he said. "And you are partly responsible for it."

"I am?" I said curiously.

"Do you remember the time we were talking about recurring dreams and you told me that for most of your life you had only three?"

"I do," I said, but he wasn't nearly finished.

"But then you said that other dreams occurred that made you realize over time that you had about 30?"

"Yes," I said sincerely, curious where he was going with his story.

"I listened carefully to what you said about dreams and I've figured out in the months that I have been seeing you that I have about 20 recurring dreams."

"Interesting," I said, still wondering.

"After you asked me to help you with Mary Bauer's case, I wasn't sure what to do. I knew I had three snitches around town that I had used regularly over the past few years. I called all three of them within a week of our talking about Mary, with absolutely no results. For two days I went to sleep wondering what to do next. On that second night, I had a dream. In the dream, my partner, Patrick, said to me: 'Why don't you ask me? I have snitches too you know.' And what he said next, sounded as if it was actually you speaking it to me. He said, 'And just like those recurring dreams, you may have a lot more snitches than you're consciously remembering and I may too. Maybe we can dig deep into ourselves to find those other snitches. Then we might have a better chance to get the answers that we're looking for.' His words woke me on the spot. I got out of bed and went directly for my address book. Believe it or not, I had not thought of this on my own. Patrick, who was probably you in my dream, told me to expand my thinking. Sure enough, I had a slew of names in there who had been my snitches years ago, some of them as far back as fifteen years. It was easy to pick out the names because I printed capital S before their names. Dr. McKenzie, I swear there were twenty-seven more snitches and confidential informants that I had forgotten about. That made a total of thirty, the same exact total as your number of recurring dreams."

"Wow," I said, reflecting on the wonder of how as a psychologist you may help someone in one area and that reasoning will bleed off and aid them in something entirely different.

"The day after my dream I started calling my old snitches and reestablishing relationships. I also asked Patrick for his list of snitches and, like he had suggested to me in my dreams, I asked him to dig deep for any of his old snitches that he might have forgotten. We put our heads together and came up with a total of forty-six names, fifteen of those names we had in common. Over the next several days we made over thirty contacts by phone and by actually visiting some of the old snitches at their last known residences. We had no luck. That's why I haven't talked to you about this until tonight. We were beginning to lose hope. Then finally we came to the name Eddie Green. Eddie is a skinny little black fellow. You'd think he was a crack addict. He's really a fast talking, very pleasant, poorly educated, dog track gambling addict, who does pretty well there actually. He's lived his whole life in South St. Pete. He knows all kinds of people. His father was a carpenter and he used to drag Eddie with him wherever he went to fix anything that was broken, or needed to be built from the ground up. Thankfully, Eddie learned the trade well. He got into some trouble about ten years ago, nothing serious, and I met him one day at headquarters on Thirteenth Street. Because he was so affable, I asked him rather casually, 'Do you have your finger on the pulse of St. Pete?' And he said, 'Yes, I most definitely do.' The more I spoke with him I realized that this diminutive carpenter might become a valuable asset for me from within key segments of the community. I taught him what it entailed to become a confidential informant, and for the next two or three years he proved extremely valuable for me."

I was tired, but Toby's story was interesting and I knew that he would soon get to the good part.

"I stopped at his old address a couple of days ago. Sure enough, he was still in his frame house on Fourteenth Avenue South and Twelfth Street. He was living alone but he told me that he had people staying there and coming and going all the time because the house was so big. What had started out as a small house had been added on to by Eddie's father every time he had a new baby or a sick old relative needed a place to stay. Now it was a two-story, eleven-room, six-bedroom home with a huge den. When Eddie's father died a few years ago, he left the house to Eddie, who was the first born and who had helped the senior Green build half of the house. Following Eddie in the family were five girls, none of whom were handy with the hammer. Eddie's next four sisters were scattered over various parts of the U. S., having followed their men. Eddie told me that each of them had a saga, and not one of them was ever likely to come back to St. Pete.

"Of course, I had told him early on why I was there, but Eddie was glib and I might even say happy to see me, as well as a bit lonely. So the words poured out of him like a faucet on full blast. But Eddie's baby sister, Natalia, had just visited him three nights ago for dinner and had brought her boyfriend with her. His name was Reubin Tatum. He was a bruiser of a man, Eddie said – about 6 feet 2 inches, 245 pounds and unusually hairy. Eddie said it was the first time he had met Reubin.

Eddie had ordered out for pizza and during the meal, the conversation flowed smoothly between the three of them. There was no shyness between them. And their conversation passed from how good Reubin's and Natalia's sex life was, to Eddie's compulsive need to gamble on the dogs, to what Reubin did for a living. He had told Eddie he preferred armed robbery over selling drugs because it gave him a bigger rush. He told Eddie as casually as if he were speaking about his computer programmer job at Jabil's Circuit, about his last three robberies, how much loot he stole and how much fun and easy the jobs were. The last one was a convenience store at Sixteenth Street and Ninth Avenue North and the one before that was the gas station and convenience store on Ninth Avenue and Sixteenth Street South, where he agitated a pretty little married lady and got $95 from her purse.

"When I heard that, I nearly jumped for joy, but I immediately became nervous because my cop car was parked on the street in front of the house and I didn't want anybody to put two plus two together and figure out that Eddie had anything to do with what I knew now would eventually happen. I told Eddie that I would take care of him financially in a few days, but I told him I wanted to get my car out of there right away and I did, heading immediately to headquarters."

Toby's barrel chest was heaving in and out as his excitement in retelling me his story increased. And though he was happy right now, I couldn't help but think that I wouldn't ever want to tangle with this guy, if I were a thug and he was upset.

I didn't want to cause angst for anybody. On the contrary, I wanted to make a couple of investigators very happy. But with the politics of human nature, you never truly know how people are going to take your sticking your nose into their business. I found out who the detectives were who were handling the case and I made an appointment to meet them the next day.

They were two detectives that I'd seen before and had heard about favorably, but I didn't know them personally. They were both your old school, hard-nosed, diligent investigators of nearly thirty years with the department, Larry Mills and Art Barclay.

I told them every detail that Eddie had told me. To my deepest satisfaction, they were both gentlemen and showed a tremendous appreciation for what I had done to help move their case along. Right now they are adding what I shared with them to the Minutia they have already gathered. They not only told me that they feel confident they'll make an arrest in seven to ten days, but they asked me if my partner and I would like to be present for the arrest. I said yes, of course. And all of this is because of you, Doc."

He used that familiar vernacular again. I liked it immensely.

"That's incredibly wonderful news, Toby."

"It'll be incredible when that SOB is behind bars."

"I agree," I said, reaching out my hand to shake his.

"It should be I who is shaking your hand, Doc," he said humbly.

"You are," I said, and we both chuckled for a moment.

"How's the not drinking going, Toby?"

"The challenge is no fun, Doc. AA says to take it one day at a time, but I feel at times that the struggle is breath to breath. How's it going for you?"

"Right this moment, not so bad. There's been so many good things happening in the last couple of days, including what you told me tonight, that I haven't thought that much about drinking. But I feel I have to be wary of what's lurking behind every corner waiting to push me into a bar or a liquor store. Is your wife doing okay?"

"We both definitely have to take that one day at a time. She's had so many scares and treatments, one diagnosis and prognosis after another, that it's a way of life for us now. It's that way of life that's still a challenge for me to accept because I love her so much. Seeing her suffer still makes me want to drink and numb my pain. But I think that everything will get better if she goes into remission. So, you see, I've got a lot to work on."

"We both do. But tomorrow is another day." He thrust his hand out to meet mine. He was a true friend. There was no denying it. We parted company with each man feeling the caring of genuine friendship.

I was high on life on my way home that night. What an incredible day it had been. I not only felt in complete command of my sobriety, I was almost giddy with joy over Toby's news that the detectives were closing in on Reubin Tatum. I knew better than to say anything to Mary Bauer until Tatum's ass was behind bars. I knew how deeply positive the news of his being off the streets would affect her. I couldn't wait to deliver the news to her as soon as it was given to me one day in the very near future. I was feeling so good that I found myself talking with my higher power. I was thanking it, primarily, over all it had given me. Then I found myself daring it to allow me to have a devil dream tonight or to have an unwelcomed visit by the Two-Knock Ghost.

"I feel too good to have a devil dream tonight God," I thought. "And I don't need to have any knocks from his cowardly, unseen little friend," I continued. "Devil dreams are supposed to occur when I'm troubled, right, God?"

To be honest, I wasn't sure how any of it really worked. I didn't know if a good day of feelings earned me or any person a night of peaceful dreams. I didn't know if you could ask your higher power for a night of joyful dreams and he would grant it. I knew nothing about the realities to the answers to those questions. What I did know was that I was communicating with whatever I thought my higher power was. It felt good. It felt restful. It felt blood pressure lowering wonderful. It was different. As I continued to communicate with my higher power during the last 30 minutes of my ride home, I felt closer to Christine.

* * * * *

Thankfully, my prayers to the entity in the upper regions or the inner strata worked, and I did not have a dream about the devil or the Two-Knock Ghost. Instead, I dreamed of music. I dreamed of sequences of notes that were hauntingly lovely, sequences that had never been heard before by any human being but me on the wondrous night of dream music. Once my brain accepted the notes as outstanding enough to pass my personal standards, it kept playing the main theme repeatedly as if on a musical loop. Little by little my brain kept adding small segments to the initial theme. Slowly, I was creating a song in my sleep.

Incredulously, I had done this before . . . but not for the past several years. As the notes tumbled into their potential resting positions, I began to think, within the dream, that as soon as I awoke, I would go immediately to the piano in the living room and write this song for Christine as close as possible as to how I had dreamed it. This is how I had done it the last time I had dreamed music. It had culminated with me presenting the completed work to Christine three or four days after the dream event.

She had always loved the songs I had written for her, each and every one. There were no exceptions. And on this night as I dream thought about Christine, my heart expanded to new degrees of love for her. Then, as the bursting of emotions occurred, more notes began to tumble profusely, seeking to find their proper logical sequence in the dream song that I was creating.

Finally, I could feel myself rebuffing the notion that dreams only last some small finite amount of seconds. Surely this dream traversed the six and a half hours of sleep I had that night. Or so it seemed. And if it had not, how miraculous it was that the human brain and psyche could create a complete masterpiece of music in less than one full sweep of the second hand across the face of a clock.

When I woke in the morning, I sprang ecstatically from my bed and raced to the piano. I turned on the tape recorder and began playing the notes as I had dreamed them. I played furiously because there had been times in the past that I had lollygagged and the dream notes slipped away as the more time passed between my dream alpha state and my waking state. That mistake would not happen on this morning. Within forty-five minutes, I had the complete song on tape, with chords, three times. I was overjoyed because now I knew I could call Christine soon. And I could share with her something of substance and beauty that would reflect the other things of substance and beauty that I had been accomplishing in the past two weeks. It had been four years since I had written her a song. Oh no! Suddenly that sentence would not leave my head. Then came the shotgun blast to my very real and fragile stomach. Before this four year stretch of years that I had not written Christine a special song, the most time that had ever passed without me having done so was a year at most. Some years I would write her three or four. That shotgun blast was another realization that had gone from my brain to my stomach pit in a nanosecond, of yet another way that I had neglected my wife.

I could not control myself. I dropped my head onto my arm that I had placed on the piano ledge above the keys and wept for several moments. Then, as if the shotgun blast wasn't enough, an irreverent freight train slammed into my brain. Rum and Coke will ease your pain. Rum and Coke will ease your pain. Rum and Coke will ease your pain. Like the rhythmic rolling of the freight train's wheels, the insidious phrase kept rampaging through my brain. My body began to shiver. The tears would not cease falling. All the good feelings of the last two days dissipated to a pool of white hot grief.

The pain stole my very breath from me and knocked me from my waking state. I was now asleep on the piano in a tumultuous state of dreamless agony. It would have been the perfect time for a devil dream. What better time to kick an eternal candidate than when he is down. But instead, next to come were the bombs.

First the shotgun blast, then the plaintiff freight train, then the bombs. *Boom. Boom.* They jolted me from my sleep and almost off the piano and the bench where I was sitting. The bombs had come from the other side of the front door. I said, "Hold on a moment," as I stumbled the few steps to the front door at the opposite side of the room from the piano. I had been startled by the bomb like knocks on the front door, but I hustled to open it anyway. I opened it. No one. The length of the balcony was devoid of people. It had happened again. The Two-Knock Ghost had intruded once more. This time when I was at my lowest ebb, having plummeted to horrific emotional depths upon the realization of another way I had neglected Christine. And the chicken shit ghost was right there ready to pounce on me when I was already flat on my back, prostrate upon my altar of shame.

I hated that ghost, the cowardly ghost of sound and fury who lacked any substance beyond its dastardly signaling device. I felt terrible in this nearly unlivable moment. But I was struck by the thud of reality. It was Thursday morning, and I had already spent forty-five minutes working on a song, two or three minutes weeping and twenty-five minutes of pitiable sleep napping. I had to go to work, work to help other people feel better, no matter how I felt. I had traded running for working on the song, but now I needed to shave and get ready to face the day with people in it. I hated the Two-Knock Ghost, but unknowingly it had done me a favor by awakening me. Otherwise, my aching soul and its attempt to hide from pain in sleep, could have caused me to be late for work. That was something I had never done. Thank you my unseen enemy.

When I got to work and saw Amanda, I immediately felt better. How could I not? Not only did I have a beautiful intelligent and pleasant secretary, but I had just driven across the lovely, small city of St. Petersburg, Florida. Sure, I knew what the problems were in St. Pete, but it was undeniable that St. Pete still possessed small city charm and was home to some of the most beautiful beaches in the States.

While driving to work this morning, I realized another way I had neglected Christine. When we first arrived in St. Pete and finally finished moving in, Christine asked me one day if we could go to the beach. I said, "Yes." I said to her, "There's a lot of choices honey. Do you have an idea of which beach you would like to see?"

Without hesitation she said, "Pass-a-Grille."

"Pass-a what?" I remember asking her.

"Pass-a-Grille, like a George Foreman Grill except with an *e* at the end. I've asked some people in the grocery store what their favorite beach is around here and most of them said Pass-a-Grille. A couple of them said Fort DeSoto. I looked up both of them on the computer and they're only a few miles apart. We could actually and very easily go to both beaches on the same day and spend a good amount of time at both locales."

I could see the excited little girl in her face when she explained what she had to me. The equally excited little boy in me answered, "Let's do it—right now—both places. Which one first?"

"Fort DeSoto."

You should have seen her face then. God, my wife was beautiful, possessed with an eternal youth that human aging could not sabotage.

We spent four hours at Fort DeSoto that day and six hours on Pass-a-Grille. The day was capped off by dinner at the three-story Hurricane Restaurant and Night Club. We each had their tasty special, a grouper sandwich.

Both beaches were vastly different from one another, gorgeous in two totally different ways. From one stretch of beach at Fort DeSoto you could look to the south and see the Sunshine Skyway Bridge. A few blocks away, but still in the Park, you look west and could see Anna Maria Island.

Pass-a-Grille was a pristine one and a half mile long peninsula filled with beautiful new and old houses with a multitude of shapes and sizes. It was very sleepy the day we visited. It was the middle of the week and there was only a spattering of cars in the scores of parking spots they had on Gulf Way from Twentieth Avenue to the tip of Pass-a-Grille.

We had the time of our lives that day. We had ridiculous fun. At Fort DeSoto Christine and I made love in the Lagoon. It was the first time we had ever made love outside. I don't know why that was, but it was a fact. It was an incredibly joyful moment for me and I think for

Christine also. Why? First of all, because I felt so much love and passion for this good, almost saintly woman, that I was able to stay within her body for well over an hour. I will never forget her little excited girl face of that day and I will never forget the womanly face of love that she gave me during that blissful hour plus inside her. A couple of times she closed her eyes for several moments and wrapped her arms tightly around my neck.

Christine had always made me feel like a man. But this day, this love making, two o'clock in the afternoon, outside, in public, with people only hundreds of feet away, was entirely different. I had never felt as much of a man as I felt on that day. I felt like a good and decent man because I was being enveloped by a woman of the same ilk. During this time we were intimate, I felt I had a handle on what the best kind of sex was, that there could ever be—because I thought I owned it that day. Thirty years with the same woman, loving her more deeply each time she presented me with a child. Loving her more from time to time when she made some random movement that she might often make, but I felt like I was seeing it for the first time. Loving her more when we were making love and she would say with a glint in her eyes, "Can we try this?" Falling in love with her all over again because she endlessly exuded the overwhelming sensuality of pure and unbridled kindness.

Yes, we had the time of our lives that day. But when I looked back on that day in its entirety, I remember seeing something now that hurt me, that I didn't understand that day. I remember a look of disapproval on Christine's face when I ordered my rum and Coke at dinner. It was there, most definitely, albeit subtle. There it was, a momentary, quickly flashed hint that she was not happy with my drinking. How many other hints had I missed or ignored throughout the years?

That day, that wonderful day when we made love in Fort DeSoto's lagoon, watched a sunset on Pass-a-Grille and ate grouper at the Hurricane, was the last time Christine and I went to the beach together. This morning, during a period of my life when awareness was falling on me like raindrops from a summer storm, I had now become aware of more ways I had hurt the woman I loved. For a brief moment I excused myself from any fault by rationalizing that within days of that memorable interlude, each of us had become entangled in the work schedules of our careers. But then I dismissed the rationalization, knowing that I had become a man of excuses and that Christine was unwilling to accept them any longer. That's why I lived at the Beaches of Paradise and Christine lived on Snell Island, 9.7 miles from me.

All that work day, which was only hours after my good news from Toby and my musical dream, I wrestled to try to gain some emotional balance between those facts and my sad awareness of more hurt that I had caused Christine. Suddenly I began to feel that my life had become somewhat of a game of keeping score. It was current good deeds and accomplishments versus poor and neglectful deeds from the past. At first, when I became aware of a past neglectful behavior, I would label it with a negative score. But after pondering it, after looking repeatedly at the cup that awareness was, I would eventually credit myself with a positive point, believing the awareness itself was a good thing. I could accept responsibility for it and try to correct the damage that I may have caused by the neglect. Then, I could stop beating myself up for it and move beyond it, learn and grow from it.

All these thoughts passed logically and swiftly through my mind between the time I said good morning to Amanda and my first client. Before that client, I buzzed Amanda on the intercom and asked her when Mary Bauer's next appointment was.

"Next Friday at 1:00 p.m.," Amanda answered most graciously, after a short pause to look it up.

"Thank you," I said.

"Do you need anything else, Dr. McKenzie?" she asked.

"No thank you."

"How about a nice cup of hot chocolate?"

It was 88 degrees outside. And still, the thought of hot chocolate soothed my imbalanced spirit even before it got here.

"That would be really appreciated, Amanda."

My next appointment with Dr. Banderas was next Wednesday at 7:30 p.m. My appointment with Mary Bauer would be two days later. I couldn't wait for time and life to pass so hopefully I would be able to give Mary news that would allay her anxieties of being hurt again by her assailant.

I felt the earth beginning to shift beneath my feet. As recently as a couple of weeks ago, I was a man of extremely comfortable habits. Even though I was separated from my wife, I had my favorite drink beside me whenever I wanted it. I had my career, my work, and my little bedroom to go into in the evenings to do my homework. I had my lazy assed self to be with everywhere I went. Compared to what I was becoming, I had slipped into a way of life that was sedentary both physically and maritally. I had slowly flattened myself into a boring, introverted alcoholic who had no right to be happy with a woman who was becoming more dynamic each day.

I was beginning to be determined to change all relevant aspects of my personality and behaviors. From now on I would try to jog in the morning. I would make time to practice on the piano. I would call my kids every week or two. I would plan for more family gatherings wherever they might be. I would stop at Sports Authority on Tyrone Boulevard and buy a couple of ten pound free weights and start toning my biceps and pecs. I would continue my visits with Dr. Banderas and continue with my trips to the Serenity Club while doing my work on my clients' behalf on the way there.

But oddly, one of the most important places I would frequent would be the live oak that Toby had shown me. Even though it was only a tree, it inspired me every time I saw it. It was a living entity imbued with strength and majesty and once, already, it had made its way into my dreams and had spared me an onslaught from the devil.

My next step was to determine when to call Christine and determine when we would meet. When we did, I would have a variety of significant news to tell her. It would all be the truth, without exaggeration, punctuated by the song I wrote for her that I hoped she would appreciate deeply.

I was enjoying my new routine. Only three things would make my life better—rekindling my love affair with my wife, getting a handle on my devil dreams, and the terrors of the Two-Knock Ghost. How childish I felt at times when I admitted I was frightened by a ghost I had never seen. Over the next three days, I called each of my children and apologized profusely for my neglect of them all those many years. I also called Christine and asked her for her schedule. When she said she was free a week from tomorrow, which was a Friday, I asked her to have dinner at the Red Mesa on Fourth Street North only four miles from our Snell Island home. I was like a young boy waiting to go on his first date with his eighth grade sweetheart.

I should have slept well Saturday night. I was doing everything right. I was even praying—in a manner of speaking, attempting to communicate with my higher power. I even fell asleep talking with it, whatever it was. I didn't label it male or female, hermaphrodite, young or old, bearded or clean-shaven. I knew as much about the appearance of my higher power as I did of the Two-Knock Ghost. But I knew that my higher power was a magnificent being, but the Two-Knock Ghost was malfeasance incarnate.

Sometime during the night, I was sitting with Christine on a white swing that was hung onto a huge branch of my favorite live oak. We were alone in a wide open green pasture with a long narrow brook that stretched as far as the eye could see in both directions, about two hundred feet in front of the oak. There wasn't a cloud in the sky and not another tree in sight. There were no rocks or boulders, no animals or birds and only the murmurings of the brook as it trickled from west to east. Christine and I were happy, holding hands and laughing as we swung beneath the branch. There were no words between us, just the silent bonds of a love that had overcome all problems.

I watched our dream swinging for a long time, not becoming bored for a micro second at the idyllic scene I was observing. Suddenly, a bolt of lightning from out of the cloudless sky hit the oak at its enormous base, split it and started it to burn. Why now I wondered? Why now when I felt that I had earned this dream by a week of good deeds, good decisions, hard work on my character. There was still nothing else in the picture but the tree, now ablaze. But dark clouds came rampaging into the azure sky. They were angry clouds, powerful and vehement as if being ushered in there by a force with evil intentions.

Through a cumulus nimbus cloud that looked like a faceless body builder on steroids, emerged the crimson Lucifer carrying his pitchfork. He too was ablaze with flame, though undeterred as he directed the clouds to give up more lightning bolts to the tree.

The live oak was helpless this night as piece by piece it ignited with a ferocity that only the devil himself could conjure. Christine and I were still on the swing, terrified that at any instant we too would ignite and suffer torturous deaths. And then it happened again—*knock, knock*—sounds differentiated from the thunder claps. But the knocks were not coming from the once idyllic scene, now ruined by Lucifer's demonism. They were coming from my front door, twenty feet away from my dream bed. Suddenly my attention was divided between how to get Christine and I off the swing, which was a high fifteen feet off the ground and what the Two-Knock Ghost might do if it got into the house and made its way to my dream.

As the oak continued to burn, I noticed the flames drawing near to the ropes that supported the swing.

"Christine," I said both logically and comfortingly, "if you scrunch down next to me, we can wait for the fire to burn through the rope allowing our end of the swing to fall five feet closer to the ground, then we could jump. It would only be a fall of ten feet, a lot better than fifteen."

"You lead, I'll follow," she said, confidently.

I liked the sound of that, even though I knew it was only a dream. The devil was still in the muscle bound cloud laughing at our plight.

Yet again, *knock knock*, this time sounding closer, as if it was at my bedroom door. "Come in already you pathetic sissified demon. What more could you do to me than the devil has already done?"

I was angry now, angrier than I'd ever been before in a devil dream because Christine was with me. I would fight with the strength of Spartacus to keep him from hurting her.

The swing jolted an inch toward the scorched grass beneath the oak.

"After we land, we get up right away and get to the brook as quickly as possible."

"Okay," she said frightened but compliant.

Knock, knock!

"Come in already!" I screamed angrily.

Christine couldn't hear the knocks. The ghost behind them was my solitary curse.

"Who are you talking to?"

"No one, Christine."

And I wasn't lying. I didn't know still, after all these weeks, who or what the Two-Knock anonymous was.

The rope burned through, the swing slid closer to the ground and Christine and I jumped. Only slightly shaken, we held each other's hands and raced for the brook. The refreshing water cooled our overheated skin and we huddled there in a tender embrace. For once, it felt like I had beaten the devil. He was still up in the muscle cloud, but I couldn't figure out why he was laughing. Christine and I were safe in cool water. We hadn't burned to death. Why was he laughing?

A moment later, he told me in no uncertain terms as he began to speak, the knocks could be heard behind him as if a demon accompaniment.

"You can have her in a dream, McKenzie, but you'll never have her in real life. I'll see to that. In real life you'll both go up in flames. There will be no brook or tree to protect you. You're higher power is a wimp compared to me. You'll have no one to protect you because you believe you have no one to protect you from me, while I have legions to back me up in my quest to destroy you."

I clung to Christine in the brook, as she clung to me. Yet I was aware it was only a dream. I wondered for a moment if she could help me fight the devil, but even in the dream I realized that in real life she had been aloof from me since I had moved out. She may not be punishing me, but I know she had high expectations for me to become a better man. I knew I was in the fight of my life, not only to win her back, but to defeat the devil in his evil nocturnal assaults and get the Two-Knock Ghost to reveal itself and face my fear of it head on.

Slowly, I watched the devil fade into the thunder cloud with only his hideous grin remaining—an atrocious antithesis to the Cheshire cat. As I held my wife in the soft purling of the cool brook, I watched the entire scene around me begin to dissipate. The flaming oak began to dissolve. The clouds turned black and slowly their blackness descended to the emerald grass inching its way toward the brook. I turned myself to face my wife and kissed her with conviction.

"I love you, Christine. And I promise we will be together soon."

In the fleeting instant of that moment I wanted to believe we would be together soon. I prayed to my higher power that we would be together soon. But I was doubtful I could keep my promise, especially as Christine and I began to fade, the last thing I saw from the corner of my evaporating eye was Satan's malevolent grin.

* * * * *

If I had not been a focused and determined man before that dream, I became an obsessed and compulsive man the next morning. I was out of bed fifteen minutes before the alarm clock clicked on to WFLA, Jack Taylor, and Ted Webb. Perfect. I walked straight to my small console piano and played Christine's new song two times, slightly up tempo to save time. I had it down now, no mistakes. Then I left the piano, put my socks and tennis shoes on and was ready for my forty-five-minute run across the street through Five Towns.

My run completed, I was ready to face the day with vigor. My bad habits were becoming behaviors of the past. And my new habits were old friends with whom I had fallen out of touch. I was being dogged by the devil and a cowardly ghost in my dreams, but I was taking steps to face them down. And even though the devil had told me that I had no one to help me, I still believed in my new relationship with my higher power and my new psychologist, Dr. Banderas.

I told myself: "Live for your new behaviors and you'll be living for the people you love and care about." Where that thought came from, I am not certain, but once I had it, I wondered about what it really meant even though I would say it repeatedly throughout the passing days.

I thought about what it actually meant to live for the people I loved and cared about, by living my new habits. Part of that concept was easy to understand, as I realized that I was already making progress to rebuild relations with Christine and my children. But what about my clients, each of whom I cared about in various ways? In my recent new age of awareness, another one hit me abruptly as I was driving and thinking at about Fifth Avenue and Fifty-fifth Street North. How many clients had I cheated through subpar thinking, considering their cases with a sluggish alcohol muddled brain? It hurt me to ponder that, but I didn't let it destroy me. The past was irretrievable. The only way I could make up for damage I caused my clients due to my shoddy homework, was to cease drinking and think with a clearer head in the future. I would do it. Night terrors aside, I doubted there was anything now that could provoke me to drink. Like the times I used to think that all other alcoholics were totally different and weaker than I was, I now started thinking that I would be completely free from alcohol substantially quicker than any alcoholic I'd ever met or listened to speak.

The next week I lived for my date with Christine and my appointments with Mary Bauer and Dr. Banderas. First came Dr. Banderas. When he asked me how I was doing, I was proud to tell him that I had jogged six times since our last visit, lost three more pounds, switched to a high protein diet, logged four and a half hours of practice time on the piano and was writing my second song for Christine in the past ten days. When I told him my personal accomplishments, I noticed a bright glint in his eyes which accompanied a wry smile. Here I was, sitting across from him in the luscious plant room, proud to tell him of my accomplishments and he was looking back at me, a man I hardly knew, exuding a sense of appreciation for those accomplishments. How easy it was for me to like somebody.

"What about your dreams?"

I recounted my singular dreams of consequence that I'd had in the past week with as much detail as I could.

"What do you think it means?" he asked me when I finished speaking.

Lazily, I answered, "I don't know. What do you think it means?"

He wrinkled his face for the first time since I met him.

"I don't think I know you well enough to venture an opinion at this time, Dr. McKenzie."

He used the more formal tack with me than the familiar Robert to make a point.

"I did notice a couple of similarities to the dreams you had previously, however. You dreamed about the devil again and as terrifying as that may have been, he was upstaged by your Two-Knock Ghost who was loud and persistent but who remained behind its protective curtain. Even though you cannot explain to me what you think about your dream in its entirety, perhaps you could suggest to me why the devil, who you don't believe in, continues to haunt you or at least why you think the Two-Knock Ghost persists in intruding into your dreams, but not revealing what it is."

I wanted to say, "That's why I'm here, Doc, to have you tell me as soon as possible what's going on with these nocturnal demons."

Again, all I could do was to shake my head no and to look totally ignorant, which I was. I thought but did not say it, "Not a very good psychologist, am I?"

"I have continued to think about your dream characters extremely often, Robert." The glint in his eyes having given way to a more serious, but caring affect.

"I have begun to theorize that your disbelief in the devil may have come as a reaction to having been introduced to him in a terrifying way as a child. Somewhere along the development of yourself as a man, you probably concluded that however frighteningly the devil was introduced to you, it was wrong to teach a child in that manner—the manner of threatening a child's immortal soul with fire and brimstone. Yet all these years later this demon is entrenched in your subconscious and wreaking havoc in your dreams. As far as the Two-Knock Ghost, my theories are more inchoate and obfuscated."

"So are mine," I answered. "It's been a multi month annoyance and I still know as little about it now as I did in the beginning."

"I will venture to say this," Dr. Banderas continued, "I believe these two entities to be somehow inexorably linked. I believe that as we research one, we will inevitably understand more about the other. What do you think about that?"

He had put forth a theory, yet he was engaging my opinion about it.

"I think you may be right," I answered, feeling exactly that.

"When you dream about one, do you dream about the other?"

I thought for a very long moment. My therapist was extremely patient with me.

"When I think about it, I would conclude that in the far greater majority of times when I dream about them both."

"That is good, Robert. You're answer supports my theory. Would you like to hear more of what I have been hypothesizing of your Two-Knock Ghost?"

"Please."

"Because of the uniqueness of the ghost, I believe that the ghost itself is inexorably linked to you, as much, if not more to you than it is linked inextricably to Lucifer."

"We'll have to see about that," I said, more surprised than disbelievingly. He was much farther along in his speculation of the Two-Knock Ghost in ten days than I was after several months.

"I don't know what conclusions that you've come to in your long years of practice Robert, or in your even longer life, but where I'm at in my thinking at the age of seventy-two, is that nothing stands alone in our minds. Everything is closely intertwined. Even the distance of years between events does not negate how closely things are connected in the confine so of the subconscious. The key to understanding these emotional proximities is to unravel them string by string until we discover the truth at the core."

He made sense to me. And it was comforting knowing that I was no longer alone in pursuing the core of the Two-Knock Ghost. My dilemma was not remotely knowing how the strings were wound around its core. I'd only had a few variations to the theme of this invisible pest. One was the loudness of the knocks. Another was whether they seemed frenzied or relaxed. Another was how many times the dual thuds had occurred within a dream. Otherwise, the Two-Knock Ghost was shapeless, formless, faceless. Was it Dr. Banderas's objectivity that had him moving along more quickly than I was in solving the riddle of one of my rude demons?

"I know that you are pondering this all the time Robert. But the prospective that I am going to pursue this from is that the devil and the Two-Knock Ghost are inseparable in your mind. You cannot have one without the other."

We continued talking with one another for the rest of our hour, with me sharing all kinds of revelations of my children, Christine, my parents, grandparents, my drinking, my practice, my childhood, my fears, my joys, my nocturnal dreams and the aspirations I had for the future.

I left there liking him more than I had at the end of our first session. I had more respect for him also, primarily because I could see him systematically turning the cup of my life over and over in his attempt to find the truths at my core.

CHAPTER 16

AT 3:30 THURSDAY morning Toby Magnessun was at headquarters with his partner, Patrick. They were both fully suited, including a bulletproof vest, meeting with Detectives Mills and Barclay. They were discussing how they were going to make the arrest of Reubin Tatum at 5:00 a.m. at Eddie Green's baby sister's house on Sixteenth Avenue and Fourteenth Street South, less than four blocks from Eddie's home. Their information on how to do this was based on a mountain of credible intel that Eddie Green had given Toby and Detectives Mills and Barclay. There had been three meetings of approximately an hour in length. Eddie explained to them that Thursday morning would be a perfect time to execute an arrest warrant because Reubin was a habitual Wednesday night "clubber" and that he'd always take Natalia, get shit-faced, dance like a mad man until 2:00 a.m., then do or sell drugs or both, then go back to the house with Natalia and collapse into bed about 4:00 a.m. Eddie had assured the detectives and Toby that Reubin's patterns were unalterable.

After extensive discussions with their superiors, it was decided that the four men in two police cars would be sufficient to arrest Reubin Tatum. Eddie had assured them that Reubin would be there alone with Natalia. There would be only one bad guy to deal with and he would be fast asleep. The detectives would enter through the front door soundlessly, using a key that Natalia had given her big brother for emergencies. She had one to Eddie's house also. Toby would wait in the back yard in case Reubin somehow made it out the back door. Patrick would wait outside the squad car in the alley blocking the get away from that slot.

They all agreed that this would be an easy arrest. The key to the front door would assure the inevitability of a successful operation. There was little or no fear from any of the four arresting officers. In fact, there was excitement and happiness, joy even, in each of them because they knew that by 5:08 a.m. one of St. Pete's most dangerous thugs would be out of commission.

At exactly 5:00 a.m., before the slightest bit of daylight graced the morning sky, Art Barclay, father of three, devoted husband of twenty-seven years, twice decorated police officer of thirty-two years, inserted the key in the lock on the front door. His partner of sixteen years, Larry Mills, also a father of three, devoted husband of twenty-three years and also twice decorated, with thirty years of service, was at his left side. One minute earlier they had commented how dark, quiet and peaceful the house looked, as if it were sleeping along with the inhabitants inside.

"Piece of cake," Barclay whispered as he turned the key.

It was pitch-black inside the room they were entering. The only sound was the gentle whirring of the air conditioner. Barclay handed the opening door off to Mills so Mills could make sure that the door opened all the way and without sound. That small task completed, both officers of the law placed their initial footsteps simultaneously inside the house. The pellets hit each of their faces with such force that they nearly flew backward out the open door. They collided in midair in their flight to their final resting spots. But they were oblivious to the colliding because both men were dead already from scores of pellets that blasted their foreheads, eyes, mouths, and necks and nestled in various parts of their brains. Death had been instantaneous. A loud sound, a flash of fiery light, then nothing.

At the instant of the blast, three men reacted in different ways. Reubin Tatum knew that he was going from sleep to a fight for his life. In the back yard, 15 feet from the backdoor, Toby drew his weapon and assumed a readiness stance he had learned at the Police Academy, gun pointed toward the back door. A hundred feet behind him, Patrick radioed for backup.

Tatum grabbed his second shotgun—his favorite weapon of choice—that was resting next to his right side while Natalia woke terrified to his left.

"Stay here and don't move," he told Natalia, not expressing concern, but as a thug who didn't want her hindering his escape route. She didn't move, except to shake and cower under the sheet. Reubin, clad only in white Jockey shorts, grabbed for his jeans and T-shirt that were preplaced on a nearby chair. His car keys were in his pants pocket and instead of putting on his regular tennis shoes, he slid on a pair of blue flip-flops. He was dressed in twenty-four seconds.

He had never planned to exit by the front door. He figured there might be more cops in the front yard, and he didn't want to see any mess that the shotgun blast might have created. According to plan, he peeked out a small separation he made between the blind slats of his bedroom window. Immediately, he saw the layout of the backyard. Toby was acutely alert with his weapon drawn. That was not good, Reubin thought. He would have to shoot his way past Toby in order to reach his old blue Saturn that was backed into the carport, its front facing the alley. He always left the driver's side door unlocked for easier access. He saw that Patrick was still in the squad car radioing for help. That was a good thing. He'd probably only have to deal with two cops if he exited right now. It wouldn't be pleasant, but it was doable. He ran wildly for the back door. He unlocked, opened it and immediately felt chips of wood smacking into his face, fragments of the door frame that Toby's first bullets had hit. Reubin raised his shotgun, pointed it, and pulled the trigger while Toby continued firing. Reubin was moving faster than he ever had. Somehow he was able to pass Toby and get into the Saturn and start it. He felt warm and wet on his left side but there was no pain, just an adrenalin rush like he'd never had before.

He ignited the Saturn and sped from under the carport as he heard sirens nearby closing in. Only one cop to beat as he cut over the grass to the right opposite the squad car. Bullets were now flying furiously from Patrick's gun. Instinctively, Reubin concluded he'd do best to keep his head down below the windows and guesstimate where the alley met the yard. Within two seconds, glass began to shatter around the Saturn and Reubin felt scores of shards hit his left ear and that side of his face. But he was still alive and his guesstimate of where the grass ended and the alley began was perfect. Now he was approximating how to keep the Saturn in the middle of the alley until he came to the side street only a couple of seconds away. He figured that there he would be safe enough from Patrick's bullets to raise up, get his bearings and decide which way to continue his getaway. Again, his estimation of where the concrete of the side street began was perfect.

"I got this shit," he said with complete confidence before he raised himself up to quickly glance out the windshield. He looked left and right, decided to go left feeling a tremendous crackling of bone and cartilage at the base of his neck. Suddenly, he could not control the car. He had started to turn left so the car continued that way at a high rate of speed for a few more yards till it careened into the curb across the side street, jarring Reubin's already excruciating head.

He was still alive but his body didn't want to function, to think. There was no more "what do I do next?" There was only dominating pain, almost crushing him onto the front seat. His brain, still barely able to perceive, heard the sirens and saw the headlights of the next police car to arrive on the scene. Maybe it was all instinct by this time, but Reubin grabbed his shotgun and opened the car door. When the two approaching officers saw that shotgun come out of the car, they opened fire and dropped big tough Reubin Tatum before he could completely exit the vehicle. In fact, so many bullets hit Reubin Tatum and with such force that his final landing spot was lying on his back on the front seat of his Saturn. Fractures of glass were imbedded in his cheek, ears, hands, legs and back.

It was 5:04 a.m.

* * * * *

In four minutes there had been four deaths. Art Barclay and Larry Mills lay dead two feet outside the house, victims of a single double barrel blast from a booby trapped shotgun, jimmy rigged to a tripwire set five inches above the floor.

The house was eerily silent, except for Natalia's barely audible whimpering. She had not yet moved and would not move until a female St. Pete Police officer literally almost pried her off her bed several minutes later.

Patrick had rushed to Toby's side a moment after he saw one of his own bullets rip through the neck of Reubin Tatum. Toby was lying on his back, motionless. His life vest was splattered with pellets but so were his neck and chin. Just enough pellets had found his carotid artery and shattered it. Toby's had been a painful death, one he tried to avoid by pressing both hands against the bleeding. He lasted ninety-three seconds, spending his last eighteen seconds in the arms of his friend.

* * * * *

At my house, Jack Harris was saying good-bye to a guest when my alarm clock went off at 6:45 a.m. I sprung out of bed with more joy in my heart than I'd had in a long time. I was one day away from two of my most looked forward to events in many years. My first was being at least able to tell Mary Bauer that the detectives were closing in on her abuser. I was hoping that I would run into Toby tonight at the Serenity Club, and he could fill me in with a little more information about the take down of Tatum. Of course I was not planning to share his name with Mary—not wishing to compromise the investigation in any way. But I was looking forward with every fiber of my being to pragmatically alleviating a significant portion of her fears. That's the same way I was looking forward to my evening with Christine. Every fiber of my being longed to be in her presence. I couldn't wait to share with her my recent awareness, my achievements, my phone calls to the kids, my change of routines, and most of all the song I had written for her.

Since my running shorts and T-shirt were already on, I hopped out of bed and turned off the radio on my way to my chair where I got into my socks and tennis shoes. In a single minute I was into the living room sitting on the piano bench. I played Christine's song at regular tempo, grabbed my keys, and headed out the door. Today I would run a little faster and maybe a few blocks longer. I felt like I had wings on my shoes that would propel me. I was happy and excited.

When my run was complete, I began the rest of my normal morning rituals. I decided to have two pieces of Publix American cheese between two toasted and buttered pieces of Publix brand honey wheat bread. I poured myself a tall glass of vanilla soy milk mixed with chocolate soy milk, headed into the living room, plate and glass in hands. I would give myself five or six minutes to eat and watch TV. I turned on the TV and flipped the dial to News Channel 8 because I enjoyed watching the Today Show and was absolutely moved every time I heard a snippet of John Williams's uplifting theme song. It was 7:55 a.m., time for the local news.

I took my first bite of my cheese sandwich as the female news caster began telling the story of the takedown of Reubin Tatum. "Three officers are dead this morning as well as the perpetrator in what was supposed to have been an easy arrest. Unfortunately, nothing went as planned as Detectives Larry Mills and Art Barclay, the first on the scene, were gunned down by a booby-trapped shotgun as they entered the house of Natalia Greene in South St. Pete in search of Reubin Tatum who was wanted as the primary suspect in a string of at least seven local robberies. Tatum, awakened by the shotgun blast, began his escape attempt by fleeing out of the back door, taking the life of Officer Toby Magnessun as he raced for his car. Tatum was killed only a few seconds later by a bullet from Patrick O'Malley, Magnessun's partner."

She continued and I listened intently. As soon as I heard that Toby's life had been taken, it felt like an emotional shotgun blasted its harmful pellets into the pit of my stomach. My eyes filled with tears, and pain and shock snatched my breath from me. This was my fault. If I hadn't asked Toby to help me, he would be alive this morning. Who would take care of his wife now? Who would love her through her ongoing battle with cancer? I knew immediately I would do something phenomenal to help her and her children—but anonymously. I could never reveal the truth to her or anyone that I was the catalyst behind her husband's death.

My morning joy had transformed into abject horror and shame. I didn't think I was a murderer, but now I knew what it felt like to be an accomplice. The death of my parents and grandparents with all of its accompanying pain came crashing into me like a runaway freight train. Christine's rejection, my pitiable nature, my pathetic thirty-year dependency on rum and Coke, my isolationist tendency, my direct involvement with the murder of my client and friend and my preoccupation with devil dreams and a nonsensical Two-Knock Ghost, took hold of me and turned me into a piece of immovable patheticness on the couch. Suddenly, there was no more me. There was only pain, which needed to be quelled.

I found myself watching the television through tear blurred eyes, but I wasn't hearing its sound. Instead, I heard the rampaging of my own inner voice saying, "You can't take this. This is too much to bear. You don't owe anybody anything right now except yourself. You need to make the pain go away. Nobody has to suffer as much as you are right now. There's comfort out there for you. You know where it is. It's only a couple of blocks away. GO GET IT RIGHT NOW!"

And I listened. First I called Amanda and told her to cancel my appointments for the day.

"Are you okay, Dr. McKenzie?" she asked me tenderly.

"Just a terrible pain in my stomach." I didn't lie.

"I think it might be a virus or food poisoning." I had to lie. "I'll try to make it in tomorrow. When you feel like you've completed your work for the day, you may leave early."

I was screaming inside at myself. Even though it was the sweet Amanda, I didn't want to talk with her. I didn't want to talk with anyone. I only wanted to stop my waking demons from tormenting me. I only wanted the stomach pain to abate immediately. I was totally living in the moment and it was hell. There was no tomorrow. There was no hour from now. There were no consequences for what I would choose to do next. Men have to do what they have to do. I was a man and I had an absolute right to do whatever it took to survive my pain. Who else was going to take care of me? Not Christine. Not my kids. Not Dr. Banderas. Not Toby. Maybe if I had chosen a sponsor, I could call him. But I hadn't even gone that deep into AA that I had picked a sponsor. Another bad choice. Maybe if I had made a friend at the Serenity Club. I had not. Another bad decision. Why was I such an isolationist? All of my life it had been me, my family, my clients and not much of anyone else. There was something else. There was rum and Coke. My friends in a bottle. I needed them now. I grabbed my keys and left the condo. I drove up Park Street to the liquor store at Park and Starkey, but it was closed. It was barely 8:30. What was I thinking? The store didn't open until 9:00 a.m. I pulled into a parking space, turned off the engine and pounded on the steering wheel at least a dozen times. I was blinded by rage toward myself and the scum bag who killed Toby. Now I had to sit out here and wait—stewing in my own excruciating juices. I couldn't control the torrent of tears that flowed from my eyes.

When I finally got home, I drank like a madman. In truth, there was no like a mad man. I was a mad man drinking. There was no sipping, no pacing. There was just downing. I got as much rum into my system as I possibly could as fast as I could tolerate it. With all my windows and blinds closed and the air conditioner humming, I screamed "SHIT" over and over between guzzles. I only hoped nobody near me, my neighbors below and beside me, and anybody walking outside the condo, would think I was certifiable.

During my intimate moment of personal depravity I only wanted the pain to go away. As the swallowing continued, I streaked closer to my goal. Oblivion. Oblivion is what I craved . . . a state of mindlessness where nothing existed. Not pain, not guilt, not worry, not hopes or aspirations, no thought of any kind. There also were no dreams of any kind. Even I would not be able to appreciate my hours in Oblivion. I merely wanted to get there as quickly as was humanly possible. I had only been there a time or two in my entire life and I might never go there again. But my goal was swiftly approaching as I could not wait to escape my real world agony. Before I entered the blackness I was seeking, I wondered if I should have bought a second bottle.

I was in my bed by the time Oblivion found me. I wish I could say that it was wonderful and that I enjoyed it, but I cannot. It simply existed and I was there. It lasted for hours and there was nothing as I had hoped for except for the very end.

I heard a voice in my bedroom gently urging me: "Wake up, Dr. McKenzie. I have something to tell you. Wake up, Dr. McKenzie." So I did, but within my dream I believed, not in my waking world.

There was Toby, standing at the foot of my bed.

"Toby!" I exclaimed both shocked and overjoyed to see him. He was wearing stunning white silk pants with a matching shirt. He looked angelic.

"I'm here to comfort you, Dr. McKenzie. There's no need for you to beat yourself up. I'm in a better place. There is no pain here. It's okay, Doc. I'm okay."

"I feel so bad," I said like a saddened child. "I don't know what to do now."

"Lead a good life, help more people, maybe do something special for my wife and kids. Alicea knows all about you. You're a topic of pleasant conversation around our house."

"Does she know I'm the reason you're dead?"

"You're not the reason I'm dead, Doc. Reubin Tatum is. And I never told her that you asked for my help to catch him. I didn't want to worry her. She's always had so much to worry about these last few years."

"I'm sorry," I told him from the most sincere crevice of my heart.

"I know you are, Doc. I am too. I wanted you and I to be friends for a long time."

"I wanted that too, Toby."

"I've got to go now, Doc. Take care of yourself and your family and look in on mine if you can from time to time. But most of all, no guilt, Doc." I made a negative face to indicate I might not be able to comply.

"Promise me," Toby said emphatically.

"I promise," I said while knowing what I really meant was that I would try my best, but it might not be good enough.

Then Toby faded into nothingness, and I fell back to sleep. I'm not certain if my Toby sighting was a dream or if I had seen his ghost. If I had been certain that it was his ghost, I would have believed everything he told me implicitly. But since I did not believe in ghosts, I chalked my experience up as having been a dream. Because of that, I placed significantly less credibility into what Toby had told me, especially when he mentioned that he never told Alicea that I'd ask him to help me find Reubin Tatum and that I had always been a pleasant topic of conversation around the house.

When I finally awoke from Oblivion minus one rather soothing dream, I wondered why I had labeled the Two-Knock Ghost with that moniker. Why hadn't I called it the Two-Knock Demon? One thing was for certain. I was not sure of any of the deepest parts of my mind. I was also not sure of how I processed information and came to so many of my vital life conclusions. And if my brain wasn't muddled enough with my sober reflections, what must it be in that horribly hung-over condition I woke up with that evening? It was 7:30 Thursday night, only 11.75 hours before I was scheduled to wake up again and begin the day when I would tell Mary Bauer about Reubin Tatum and take Christine out for what I thought might be the most important date of our lives to this point. I couldn't do it all. I could see Mary, but there was no way I could take Christine out and bestow upon her the love she deserved, combined with the high degree of spiritual upliftedness I felt as recently as this morning. I got out of bed and went directly to the kitchen counter where I believed my rum bottle to be—not to drink any but to throw away whatever was left. The bottle was where I had left it, but there was no rum in it to discard. I had drunk it all. That explained why I felt so monstrously ill.

Though I was feeling lonely, I knew I had to call Christine to cancel our date for tomorrow night. I could never recover fast enough to show her the new man I had become, at least through almost eight o'clock this morning. As I drank a tall glass of apple juice with seven ice cubes, I dialed her number. Fortunately, she answered, the sensitive voice I longed to hear more than any other.

"Hello," she answered simply, after the first ring.

"Hi, Christine, it's Robert."

I had tried to be neutral in my vocal affect, but she picked up on something immediately, knowing me better than anyone in the world.

"What's the matter Robert?" she asked plaintively.

As soon as I heard the concern in her voice, I realized that was both exactly what I needed to hear and what I didn't need to hear. I crumbled, almost hanging up the phone before I spoke another word.

"Some things have happened in the last few hours, terrible things, that make it impossible for me to see you tomorrow night." I spoke through a tumult of tears and with a voice that uncharacteristically quivered.

"What things, darling?"

Darling? I was darling now when I felt like yesterday's garbage?

"Have you seen the local news today?" I asked, my voice barely able to sustain itself.

"Yes."

"Did you hear about the police officer that was killed?"

"I thought there were three."

"You're right, Christine. There were two detectives that were killed coming in the front door and a cop that was killed in the backyard."

I paused a moment as my wife listened silently.

"The cop in the backyard was my client and I dare say, my friend."

I gasped for air and spit out, "The way that he died is killing me because I think I am responsible."

"I'll be right there, Robert."

"No, Christine. Please don't. You don't have to do that."

"I'm going to wash my face and drive right over there. I'm hanging up now. I'll see you shortly."

Her voice had transitioned from genteel caring to the adamant drill sergeant who had made up his unbendable mind.

"Thank you, Christine." Click.

I immediately got up from the couch in the living room and put the empty rum bottle in the garbage under the sink. As soon as I closed the cabinet door, I thought, "That isn't enough." I took the half-full plastic Publix grocery bag out of the waste basket, tied it and took it downstairs to a trash bin in the breezeway of my building. My head was throbbing and I was nauseas, but I came quickly upstairs, peed like a race horse, then got into my shower and tried to scrub the stains of the day away. I brushed my teeth and used Listerine sumptuously. By the time Christine arrived, I was feeling a touch better physically, but emotionally I was feeling overwhelming shame and guilt over Toby's death and how I had reacted to it. Christine's coming over was not what I had planned. In some ways, it was the antithesis of what I wanted now. I awaited her visit with a combination of hopeful anticipation and dread.

When Christine arrived, I felt like she had come to pick me up out of the snow like the first time we met. A little over an hour ago I was in oblivion and now I was being seen by my favorite person as I crawled through the emotional nadir of my lifetime.

Word by honest word, it all began to tumble out from me to her. Selfishly, uncontrollably, I dominated the conversation with my story. I told Christine everything, how I almost hit the woman on the bicycle on Madeira Beach, how I realized that I was an alcoholic. I told her of beginning my journey through AA, my new running regiment in the mornings. I told her about Toby and the live oak—almost all of it coming as genuine tears streamed down my face. Finally, after over thirty minutes of abject sadness, I told her about my new psychologist and how I chose him out of the phone book. When I told her his name, she giggled outright.

"Really," she said. "What are the odds of that name popping up?"

"A million to one," I said, smiling for the first time since my morning run.

I shared with her the reasons why I had chosen a psychologist and she easily understood my terrifying devil dreams, but was baffled by my preoccupation with the Two-Knock Ghost. I explained how I had completely broke down and destroyed everything I'd worked so hard to build up the past three weeks when I heard about Toby's death.

Throughout every minute of my story telling she held both of my hands in between hers. The tenderness that I felt coming from her was overwhelming and though I had begun the stories feeling like pond scum, I felt remarkable joy being in the presence of and being affectionately hand held by my wife.

Then she said something that uplifted me more than I could have ever anticipated would happen this night of incredible sorrows.

"Robert, you haven't destroyed everything you've worked for these past three weeks. You've stumbled, that's all. Many people who struggle with alcohol stumble in recovery. It isn't the end of the world for you honey. It's part of the process unfortunately. But after everything that you've told me, I can easily and completely understand why you faltered. You're a sensitive man and you felt unbearable grief and guilt. Those two emotions are often untenable in the confines of the human heart when felt to the depth you felt them. And, Robert, you need to know how proud I am of what you have accomplished recently. There is no reason why you can't pick up tomorrow where you began today."

The support she had given me was the greatest gift a man in my position could have hoped for. It was time for me to try to return the favor.

"Christine, I did something for you about a week ago that I haven't done in a long time. In fact, it was the primary reason why I wanted to see you tomorrow night."

She looked deep into my eyes without removing her hands from mine. It was the kind of look that reaffirmed not only were we connected, but that we would be true friends and mates till time ran out on this plane.

"What is it, Turf?"

She saw the old me in that last gaze between us. She saw something of both the beginnings and the high points of our thirty-five years of love. She was convinced that something special was coming.

"I wrote you a song, Christine."

Her eyes began to water.

"I'm sorry that it's been so long since the last one," I said humbly. "But I promise it will never be that long again."

"Don't apologize, Turf, just play it for me please."

I had given Christine a myriad of types of gifts throughout the decades—clothes, china, perfumes, jewelry, art. But nothing pleased her more than when I wrote her a song. She would transition from whatever mood she was in to a warm, almost feline creature who was about to receive a surprise from the great beyond. Tonight would be no different. I could already feel the actual warmth of her caring through her hands, but when I told her I had written a song for her, a burst of glee shot spontaneously from her eyes. Across from me was the twenty-year-old absolute romantic and idealist, and the fifty-five-year-old romantic and idealist whose eyes had not glistened like this in nearly three long years. Her temperature had actually spiked when I told her about the song. I could feel it through her hands as soon as I told her. As I looked into her expectant and joyful eyes, I made up my mind that my number one priority for the rest of my lifetime would be winning the deepening love of this woman.

I walked away from her tender hands to the piano bench, sat down and began to play. Though I focused on the keys and the passion required to interpret the music correctly, I couldn't help but to raise my head from the piano keys and look upon my wife. Her eyes were glistening like the facets of sapphires in close proximity to diamonds. The moisture in them created more facets and I almost became lost in them while forgetting the music. Though her beauty was driving my distraction, my focus shifted back to my playing, as I summoned a reserve of passion for the song's conclusion. After two minutes and forty-three seconds of actual playing time, my song for Christine was concluded. For a moment we were silent.

"Did you name it?" she asked.

"That's your job, Christine."

Over the past thirty-three years, for some unknown reason, I had never named the songs I wrote for her. I guess it probably started with that first one when I was so excited to play it for her, but I hadn't titled it yet. I played it for her and she asked her usual, something like, "What'dya name it?" And when I told her I hadn't, she popped out with, "Can I name it?" I said, "Sure." And a couple of days later she came to me like a happy little kid and said, "Blue River." And I said, "I like it!" That's how her naming songs began.

"Will you do me a favor, Turf, and play it again?"

There was that old nickname.

Wordlessly, I turned back toward the piano and played her song again, bringing more passion through my fingertips for the second rendition. This time when I finished, my tiny wife surprised me again. She got up from the couch, walked to the dining room table, grabbed a chair, carried it over my laminate floor and placed it directly behind me and the piano bench.

"Would you play some of the other songs you wrote for me till you get tired?"

"I haven't practiced them in a long time," I said shyly.

"You'll be okay. They don't have to be perfect."

When I turned back around to play, Christine scooted her chair so that it butted right up to and touched the piano bench. Then she put her head on my back and wrapped her arms around my recently less paunchy belly. For a man who was feeling as miserable as I was earlier in the day, I was feeling warm and fuzzy in this moment, which I never wanted to end. But it did, forty-five minutes and eight or nine songs later when I felt Christine almost slide off my back and onto the floor as she drifted into sleep.

Slowly and carefully I pushed my back against her body, making certain my wife was sitting safely against the back of her chair. Then I turned around, stretched a bit, reached down, picked up my 102-pound bride, carried her into my bedroom and placed her gently on my bed. Christine probably was never aware of the experience, but I was, as my heart soared when I felt her warm breath near my nose and lips. I wanted to kiss her, but I did not because this was not a moment for our lips to meet. It was a moment for me to carry her to the bedroom like a father carries a sleeping child from the car to the bed after a visit to Grandma and Grandpa's house. As I carried my wife, I remembered the last time I had done so. It was 1971 and we were on vacation in South Haven, Michigan. We had both had a day of adventuring in several towns including Saugatoulk and Holland. By the time we got back to our cabin—the Chalet Afterglow—located on a high bluff near the lake, Christine would not wake up to my urgings. So I carried her inside.

Thirty-three years ago already. Where had our lives gone so quickly? I looked upon the sleeping woman lying on top of my sheets. After I brushed my teeth, I spoke silently within myself to the devil. "You're wrong about us," I said confidently. "Christine's and my relationship will never go up in flames because you won't destroy me, no matter how hard you try. You see, I realize I'm a damaged man now. But I know I can repair myself. Nice try with burning the live oak in my dream. That bothered me immensely, but I know that the next time I go to see it. It will still be there, thriving. You don't have the power to destroy even a tree in real life, much less a man or a relationship like ours. That's why you torment people in their dreams, because that's all you've got. And tonight when I go to sleep, I've got the sweetest, kindest, most caring woman God ever created, lying beside me. What have you got? Nothing but demons surround you. I've never heard of Mrs. Devil."

I chuckled as I concluded this complex day with what I thought was some pretty good mocking of Satan.

CHAPTER 17

WHEN I AWOKE the next morning at 6:45 without the aid of my alarm clock, which I had forgotten to set, Christine was already gone. Not knowing her current schedule, I could only assume that she had to be at work early and was aided in waking by her ever vigilant body clock. On the bed where she had slept for the first time was a note on eight and a half inch by eleven inch lined paper that said, "Dear Husband: Thank you for sharing so much so honestly last night. I am proud of you for all that you have accomplished in the past few weeks and I'm certain that your setback yesterday will not deter you from any of your goals. For too many reasons to mention right now, the new song you played for me last night is my favorite ever. I'm calling it 'The Haunting.' Call me later this evening and we can talk about it. I love you, Robert. C."

There she was again. The old Christine who was 100 percent supportive of me, appreciative of my depth, honesty, and creativity, upon which she placed high value. She could not have known this, but her note to me had also mocked the devil.

Even though Christine's loving nature had energized me, I still felt the drag of yesterday's sorrows. Though I had remained in my running clothes from yesterday morning, it was not easy to pull my hung-over body out of the condo for a morning jog. But I did it, realizing that this was the first day again, of the rest of my life and I was determined to live it based on my improved standards.

During my jog my head ached behind my eyes and up toward my temple, but I overcame it with thoughts of Mary Bauer and our early afternoon meeting. Yesterday, when I called Amanda and told her I wouldn't be coming into work, I had currently been thinking that there would be no way I would be able to face Mary with the mountain of crap I had rotting my brain. I was already planning to call the office before Amanda got there Friday and tell her that I'd be coming back Monday. When I called Amanda yesterday I was envisioning a complete downward spiral. I knew I would be shattered because I was returning to drinking. On top of that I would have to face Christine and break our date. That would have crushed me. I'd feel badly that I let a few clients who depended on me down. It would simply be one larger negative on top of another and I would be beneath all of them with my trusty rum and Coke trying to drown my sorrows.

Christine's tenderness and compassion changed not only my working plans for the day, but the level of determination I would have as I faced my future. One night of being in the presence of Christine's love and encouragement had reminded me of my primary reason for striving to be a better and sober man.

After calling at exactly 8:00 and telling Amanda I would be in soon, I felt a renewed vigor to meet the day. I drank two eight ounce glasses of apple juice with several ice cubes in each glass and made a tasty cheese and toast sandwich.

"Are you feeling better, Dr. McKenzie?" Amanda asked me as I bounded into the waiting room with unusual enthusiasm.

"I am, thank you very much."

"Hot chocolate this morning?"

"Yes please."

"Coming right up, sir."

Normalcy recovered.

Mary was my first patient after lunch. I had not done my usual note writing the night before so I had nothing planned to say to Mary. It was one of the most important sessions with a client that I had ever looked forward to, and I was unprepared. For an instant, that scared me. But only until it came to me almost immediately, that speaking to her logically and from the heart would be sufficient.

When Mary came into my office, I felt markedly sorry for her. She had been through an ordeal that had forcibly dashed her emotions into a lingering hell. She was a petite woman of courage and conviction who, through no choice of her own, was being tested by life in a complex way. I knew that she was constantly asking herself, "How do I overcome what happened to me and be the best wife and teacher I can be, when I fear each day that he may find me and do worse to me?" Today I would alter one aspect of her hypothetical question.

For some reason I will never understand, it was a soft entry into our conversation that day. We were both very quiet, almost somber.

"How are you today, Mary?" I asked, to begin.

"Physically, pretty well, Dr. McKenzie, but mentally about the same, less than adequate."

"I have something to tell you that might brighten your spirits a bit."

"What's that, Doctor?"

"Have you been watching the news the past thirty hours or so?"

"Yes, a little, the usual."

"The bad guy that was killed in St. Pete, Reubin Tatum, was the man who assaulted you in the convenience store. He'll never hurt anyone again."

"He's gone? You're sure it was him?"

"I'm positive. I have a friend in the Police Department." It was a white lie. I had a friend in the PD.

"I saw when the detectives who knew Mills and Barclay were so mad that they grabbed the case files and rounded up the other two gang members."

I hadn't really heard that. "That means that any of your fears of ever being hurt by any of these guys again can be put to rest."

"What if they get out in a few years?" She was still frightened.

"I read in the St. Pete Times a few weeks ago that the St. Pete Police believe without a doubt that the gang was responsible for the shooting death of the Indian store clerk at the Shell Gas Station at 18 and 34 South. In Florida, when you participate in a felony which results in a death, it's the same as if you pulled the trigger. The sentence is always life without the possibility of parole."

She shook her head lightly twice in a yes movement as she squinted her eyes and looked outside the window to the water. She was still squinting and in deep thought when she forced herself to speak with her softest voice of any of our sessions together.

"Do you really think this is the end of it, Dr. McKenzie?"

"Without a doubt," I said strongly but fused with tenderness.

She was looking at the water as if gaining strength from its sight. When she turned back to make eye contact with me, a single tear slid down the left side of her face.

"Thank you for telling me that doctor." Her volume remained on soft.

"How do you feel knowing those guys can never hurt you again?"

"It makes me feel." She paused and looked out toward the water again. She was in deep thought. Then she finished her sentence with a single word, *different*. And that was it. She didn't smile. She didn't say that she felt safe again. I was disappointed. I had expected something from her. I expected smiles, at least one. I expected joy. I expected sighs and words expressing relief. But I didn't get any of it. Again in my life experiences, I was reminded that one can never fully know how someone will react to what you tell them, especially when you expect to ease someone's embedded pain with a few words, no matter how powerful you think those words will be.

I realized immediately that I had much more work to do with Mary. I was certain that someday she would be happy again; it just might not be on this particular Friday afternoon. I got over my disappointment in a flash and went right back to work.

"Is there anything else that you would like to talk with me about today?" I asked.

Now she perked up a bit.

"My husband and I have been talking about going on a cruise for the past few days." She smiled guardedly.

"You have!" I said delightedly. "Where to?"

"The Bahamas."

"How long?"

"Seven days, not long."

"How did it come about?" I asked, pleased to be talking about such a potentially happy adventure.

"He asked me."

"Wow, how nice."

"It was nice. He totally surprised me."

She had turned her volume up and I could tell that any moment she would ask me what I thought about it.

"What do you feel about a trip like that?" I asked, keeping positivity in my voice.

"Up until today I didn't feel good about it. I felt like I would be running away, almost as if I was being forced by those robbers to leave my home, just to have some peace of mind. But then in seven short days I would have to return to my home, but those guys would still be here. I never told you in this way before, Dr. McKenzie, but I love St. Petersburg. It's a beautiful little city and those guys robbed it from me. Home is supposed to be where you feel safe. They stole my home from me."

"But things have changed today, right?"

"They have, and that's why I feel so different on so many planes. When you first told me about Reubin Tatum and his thug buddies, I almost could not compute the reality of it. Fear had wrapped itself around so many aspects of my life so tightly, that when you told me the story, the fear didn't unwrap instantly. It still hasn't. But I'm beginning to feel better because of the logic of it. Those guys are gone and its illogical to fear that they could ever hurt me again. But what I am feeling is that fear inside me has taken on a life of its own. Its separate from the robbers and it wants to keep me bound up within it. Do you understand what I'm saying, Dr. McKenzie?"

I not only understood, but I related what she said to my life and how fear had bound me, how I carried it around my waking days dreading the next dream onslaught of the devil and the absurd taunting of the Two-Knock Ghost.

"I understand, Mary. I truly do."

"It's as if fear itself has become a new dimension of me, an integral part of me. It's made me short-tempered with the children at school, crabby with my husband, withdrawn from my mother and father, more distant from the people at my church. You would think I might have reached out to those people for support. But I've gone the other way. I've retreated inwardly. And even though it's lonely in here by myself, I'm not sure how to get out. Even the news you shared with me today only makes me feel a little better. How do I get out of my fear head and get back to being my old self again?"

She was looking directly at me with eyes of yearning, expecting a profound and immediate answer. I don't know how long I paused before speaking to her, but my first thought after she asked me the question, was that I felt so inadequate this moment to answer what was probably the deepest and most sincere question of her adult life. I went for the obvious.

"Going on the cruise would undoubtedly help, Mary. Now you and your husband can look at it as a celebration of your new peace of mind. Do you love the water?"

"Very much."

"Do you love to travel?"

"Ditto."

"Do you love adventure?"

"Yes."

"You see, all those things are things you love. You will be pursuing things you love and that is the way you will overcome your negative self and become happy again. You must absolutely fill every aspect of your life with the things and the people you love. Gradually, the fear will dissipate because fear cannot coincide with an abundance of love."

"You're right, Doctor. I know that intellectually."

"All change for either good or bad starts with a single thought, Mary. If you believe in the concept that I just shared with you, you'll start pursuing what you love post haste."

"You're right, Dr. McKenzie. What you told me today has given me the motivation to pursue love and break out of the prison I've been living in all these weeks."

She was sounding more optimistic. And I was feeling better about the session now than when she had first said, "I feel . . . different."

We continued talking, but much more lightly than the conversation had been up to this point. I even asked Mary if she had thought of anything she might need to buy for the cruise. She told me that she needed to buy two new bathing suits. When I asked her if there was anything else, she shifted gears and answered: "I need to lose the ten pounds I've gained since this ordeal began." She giggled nervously when she said that. Then she said: "You may have noticed." I said: "I have not." Then she said: "You're so kind, Doctor." But I hadn't noticed. Since I had met her several weeks earlier, I had always been a student of her face. I looked at it constantly for any hint, however subtle, as to how she might be feeling deep inside. I searched for the truth of her affect, the depths of her sadness, the degree of her fears, how she was feeling each moment. I never noticed the extra ten pounds. And I wondered if I could ever notice that little weight gain on any of my clients.

When we came to the end of our session, Mary surprised me by showing me the only piece of physical affection she had ever shown me. When she said good-bye, she reached out to shake my hand the same way she had shaken it at each previous conclusion, but this day she placed her left hand on the right side of my right hand as she shook it with her right hand. Instantly, my hand felt like the cream filling between the black crunchy parts of an Oreo cookie. It was a good feeling—a genuine gesture of appreciation from a grateful client, one of the kinds of moments a good psychologist lives for.

Then she said, as she held her left hand firmly against mine while she maintained her grip with her right hand: "Thank you, Dr. McKenzie. What you shared with me today has helped me to turn the corner toward more normalcy." She removed her hands. "I've never been good at showing my emotions on the surface, so you may be a little confused as to what I am feeling. But I'll tell you and this comes from deep within me, I not only feel different, I feel better. I'm learning new things all the time, how to be a braver woman, a better wife, teacher, and person overall. You've been an integral part of that growth."

Then she turned and headed for the door. I was silent, allowing her to conclude our session with the final spoken words.

When she left the room, for the first time since I had met her, I believed that she would not only have a good life, but a great life.

With Mary gone, I was alone again with my thoughts. I still had two clients to see, but I kept looking past them somewhat selfishly, to my phone call in four hours or so to Christine, my next session with Dr. Banderas, beginning a new run of sober days and contemplating how I would square off against the devil in our next dream and how I would motivate the Two-Knock Ghost to reveal itself the next time it came calling.

Before I left the office at about 5:45, I called Christine.

"I have a couple of filet mignons that I bought at Publix on sale Thursday, a cobb salad, some macaroni and cheese, and a package of mushrooms, if you would like to come over and share dinner with me."

"I'd love to," I answered, as thrilled as a sixteen-year-old going on his first date. I know I've said that or something like that before. But it is what I truly felt.

"Are you still at the office?" she asked.

When I said "yes," she said, "Good, then you don't have to drive across town to the condo. You can just shoot over here from the office. You can come whenever you want."

"I called you as I was planning to leave work. See you in fifteen, okay? Can I bring anything?"

"Nope, and I have plenty of apple juice."

"Yummy," I said and then something popped out as if we had never been separated, "I love you, Christine."

"I love you too, Turf."

Then she put her phone in its cradle.

Twenty-four hours ago I had been in oblivion—a place and condition in which I thought I needed to be. Tonight I was back to living in hope.

My evening with Christine was memorable. It seemed like she was sharing a duality with me. One part was thanking me for what I had accomplished in the three weeks prior to my fall from grace yesterday and the other part was strongly encouraging my future endeavors.

It seemed that night that we talked about everything. I was not selfish. I asked her about her job and she told me myriad stories about how she helped people in dire need. I also boldly asked her if she was happy living without me. Whereupon, she answered, "No, silly. I miss you terribly. But now that you're serious about getting your life back on track, we don't have to wait too long to get you back home, right?"

Considering that only yesterday she had seen me in my personal nadir, I thought her words were pretty magnanimous. I realized that what Christine had wanted from me was totally logical and fair. Above all else, she wanted me to realize that I had a problem with alcohol. She needed me to admit, primarily to myself, that I had gradually slipped from being the man I had been in the past, not due to normal aging, but due to all the subtle and negative effects of what a chemical addiction could do to a person. She wanted me to grasp what those changes had been and begin to turn the tide to alter those resulting behaviors. She didn't expect me to turn back the clock, she was happy to be with a fifty-five-year-old man. She simply wanted me to change a variety of behaviors and become the best fifty-five-year-old man I could be. During the past three weeks as new awareness of how I had shortchanged Christine became almost a daily theme, I became aware of what my wife needed and wanted in the future. She wanted and deserved a running partner. She didn't need a man who isolated himself in his room most nights, no matter what his reasons. She loved not only the music that I wrote for her, but that it came from a place of deep caring within me. She had every right to expect those things and many more from me. The two nights we were spending together showed each of us how much the other cared and the extent to which we would go to love our mate more deeply in the future.

At one point in the evening, long after our dinner was enjoyed and the dishes were cleaned and put away, we were sitting together on the couch. We were each snacking on a regular flavored Klondike bar with a huge glass of apple juice on the side when I decided to exert myself with profound and complete honesty.

"Christine, I wish I could come home tomorrow. But there are a few things I need to share with you that will greatly affect the time table for that return."

She looked into my eyes with unwavering intensity.

"There are four things that I don't want to bring back home with me. One is alcohol. I can promise you that I will never bring another bottle of alcohol into this house again. I know myself I don't want to make promises I can't keep. Have I ever broken a promise to you?"

"No."

"The next one is my devil dreams. I don't know what will be harder, giving up alcohol or getting rid of the devil dreams. Even though they are very personal, they always leave me with a negative emotional residue. You don't deserve to be around that when it happens. It's the same thing as a hangover but on an emotional level."

"Then there's the Two-Knock Ghost. I don't know what it is or why it is, but it frightens me because I think it is going to exacerbate every bit of suffering I've gone through with the devil by a multitude of fold."

"Finally, you don't deserve an isolationistic husband. For almost thirty-five years I've been going to my bedroom to work almost every night. For most of those years I felt justified in doing so—rationalizing that it made me a better psychologist to be super prepared for each of my clients. But since I've been on my own in the condo, I've realized more that I've always felt loneliness when I first went into that room to do my work. Something's wrong with me to cause me to feel that way time after time. I'd like to find out what it is. As far as I can figure, I have absolutely no reason to feel that peculiar type of loneliness. I had great parents, super grandparents, met you young and we were always close, and had three great kids. There's no reason for that emptiness I feel when I go into that bedroom. But those last four things are big reasons why I hired a psychologist. I'd like to come home free from all of those conditions. Those are my four personal demons, Christine, and you don't need to be subjected to any of them."

Christine's eyes were glistening with love for me.

"Thank you for being so honest with me. A few months ago when I sent you away, I asked you not to come home until you were a changed man. In these past two days you've let me know that you've identified your demons. That is amazing, Turf. You're so far ahead of many people who never identify their demons and consequently can never work through and conquer them. Everyone has demons."

"Even you?" I asked, somewhat stunned.

"Even me, Turf." She kept calling me that nickname seldom used in recent years, reminding me of that time when I was young, strong, happy go lucky, sporty, believed the future was golden before me. I watched her closely as she spoke, noticing in this moment her roundish, pretty, naturally puffy lips. Then my eyes went to her hair, seeing several more grays among the blacks then when I left the marital household a few months ago.

"Like what? What demons could possibly torment you?"

"Yours."

She paused for a poignant moment holding my eyes with her magnetic gaze.

"All of your demons now belong to me as well. And as long as it takes for you to feel you have conquered those demons is as long as I have to wait for you to come back home, the man that you and I both want you to be. And that leads me to my worst demon of all."

She paused again, sadder than a moment before when she told me that my demons were hers.

"What's that, Christine?" I asked, kindly.

"I thought that you might know this one, being that you're a pretty good psychologist."

"I really can't imagine. Tell me, please."

"Losing you, Turf. The fear of losing you to anyone or all of your demons is my greatest demon."

I was looking deeply into the vast reservoir of love Christine held in her eyes for me. They were different eyes that had firmly sent me packing a few months earlier. I knew it had been done for me and our own good, but in spite of my egregious stumble of a day ago, much of that good had already been accomplished. Christine had evolved not in the same way that I had, but she had evolved. She had studied me closely the past two days and had seen enough to conclude not only that I was on the right path, but that now was not a time to be harsh with me, but to be loving and supportive. Her eyes alone gave me the desire to speed up my healing so I could get back to her as quickly as possible. I wasn't thinking of myself now, while focusing on the connection that was our mutual gaze, I was thinking of her, of minimizing her having to ponder the demons I had revealed to her.

"Can I stay the night, Christine?"

She didn't say anything, simply slowly shook her head yes, while her intrepid eyes whispered, could there be any other answer.

* * * * *

The next two days were a symphony of kindness between us. We shared Saturday breakfast at home, Saturday dinner at Lee Gardens on Fourth Street North. Sunday I treated Christine to a marvelous brunch at Shepard's on Clearwater Beach, spent the day relaxing on the beach two blocks away, then showered, freshened up as best we could, put on the nice clothes we had worn to lunch and capped off the weekend with another wonderful meal at the Salt Rock Grill, a few miles south of Clearwater Beach.

Without even speaking about it, we were both thinking that it would be best if I drove back to the Beaches of Paradise after I dropped Christine at home after dinner. That would allow each of us a few hours to transition comfortably to our individual routines, which had been joyfully interrupted the past two days.

How could I know driving back to our beautiful home on Snell Island that one of the most magnificent moments of my life awaited me before I left Christine? When we arrived there, I went to our bedroom, grabbed a few casual and tee shirts, a pair of dress shoes and a few newer pieces of underwear and socks to take back with me to the condo. I was only in the house five minutes. Christine had come upstairs too and was in our bathroom brushing her teeth when I said, "Honey, I'm just about to leave," as I stuffed the items I had gathered into one of the many travel bags I owned.

Before she rinsed the toothpaste from her teeth, she said, "I'll be right down to join you and say good-bye."

I carried my things downstairs and placed the bag a foot and a half in front of the front door. By the time I turned to start for the living room, she was right behind me. I had heard her bare feet bounding quickly over the carpeted stairway from the second floor.

"You're cute," I said, feeling boyish and I looked into the girlish glow in her eyes.

"Thank you, Mr. Turf," she said playfully.

Mr. Turf . . . I wondered, where did that come from?

Prompted by a boyish urge, I bent downward slightly and with a wraparound hug I lifted my beautiful wife off the ground. Instinctively, she wrapped her arms around my back. My boyishness dissolved as Christine rested her head on top of my shoulders, nestling it tenderly, as if it was a gift against my neck. And there it was, the moment I will remember till the day I die. It was the "Endless Moment," the boy in me again becoming the man who fate had entrusted with the care of this lovely soul he held in his arms. It was the "Transforming Moment" because until it occurred, I was still feeling residue of shame for my Thursday slide back into the bottle. In this lingering moment I felt power flowing into my actual body and my spiritual and emotional self. Some of it was flowing into me from my wife, like she had an on button that she had flicked into position which allowed a palpable electrical love to flow from her body into mine. As I held her during the "Eternal Moment," I felt like the star of a great romance novel that had been made into a movie. In this scene, the camera circled us quickly a multitude of times, revealing the depth of feeling the hug expressed from mate to mate from every angle. Some of the power was emanating from beyond the magnificent hug. I thought it might be coming from my higher power, God, the universe—from some entity greater than I. And I thanked it repeatedly, knowing with certainty that I would win in the end. Undoubtedly there would be a struggle, but I would learn from it things I did not know about myself. They would make me a better man, husband, father, psychologist. I would conquer the devil dreams, identify the Two-Knock Ghost, beat alcohol and figure out why loneliness always accompanied my isolationist treks to my bedroom. Through my hug, I soundlessly told my wife of the profound depths of love I had for her and assured her that in a short period of time I would figure out all of my challenges and return home a better husband than I'd been since the night of my twenty-fourth birthday.

I chose not to pursue my wife's lips. If she was feeling anywhere near what I was, the hug was more than enough. It was a novel in an instant, a history, our lifetime in a moment that would not end. Christine did not move. She clung to me like a child holding on to daddy. But this was a wonderfully loving woman who had not moved a centimeter since she had nuzzled her head into its current resting position several minutes ago.

When gravity began to suggest it was time to put Christine back down on the ground, I listened carefully to what my wife was telling me she wanted me to do, how she wanted the Eternal Moment to end. It was her complete lack of movement that prompted me to carry her to the couch where with my right hand I positioned a large throw pillow upon which I would place my head. Then carefully I positioned my butt on the couch, slowly lowered my body to the pillow and cushion, with Christine immovably onto my body. Then I lifted my legs, with shoes on, onto the lower portion of the couch.

Christine never moved. Her hands were clutched around my back. Her head was tucked into the 90 degree corner between my head and shoulders. I moaned appreciatively as I felt the soft brush of her lips against my neck and smelled her fresh breath going in and out of her in a regular peaceful rhythm. I had no idea whether Christine was asleep or barely clinging to consciousness. But wherever she was between the two worlds, she was serenely comfortable. I would not disturb her. As a result, the "Unending Moment" continued. Holding my wife in this way was freezing time, as negative thoughts evaporated and my fading conscious mind could only focus on the profundity of the moment I was sharing.

I had never felt more powerful in my entire life. It was determined power, the kind of power a person feels preceding a series of life altering actions. It was the power of knowing, of knowing the outcome of future events before their unfolding. During this "Elongated Moment" while enveloping Christine in my arms, I realized that this was the most real and important aspect of my life and that in my future I must cherish and nurture the woman on top of me with every fiber of my being. The devil dreams and the Two-Knock Ghost were just dreams. Obviously, though I didn't know what had caused them, they were obviously the result of things from my childhood that had frightened and hurt me. I knew enough about psychology to know that much. And my recurring loneliness and my isolationist tendencies, could they all possibly be tied together somehow?' I had never considered that before, but in the Moment of All Moments my mind was soaring. For a while it seemed free of all encumbrances. There was no doubt, no worry, no guilt or sadness related to Toby, no devil fears, not even curiosity as to the nature of the Two-Knock Ghost. I was trying my best to be in the moment, to participate fully. What was emanating from Christine to me was all the powerful energy of unbridled love. If it is true that God is love, then I was holding God tenderly beneath my hands and arms.

Unknowingly, I fell asleep. It was dreamless until, after several hours, the live oak appeared in its idyllic scene amidst the resplendent green grass with the babbling brook in front of it under a clear blue sky. Christine and I were sitting on the swing holding hands. Her head was resting on my right shoulder. This time the swing was attached to the same branch, but it was much closer to the ground, the perfect height for us to scoot onto and off it. The tree was healthy again and thriving. The swing was new. Nothing was burned and the grass was glistening under a morning dew. The temperature bordered on the cool side, but overall was pleasantly mild.

Our dream selves were not speaking to one another, but it was evident that we were communicating deeply, from a realm beyond the silence. A slight breeze gently moved the swing forth and back, forth and back. There was a finality to the picture, like it was the last scene to a happily ending love story where the character's body language was saying: "And they lived happily ever after." As I observed the dream, I thought it out of place in the sequence of my real life. Certainly this was too early for the seeming finality of this scene. Much work was left to be done by me to improve myself, and until tonight I had no idea what work Christine might have to do with her issues, many of which had been caused by me. I felt a flash of shame pass through me as I considered how selfish I had been with her, how spiritually unaware I was of so many things. I thought, while watching the lovers on the undulating swing, that it would serve each of us better if I could return home to Christine with a few more awareness within my being. What they might be, I had no earthly clue.

That was the totality of one dream that night of "My Everlasting Moment." There was no devil, no suspicious knocks, only the dream as I have described it. I took it as much needed and appreciated encouragement. I thanked my higher power for it. Eventually the scene faded to black and sometime after, I awoke. Christine was still above me, though she had shifted her arms. They were no longer around me, but rested against my sides with her hands upon my shoulders. With a momentary, yet pervasive sadness, I decided that it would be I who ended "The Hours Long Moment" and head for the condo.

With utter gentility and tenderness, I shifted my weight from the couch as I carefully slid Christine from my body. I cradled her head in my hands and set it upon the same pillow that I had been sleeping on for the last seven hours. I had not awakened her. I checked my watch, 3:00 a.m. I felt remarkably rested, didn't want to take a chance of waking Christine, so I didn't even kiss the back of her head like I wanted. Instead, I tiptoed to the hallway by the front door, grabbed my travel bag and walked out the door, locking it before driving off. For as long as I could see the house, I kept looking into the rearview mirror, realizing that the woman I had left there might very well be my higher power. If not, at least my far better self.

CHAPTER 18

I THOUGHT ABOUT alcohol a thousand times a day, but every time I thought of it, the word *no* came leaping to the forefront of my mind. The word *no* became a soldier, a warrior of mythical proportions, there to protect me from myself and from any bottle of rum I might ever consider to procure. The soldier held his brilliant sword ready to swing it on my behalf against my weaker self. It was easy to continually implore the redundant no warrior to assist me. It was necessary and effective.

More than the warrior no, my greatest ally was focus, a near God. From Monday morning until life would end for me one day, I needed to stay focused on behaviors that would make me a better man: Running, writing music, staying out of my bedroom to work on my client notes, conquering my addiction to alcohol, ending the devil dreams, identifying the Two-Knock Ghost, developing my relationship with Christine and my children, figuring out something wonderful to do for Toby's wife and their children, and developing more insights into the true nature of myself and humanity. These were the multitude of worthwhile ventures I needed to focus on. How many things I had to ponder that held more prominence than whether I should have a drink.

Soon it was Wednesday evening and my appointment with Dr. Banderas. Though I was not seeing him for his assistance in helping me conquer alcohol, I told him of my Thursday collapse immediately upon beginning our session. I explained to him that Toby had been my client and how I had solicited him to help me find Mary Bauer's nemesis. I explained my guilt, although almost miraculously much of it had abated, and I told him of my visits with Christine and how they had helped me deal with my initially rampant angst.

"Marvelous," he said after I had spoken nonstop through 25 percent of our session. "If Christine had not come and given you her love and support, you might have gone on a four day binge, right?"

"That's what I felt like doing before she joined me at the condo."

"It is wonderful that you now know that you have that depth of support because you will be fortified by it as you face the difficult work that lies ahead of you."

It was a complete diversion from what we had been talking about, but I was so curious about his answer to my next question that I went right for it.

"Have you thought anymore about my Two-Knock Ghost?"

"I have," he answered quietly while shaking his head. "And rather extensively I might add."

I wondered what he could possibly mean by rather extensively, considering the details I had imparted to him were so limited. Two knocks here, two knocks there, hard knocks, soft knocks, frenzied knocks, always two by two and no showing of itself, not even for a single instant, ever. Countless intrusions on the outer peripheries, but never an entry. How could he have pondered that extensively?

"I held up what I knew about your Two-Knock Ghost as if it were a cup and I wanted to see it from every possible angle. I began looking at the cup not only as the actual ghost, but I factored in each back story you've ever told me about how hard it knocked, when it intruded, how many times it knocked, etc. Here are some of my hypothesis. Number one, the Two-Knock Ghost is particular to only you. No other of my patients has ever expressed anything close to being plagued by something like that. Next, there is a reason for its existence. Until now, you have always considered the knocks as precursors of impending doom. What if the knocks are a sign of good manners?"

"Good manners?" I was stunned.

"How many times would you estimate the Two-Knock Ghost has infiltrated your personal space?"

"Two hundred," I answered.

"And it's never come in?"

"Correct."

"In my thoughtful meanderings about the possible intentions of this shy ghost, I have considered that the creature may be knocking in order to ask your permission to enter your dreams."

I hung upon his every word. He had done it, not solved the riddle of my ghost, but he gave me a completely different perspective from which to look at Two-Knock. And it was both less frightening and spiritually refreshing. In fact, what he said might only have been one of countless possible clues, but it reminded me that sometimes the truth of something is the complete antithesis of what it appears to be. But Dr. Banderas had said it and suddenly I had something else to consider. A well-mannered ghost? Okay, but come on.

"Any other thoughts about it?"

"Yes. Do we both acknowledge the fact that most of the things that plague us as fears in our waking life and in our dreams are a direct result of situations that occurred in our youth?"

"I agree that for the most part that's true."

"Then let's proceed. Is there anything you can remember about your childhood where someone tried to frighten you about ghosts? Before you answer, think very hard, take your time."

I began scanning my entire childhood beginning with my first memory of falling off a large purple tricycle and bloodying my face on the concrete when I was about four. I recalled my school days, my friends, my teachers, who were usually nuns, and they never talked about ghosts except the Holy one. I thought about the camping trips with my parents and my Boy Scout buddies. Lots of ghost stories came up. Some of them were horrifying, sometimes a little funny while they were scaring the daylights out of me, but I never put any credence in them. They were just stories. I allowed them to frighten and amuse me in the moment then I moved on. I didn't believe in ghosts.

"There's nothing, Doctor."

"There is something, Dr. McKenzie, and it's our job to find it together. Now if there is nothing that you can recall then perhaps our strategy in how we perceive the ghost must change. Have you ever considered that the Two-Knock Ghost may want to help you, that it might be friendly?"

Well mannered and friendly? I kept the somewhat comical thoughts to myself.

"What do you think about my last hypothesis?" he asked after the silence between us lasted too long.

"I haven't had enough time to analyze it," I answered, telling the truth.

"Let me help you. By applying some principles of logic, I might help you see the ghost in a different light. Tell me, how long has the ghost been bothering you?"

"About four and a half months."

"Earlier, you said that it's made its presence known in your space over two hundred times, correct? So about 140 days, 200 visits. Has the ghost ever physically hurt you in a dream or in real life?"

"No."

"But you're afraid of it."

"Yes."

"Why?"

"Because, most of the time I hear it, it's accompanying a devil dream and it's the most horrendous moment of my entire life."

"But the ghost has not hurt you, correct?"

"But I know it will." I answered his question like a frightened child.

"I must challenge your assumption, Dr. McKenzie," he said intensely, looking every bit and more of his seventy-plus years.

"Right now you are projecting your greatest fears onto an entity you do not even know. You are fearing the unknown and have been doing so since the beginning. The ghost now knows that you consistently fear and reject it. If it ever had the desire to assist you in some way, but feels rejected by you, it may never get the chance to help you and it may keep knocking and annoying and frightening and haunting you forever."

Boy, this guy had a vivid imagination. I was speechless. He saw it immediately as the first second passed when he finished speaking.

"I see you're speechless," he said after eleven more seconds had passed. "I must tell you that I have a reputation for getting my clients into this condition on numerous occasions," he said with a twinkle in his eye and looking younger. "May I boldly suggest that you dig deeply within yourself to find your bravery? Then, once you have, you will be able to begin retraining your conscious mind to at least accept the possibility that the ghost is an ally and may want to help you and not hurt you."

"I can see the logic in your thinking, Dr. Banderas," I said reluctantly. "But the difficulty lies in the fact that your idea is 180 degrees opposite of what I've been thinking all along."

"Therein lies the work that you will have to put in, Dr. McKenzie. It will not be easy for you to change your perception of your ghost, but the process of change is always started by a single thought. That thought doesn't always have to originate with the person that wants to make a change. In this case, it has been I who has implanted the thought within you. Now, it will be your task to inculcate that concept into your thinking as something you embrace as viable. The next step will be to invite the ghost in when it knocks again. If it comes in, you will see it and know what it is and finally figure out what roll it has in your life. If it does not enter your dream, we will keep turning the cup and come up with new ideas and new strategies. I can assure you that my next ideas will be far less than 180 degrees from your rationale zone."

New material, I thought. I always liked new material. Whether it came from a comedian, a president, Christine, my kids, or in this case, my psychologist.

I knew Dr. Banderas expected a remark from me. He very much deserved it. He had put a great deal of thinking into my behalf.

"Dr. Banderas, I will go home tonight and begin thinking about everything you have suggested, I promise." I was being 100 percent sincere.

"Dr. McKenzie, there is one more topic I would like to share with you. No matter how expansive and limitless the human mind may be, where so many aspects are unknown to one another, it may also be compared to a tiny box where everything is intimately related, even intertwined with everything else within the box. There is nothing random, nothing that stands alone. This is one of many dualities which exist in the human mind. In your specific case, I am considering your ghost, the devil, your seemingly inappropriate loneliness, your isolationist tendencies and lastly your drinking. I am curious as to what your mind will ultimately reveal to you about how these elements of your life are related, or if they are related at all."

Dr. Banderas's voice was fracturing as he spoke. I assumed he'd had a long day and was tired. During his last few sentences, the twinkle was gone from his eyes. His thoughts were deep and serious and when he spoke them, he looked every bit of the seventy-two years that he was. I noticed the lines on his face, deep furrows in some places. I wondered how he'd developed each of them. Were they the result of a half century of profound contemplation as he had been doing for me? Or had sadness put them there? Had his personal failures put them there? Or was it simply a fluke of genetics? I concluded that it was probably a combination of all these things and maybe more. I enjoyed looking at the man's face. It was contemplative, intense, yet serene and kind. He had, only moments before, spoke of the dualities of the human mind and now I was considering the complex nature of his facial roadmap. In the next few seconds I searched the contour of his face. I felt honored to have chosen this man as my therapist. Then I spoke.

"I am impressed with your thinking on my behalf, Dr. Banderas. I have no idea what will come of it, but I promise I will consider every aspect of what you have told me."

"That is all I can hope for sir," he said.

There were a few more sentences that passed between us that Wednesday evening, but I've shared with you what was more important. Dr. Banderas had given me an entirely new perspective from which to look at everything that had been bothering me for a long time. Now, in good faith, and as directed, I would force myself to be open to his suggested possibilities.

I felt so comfortable in the lush jungle office that I didn't want to leave. But when I did so, I put a smile on my face and shook Dr. Banderas's hand. I was looking down to his eyes that were several inches below mine. He was smiling a little Munchkin like smile. His eyes sparkled with the knowledge that he had contributed something unique to my thinking. Even though I stood a full eight inches taller than Dr. Banderas, as I walked out of his office I felt myself intellectually and spiritually looking up to him as if he were a giant of a man.

Dianne was still working, obviously tired, but pleasant as always.

"Same time next week, Dr. McKenzie?"

"Yes, ma'am," I said.

I wrote her a check, handed it to her, said good-bye and left, immediately heading for the Serenity Club. It was my first time to go there since last Wednesday. I had attended meetings Monday and Tuesday nights, but I had gone to a different venue, this one on Forty-Ninth Street North, much closer to my condo. I was afraid to go back to the Serenity Club because I thought that the memories of Toby would tear me apart and work against my sobriety. At the new place, there was a guy there with a big nippy dog. The first night I tried to pet it, but the dog growled, then snapped at me in the lobby. At break time, I watched the dog nip at six or seven people. It annoyed me. The next night the man with the dangerous dog was there again. I stayed away from them, but my curiosity kept my eyes glued to them. The dog nipped at almost everyone it passed. There was a viciousness about the animal and an "I couldn't care less" attitude in the owner. I was appalled that the man was allowed to have the dog with him. It wasn't a service animal. I didn't want to speak up about it because I was the newbie. I decided Tuesday night when I left the Forty-Ninth Street meeting place that I would return to the Serenity Club no matter how I felt. I didn't want to see that dog tear into someone one day.

As I drove to the Serenity Club, I enjoyed working on my approaches to my clients for Thursday. It was 8:30 already. The meeting started at 9:00. I didn't have time for a relaxed dinner so I stopped briefly at a McDonald's and grabbed a super-hot filet of fish and a diet Coke. But what I thought about most that night on the way to the meeting, even when I was contemplating my strategies to utilize with my clients, was how much personal work I had to do. There was unfinished business everywhere. In fact, it seemed as if my entire life was unfinished business. While I pondered that, I came to believe that my entire future life was unfinished business. But all of that was too immeasurable to fathom. I needed to focus on the here and now. I reasoned that I had two battlefields; one was practical, one was mystical. I couldn't do anything about the devil dreams or the Two-Knock Ghost, but I could absolutely break down what had to be done on the pragmatic level. First, I needed to do whatever it took never to drink again. Second, I needed to figure out what to say to and give to Alicia Magnessun. Third, I needed to consistently increase my respect and affection for Christine. Fourth, I needed to be a more consistent and caring father. And lastly, I needed to put it all together, everything I would learn, and become a better psychologist and human being.

I decided as I found a parking space a block from the crowded Serenity Club, that over the next few days I would jot down a variety of ideas relating to Alicia Magnessun and present to her my final words and gifts within two weeks of Toby's funeral, which had been scheduled for Saturday morning, nine days after Toby's death. I wouldn't miss the funeral for the world. Strangely, but unbelievably lovingly, Christine would call me at the office and ask me if I would like her to be at my side for the funeral. I would say yes, and we put our plan into effect, which included dinner and an overnight on Snell Island on Friday night.

But it was still Wednesday and I had to face being at the meeting knowing that Toby would not be there tonight or any other night ever. I knew a rum and Coke would take the edge off all my miserable feelings. I felt vulnerable as I thought that I would forever crave a rum and Coke. After a rum and Coke or two or three, they would always take the edge off my anxiety. My toughest job in my future life would be not to surrender to that nagging knowledge.

I didn't speak at the meeting. It wasn't because I didn't have anything to say. It was because my story of Toby and Mary and Reubin, the shootout and my wanting to be friends with Toby, was too complicated, too convoluted. I listened instead to everyone else's problems and there was escape and comfort enough in that.

I stayed through the entire meeting, my mind consistently wandering to thoughts of Toby's wife and children and what kindness I could do for them. I made up my mind that I would never tell Alicia that it was I who had asked Toby to help look for Reubin Tatum. I decided that, based on the current popular phrase, "too much information." In this case, I felt that revealing to Alicia that Toby was my client and friend, and that I thought that someday Christine and I, and she and Toby would probably have become friends, was enough. My greatest fear in regard to Alicia was that Toby had told her all about my request, and she would despise me from the announcement of my name at her front door.

I thought about what amount of money I would give to her and the children. That seemed the easiest part of all. With the insurance money I had received from the deaths of my parents and grandparents, I had become fairly wealthy at a young age. And with Christine's keen mind and the thirty years of ongoing assistance from her father's keen financial mind, we had doubled our holdings a few times. I didn't want to make her feel like I was giving it to her as if she were a charity. On the other hand, I didn't want to arouse suspicions in her either, that I might have had something to do with Toby's death and I felt guilty. She would have been 100 percent correct about my second line of concern. I prayed to God to let her be ignorant of this one fact of her husband's life. God forbid that my showing up at her home would hurt her more. Then I felt my shame and worry urging me to take a drink of rum and Coke. Just one. I could control it. The pain I was feeling right now wasn't that bad. A few ounces of ice cold rum and Coke would make it all better. These thoughts passed through my mind in their entirety until I thought: "And yeah, a single drink right now could ruin your life. Is it really worth it, no matter how cold and tasty and comforting it might be?" Of course I answered no. But the thought of thirst had to be replaced. I decided that on the way home I would stop at a 7-Eleven, buy a tall drink glass, no matter what it cost, fill it with ice, then buy however many small bottles of apple juice that it took to fill that soda glass. Now I was craving freezing cold apple juice. I had beaten back one of my demons again. I wondered how many thousands of these mental skirmishes I would have in my future; then I thought about the tree.

My mind had been cluttered with thoughts moving faster than clouds on a windy day that I hadn't thought of the live oak until the meeting was almost over. Immediately, I decided I would go to see it this night. I was surprised a few minutes later, when actually leaving the meeting, two or three people said hi to me in a very friendly way and that two different people unbelievably said to me something to the effect of, "We haven't seen you for a few days." I was touched that people might have missed me. Then I wondered what they might be thinking and may have already said about Toby.

The short drive to the live oak was, for the first time, heartbreaking. Seeing it was worse. Before I got out of the car I was overcome with emotion, dropped my head to the steering wheel and cried the heaviest tears I had in decades. When my waterworks ceased, I got out of the car, leaned against the right quarter panel and gazed at the tree that had made its way into my dreams. It was so broad, so stately and majestic as it continued to spread itself out over the street and three neighbors' homes. It was all that I had left of Toby—something spectacular that he loved. Why should I feel so sad? The tree was still here, enriching the lives of everyone who saw it. I should be thankful that Toby thought enough of me to show it to me. I was being uninsightful thinking that the tree was all I had left of Toby. I had all the memories of our talks. I had helped him begin AA and to feel that he was gaining control over alcohol. Most of all, I instinctively felt that he knew that I was his friend. And I knew in my heart that had he lived, developing a friendship with Toby outside of the office was something I would have not been able to deny.

Someday I would show Christine this tree. If there was an opportunity, I would show each of my children. And the tree would add more people to the list of lives it had enriched. After my initial sadness here tonight, I began to feel joy again for being able to look upon such a powerfully beautiful living thing. Once again, inspiration flowed from the tree into my being. The inspiration was encouragement to be a better man, to be stronger, to broaden my horizons, to conquer my demons and to help others conquer theirs.

Nine minutes later I was enjoying the apple juice drink that I had fantasized about during the meeting. It was wonderful. Over all, I thought I had a pretty good day. I worked, helped people there, had a great session with Dr. Banderas, attended all AA meeting, did not have a rum and Coke, saw the tree, and was unwinding my day with icy apple juice on my drive home. I was feeling confident that I would enjoy a demon free sleep and wake up refreshed for my Thursday morning run. I was wrong again.

The first few hours of my sleep were indeed peaceful. Then the devil boldly intruded. This time Lucifer was a cruel Nazi guard and I was a frail Jewish prisoner of war in an unknown concentration camp. Both the devil and I were in a courtyard, completely devoid of any other people. I was locked in a stock, my hands and head sticking out in front of a wooden grate that was latched so I couldn't escape. The back half of me was on my knees on frozen earth. I was shirtless and shivering as falling snow settled on my back and hair. The devil guard was standing before me with a whip.

"It has come to my attention that you have sought help from outside the camp in order to facilitate the termination of your imprisonment here."

Though it was a dream, I concluded quickly that he was referring to my seeking counseling from Dr. Banderas.

"Yes I have," I said as cockily as I could muster.

"That is unacceptable Prisoner 92719. For that you must be punished. Ten lashes with a whip."

Already the cold was unbearable. I felt my eyelashes begin to freeze. Though I had acted cocky a moment before, I wondered how I could possibly endure ten lashes from my jailer. The devil walked behind me sneering. He raised the whip. My body tightened and I clinched my teeth. As the Prince of Darkness began to swing the whip toward my body, I heard a pair of frenzied knocks. "Goddamn it, not now!" I said at the same time the whip lashed my back. Upon the strike, the whip had curled around my ribs and reached the middle of my chest. My skin was torn from me and I could feel the bloodletting quickly from my wound.

"Why now you asshole?" I yelled at the Two-Knock Ghost, directing more anger toward it than toward my purveyor of pain. "Do you want to come in and join the fun?" I had fallen back to my same old way of thinking.

A second whip strike. This time my breath was stolen completely from me as fresh skin was ripped from my body again.

Then came two more knocks. I screamed a blood curdling scream, partly in complete fear and frustration and partly to frighten Two Knock away. My head lowered as far as it could toward the ground as my dream body felt more pain than when the devil began to eat my face many nightmares ago. My soul was crashing into its deepest ever pit.

"Come in," I said, barely audible while questioning whether I could live through eight more strikes from the whip, remembering Dr. Banderas's advice. "I have nothing left with which to resist you. Come in and reveal yourself. If you're evil, then you can assist the devil and finish me off right here, right now. If you're a friend, I need you now more than ever."

I screamed with excruciating pain as the third strike ripped across my spine. Instead of staying down, my head snapped upward toward the gray sky. Suddenly, a warm wind blew the snow away and a single illuminated and glowing gold and yellow door appeared in the southeastern sky above. I maintained my fixed gaze, fully expecting an army of Satan's Nazis to come running through it. I knew the devil enjoyed big productions. Why not now? He turned to look, but not as if he expected to see what was happening. The door burst open and a man and woman flew through it with incredible speed. They were dressed in white leotards like the ones Olympic gymnasts' wear, and they headed straight for the Prince of Nazis. They landed firmly on the ground, their backs before me, and with the rage of angels, began beating the devil unmercifully. Satan was helpless beneath the pummeling. As the onslaught of punches continued, all of the devil's blood splattered away from the wild couple, so their garments remained pure white during their entire attack. Then the woman bent down and picked up the whip. The man had punched the devil into a submissive position on the earth. He had weakened the demon, enough that he was able to hold it to the ground by forcefully pushing down upon his head. Then the woman began snapping the whip across the earthbound devil's back. I saw him writhing in agony with every strike, his head raising up enough that I could hear his screams.

Upon the sixth of the woman's whip strikes to the devil's back, buttocks, legs, and feet, the devil Nazi summoned enough power to push himself off the ground and out of his holder's hand vice. But instead of attempting to fight back, the devil arched his back, throwing his head toward the still open and glowing door and screamed a defeated whale. My imprisoned body actually felt the sound waves from his cry. Then he vaporized.

The woman dropped the whip and walked proudly to the man. He took her hand as she helped him stand. They embraced as if celebrating a victory, then capped it off with a gentle, slightly lingering kiss. Then they turned and began walking toward me. It was my parents.

"What the . . .?"

"Robert, you finally let us in," my mother said while flashing her beautiful and long missed smile.

"Mom! Dad! What are you doing here? I've never dreamed about you before. Why are you here now?"

"We have much to tell you son," my father said as he opened the stock which entrapped me. "But we can't tell it all to you now."

He lifted my abused body out of the stock and placed me on the ground with my head in my mother's lap.

"The place where we come from has very specific rules and we only have a moment here now before we'll have to leave."

"But you only just got here," I said while acutely feeling the pain of my injuries.

"We can come back again, Robert, if you'll only let us in when we knock," my mother said. She was touching the wounds on my chest and shoulders and when she did so, the torn and battered skin miraculously healed.

"Let me help you son," my father said, as he gently turned me over so my mother could heal my back.

They were younger than I was, in their late forties—the exact ages they were when the drunk driver killed them. And my dream self was fifty-five. The same age as my real self—the dream observer.

"Did you come from heaven?" I asked as I sat myself upright to the right of my parents.

"Not exactly," my father said.

"We haven't seen the light yet," my mother said matter-of-factly. "We know we will, but we've got unfinished business with you. When that is completed, we can advance to the next level, whatever that might be."

I felt so lucky and safe near them. I leaned over and hugged my mother first.

"I love you, Mom. I've missed you. Thank you for saving me from this nightmare with the devil."

"You're welcome, Robert. That's what we're here for. By the time we say our final good-byes, many questions will be clarified for you."

I stood up, walked to my father and extended my hand to help pull him upright.

"You look very handsome and studly in that uniform, Dad," I said as I hugged him tightly, "Like a superhero."

"I've always wanted to be that for you, Robert," he said as he kissed my neck.

"Is that it now, for my devil dreams? Have you two finished him off?"

"We don't know that for sure, Robert," my father answered. "What you dream about is partly a mystery of nature. No one can ever say for certain what you will dream about tomorrow night."

"We can only assure you that we will be back again until we have told to you what we must," my beautiful mother added. I had forgotten how wonderfully lovely she was and how handsome a couple she and my father were.

"Just let us in the next time we knock," my father said with a smile.

"And stop being afraid when you hear us knock," my mother said, mock scoldingly.

"I will, Mom, I promise. But why . . ."

"We have to leave, son. We're being beckoned." My father always called me son. My mother never did. It was always Robert.

"Do you have time for a kiss good-bye?" Both my parents said yes simultaneously. My mother kissed my left cheek and I kissed her right. That was our kiss ritual in real life. My lips had never touched my mother's lips. A moment later, my father kissed me on the left side of my neck where the shoulder starts to jut out. He blew a long and tickling fart sound. Then I kissed my father on the right side of his neck, blowing a loud and tickling fart sound as well. That was our kissing ritual. It saddened me to remember that the last time I had said goodbye to them this way was thirty-one years ago.

Then they held hands as they turned away and floated upward through a now blue sky to the still golden glowing open door. When they passed through, the door closed and faded away.

I could not believe what had just happened. Both my dream self and my observer self—the real me—were in shock. The Nazi prisoner was totally woundless. He was wishing he could have completed the question he was asking when his parents announced their ascension. It was going to be, "But why do you only knock twice when you want to come into my dreams?" But he had not because time did not permit. He stood there wondering about what had occurred. But he felt remarkably soothed by his parents' appearance and completely hopeful that they would return again quickly. The dream ended and a few minutes later I awoke. Instantly, I felt everything my concentration camp character had felt, not as if it had been a dream, but as if the events had really happened to me.

I dismissed trying to dislodge my waking self from my dream self. Things were complicated enough and I began the process of sorting through the dream with my conscious questions.

"Where had my parents come from? Why had they not aged? What more than by combating the devil on my behalf and telling me they loved me could my parents have to reveal to me?" They had been the most open communicative and forthright people I had ever known. My parents were the Two-Knock Ghost?

The questions, that could only be answered by my parents, kept coming relentlessly. Though they seemed endless and wanted to dominate my day, I had to dispel them and work with my clients and call Christine and Dr. Banderas and tell them what had happened. As I ran this morning, I felt lighter and happier than I had in years. And I thought it odd that I truly believed that what my parents told me in a dream—that they would return and tell me things of import—was the truth, not merely isolated dialogue from a random dream.

When I returned to the condo, I played the last song that I had written for Christine on the piano, showered, and shaved and headed for the office.

I was absolutely ecstatic when I greeted Amanda who was sitting at her desk looking resplendent in a red dress with black trim at the bottom, the pocket and the edges of the short sleeves. All the way to the office from the Beaches of Paradise, what I thought about was how lucky I was, how bright my future could be.

Amanda reminded me of my schedule and even though it was almost 90 degrees outside, I said yes when she asked if I wanted hot chocolate. Then immediately I thought she must think I was an odd duck because of that little quirk.

The day went smoothly, as had thousands of similar days before this. I equated the experience to the movie, *Ground Hog Day*. It was nothing special, just my typical day with few deviations. But today my highlights were my two phone calls. The first to Dr. Banderas at noon, and the second to Christine at 5:30. I was fortunate enough that when I called Dianne to ask if Dr. Banderas would speak with me, she asked him and he had said yes—even though I was interrupting his in-office lunch.

"Hello, Dr. McKenzie," he said pleasantly. "It is interesting that you are calling me the day after your appointment. What has happened that you wish to share with me?"

"Dr. Banderas, I took your advice and let the Two-Knock Ghost come into my dream last night."

"And what did it turn out to be?"

"It was my parents."

"So it was not something malevolent?"

"On the contrary, they absolutely saved me from incredible pain in what started out as a horrendous devil dream."

He asked me to describe the dream in detail, which I did. When I finished, I asked him what he thought.

"It was a beautiful dream. It took courage for you to finally, if not somewhat reluctantly, invite the ghost in, not knowing if its intent was to harm you. By doing so, you have taken a giant step forward in your recovery. I'm not sure that I believe in ghosts, but I believe in dreams. And in this case, I believe that Two Knock will return and reveal more. And if it does, you must tell me every detail because the facts of your dream may alter the way I perceive the universe."

"I never expected you to say that."

"We are all each other's teachers, Dr. McKenzie, as you probably already know. But I am certain that your parents will return because they always returned when you did not invite them in. They never gave up before. Why would they give up now, when they finally made contact? It will be the sum total of what they tell you that will influence you so much that it may change your life. And as you reveal the facts in their most minute detail, that is what may alter my perception of the universe as well."

"I promise I will keep you abreast of any dream I have of them, Doctor. And thank you for making me feel like everything I tell you is fascinating and important to you."

"It is, Dr. McKenzie. Each tiny piece of the puzzle that is your dreams is fascinating. But what picture will be revealed when the puzzle is put completely together is what we both anxiously await."

"Thank you, Dr. Banderas."

"You are the utmost welcomed, Dr. McKenzie."

He sounded kind, but I also detected a bit of tiredness in his voice. I wondered for a moment how hard he worked. If he put as much effort and energy into each of his clients as he did for me, he would have every right to be tired. Thinking deeply of the right things to say to people when they are in mental distress or agony can be exhausting. Dr. Banderas was a strong and gentle soul. I could feel the weight of his ponderous mind, which was not unlike mine. I felt we were kindred spirits. He was intelligent and kind. I respected him and genuinely liked what I could see of him as a person.

After I hung up the phone, it was back to work for me. But no matter what I did, the predominant thought in my mind was when will my parents return to my dreams. The answer didn't come soon enough.

Monday night came and went, no dreams of note. Tuesday night was the same. Wednesday nothing, except for my meeting with Dr. Banderas.

I was very excited to see the man who had suggested that I invite the Two-Knock Ghost into my dreams. After a playful interaction with Dianne, I entered my psychologist's plush office. Dr. Banderas stood as I entered. He held his hand out to shake mine as I strode across the room.

"Success," he said, as we squeezed palms. "A good beginning, that's what I like."

"It's a start for sure, but I wonder where we go from here?" I asked.

"We wait," he answered, "patiently and appreciatively of what they have shared with you in their first visit. I don't think you can hustle ghosts along," he said with a twinkle in his eye and a slight smile cracking onto the right side of his shut lips. "They live in their own time and space and we must respect their comings and goings, as they obviously have their own unique agenda."

I enjoyed listening to how this man articulated his thinking. For somebody who had told me he didn't believe in ghosts, he sure seemed to know how to show them courtesy.

"I am the psychologist and you are the client in this relationship, but I am extremely excited to hear what your parents have to tell you, hopefully in the very near future. I don't think I've told you this yet, but sometimes when I'm finished dealing with a client with an interesting case, I dream some kind of dream directly related to it and sometimes I wake up thinking about the facts and circumstances of a case and often lay in bed thinking about it. I've lost thousands of hours of sleep over the years because of this reality."

"I hope you don't lose too much sleep over my case," I said with a twinkle in my eye.

"On the contrary, Dr. McKenzie. I hope I do. Your case has become one of my favorites ever, and now the dream ghost has revealed itself and it's friendly. When I think about my cases during the day, I am always distracted by something or someone, Dianne, a phone call, an emergency. But when I lay in bed and think about things, I am rarely distracted except maybe for my dear wife getting up to go to the bathroom. I even gave a nickname to that type of rumination. I call it, 'wee hour thinking.' And I want to assure you that though I have lost sleep, I have not lost those hours. In fact, I have gained something because most of the time I do my best work while lying flat on my back in bed during 'wee hour thinking.'"

"What have you gained, Doctor?" I asked, feeling intense curiosity.

"Mostly insight, insight into the minds of my clients, sometimes my own mind and often into the nature of the human mind in general."

We talked like that for the rest of the hour, like two men getting to know each other piece by complicated piece. The more he spoke, the more I drifted into that space of wanting the man to be my friend. There was nothing new, nothing earth shattering in our conversation. The predominate theme was his encouraging me to be patient about my parents' return. Also, he encouraged me to be joyful about my dreams and my life in general because not merely one breakthrough was about to happen, but many.

I trusted him and I bought his encouragement and superimposed it upon that which I was producing for myself.

Then Thursday night, nothing in the way of notable dreams.

Finally, it was Friday. I knew Friday would be exciting. Mary Bauer was scheduled for 11:00 a.m. I couldn't wait to see how she was feeling after our last intense conversation.

When she came into the office, I couldn't believe my eyes. The ten years she had aged in the last several months were gone. Her cheeks were rosy and her skin was sun-toned, as if she had spent hours on the beach in the past few days. She was smiling and pretty. The sad scowl which had zapped her of her natural good looks since I had known her had been vanquished by a blithe spirit from within her.

Dr. Banderas's jungle had influenced me and I had recently purchased seven plants from a greenhouse on Central and about Sixty-Eighth Street. They were the first things she commented on as she almost bounded through the door.

"Wow, Dr. McKenzie! Your plants are beautiful. They really liven up the room."

"Thank you, Mary. You look marvelous. To what can we attribute this change for the better?"

"When you told me that Reubin Tatum was gone forever, I took that to heart, Dr. McKenzie. Each time I thought about that and felt better. Then, every time I thought about the rest of Reubin's gang being gone forever, in a cell, I felt better still. I have much to thank you for. You have given me my life back."

A sharp pang of pain hit my stomach and immediately I thought of the soothing effects of rum and Coke. I had given Mary her life back, but I had cost Toby his. For a moment I continued looking at Mary Bauer squarely in the eyes while slowly nodding my head, but not hearing what she said. When she seemed to be finished with her next spoken paragraph, I guessed at what to say to her next.

"How have these improvements in your happiness level influenced your relationship with your husband?"

Mary Bauer was a shy, private person. What she said next surprised me.

"We made love two times this week. Both times it was filled with tenderness and passion. And it was I who initiated almost all of the passion. It's not that my husband had become disinterested in me. It's that he had become tentative in his approach to me because he knew I was hurting emotionally. I knew that I had forced him into that behavior and I wanted to make it up to him. I felt safe with him, loved and adored by him, and I felt free to give of myself. It was the first time I'd felt that way in a long while. I feel like you've helped me to reclaim my marriage too."

Another pang hit my stomach. I had helped Mary Bauer to reclaim her marriage, but I had caused the destruction of Toby Magnessun's. I wished I had a bottle of rum and Coke in the office, so as soon as Mary left, I could take a drink and put a Band-Aid on the massive guilt wound that I had. It was yet another of those thousands of skirmishes I knew I would have in my battle to stay sober. I quickly dismissed my desire for alcohol and tried to replace it by feeling some joy that Mary and her husband were mending.

"What about the cruise?" I asked.

"We're going. I won't have anything to worry about while we're gone. We're so excited."

She was ebullient. I was genuinely happy for her.

"Dr. McKenzie, there is one thing that is bothering me. It's new and it's extremely difficult for me to tell you."

"If you really don't feel comfortable, you don't have to tell me."

"I know that Doctor, but I have to."

She paused and swallowed hard.

"I want this to be my last session with you. School's out, summer's almost here. I'm feeling better. My husband and I are going on a cruise soon. I don't want to think about pain anymore or negative things, specifically, my problems. I didn't have any therapeutic problems before Reubin Tatum. I was very happy. I want to be that woman again. I know I can access her now. You've helped me so much and I thank you for your kindness, logic and consistent encouragement. But I want to look forward, not back. You helped me to move off the horrible spot that I was stuck on. I hope I'm not hurting your feelings by wanting our sessions to end Doctor, but you understand why I'm thinking this way, right?"

She was speaking with a profound fusion of intensity and sincerity, and though it was a difficult moment for her, I could see the strength and confidence of the old Mary I had never seen, emerging.

She would never know the great loss that had been incurred in order to deliver to her the comfort she deserved.

"Of course I understand, Mary," I said after what might have been too long of a pause. "I'm proud of how far you've come so quickly. If you're happy, then I'm happy. If you've made up your mind already, about all I can offer you is to be here for you if you ever need to return for any reason."

"Thank you, Doctor," she said, apparently relieved she didn't get an argument from me.

We talked out the rest of our final hour with rather superficial conversation. It was actually highlighted by Mary's telling me of five new dresses she had already bought for the cruise. She regaled me with glorious details about colors, patterns, lengths and cuts. She spoke quickly as she described the clothes she couldn't wait to wear for her husband. She told me that she wouldn't show him the outfits before she wore them on the cruise. She wanted them to be a surprise. She was giggly as she spoke. All I could do was sit there and watch in amazement at her reacquired joy.

When she departed my office, I felt sad and lonely, the way a person often feels when they finish a good book they took their time reading. I usually felt similar to this when a client reached the end of their time with me. And I wanted a drink. When I was drinking, I never thought about alcohol during my working hours. But now, because I hadn't been drinking—except for my one collapse—it seemed that with every twinge of negative emotions, my body was overcome with cravings for liquor.

I picked up the phone and called Christine. Fortunately, she was at work on a break and able to talk. I asked her if I could take her to dinner, maybe to Lee Gardens, the Chinese Buffet on Fourth Street. She said yes and I immediately felt better.

That night dinner was wonderful. We knew all the waitresses and the hostess, and they knew both of us by our first names. I told Christine about my dream and how the Two-Knock Ghost finally came in and that it was my parents. She listened with interest to every word. She asked me also, if I had any stumbles during the week and I told her no. She smiled.

Throughout the night Christine and I were affectionate with each other. In the car and on the short walk into the restaurant, we held hands. Inside the restaurant we got a booth and decided to sit side by side. There, the affection continued. Often I would rest my hand on her leg and equally as often, she would rest her hand on my leg. It was almost as if we were a young couple again.

I would listen to stories about her job as intently as she would listen to details of my life. The smooth flowing of the equality of our sharing was so wonderful that at one point during dinner my eyes welled with tears as I thought about it. Everything I had ever wanted in life was wrapped up in this tiny woman sitting next to me. Christine noticed my eyes.

"What's the matter, honey?" she asked tenderly.

I simply shook and lowered my head as my eyes closed.

"You're happy right now, aren't you, Turf?" There it was again, my old nickname. And a greater flood of emotion came upon me forcing tears from my eyes like parallel rivers of liquid emotion. I nodded my head yes this time. As Christine reached around my neck and hugged me tightly before kissing me lightly on the neck, the way my father did, but without the funny sounds.

After dinner, during which we consumed at least 30 shrimp each, I drove Christine the short ride back to our home on Snell Island. I parked the car in the driveway and accompanied my wife to the front door and right into the house. We did not need words between us to ask and answer whether I would spend the night with her. It was understood between us in an inner space that was never wrong.

We brushed our teeth at the same time, then Christine put on a pretty pink teddy, and I put on a pair of solid blue cotton pajamas. We were in bed within thirty seconds of one another—Christine first, then me. I snuggled up behind her, curled my body around my resting sweetheart, then brought both my feet up, so they were playing with hers. We were cozy beyond belief. There were no covers above us. The air conditioning was set at the perfect level. We were together and tender, two people who'd had interesting and tiring weeks. Within three minutes and without a word having been spoken or a single kiss being shared. That is how we fell asleep.

Sometime during an undisturbed night of quality sleep, the real excitement began. Thankfully it wasn't a devil dream. I hadn't anticipated having one because they were extremely rare while sleeping with Christine. My favorite live oak appeared. It was recurring in its most recent position as the centerpiece of the tranquil rustic scene. The tree was in front of the creek that ran through the entire scene and the grass was the green of a million emeralds and the sky was a cool blue and cloudless. The white swing was hanging from the tree's lowest branch, and I was sitting on it pensively. I was holding my notebook from work, working on what to say to tomorrow's clients. All of a sudden like a thunder blast from a clear blue sky it broke the moment of tranquility I was enjoying and scared me for an instant. Two knocks, that's all it was. The sounds of the knocks had been augmented by some unknown power, but this time I knew what it was. I looked to the sky where I heard the knocks emanate and said, "Come on down," in an announcer voice, like they do on *The Price is Right*. In a moment the golden glowing door opened and my parents passed through, this time floating down to where I was sitting on the swing. They stopped and stood before me smiling sweetly, my father carrying a large picnic basket, the kind that opens at both ends. My mother spoke first.

"We thought you might be hungry, honey, so we brought a picnic lunch to share while we all chat." I jumped off the swing while my mother pulled a sheet, the same cream color as I wore in my dreams, out of the basket and spread it on the ground. Then each of us sat on it as Mom and Dad took out my favorite foods one by one. I was so happy to be there with them, but one thing was very strange. It was weird being older than them. No one said a word about that. The fact that I had aged and they hadn't was just accepted because I was still living life on earth and they had obviously been in a place where you didn't age. Because of that, we accepted each other for the way we were, but it did raise my curiosity about where they had been all these years and where did they come from these two welcomed visits? Because of my wondering, I asked them my first question.

"Where have you been, Mom and Dad—heaven?"

"Not quite, Robert," my mother answered softly. "We've been in a place called Respite. It's a lovely place where people who have unfinished business with their children or other loved ones go."

My father spoke next. "Respite is a place where people who have caused damage unwittingly to their children and loved ones wait for their loved ones to become in crisis mode because the damage becomes too much to bear."

I was shocked. "Are you saying that you and Mom caused me damage?"

"We are, Robert," my mother said softly. "We're here now to reveal what we did to hurt you."

"But how did you know you hurt me? I honestly don't remember anything but good things that passed between us."

"We always tried to be wonderful with you, Robert, but we were not perfect parents," my mother continued.

"But how did you know you hurt me? Was it some kind of mutual spiritual awareness? Or was it a person from Respite who told you?"

My father gently took over the conversation as the three of us began eating barbeque flavored fried chicken, corn on the cob, coleslaw and baked beans—everything tasting exactly the way those foods tasted when Mom made them while she was alive.

"When we died, son, we saw a white light. It wasn't a brilliant light, but it was the only one we saw, so we followed it. We passed through an unusually lit vortex that was comprised of all the colors of the spectrum. We passed it thinking that this was the eighth wonder of the world, or the first wonder of the world beyond. We were both traveling through the rainbow vortex at the same time, holding hands because we had died at the same instant. We were just lucky to be traveling through the vortex together, I guess. All of a sudden the vortex slowed our speed little by little, until it deposited us on a white cloud that was strong enough to walk on. I was certain we were in heaven because everything I was experiencing was really cool and the laws of physics didn't apply."

Then my father spoke again. "A hundred feet ahead of us was a great white wall that looked like it might be the outer enclosure of heaven. But directly in front of us was a huge golden gate with a giant gold knocker on the right side of the gate. There was no place else to go. There were only clouds at the base of the white walls. We walked to the gate, knocked with the knocker the way we always did when we were alive. First, I banged it once," my father paused and looked at my mother.

"Then I banged it once," my mother said.

"The gate opened immediately," my father continued, "and standing on a cloud waiting to greet us was an angelic man I thought for sure, for a moment, was God. He said, 'Welcome to Respite McKenzies.' He explained to us what Respite was and explained what we had done to hurt you and expressed his confidence in us that we could rectify the situation when the time was right. Now is the time."

My father had said so many things that brought questions to my mind, but the thing that he had spoken that intrigued me the most was when he said that he had knocked with the knocker once and that Mom had followed doing the same thing. Two knocks coming upon Respite. Two knocks before saving me from the devil. Two knocks today. Countless two knocks that I had ignored or that had frightened me to death.

"Dad," I asked with an incredulous look upon my face, "why always the two knocks?"

"Son, when I was in basic training in the air force, I was taught to only knock once on my drill instructor's door if I needed something. Knock once and wait. No matter how long it took for someone to answer that door, knock twice or more when you became impatient and you would have to face embarrassing repercussions from one or more GIs."

"When I returned home after my tour of duty, I told your mother that story. She liked it so much she said . . ." He paused for a moment and he smiled at her as she finished his sentence. "Everywhere we go that we have to knock, why don't you knock once and I'll knock once. That will be one of our own things."

"And that's what we did from that day forward until the night we died," my dad said.

"Don't you remember that, Robert?" my mom asked.

"I have no conscious memory of that guys," I said sincerely. "None."

My mom had brought apple juice for the three of us. Before I was born, it had been my dad's favorite drink. He got my mom into it. She liked it and when I came along, I loved it too. Time was passing slowly in the dream. My parents and I were enjoying a real picnic. There was only joy and one answer already to one of my deepest mysteries. There were no menacing clouds or lightening, no devil in sight. I was thinking, "I dare him to come into this loving scene after my parents kicked his ass in the concentration camp." My father spoke next, as I took a drink of cold apple juice.

"The main reason we are here to see you, son, is also the main of two reasons why we were assigned to Respite instead of heaven. Your mom and I made a bad decision in regard to you when you were a very little boy. We thought we were doing the right thing at the time, but we weren't. We found that out when the Gate Keeper explained it to us."

"What was it, Dad? I don't remember you or Mom ever doing anything to hurt me."

"Son," my father said softly, "when you were two years old, your mom and I had a baby girl. We named her Lena in honor of your mother's grandmother who had the same name. Lena was about two months premature. She was the tiniest of infants, and she was born with a serious heart defect. But she was a fighter and against all odds she was allowed to come home to us when she was six weeks old. We put her in a crib in your bedroom and it worked out well because she was a well behaved baby and maybe too because she was weak, she usually slept through the night and didn't disturb you. From the first moment we brought her into your bedroom you were fascinated with her."

The tag team conversationalists that my mother and father were switched to my mother.

"You would go to the side of the bassinet and stand there for the longest time watching her. Then you wanted to rub her head and face and we both taught you about her soft spot and that when you touched her you had to be extremely gentle, almost as if your fingers were feathers. You would spend hours in that room with her, fascinated with her breathing, her falling asleep, her waking up, why she cried, how she moved her tiny fingers. From the time we brought her home there was no doubt that you spent more time with her than any other person. You doted on her as much as a two-year-old boy possibly could. You even asked us if you could feed her and we taught you to sit on a chair outside the bassinet that was the perfect height for you and you would hold that bottle in her mouth and sit there like a statue until the bottle was empty and you would call out for Mommie."

Dad's turn.

"But Lena was a weak baby. She had to go into the hospital for periodic procedures. When she was gone, you would spend long periods of time in your room. You would look at Golden Books then you'd get up to check the bassinet to see if Lena had magically reappeared. Then you would color and after a while you'd check the bassinet. You might play with your toy instruments or your big Tonka truck or your small Tootsie Toy cars that were from my childhood. But no matter what you were doing, you would always stop yourself and check to see if Lena had returned."

"When your mom would finally carry Lena home from the hospital and put her in the bassinet, you would become the happiest little boy there ever was."

Then my mother said, "While Lena was away at the hospital you would always ask us, 'When that little baby coming home again?' And as the first year passed completely by you started asking, 'When that baby gonna come outside and play with me?' But Lena was so sick because her heart problem never got better and never went away. A few days after Lena turned one and you were just slightly past three, we had to take Lena in for another procedure. This time her weak little heart couldn't take it. She died and never came home again." Mom's eyes welled with tears even after all the years removed from Lena's death.

Dad continued when he saw Mom's tears, "But that didn't stop you from asking about your baby sister. Time after time, day after day, you would ask, 'When that baby coming home again?' No matter what answer we gave you, your questions never stopped. Shortly after Lena died, your mom and I decided to take the bassinet, all her clothes and her precious toys out of the room and put them in storage in the attic so you wouldn't think about her so much. But you still continued asking. One time we told you that Lena had gone to heaven and you asked, 'What's heaven?'"

"We talked it over between ourselves and decided about three months after Lena died never to talk about her again, because we knew that even though you were merely a little boy, you were hurting over the absence of your sister. You asked about her for over a year. Every day you would go into your bedroom and sit on your bed reading or playing with Linkin Logs or your Erector set for hours."

Dad's turn again.

"I'd go in your bedroom to see what you were doing in there so long. You'd say, 'I'm waiting for Lena to come home.' So I'd ask you to come outside and play baseball with me. You'd always say yes. Then we'd play catch and I'd pitch a baseball to you and you got pretty good at throwing, hitting, catching and fielding. When you were three, four, five we would play in our backyard, but after you were six, I promised I would take you to the 'big boy' park. That just happened to be Mark White Park—right across from Bridgeport's famous quarry. Then on an unused diamond, I hit thousands of ground balls and fly balls to you. And every once in a while we'd hear them blasting in the quarry and we'd feel the ground tremble beneath our feet. Do you remember that, Robert?" my father asked proudly.

"I do," I said thankfully with a warm smile upon my face.

While my dream father—half of the Two-Knock Ghost—seemed to relish his memory of our ball playing, my mother chimed in.

"After about three years, we thought that you had forgotten Lena. You behaved like a perfectly well-adjusted little boy, who was growing into being a wonderful young man. But the Gate Keeper told us we were wrong, that you had pushed your pain regarding Lena deep into your sub conscious, that someday it would catch up to you and cause you immense grief. We were explained that when your time of pain arrived, that would be our time to come to help you."

The three of us had finished the main part of the meal and we were enjoying Mom's famous lemon meringue pie.

Dad continued, rather ominously. "Son, there is one other reason why we are here and it is not pleasant. Through all of your boyhood we sent you to Catholic school. From first grade through fifth grade you attended St. Anthony's at Twenty-Seventh and Wallace. In the summer between your fifth and sixth grades, we bought a house on Thirty-Second and Low, only four short blocks from our Union Avenue house but from sixth through eighth grades you were enrolled in St. David's on Thirty-Third and Emerald. Do remember those facts, Robert?"

"I do," I said once again, as a river of memories from each school came flooding into me.

"The problem was your second grade nun, Sister Mary Timothy. She was a very devout, overly zealous, utterly unhappy and punitively oriented teacher. She was always talking about the devil, teaching her students about how the devil was always watching you, relentlessly stalking you, always tempting you to turn away from goodness to the Dark Side, long before Darth Vader."

"How did you know about Darth Vader? Didn't you die before Star Wars came out?"

"We did in fact, but the Gate Keeper allowed us to see what was happening on earth from time to time. It was like watching a news reel for your mother and I. But back to Sister Timothy. She used to have special little classes for the girls only and special classes for the boys only. God only knows what she told the girls, but you would come home and tell us what she told you and some of it was pretty disturbing to us. Here's some of the things she told you. If you masturbated the devil would punish you. If you had sex before marriage, the devil would punish you. I didn't even know if you were old enough to know what sex was, but she taught you about Lucifer none the less. She told you that if you got divorced, or hurt your wife, or if you became a drunk, the devil would find horrible ways to punish you. You would come home and be absolutely terrified of the things about the devil and his brutal punishments that Sister Timothy would tell you."

"We almost went to speak with her on a couple of occasions," my mom said, "but at that time of our lives we believed the nuns spoke the true words of God like the priests did. As we grew up ourselves, we began to think that might not be the case. We found so many things we began to believe were inconsistencies. One of them occurred when we realized that when a movie was too brutal or too frightening or both, the Catholic Church might condemn it so you wouldn't go to see it. But there was never a limit on what the nuns and priests could preach to you about what the devil and the fires of hell could torture you with for eternity. Your father and I came to believe that stories of the devil and hell could be infinitely more damaging to the psyche of a young child than practically any movie. Threatening someone's one and only eternal soul as a young child by a creature as hideous as Lucifer could stick with a child for the rest of his life."

The rotational conversation continued when my dad said: "By the time we realized these what we believed to be awareness, it was too late. You were growing into a beautiful young boy and Sister Timothy was long gone. We thought you had outgrown her scare tactics. But when we died and went to Respite the Gate Keeper told us we were wrong. He told us that what Sister Timothy told you, not once, but scores of times, had hurt you deeply and would catch up to and damage you even more deeply later. He very lovingly told us that we should have admonished Sister Timothy the first time she ever frightened you and you came home and told us about it."

"Quickly, the years went by. We had asked the grandparents and the older folks in the family never to speak of Lena again and no one ever did. It was as if Lena had never existed."

"So we hoped," Mom added contritely. "But she had existed, and that's where we went wrong."

The real me couldn't believe what was happening. The dream me couldn't believe it either. The Two-Knock Ghost was my parents and they were explaining why I was so screwed up, under my favorite tree while sharing my favorite foods. Beyond that, I believed that this was the most dialogue I had ever experienced in a dream. I was certain that I would remember all of it, just as I remembered notes I had dreamed then woke up and played them on the piano. But was what they were telling me true? Or were they just spoken words without meaning. It was after all, a dream. How could I prove or disprove any of it? I was fighting to cling to every fact so I could begin to research everything tomorrow. Certainly it would be easy to check the birth records for a Lena McKenzie born in Chicago in mid to late 1950. I was born in Luis Memorial Hospital. There was not any reason, I assumed, for my mother to choose a different hospital for her second child. And finding whether Sister Timothy was my second grade teacher would be a snap. No doubt the mammoth Chicago Archdiocese would have that record somewhere."

"How did you like the meal, Robert?" my mother asked.

"It was wonderful," I answered. "But the conversation was better. Besides, how did you prepare all that stuff in Respite?"

"We have a great deal of tiny little miracles there, Robert, especially when we appear in a dream. That affords us a great deal of flexibility in our cooking process. Almost anything is possible." He had a wry smile on his face as he often did when he tried to make me laugh. I smiled. That was it. As soon as I did so, my mother's happy face was replaced with immediate sadness.

"We have to leave now, Robert," she said softly.

"Will you come back again?"

Dad answered, "That depends on you and how you handle the information we've shared with you and whether the Gate Keeper tells us our work here is finished. It's been a wonderful blessing to see you, but your mom and I are excited to see what lies beyond Respite."

"I understand completely, Dad, but if I get to see you two again, that would be a true blessing for me."

Cleanup of the picnic site was fun to watch. Mom opened the top of the big picnic basket and one by one things started lifting themselves in slow motion, as if in a Disney movie, and placing themselves neatly into the basket. As I watched, I thought that the only thing missing from the scene was accompanying music. I thought of the song "The Sorcerer's Apprentice" and played it in my dream mind as the eating utensils floated weightlessly into the basket. The finale was the folding in on itself of the cream colored sheet, which had been placed on the lush grass to hold the food. My music ended perfectly as my mother closed the lid. Then she came to hug me and we gave each other our perfunctory kiss on each other's cheeks, then my father came over and hugged me while we blew fart kisses on each other's necks with our lips and laughed hysterically when we did it. Strange, I always thought of my father as an extremely sophisticated man, but not when we were making fart sounds on each other's skin. Then we quickly switched sides, blew some more fart sounds, and laughed even more the second time.

"I love you, son," he said, still smiling.

"I love you, Robert," my mother said elegantly.

Then each of them grabbed a handle of the picnic basket simultaneously and began floating backward slowly toward the golden glowing open door that rested in the southeastern sky.

"I love you both," I said from the depths of my soul, knowing that they had sacrificed years of eternal bliss for the opportunity to help me when I needed it the most.

The Two-Knock Ghost was gone. Perhaps never to return, behind a door that I could not access no matter how diligently I might try. How I wished that I could see them again, if only for a moment, to tell them what I had done with their information. But now it was my turn to find out if what they had told me was the truth or merely the absurd fiction of a dream.

CHAPTER 19

THE NEXT MORNING I told Christine everything I had dreamed the night before. She reacted both skeptically and cautiously, telling me that even though the Two-Knock Ghost had revealed itself and shared all the information that it did, that wasn't reason enough to believe that what they said was true. I told her, "But, Christine, what if I find out that Sister Timothy and Lena were real?"

"I'd be very shocked indeed," she answered.

After breakfast, I realized that upstairs in one of our closets in a guest bedroom was a huge box with all of my report cards in it, along with some of my elementary school drawings, special awards—mostly for winning spelling bees and trivia related to my class subjects. The awards were mostly what we called Holy Cards, with pictures of saints on one side of them, with usually a prayer on the other side, or a story about that particular saint whose picture was on the opposite side. Sometimes we would win cards that we were taught were Relic Cards, cards that had a piece of a saint's clothing or a fragment of one of their bones or a piece of something they owned. I loved winning those cards until a classmate that I admired told me that if someone added all the wooden pieces of the True Cross that the Catholic Church had given away in Relic Cards, the total would be as big as the Empire State Building. Whether that statement was true or not, it ruined my love of those cards. She might as well have told me that if they added all the pieces of bone fragments of the saint that they had given away, the saint would have been as big as Paul Bunyan or King Kong. My friend's statement just destroyed it for me because I looked up to and admired her, because she was smarter than I and her Holy and Relic Card winner's collection dwarfed mine by about three to one. I think her name was Marilyn Minko. Anyway, I saved the cards, mostly because I had won them and I liked the stories of the saints.

I found the box easily, though I hadn't looked into it for years. I carried it onto the bed, sat my back against two pillows and opened the box. Exactly what I thought was in there, was. There must have been fifty Holy Cards, an old scapular, a couple of text books, some poorly graded art work from my elementary years, and every single one of my report cards from first through eighth grade, sitting right on top of all that stuff in no special order. I picked them out of the box as I felt my heart begin to beat faster in my chest and a multitude of butterflies flit like crazed pixies in my stomach.

I didn't care about looking at my grades or to see my bad marks in deportment. I only wanted to see who signed the front of each card, who my teacher was. First card, eighth grade, Sister Ann Therese. I figured I'd check all the grades and signatures in case the Two-Knock Ghost had been right about the name, but mistaken about the grade. Second card, sixth grade, Sister Mary Mark. I remembered that she was pretty and that I liked her, probably because she liked me. Then I took a moment to reflect on the beauty of Sister Ann Therese. She was the loveliest nun I had ever seen. I remember that once a handsome priest came to see her at school. They were about thirty-two years old. She had told us they were friends in her life before the convent and his life before the seminary. They played a duet on guitars and sang together as though they had done it a hundred times. I remembered how she looked at him nostalgically, almost romantically, while they were performing for us, looks that made me wonder then and they made me wonder now, all these years later.

Next report card, third grade, Mrs. James Olek. She was pretty too. She had been my only secular teacher. I met her daughter one summer when I was working at Benton House and asked her if her mom taught third grade at Saint Anthony of Padua's fifteen years ago. When she said yes, I felt happy. When she told me that her mom would be at the Benton House Bazaar in two weeks, I was ecstatic. When I saw Mrs. Olek at the bazaar she recognized me immediately, came right up to me and kissed me on the cheek affectionately. I was twenty-three and married. She was thirty-seven, married and gorgeous, with long blond hair and deep blue eyes and I melted into a tiny grease spot on the floor. She told me that she always thought I was a good boy with a big heart because I would always fight the bullies when they would start beating up on the weaker kids.

"I had to admonish you for fighting back then because it was my job and you were quick to your fists. But secretly I was always proud of you for standing up to and decking a few of those guys because they deserved it. If I remember right, you never lost a fight, and when you beat up a bully, you became friends. Do you remember that, Robert?"

"I do, Mrs. Olek."

"About my last name, Robert. It was originally Mrs. James Oleskevich. We shortened it to Olek back in the day because Polish people were being prejudiced against and were having difficult times finding jobs."

"I remember you were pregnant most of the school year and you left school in March of 1956 to have your baby. Was the girl that's enrolled in the summer school program here at Benton House that baby?"

"It sure is, Robert. That's my oldest daughter, Jane. I also have another daughter and a boy."

I only remember two other facts that she told me that her husband Jim was a lawyer and that about half of those bullies that I fought in the Third Grade went into organized crime in Chicago and wound up in prison with lengthy sentences. When she left, she kissed me again, ever so gently with great affection. I can still smell her perfume in my memory. Oh how deeply I was in puppy love with my third grade teacher, Mary Jane Olek for nearly the whole school year in 1956 and for one glorious hour at the Benton House Bazaar in 1971.

Report card number four, second grade, and there it was, in tiny little chicken scratch but to me the most important signature I had ever seen—Sister Mary Timothy. The Two-Knock Ghost had been right. Suddenly, the images of Sister Timothy besieged me. She was the antithesis of Sister Ann Therese and Mrs. Olek. She was old and wrinkled with ugly buck teeth. She had a penchant for falling asleep in class and would say, "Huh?" When somebody would go to the front of the class and wake her. Her mouth and eyes would open at that instant. Her buck teeth would thrust forward when she blurted, "Huh?" And at that very same instant the entire class would erupt into laughter. I had forgotten that scene for many decades, but in this present instant of remembrance, I recalled that I had witnessed the scene with different student wakers at least one hundred times.

Poor Sister Timothy, I thought. She was old, bitter, frail, and in failing health. I envisioned her living a loveless childhood, never dating as an uncomely young woman and finally falling in love with and marrying Jesus because He was the only One who would have her. I suddenly remembered her nearly goose stepping awkwardly back and forth in front of the classroom like a frustrated Nazi when she was on one of her devil rants. I saw her now in my mind's eye and she was frightening. I wondered how many children's nightmares she contributed to with her devil tales. And I wondered how many of those children grew into adulthood still dreaming the nightmares and wondering where the Hell they came from.

But again, there she was, Sister Timothy, the perpetrator of the origins of my nightmares, proving that half of what the Two-Knock Ghost had told me was correct. Monday, I would find out if Lena was real.

Five minutes later, I was telling Christine what I had discovered about Sister Timothy, Mrs. Olek, and Sister Ann Threse. I showed her my second grade report card and Sister Timothy's signature but for some reason, Christine was more concerned with my Mrs. Olek story.

"Do you remember that I was there that night at Benton House and that you introduced me to Mary Jane Olek?" she asked me playfully.

I said, "No." I really had no clue.

Then she teased me when she said, "I could tell by the look in your eyes that you were really smitten with her, so I asked you if you were in love with her and you said, 'Yes, since I was eight but even more so after tonight.' But I let you keep your crush for her because I never thought it would interfere with our marriage and it never did."

We both laughed heartily then kissed what I would call a "happy kiss," separated and continued with our day.

My mind was focused and poignantly directed. I wanted to find out now if Lena was real. I didn't want to wait till the public offices opened on Monday. I wanted to know now. But I wanted to be attentive to Christine too. She had told me that she wanted to go to quiet little Gulf Port Beach for the afternoon, then have dinner at the Back Fin Blue Café. That was fine with me. Hanging out with my wife today was the most important thing in the world to me, but finding out about Lena was priority too. While we were getting ready to go, I silently pondered how I could find out about Lena. I wondered whether I could find an older relative who might know the answer. The more I thought about it, the more I realized that everyone from that era was either dead or forgotten. I remembered, joyfully, how we used to have the most wonderful family get-togethers in the mid and late 1950s. I'm talking huge family gatherings with second and third cousins coming and distant relatives I might see once a year. My cousins' fathers, my uncles, all great guys, would drive up in their big beautiful straight eights or their snub-nosed Studebakers or their monstrous Hudsons, park, exit their car with chests puffed out with pride for their automobile and their family. They would play baseball with us and toss a football around. I still remember Uncle Philly playing the catching positions during our baseball games while smoking his ever present Garcia Vega Palma cigars.

I thought of all the old times, of someone who might know of little Lena's existence. But as I recalled the old timers, I realized that the ones that had been forgotten by me were forgotten because when we had those huge family gatherings I'd usually be hanging out with the little kids about my own age and a few uncles and my grandpas and grandmas. But as the sixties rolled through, the enormous family gatherings became fewer and fewer. By the 1970s they were virtually nonexistent. In fact, the last of the mammoth family gatherings I remembered was at the funeral for my mom and dad and Dad's mom and dad in 1972. I strained deeply to remember those faces from thirty-two years ago. But I could not remember anyone who could help me.

Then, while I was putting on my bathing suit and feeling better about losing a third of my paunch, my mind recalled when Toby told me how he had looked through his old address and phone book for possible informants. I decided to get my old black phone book which was still in my bedside table drawer and look through it on my way to Gulf Port. I told Christine what I was doing and she wished me good luck genuinely.

I asked her to drive, which she did happily. As we drove, I began looking through my old phone book hoping to find someone beyond my conscious memory who could help me. I began with the *A*s and chuckled that the last time I did this kind of thing was when I went through the Yellow Pages and found Dr. Banderas. This time, however, I sailed quickly past A, B, C, and D, amazed at how many names I no longer remembered and how many of my family had passed away.

E, F, G, H, I, J, K—nothing. Ten letters into the alphabet of names, I was feeling a bit disconsolate, but I continued. L, M, N, O, P. Still no names jogged my memory. Q, R, S. OH MY GOD, MONA SILVERI! I had not thought of her in years and I had not seen her since my parents' funeral. My mother's mother, Rita, had a sister, Maria. She had a beautiful daughter. Her name was Mona. She was my cousin.

She was a tall, beautiful, flaming redhead, who I loved dearly when I was a child because she was always so kind to me. She had married an Italian fellow named Anthony Silveri. Everybody used to call him Tony Sil. He fashioned himself a cowboy and farmer. He married Mona in Oak Lawn in 1958. Mona was twenty-four then. He was twenty-eight, well-educated and tightly connected to Mayor Daley and the awesome Daley Political Machine. He held an extremely well-paying job with the City of Chicago in finance and every election season, worked tirelessly to help Richard J. Daley become Mayor once again. Tony Sil kept his city job till he was forty-five. He had saved every penny he could since he started working as a bus boy at El Bianco's in Cicero at the age of fifteen. His dream was to own a horse farm and raise corn because his favorite food was corn on the cob. Sounds strange, but that's just the way it was.

When Tony Sil had enough money to pursue his dream, he bought eighty-six acres outside of Grass Creek, Indiana. A modest five-bedroom house rested near the middle of the property with a long winding driveway that led up to it. The five bedrooms worked out perfectly because by the time he and Mona purchased the farm, they had four children and they all lived at home. Each one got their own bedroom. Mona was as excited to have a corn and horse farm as her husband because any dream of his was her dream also.

I remember it was big news in the family when the Silveri's bought their dream farm. I also remembered that Mona had worked strenuously, mostly waitress jobs, and had contributed thousands of dollars to their marital dream. She was the rare woman who could raise her children well, work a ten-to-twelve-hour shift five or six days a week, be a great wife, sleep four and three-quarters to five and a quarter hours each night, and get up and do it again day after day, year after year without complaint. Joyfully even. Thankful to the God she believed in for everything that she had.

I thought Mona could help me because she had known me my whole life. When I was two, she would have been sixteen and the birth of a baby girl in our family in 1950 would be huge news that would have dwarfed the news of when Mona and Tony Sil bought their farm—and everybody knew about that. Certainly Mona would remember if Lena had been real.

It had been nearly two decades since I had communicated with Mona. I had heard that Tony Sil had passed away at age sixty from a massive heart attack while riding his favorite horse, Fire Brand. Christine and I took a ride through Grass Creek to the Silveri farm and attended the funeral. Mona was still pretty, but of course she had aged and looked pale and drawn from her recent sorrows. Still she was very kind to me and I remember thinking at the funeral, which was held in her living room, that Mona and I had a real bond between us and we would always be friends.

But I did nothing over the years to nurture that bond or our friendship. The result was that we fell completely out of touch. I knew nothing now about her life or even if she would still be alive. She would be about seventy now, and I wondered when I looked at her address and phone number if they would be the same after all these years.

But I had found it, and I would dial that number when Christine would be taking her usual nap on the beach. For a moment, however, I closed the old address book and started to show Christine some quality attention. Two and a half hours later, Christine was asleep in her beach chair. I grabbed my cell phone and walked about a hundred feet away to a free-standing silver metal swing which rested under the branches of a couple of trees. My place on the swing felt kind of private, even though there were a few people around. I began dialing the number with a mixture of trepidation and joy in my heart.

"Hello." My god, I recognized her voice. "Mona, it's Robert McKenzie."

"Good Lord, Robert, where have you been?"

She coughed about twenty times.

"Just living life, Mona. How are you?"

"I'm doing great. I just bought a house as an investment property."

It was 2004 and the average person could still do that and make some money. Sadly, in a couple of years she would find out just how upside down she would become with that investment. But in this moment she was happy, so I was too.

We spent the next few minutes talking pleasantries about how everyone in each family was doing. I kept my answers short because I only had one question to ask her that had any real import other than how she was feeling.

When I felt that the basic pleasantries had been answered, I began my exploration.

"Mona, I had a bit of a selfish motive for calling you. I need to know if you know something about my distant family history." I felt myself pause, an almost literal nervous lump in my throat.

"What is it, Robert?" she asked and coughed again about ten times.

I couldn't believe how stressful asking my next question was.

"Did I have a baby sister when I was about two years old who died about the time I turned three?"

It was Mona's turn to pause. I could sense the stress that she was beginning to feel through the silent line. Then she proved it a moment later when slowly she began to answer my question.

"I don't really begin to know where to start to answer that question. As simple as the answer is, there is a secret attached to it that makes the answer complex."

Mona paused again. I could feel more stress within her, more hesitancy.

"Why is it complex, Mona?"

"Because in 1951, my parents asked me never to talk to you about something very important because they wanted to spare you from any emotional hurt."

"Was it about the fact that I had a sick baby sister and she died when she was about one?"

There was no pause.

"Yes."

"Was her name Lena?"

"Yes it was, Robert. How did you know that?"

I told her that my parents had told me the details in a dream. I chose not to tell her they were the Two-Knock Ghost.

"It must have been an awesome dream," she said while coughing.

"It was."

We talked for a few more minutes. She told me that Christine and I would always be welcome to come and stay for as long as we liked; there were four bedrooms not being used because the kids were all grown and living their lives elsewhere.

"I promise you, at least I will come up there and spend a week with you next March."

"If Christine can get some weeks off, I'll bring her. Deal?"

"Deal."

I thought that was the perfect place to end the conversation.

"I'm going to sign off now, Mona. I'm at the beach with Christine, and I want to go back to my beach chair and be there when she wakes from her nap. And speaking about bedrooms, we've got empty ones here too. You're more than welcome to come here if it gets too cold for you up there."

"Thank you, Robert. I'll keep that in mind."

"Thank you, Mona. You shared something with me that I needed to know. I wish you the best of life and I promise to keep in touch. Good-bye, Mona."

"Good-bye, Robert. Take good care of yourself."

She was gone. And I had my answer. The Two-Knock Ghost had told me the truth—in a dream no less. I was ecstatic. I couldn't wait for Christine to wake so I could tell her the news. As I returned to my comfortable beach chair, I reflected on my conversation with Mona. I realized I had invited her to come for a visit as if I were still living with Christine. Having done that, I thought it must have been because I believed deeply within myself that I would be back in my home by winter. I certainly hope so.

I sat next to Christine for forty-three minutes before she drifted from her sleep of an hour and a half. As I expressed in this story before, I felt like an excited child as I explained to Christine my conversation with Mona.

"My ghosts are real!" I told Christine. "No wonder I was drawn to the bedroom. Deep down, in places I didn't even know existed, I was always waiting for my little sister to come home. That phone call explains why I always felt loneliness when I first went into that room. That absolutely explains it. There's no other explanation. That has to be the reason because otherwise my life was almost perfect. And the fact that I chose the name Lena—where did that come from?"

"I can't answer that," Christine said, showing some fascination with my story. "But it seems as if the Two-Knock Ghost is a bit of a different kind of miracle that has happened to you in your dreams."

"First Sister Timothy and the devil then Lena dying when I was three. I guess the alcohol was anesthetizing me for more than just the death of my parents and grandparents.

Christine said, "I think you're right, Robert." Then she reached for my left hand with her right as we both laid on our beach chairs contemplating our own personal thoughts until we left for dinner about two hours later.

My head was filled with two things that night. First I was spending my second consecutive loving weekend with Christine, who like fine wine was becoming better with the passage of time. Second, I couldn't wait to talk with Dr. Banderas Wednesday night. I would tell him every detail of my magnificent dream about my parents. I would ask his opinion and enjoy his unique insights and I would thank him for encouraging me to invite the Two-Knock Ghost into my dreams. The way I set up how I told him about the Two-Knock Ghost, how could he have possibly concluded that the Two-Knock Ghost might be friendly?

But tonight it was time to focus my attention on Christine. I made points with her when I recommended she try the locally famous corn chowder soup, and she loved it. Then throughout dinner I shared jokes with her that I'd memorized off the internet, talked about our children, asked her in great detail about every aspect of her job. I wanted her to talk abundantly, about everything she did. She told me her own funny stories about the people she worked with, elaborating while giggling a great deal, about a few doctors who couldn't even tie their own shoelaces without the help of nurses. Oh God, how I simply loved to watch Christine talk. Her eyes were always glistening, especially when she told me stories about people whose lives she had a direct hand in saving.

As our sharing continued through Saturday's later day hours, I could see us returning to a relaxed normalcy that neither of us had experienced in years. The flow of our conversations, our quiet times, the transitions we made from being at the beach to leaving, to showering together outside, going into separate bathrooms and changing from our bathing suits to our evening wear, sprucing up, meeting up again, then driving to the Back Fin Blue and having a wonderful dinner; it was all smooth and fun. We talked and giggled, took a swim out past the buoys and even beyond a couple of sailboats that were moored about two hundred feet south of the buoys. We were enjoying each other's company as answers and lifestyle changes were happening to me, which impacted Christine just as much, but in a different way than me. I believed she felt she was being more loved by me, that I was being more attentive to her as a complete person, more interested in genuinely asking her about every aspect of her life. I could admit to myself now how the alcohol dimmed all of my senses and turned me into the opposite of a loud mouthed drunk. I was a quiet introverted drunk—and even that fact made me think that I was exempt from any responsibility for hurting my kids and my wife. One of the things I thought about when Christine asked me to leave the house, was, "How could she ask me to leave? I never even raised my voice to her or the kids." How could I? I was drunk and half asleep or sound asleep by the time Christine came to bed. How many of those nights did I not even kiss Christine good night. And there I was, when I had first been cast out by Christine, thinking about how great of a husband I had been. And how great of a father I had been. But I realized I hadn't been either. I was, almost every night, simply a sad, shy drunk, who isolated himself from the people he loved most.

But things were changing now. I was spending my second weekend in a row with Christine. We had not made love, but we were loving each other continuously, sharing genuine affection each moment of every day we were together. We did not yet speak of my returning home, but it was now understood, but unspoken between us, that it was only a matter of time.

* * * * *

Wednesday night at 7:30 couldn't come soon enough, but it did. Finally, it was my time to share my dream with Dr. Banderas and moreover, see what he felt about it. Loyal Dianne was working late as usual when the Doctor had patients at night.

"Dr. McKenzie, how are you doing tonight?" She greeted me as if I was the first person she had seen in weeks.

"I'm well, thank you, and happy and excited to see Dr. Banderas. How are you?"

"I'm wonderful thank you, and Dr. Banderas is excited to see you too tonight. He told me that this afternoon. Let me buzz him and see if he is ready for you." I respected her friendliness and her professionalism.

"Dr. Banderas, Dr. McKenzie is here. Are you ready for him?"

"I've been ready for him all day, Dianne. Thank you, and send him right in."

"Yes, Doctor."

She walked the few feet to the door to Dr. Banderas's office, opened the door, held it for me, and closed it as I passed her into the jungle.

"Hello, Dr. McKenzie," he said before I could say my hello first.

"Hello, Dr. Banderas. How are you?"

"I'm just a touch tired near the end of a long day, but before I ask you the same question, I want to tell you that I have had a strange, almost psychic feeling since Friday night, that you have wanted to share something extremely important with me."

"You are correct, sir," I said emphatically, but playfully.

I noticed dark circles under his interested eyes.

"Well, sit down, get comfortable, and tell me what you experienced."

I sat in one of his comfortable leather client chairs and felt complete comfort immediately. I waited for him to become comfortable in his much more expensive leather chair before I began.

"I had the most incredible dream I have ever had in my entire life a few nights ago, and I have been utterly anxious to tell you ever since."

"You've got me on the edge of my seat with anticipation. Let's hear it." He clasped his hands in a gentle closure on the middle of his lap.

"You remember how I told you the Two-Knock Ghost revealed itself to be my parents?"

He nodded.

"They came back. This time they brought me a complete picnic from Respite while I was relaxing in a dream under the live oak." Slowly, I described my dream to him in every detail. I shared with him every word my parents spoke to me. I was sure that I didn't miss any, marveling at how a human being could memorize so many words from a dream after hearing them only once. I thought for a moment when I considered that, how different it was when I heard notes. They would repeat themselves countless times, as if they were asking me, "Are you getting this? Do you like this sequence?"

When I finished the retelling of my dream, he asked me very simply: "How did you feel afterward?"

"I felt fantastic. I felt the tremendous love of my parents. I felt great joy, wonder, and relief at the things they told me, but most of all I was overwhelmed with curiosity whether Sister Timothy and especially Lena, were real."

"Did you satisfy that curiosity?"

"Indeed I did, Dr. Banderas. The very next day I found the box with all my old report cards in it and BAM, there it was. The fourth card I looked at was second grade and Sister Timothy. The Two-Knock Ghost remembered what I had long ago forgotten."

"And what about Lena?"

"For that I looked through an old phone book to find an older relative who I was close to, who might recall her. I remembered Mona Silveri and when I asked her, she confirmed that my parents had Lena and that I'd had a little sister."

I explained to him that the reason my parents did not want to talk about Lena ever again after she died, was they sincerely believed they could spare me a great deal of pain by hiding the truth from me. Apparently, they were wrong and were told so by the Gate Keeper.

"Do you mind if we look at the dream as a cup, Robert?" he asked, his hands still folded in his lap.

"No, sir," I said, knowing that his take on my experience would be interesting. "I must begin by saying that in no way will my comments attempt to denigrate the depth of importance and meaning that your dream has had for you. There is no doubt that this was the quintessential dream of your life to this point. It has impacted you more than even most of the experiences of your waking life. But I'd like to suggest that we look at the dream from a different point of view. I believe that when you were a little boy you were deeply wounded by the death of your little sister. When your grief wasn't worked through by your parents not talking about it until you were healed from the pain Lena's death caused, you unconsciously pushed your pain deep within your subconscious mind. Over the years that pain was compacted by all the other pains that you experienced in life, most notably the death of your parents and grandparents. We both know now that the longing for your sister to return is the reason why you felt loneliness every time you went into your bedroom to work for your clients. We now both know that your longing for Lena to return is the reason you would spend so much time in your bedroom. You continued to repeat the pattern long after you had consciously forgotten that Lena had ever existed. When you were sent away by Christine, that triggered the guilt you had for failing her and that in turn triggered the devil dreams, as inspired by Sister Timothy. She had frightened you so much that you blocked conscious thoughts of her for decades. But the fears that she bestowed upon you lived deep within you all those decades as well."

"But now I would like to suggest that something may be happening in your dreams that goes far deeper than you have ever imagined."

His face had become extremely serious—the most intense he had ever shown me.

"There is a theory, as you may already know, that states that every character in your dreams is you. If we hold up the cup of your dreams and look at it that way then your parents and the devil are all really you trying to reveal something to yourself. In the case of your parents revealing the things they did, it is absolutely clear what you were trying to reveal to yourself because the Two-Knock Ghost—your parents—you, were very specific. In the case of the devil, things became more complicated. In its simplest form, it could be that you formed a horrendous way to beat up on yourself for hurting Christine. Your choice of the devil came from deep within your subconscious where all the admonitions from Sister Timothy were stored. The death of Toby, your unhoped-for binge a couple of weeks ago, your admission that you were an alcoholic, the telling to you by your children that they missed you when you spent so much time in your bedroom, all these profoundly emotional occurrences stirred up the part of you where your subconscious agonies lived. The appearance of the Two-Knock Ghost even preceded most of your recent awareness. Why it appeared when it did, is anybody's guess, but the fact that it appeared indicates that somewhere deep within yourself, you were desperate to resolve the issues that were plaguing you in your subconscious. It may have been that your parents were truly the Two-Knock Ghost which came from Respite to help you. It may have been that unknown to your conscious being, your subconscious mind created the Two-Knock Ghost to be the purveyor of the facts of your childhood that you have imparted to me. You may have molded it to reveal these hidden facts to yourself by your parents because you loved and trusted them. But the facts that were revealed to you by the Two-Knock Ghost were facts you already knew but were submerged deeply within the mire of your subconscious."

What he was saying made a great deal of sense. But I didn't want to believe it. To me, the Two-Knock Ghost was just who it said it was—my mom and dad. I did wonder why they limited themselves to my dreams. I thought if they had appeared in my waking hours that would have been more ghostly behavior. I was feeling a bit bewildered, and it was beginning to show on my face.

"There is no absolute truth in what I am saying, Dr. McKenzie. They are merely some of my conjectures about your friendly ghost and your unfriendly devil. The bottom line is that you will always have the right to believe whatever you wish to believe about your dreams. The final interpretation will always belong to you. I am merely purporting an alternate theory."

"I understand, Doctor. I will definitely think about what you have said. I can tell you right now that you have shaken up my conscious mind today as much as you said all of those life experiences have shaken my subconscious mind."

"You are an extremely creative person, Dr. McKenzie. Your dreams show that. You have spent so many hours attempting to create profoundly helpful strategies to suggest to your clients who are mired in their own ruts. But now, as you face conquering alcohol, you must take the time to research your own mind for the truths that will free you to be successful in the ensuing phases of your life."

"I will, Doctor. And we can talk about the conclusions I come to next week when we meet again."

He relaxed his furrowed face.

"I will look forward to that with joyful anticipation. Then he smiled. It was then that I noticed again his overall look of tiredness and I told him so in the middle of our conversation. I said, 'Dr. Banderas, you look tired,' as I wondered if the man ever got enough sleep.

"I am." That was all he said, as he smiled, closed his eyes for a moment and nodded his head a single time.

The remaining part of the hour I spent telling him about the second wonderful weekend in a row I shared with Christine. Time after time he told me how happy he was that I was rekindling my love with Christine. Each time I looked deep into his eyes and they were filled with genuine happiness.

After we had exhausted conversation about Christine, Dr. Banderas segued smoothly into his next question.

"Dr. McKenzie, how are you doing in your efforts to conquer alcohol?"

"Okay. I honestly believe I think about drinking a few times every day, but I don't give into it. The busier I am, the less I think about it."

"Have you discovered any triggers that cause you to crave alcohol?"

"Yes, sir, I have." I paused for a moment feeling a little ashamed at having to share such a vulnerable aspect of myself. "I crave it most when I'm hurting terribly emotionally or when life slows down to a crawl and it's evening and for a moment I feel I have nothing to do, but mostly it happens when my emotions are at a low ebb."

"May I speak freely about that with you, Doctor?" he asked politely.

"Yes," I said. "Please."

"Each of us is our most vulnerable when our emotions are ebbing lowly and we are alone with nothing to do. Christianity says that an idol mind is the devil's workshop. But if you take Christianity and the devil out of that equation, it can still be said that when we are quiet and hurting deeply emotionally, that is the time when the most negative of thoughts can flow into your mind and cause you to feel hopelessness. That is the perfect time for a drink, to calm your nerves, to divert your brain from its pain."

"I will put forth now, that love and creativity will carry you through those moments to a life of being alcohol free."

"How Dr. Banderas? How could those two things keep alcohol from me?"

"In reality, Dr. McKenzie, it will be the choices you make that will keep you alcohol free. But love and creativity are, in my opinion, the two most powerful emotions on the planet and in times of crisis they can be your greatest allies."

"I've never heard of creativity referred to as an emotion," I said, somewhat strained.

"In the far greater majority of the corners of the earth it is not considered an emotion. It is merely a personal conclusion I came to during one of my many sleep-deprived nights."

"How did it come about?"

"I was contemplating God and the concept that many people believe He is love. I could wrap my head around that rather easily because as human beings we seem to receive the most joy when we are sharing love on any level. It is somewhat Mr. Spock—like logical, that we would associate God absolutely with the finest emotion. As I continued to contemplate, I wondered what qualities he might have that made God unlike any other entity in the universe. The conclusion I arrived at was that God was a compulsive creator. Okay, maybe not compulsive but driven, prolific, layered. And I don't mean simplistically like the God of the Bible who only created for six days—even though each of those days may have taken millions of years—then hung up His creative paint brush. I came to believe that God had created before He created our universe and that since He created our universe. He has created many more universes, a multitude of realms and dimensions that would be unfathomable to us. I came to believe that one of God's greatest gifts to us was to give each of us an infinite river of creativity that we can access at anytime. This flow of endless creativity is flashed before us every night in our dreams in our waking days, each time we create something beautiful rather than to destroy something, we are coming the closest we can to true love, to God if you will."

"So now it is time for my little trick. This was developed while reflecting on your specific case during a recent night of ruminations. This is what I want you to do from now until forever whenever you need a drink. I want you to immediately think of the love that you have for Christine and your children and the love that they foster for you. Then, think of your clients, how much you care about them and how they need you to be clear headed when you contemplate how to help them. Then think about your music and how much you love to create songs for your beloved. I want you to think about new notes for your next masterpiece of music for her. Then I want you to flip the switch and start to think of all the types of creativity there are for you to tap into right at that moment. Think about what you and Christine will talk about that night, or what you might have for dinner or if she'd be interested in a game of 500 Rummy or Four Score. Think about what to buy your kids for Christmas or their birthdays. Consider if it's time to begin your memoirs. I want you to flood your mind with every possible creative thought that you can summon. Those thoughts fused with your reflections on the people and the things that you love will help you feel connected to your Higher Power in a pragmatic way. This approach, I believe, will help to carry you through those difficult moments of craving."

When he finished, he seemed exhausted, as if as he was speaking, the gas was disappearing from the tank and now it was gone.

"Thank you, Dr. Banderas. You've given me a great deal to think about. I am looking very much forward to our next meeting where we can theorize some more."

"I'm looking forward to it, I believe as much as you are. Yours is an interesting case. Every few years someone comes to me with a series of conditions I would rate unique. It is a person with an unusual reality which intrigues me, makes me think and question things more, causes me to have more sleepless nights. Your Two-Knock Ghost is one of those unique entities that I have contemplated deeply and will continue to do so in the future and as time passes I will share with you my perspectives as they evolve. Together we will expand our understanding of the ghost considerably."

I stood to leave, stretching my hand over his enormous desk to shake his much smaller hand.

"Take good care of yourself, Dr. McKenzie," he said as our strong grip was locked.

"You take good care too, Dr. Banderas."

He nodded his head slightly as he often did and he smiled as if to say thank you. We released our clasp and on my way out of the office, I couldn't help but to reflect on how beautiful it was there in the jungle.

Once I was in the waiting room, Dianne quickly asked me, "Same time next week, Dr. McKenzie?"

"Absolutely," I said with a huge grin on my face.

As soon as I left the waiting room, I began thinking creatively. I began by asking myself, where could I be the most creative in my life right now? The answer was that I needed to take care of business with Toby's wife, Alicia. At first I thought I would drive to her home, introduce myself and present her with some type of magnanimous gift. Then I began to question my motives for wanting to see her in person. Certainly I had no romantic interest in the woman. But did I want to meet her to apologize somehow for having had a hand in causing the death of her husband? Certainly I could not begin to put myself into a position conversationally to even get close to suggesting that I had anything to do with Toby's death. Resentment might be borne instantly within her and that might lead to defeating my reason for going there.

As I drove across town toward the Serenity Club, I thought about nothing else, but how to give this deserving woman something of myself that would benefit her and the children while simultaneously assuaging my guilt for having put Toby on the path to meeting up with Reubin Tatum.

My thoughts around this type of creativity were hurtful, even though I knew that ultimately whatever I gave her would be deeply appreciated and appropriate. As I approached the Serenity Club, I had not yet finalized my gift plan for Alicia. I decided to change my routine and drive to the live oak. There, maybe I could find peace to ease my chaotic thoughts that would absolutely distract me from whatever was going on around me at the meeting. I parked in front of the Church of the Assension and looked at the live oak. It was strong and muscular, like Toby. I not only began thinking about him but I started to consider saying a little prayer to him, ask for his advice. If he gave me some, maybe my consternation over the correct way to approach Alicia might dissipate.

As I scanned the limbs of the huge oak tree, I thought, "What if Toby had told her all about me—everything that he could? Then I appear at her door and introduce myself. I could create a catastrophe." At that moment I formulated a prayer to Toby. At the same time, I asked my Higher Power—my God concept—to work in tandem with Toby and help provide a solution to my problem.

As I sat in the car gazing at the tree's majesty, I wished Toby could have been buried beneath it. He would have liked that.

"Do it anonymously," he said.

I thought I heard Toby's voice.

"Toby, is that you?" Then I heard it again, but not as Toby's voice, but as we humans hear a thought that enters our head.

"Do it anonymously!" It seemed louder this time than a moment ago when in my reverie I believed it to have been uttered by Toby's voice.

My reasoning now took over. Anonymity was the answer. This way nobody would be embarrassed, or angry, or hurt. I imagined Alicia receiving an innocuous letter in the mail, opening it and finding a cashier's check in it with a typed letter that said, "Use some of this toward the kids' college fund and use the rest for a vacation for you and the kids. Toby was my friend and he always spoke about how much he loved you three." Unsigned.

That was it. Done deal. I would put the plan into motion tomorrow. I was ready to leave for the Serenity Club when I heard another voice in my head.

"How much?"

That was a fair question. A thousand? Two, three, four thousand dollars. Hardly! School would not be cheap in a decade and even a jaunt to Disney World for a week could be kind of pricey. Five, six, eight? Those numbers sounded too puny for the situation but when I went around the corner of my mind and considered the right number for the first time, it sounded perfect. I would send Alicia a check for $10,000 with a letter suggesting, to some degree, what to do with the money; but knowing full well that Alicia would have the final say about how the money was used. I would never know how the money would be spent. I was okay with that. I had come to know and trust this woman through her husband who loved her, who adored her.

My problem solved, I used a heavy foot to get me to the Serenity Club. There I opened up like a desert flower after a spring rain. When I got the opportunity to talk, I did—more than I ever had anywhere before, about myself. It seemed like I talked incessantly. I told everybody about my devil dreams and how I thought the Two-Knock Ghost was an evil entity before it revealed itself to be my parents. I told them about my psychologist, not his name of course, and how he encouraged me to willingly invite the ghost in to reveal itself. I told my story, as much of it as I could recall. You could have heard a pin drop in that auditorium. Everyone was interested. Finally I told my audience how happy I was that so many wonderful things around me and within me were happening. There was no part of me that acted cocky about what I was experiencing. Everything I said was coming from my heart. I concluded by encouraging everyone not to be afraid to meet their demons head on because that would be the only way to defeat them. Then I genuinely offered my help to anyone anytime if they felt they needed it.

On my way home, I began thinking about Alicia and the anonymous check and letter I would send her tomorrow. Then I thought about calling Christine, asking her if she was still on the same weekend off schedule, and asking her if she would like to spend a third weekend in a row together. And finally, I thought about as many of Dr. Banderas's opinions as I could, especially his comment that every character in a dream is the dreamer. Of course I had known about the concept for decades but until he reminded me, I hadn't thought of the concept in relation to my dreams. As I approached the Beaches of Paradise, I looked forward to the next time the Two-Knock Ghost would appear. I was developing some poignant questions for it.

* * * * *

I had another wonderful weekend with Christine. Friday night we drove all the way from Snell Island to Ulmerton and had dinner at Golden Coral. It was one of Christine's favorite restaurants. Boy, could she pack it in for a tiny woman. It amazed me that she had almost the same figure she had when I met her over thirty years ago.

Saturday we went to the north end of St. Pete Beach to an art fair where a variety of vendors were exhibiting their creations. For dinner we ate outside behind the Don Cezar.

We ran together both Saturday and Sunday morning. Then Sunday we drove to Tampa and first went to Lowry Park Zoo, then capped off the day with a multi hour fun time at Busch Gardens. I think it was our best weekend ever, with Christine acting more or less as the activities director. During that weekend with Christine I was reminded how much there was to see and do and share with your mate if you were happily married.

Every time we sat down to eat, I thought about ordering a rum and Coke but I dismissed those thoughts quickly, often using Dr. Banderas's suggestions. I thought first of my love for Christine. What was worth more—a successful marriage or a drink? Then I would try to create some fun or stimulating conversation with Christine. It worked. We stayed busy together, and I kept the demon of alcohol locked deep in the basement of my mind. Genuine affection was returning to us. We held hands everywhere we went. We gave each other little kisses fifty to sixty times each day. We snuggled on the couch Saturday night and watched *The Shawshank Redemption*. We held each other tightly at night in our king-sized bed. Only one thing was missing. We had not made love since Christine had asked me to leave. I believed that would happen when I came home to stay, when Christine felt that all was right with us.

* * * * *

After the weekend, I got busy. By Tuesday lunch I had typed a letter to Alicia Magnessun and secured the cashier's check for her. I typed her address on the envelope, walked the few blocks to the little Post Office in the tobacco store near Publix and mailed it. She would get the letter Wednesday, the same day I would see Dr. Banderas. Since I had not had any devil dreams and the Two-Knock Ghost had not revisited me, my primary question for the session would be, "What is your advice as to how to ask Christine when I can come home?" I knew I was a novice in my sobriety, but I also knew myself—I thought—and if I promised myself and Christine that I would never take another drink, I never would. I had never broken a promise to Christine and I wasn't about to start now when I was so desperate to get back home and make things work better than they ever had before.

* * * * *

Tuesday night, the devil attacked me again. This time in my bedroom where I was wearing the cream-colored pajamas under the cream-colored sheets. He was sprawled back against the ceiling; his hysterical laughter woke the man in the cream pajamas. When he ceased his laughing, he started criticizing me. "You're so prideful, aren't you, Mr. Big Shot? Everything going your way now. Good times with Christine, haven't had a drink in a few days, good sessions with your little psychologist, running every day, so many strategies for how to improve your life. You really think you've made it, but you're just a baby beginning to crawl. You have no idea the torment and temptations I will send you through the years that will knock you off your cocky perch. I think I'll come down there right now and eat your face off."

Knock, knock, loud and powerful. Both the devil and my dream self reacted to it.

"Come in," I yelled. And there they were emerging through the glowing door in all their splendor. My beautiful, powerful, loved beyond comprehension—parents, the Two-Knock Ghost.

"Be gone, Satan," they said in unison, in the name of the Creator of the Universe whose power commands you to hell."

The devil, still pinned to the ceiling, was no longer laughing. Instead, the look on his face recognized my parents' power. Then an ever so slight altering of his eyes indicated that he really didn't want another beat down from them. Without a fight he merely retracted through the ceiling and the room belonged to my parents and me. I sat up in bed as they sat on each side of the end of the bed facing me. We were a triangle of family.

"Thank you for saving me again. It's no fun having my face ripped apart."

"We understand, son," my father said.

"But we can't come to rescue you anymore, Robert," my mother said. "It's time for us to go to our next level."

"But why so soon, only after three visits?"

"We've told you everything we need to tell you son," my father added calmly. "And we've watched you take hold of and run fast with the information."

"Your life is swiftly becoming what it should be, Robert," Mom said. "No one can assure that you will never dream about the devil again or take another drink, but we both can assure you that you are in the process of taking control of your life again. As you gain strength in doing so, the devil dreams will lessen as will your dependency on alcohol."

"Our work is finished here, son," my father tag teamed. "The Gate Keeper told us it's time to leave Respite. You're on your own now to find your own way with the information we've given you."

"I'll miss you immensely," I said. "It's been kind of fun having you around for a while, knowing it was you who were knocking on my doors."

"We will miss you too, Robert," Mom said sadly, "but just as I said, there are no guarantees about devil dreams or drinking, there are no absolutes that one or the other of us won't appear as characters in your future dreams. We simply will no longer be the Two-Knock Ghost as you call us. Two Knocks' work is done. You know we both love you dearly."

"I know, Mom."

"It's time to go, son," Dad said as he began to stand. Mom rose also, and they both approached me as I was sitting up against the headboard. Mom bent down and presented her cheek and I kissed it tenderly then she hugged me. Then my father and I blew farts on each other's necks and then he bear hugged me surprisingly. He walked to the opposite side of the bed and took my mother's left hand in his right as I imagined he had done a million times. And without saying another word, a golden glow surrounded them as they floated backward through the bedroom door. The last acts of love they gave me were a smile from my father as my mother blew me a kiss with her right hand.

My dream self sat upright against the headboard for what seemed to be several minutes. I was thinking about what had just happened. First of all, an entity I believed was a monstrous evil turned out to be a tremendous ally for self-realization. It had come three times and now it was gone. The man in the cream pajamas had a heart full of joy at having shared so much with it and a heart full of sorrow at its departure. Gradually, my dream self slid down beneath the sheets and into sleep.

The next morning I awoke refreshed, looking forward to Dr. Banderas and spilling my guts about the week I'd had and about how I had considered his interpretation of my dream. I ran for a solid thirty minutes, mostly up and down the variety of streets in Five Towns. When I got back to the condo I immediately put a towel on the piano bench and played the song I had most recently written for Christine. While doing so, I felt vague and haunting notes inside my head trying to form themselves together—the initial seedlings for my next song for her.

I felt great. The devil's taunts of the night before weren't lingering negatively like they used to. Satan was wrong. I and everyone who loved me and cared about me was right. I had too many wonderful things and people to live for not to develop myself into a better man. I would drink no more rum and Coke and I would not go to my bedroom for hours on end, ignoring Christine. I would no longer feel the loneliness as I walked to the bedroom each day, for now I knew that I had had a little sister and that when she died, I longed for her return. I thought that I might even try to forgive Sister Timothy for scaring me half to death, but not today. I was too excited to see Dr. Banderas.

As I breezed across town I thought about my clients for the day and I wondered if Mary Bauer had taken her cruise yet with her husband. I hoped she was progressing well with her newly found peace of mind. I even looked forward to seeing Amanda, my eternally effervescent and efficient secretary. And lastly for the morning, I looked forward to my hot chocolate even though it was 92 degrees outside.

"Hello my sparkly one," I greeted Amanda.

"Bon jour monsieure," she responded from behind her desk.

"Como talle vous, madame?"

"Sava bien, boss."

I cracked up. We had fun like that almost every day. Another reason to be sober. She handed me a list of my clients for the day and as I walked with it to my office, she asked "hot chocolate?" And I answered, "Most definitely."

Morning was a joy, two senior citizens with similar problems of coping with life and loneliness after the death of a spouse.

At lunch I walked five blocks to buy a Polish sausage and Orange Crush from Joy, my favorite vendor. Always the ebullient soul, she was once again this sunny early afternoon.

"May I have a Polish sausage without the bun please and an Orange Crush?" I asked.

"But of course, but if you're going high protein, then there's a heck of a lot of carbs in that Orange Crush."

"That's right," I said. "How about a bottle of water then?"

"Deal."

In the next few minutes she filled me in on all the little and big things going on in downtown St. Pete. It was a hot as hell afternoon and she was dripping with sweat, but I hugged her anyway as was our custom, and I didn't mind a bit as behind her thick glasses was a dear kind soul. She was a hot dog selling fixture downtown and by far the best one, in my opinion. She was yet another reason for me to live and to enjoy my life. I was so happy this early Wednesday afternoon. I felt like a kid in a candy store and all of downtown along my Central Avenue walk to and from my office was the store. I felt like there was something for everyone there. Three bites of Polish sausage and two swigs of bottled water into lunch, I said good-bye to Joy and walked a couple of steps across the street to the little antique junk shop run by an eighty-two-year-old Italian named Arturo. I asked him if he had any baseball cards and he turned around, reached up to a shelf behind him, about eye level, and pulled down a stack of about fifty cards. My first thought was that the cards couldn't be very good because a cardinal sin among baseball card collectors is to rubber band your cards. My second thought was yuck. The first fifteen cards were from the 1990s—an era in which they made so many millions of cards, that I had little interest in any of them.

But then a 1981 Kirk Gibson popped up with the little baseball cap in the corner. Then a 1976 Carlos May, then a 1959 Brooks Robinson. Get outta here. You've got to be kidding me. That was his Rookie card.

I looked at it carefully and quietly, so as not to draw any attention to the fact that I liked it. It did not have a crease of any kind on either side. Its only real flaw outside of the 60-40 off centering were two faint rubber band marks on the side. A few cards deeper, I found a 1952 Bowman Roy Sievers and behind it a 1957 Billy Pierce. I was ecstatic but I kept that emotion tightly in check. I asked the old guy, "How much for this little stack of cards?" Arturo who obviously knew nothing about baseball cards, answered "$20" immediately. I said, "Ouch." And he said, "Okay, then $15." "You've made a sale Arturo." He took the money and I left the store matter-of-factly, knowing full well that the value of the Brooks Robinson Rookie card was worth several times the $15 I had paid for the whole stack.

As I opened the door, I realized I had one more question for Arturo. I said, "Hey, Arturo, do you know anywhere close by where I might be able to find some baseball memorabilia?" He said, "Yes, there's a little alley way that goes all the way through the building from Central to First Avenue worth. The guy who uses that alley sells all kinds of stuff. That might be your best bet. It's only about 100 feet toward Seventh Street."

"Thanks, Arturo. I'll stop back again."

"Thank you, sir. Have a nice day."

"You too."

I looked at my watch and noticed I still had thirty-two minutes before I had to be back to the office. I walked the one hundred or so steps to the alley which was super easy to find, and went in there to explore. Scores of baskets lined the walls, filled with mostly junk, I thought, but with some interesting items mixed in. There were brooms, pictures of all kinds, ice trays that went back to the 40's, two wet suits, tennis rackets, baseballs, hats of all sizes for men and women, coloring books, new and older Golden Books, toy pistols and rifles. You get the idea. In one of the baskets I noticed an old baseball bat. I picked it up to look to see if it was a signature model. It was a Johnny Bench model. Here came the same excitement. The little boy in me was jumping with joy. The middle aged man in me was as cool as a cucumber. "How much for the old bat?" I asked the proprietor in the Hawaiian shirt and Panama hat.

"Four bucks," he said. I pulled out two two-dollar bills and gave them to him. "Don't see these around much anymore." He said, as though I'd given him a treasure. "Thanks," he said happily. "Thank you," I responded a little more appreciatively knowing it was I who got the real treasure.

I walked the one hundred steps to the end of the block, crossed the street as happy as I had ever been, knowing that I was finally moving in all the right directions to becoming a better man. And yes, that was important to me. I gave Joy another hug, wished her a prosperous day, then walked the five blocks to the Bank of America Building.

I greeted Amanda as friskily as if I was a college kid and she was a coed. Then I went into my office and felt like an encouragement king with my one o'clock appointment, a Yellow Cab driver who had been robbed at gunpoint by an unusually well-dressed yuppie couple. He had trust issues with everybody and was going through some serious post-traumatic stress.

When he left, I had a free hour between two and three and was working on my notes for my three o'clock client. At exactly 2:47 p.m. Amanda buzzed me.

"Dr. McKenzie, it's Dianne from Dr. Banderas's office for you."

"Thank you, Amanda," I said and went right for the blinking button.

"Hello, Dianne!" I said with a level of joyful energy I had within me all day.

"I'm afraid we have to cancel our appointment for this evening." Her voice was quivering like I'd never heard it, so I altered my vocal level to match hers.

"What's the problem, Dianne?"

There was a slight pause, as if she was clearing a lump from her throat.

"I'm afraid Dr. Banderas passed away today, just a little while ago while working in his office."

"How did it happen?" I asked calmly, although the news devastated me.

"He looked like he just fell asleep in his chair. I'm guessing he had a heart attack or an aneurysm. I probably will never know. He had a break between his lunch hour and his two o'clock. I never bothered him while he was working that way unless it was an emergency. When I buzzed his office to let him know his two o'clock was here, he didn't answer. I got up, knocked on his door—no answer. I went in and there he was, sleeping peacefully in his chair. When words didn't wake him, I touched his shoulder. He didn't move. I noticed an awful pallor in his face, so I grabbed his cold wrist, felt for a pulse and within seconds of finding no pulse, I dialed 911. Your file was open in front of him when he died. I must tell you that since he met you, he would often tell me that you were his favorite case." I was almost in tears of profound sadness, but for Dianne's sake I remained calm.

"I probably won't be seeing you again, but you were a wonderful client and I want to thank you on behalf of Dr. Banderas myself."

"Thank you, Dianne. It was a pleasure interacting with you and Dr. Banderas too."

"Take care, Dr. McKenzie. You know, there's a chance someone else will take over this practice. Would you like me to call you if that happens?"

"No, thank you, Dianne. I'll go it on my own for a while."

"God bless you, Dr. McKenzie. I've got to go now. I have so many more phone calls to make and the Paramedics are still here and want to ask more questions. Good-bye now."

"God bless you too, Dianne," and there was a click on the other end.

I buzzed Amanda immediately, still composed. "Could you please hold my calls till my three o'clock gets here, Amanda?"

"Yes, Dr. McKenzie."

There were seven minutes before 3:00 p.m. that afternoon. Seven measly minutes to quell my raging grief and present my new client—an important deserving person—with an upbeat therapist who owned a clear head.

Six minutes. Too late to cancel, but how could I possibly do this? I had imploded. Hooked inside and anything worthwhile left to give could not be seen within the black hole my heart had become.

Panic sped into an emotional black hole from which nothing seemed possible to escape. As the seconds ticked speedily past, my body began to literally shake. I was Jonesing for a rum and Coke to calm my nerves. For an instant I actually wondered if I had long ago hidden a bottle in the office and forgotten about it. I had not.

Then suddenly it hit me, with slightly less than two minutes to go on the play clock. It was a promise I made to Dr. Banderas whenever I felt compelled to drink, I first had to think of all my wonderful reasons to live. So I did, even though I was panic driven. I first thought of

Christine, the wonderful, powerful, dynamic soul whose well-being had been entrusted to me by my marital vows which meant everything to me. Then I thought of my three children, how much I loved them, how different they each were and how worthy they were of my love, attention and encouragement as they journeyed through the ensuing phases of their lives. I thought of my clients and how much I cared about each of them. Then I thought about the memories of Toby and Dr. Banderas—how lucky I had been to have had both of them in my life, if even for a short time. Both men had cared for me. One gave his life for a cause I had asked him to believe in. The other had probably worn himself out by losing countless hours of sleep by pondering what the Two-Knock Ghost meant to my life.

And as the clock ticked down below the final minute before Amanda would buzz me for my next appointment, I kept my promise to think of how to be creative within the context of the things I cared about. I hit immediately on my next client, Nicholas Charles, a white kid from a tough part of South St. Pete, who was dealing with his affinity for all kinds of drugs. Charles was a quiet and shy boy. Because of that, he was an easy target to be bullied by several gangs at Gibbs High School. Those gangs, I learned from Charles, were very skilled at picking out the kids they thought were the weaker ones. But with my client they were gravely mistaken. Though quiet and shy, he had a penchant for fighting back and quite well. He had been the product of an abusive upbringing and did not like bullies. He had been living in Foster Homes since he was twelve. Recently, during a bullying session with multiple boys harassing him, one of them made the mistake of slapping him in the face. Charles put the much larger slapper in the hospital with multiple facial fractures. Because several witnesses backed up his story of being tormented then slapped, Charles did not face the discipline of a suspension. But the courts knew he had a leaning toward using his fists. That's why they ordered him to see me. It was not only my duty to try to save him, but my sincere wish.

Then buzz. I shook in my chair when I heard the buzz from Amanda. Though the sound startled me, I wasn't panicking anymore. I had work to do and a boy that needed caring. Life goes on, even immediately after you lose someone you care about. Sometimes life is moving so fast that you must grieve between the bursts of activities it sends you. The speed of life does not wait for you to overcome your sorrows. It does not care about you. It is not a living being, as you are. It is simply reality that must be dealt with. It has no soul.

"Send the young fellow in," I said back to Amanda.

"Right away, Dr. McKenzie," she said to me in her marvelous dual voice of professionalism and playfulness.

I was back to work again. I felt better. I thanked my Higher Power for helping me through another skirmish, no, a major battle.

Later I called Christine and told her Dr. Banderas had passed away. She asked if I wanted to come over tonight. I said no thank you. I told her I wanted to see if I could handle my grief on my own and not drink. I told her that this would be a big test for me and if I made it through successfully, it would give me a more solid baseline of confidence to face my future.

"Do you want to come over Friday night and spend the weekend?" she asked with a tone of hope in her voice.

"I don't think so," I answered. "I want to see how long it takes me to get through the temptations to drink because somebody close to me has died."

"Will you keep me informed on how you are doing?"

"How about if I call you every couple of days?"

"Okay, Robert, if that's how you want to do it."

"Thank you for understanding, Christine."

"I love you, Robert."

"I know you do, Christine, and I love you more than anyone on the face of this earth. But right now I want to challenge myself to see how much I love myself."

"I understand, Robert," she said, speaking more formally than when she called me Turf.

"I'll call you in a couple of days, honey."

"Good-bye, Robert."

* * * * *

I faced the next few days with some confidence but with more tentativeness. The temptations to drink were everywhere. They lurked in every crevice of my day. No matter what I was doing, I kept thinking about Dr. Banderas's death as a terrible loss. I had just begun to interact with the man. With Toby I'd had several months to interact. With Dr.

Banderas I'd only had far too few weeks and he really hadn't answered many questions for me. His conjectures and surmising had raised more questions in me that now I would be forced to answer on my own. I would not elicit the services of another psychologist.

Over the next several days I realized that the only way to prevent myself from sinking into a pity pit when thinking about Dr. Banderas, was to think of everything that had gone between us as a game. Even the questions he had raised in me about the Two-Knock Ghost were gifts he had given me. When I realized that, I immediately thanked my Higher Power for anyone who ever raised a question for me to ponder one of life's mysteries.

I called Christine faithfully every two evenings. Each time I told her that what I was experiencing was a slow process of self-exploration. And I told her most importantly that I had not drank alcohol. I continued my visits to the Serenity Club and to look at the live oak once every few days. There, I would mull over my life, which had gone through so many upheavals lately, and contemplate how to face my future with the courage and dignity not to be dependent on alcohol.

It was late one night while parked in front of the Church of the Ascension and looking at my favorite tree, that I began to look at the Two-Knock Ghost differently. First, I asked myself, "Aren't ghosts something people see in their waking lives? Don't they terrorize you when you have nowhere to run? Can't they find you wherever you think you could hide?" At least in a dream if things got too bad you could wake yourself up. I didn't even believe in ghosts. After all I had still never seen one in my waking life, I believe in the Two-Knock Ghost, but it had manifested itself only in my dreams. I asked myself, "Why had I named it the Two-Knock Ghost?" I didn't have an answer. I thought about how Dr. Banderas had reminded me to keep turning the cup of an experience around and around until you see the experience in its entirety. Unravel the experience string by string until you see the experience through to its core.

For all the years of my adult life, I had not thought of Sister Timothy but she was in my mind, embedded in there with all her devilish terror tactics. Leaving Christine had freed those dreams to come squiggling up my emotional chutes from deep within my subconscious.

And what about my little sister Lena? No matter what my parents did to protect me from the pain of Lena's death and to help me completely forget her, I remembered her, just deep within myself, unknown to my conscious recollections. And I hurt about her every day. Her loss was the first experience that sensitized me to how deeply death can impact even a small child. It possibly was my first step to becoming a psychologist because I hurt for people who have loss.

Was the Two-Knock Ghost really a ghost if it appeared only in my dreams?

After nearly three weeks and nine calls to Christine, I called her one night and told my wife that I wanted to come home, forever. I had unintentionally used a tone of voice that Christine had never heard. It was strong, confident, determined, and undeniable.

"If you truly believe you're ready," she said.

"I do," I answered with no change in my vocal tenor.

"When?" my wife asked gently without anxiety.

"I'd like to spend this weekend with you then go back to the Beaches of Paradise after work Monday, pack and move back home next Saturday."

"Okay," she said. "Let me know if there's anything I can do to help."

"You have enough to do. I can handle this on my own, although I've already decided to use Eight Brothers Helping Others because I like the name." Then my mind shifted oddly to something Dr. Banderas had told me about creativity. And just as instantaneously as the thoughts of Dr. Banderas popped into my head, this popped out of my mouth to Christine. "As soon as I get home, I'd like you and I to start planning a vacation together. I'm thinking about a cruise. We've never been on one. Would you like that?"

Here came the little girl again and the girl I fell in love with.

"I'd absolutely love that, Turf," she said in a voice not unlike a six-year-old getting news she was going to Disney World.

"I'll see you Friday night," I said.

"I'll see you, Turf. Be well."

* * * * *

The human mind has always amazed me. How deep it is, how complex, pliant, breakable, resilient, how layered. How impressionable. It seems as if everything you see, hear, taste, touch, and feel, leaves an indelible imprint upon you, whether you realize it or not. Everything comes into you from a slightly different angle making you the only one of your kind in the entire universe.

As I pondered the minds of others, I pondered mine. Something may have surfaced from an unfathomable depth to reveal itself and help me to identify parts of my being that were damaged. I wanted to believe with all of my emotional heart that my parents were the Two-Knock Ghost, but the ideas of Dr. Banderas that even I had known before meeting him, kept repeating themselves in my thoughts. "What about that theory that suggests that all of the characters in your dreams are you?" Now, I want you to understand this, I don't believe that everyone in your dreams is you, as an absolute truth. Dreams are too complicated and even random to be explained the same way 100 percent of the time, and I do not think that Freud or Jung or the Sleeping Prophet has identified everything there is to know about dreams. I think humanity is still learning how to interpret dreams as each of us is attempting to understand our own. But if I did consider that the Two-Knock Ghost—my mother and father was me in my dreams. What might I think about it? I have my own interpretation. I have the right to my own, don't you think?

I started to break it down theoretically. If each of my parents was me, then it was me telling me the story of Sister Timothy and Lena. That would mean that I had remembered everything but those memories had found a hiding place multiple layers within my subconscious.

Still, I wanted to believe that the Two-Knock Ghost was my parents. I clung to that thought as my primary belief of what the whole experience was about. Dr. Banderas's ideas were my secondary considerations. It was comforting to me as a human being to have seen my parents the way they appeared when they saved me from the devil Nazi, It was one of the greatest moments of my life. It did not detract from the thrill of the event merely because it was a dream. I blew fart kisses on my father's neck. That was fun. That made sense. It did not make sense that if everyone in my dream was me, that I blew fart kisses onto my own neck. They both had hugged me and told me they loved me and missed me. They told me about Respite and why they had to stay there and wait for the right time to rescue me. It all made perfect sense to me.

Then my internal psychologist picked up the cup of the entire experience and turned it yet again trying to break it down to its core. I honestly didn't know what the truth was, but I deduced that just because my parents had rescued me a couple of times from Satan and scared the living crap out of him, that didn't guarantee that I'd never have another devil dream. And if I did have one or an occasional one, I would just have to deal with it because I did not know how to eradicate those dreams. As I continued to turn the cup, I realized how easy it was for a human being to be tormented by something they didn't believe in. I realized more deeply how careful adults need to be when they teach children that something heinous is absolute truth. Freddy Kreuger is scary. Jason is scary. Chuckie is a little runt punk. But they only kill your body. The devil torments you with the threat of possessing your eternal soul and torturing it for every second forever.

It fascinated me how many times I could turn the cup and from how many angles I could look at each human experience. I wondered if my Higher Power, God, turned the cup that way when He evaluated the life of each human being.

* * * * *

A few days later I was living in my home with Christine again, feeling cozy and loved. I also felt honored that my wife believed in me and the progress I was making that allowed me to be welcomed home. Was I nervous about being there? Was I unsure of my ability to be creative as a loving husband? Was I worried that I might slip and have a drink again? You bet I was. After all, I'm just a man. I can falter, as can we all.

I was also determined to show Christine the love she deserved from me. I was determined to keep my promise to never drink again. I would include my children more in our lives. I would become a better psychologist because now I was a more aware man. I would put many more plants in mine and Amanda's offices and think of Dr. Banderas each day I worked within my jungle. Every year or two I would send a little more money to Alicia while her kids were still growing and even when they were in college. I would think about Toby often and always believe that he was a true friend who laid down his life to do a favor for me. I would think of Mary Bauer, who I never saw again after her final office visit when she was so determined to make it beyond that meeting on her own. I hoped she would send me a Christmas card each year to keep me up to date about her life. There was no doubt I would send one to her. I would think of the live oak, show it soon to Christine and someday to each of my children. I would try to take my life one day at a time, or sometimes when things would get tough, from breath to breath. I would soon change the location for my AA meetings. The Serenity Club was too far from Snell Island and now that I was back at home with Christine, I wanted to spend every possible moment with her. I honestly didn't know if I would get a sponsor or even how far into AA's program I would go. Those and so many more questions would be answered in my future.

I would think of the Two-Knock Ghost. I would always be thankful that it never gave up trying to coax me into letting it into my dreams and how Dr. Banderas encouraged me to take an entirely different tack and consider it a possible friend. I would honor my long dead parents for their eventual appearance. I would always be so utterly thankful to them for what they shared with me in real life and in how they rescued and loved me in my dreams. I wondered if I would ever see them again. I hoped I would.

Finally, because it was my nature to go as deep as I possibly could into the wise workings of the human mind, I would forever wonder what and who the Two-Knock Ghost really was. Was it even a ghost because it appeared only in my dreams? Or was it absolutely a ghost because it haunted me time after time before it finally revealed its message brought from the faraway place called Respite? Or had the circumstances of my life sent a grenade into the solidified mass of the subconscious of my early life, causing long buried memories to drift creatively to my dreams in the room next to my consciousness? I thought of the Gate Keeper. Could he have been me keeping the secrets of my past locked away until the night I was ready to reveal them to myself? What if the Two-Knock Ghost had simply been me all along?

CPSIA information can be obtained
at www.ICGtesting.com
Printed in the USA
FSOW01n1452010217
30274FS